Thunder of the Gods

By the same author in the *Empire* series

Wounds of Honour
Arrows of Fury
Fortress of Spears
The Leopard Sword
The Wolf's Gold
The Eagle's Vengeance
The Emperor's Knives

Thunder of the Gods

Empire: Volume Eight

ANTHONY RICHES

HODDER &
STOUGHTON

First published in 2015 by Hodder & Stoughton
An Hachette UK company

1

A CIP catalogue record for this title is available from the British Library

Hardback ISBN 978 1 444 73196 5
Trade Paperback ISBN 978 1 444 73197 2
E-book ISBN 978 1 444 73198 9

Typeset in Plantin Light by Palimpsest Book Production Ltd, Falkirk, Stirlingshire

Printed and bound by Clays Ltd, St Ives plc

Hodder & Stoughton policy is to use papers that are natural, renewable
and recyclable products and made from wood grown in sustainable forests.
The logging and manufacturing processes are expected to conform to the
environmental regulations of the country of origin.

Hodder & Stoughton Ltd
338 Euston Road
London NW1 3BH

www.hodder.co.uk

For Vivienne Maxwell, David Mooney and John Prigent –
the triumvirate who make sure my mistakes
never reach your page.

ACKNOWLEDGEMENTS

As usual with the *Empire* series, what looks to the reader like a leisurely progression through the provinces and events of late second-century Rome is in reality a book-by-book refinement of the author's existing knowledge, as each story's location and plot requires a more detailed understanding of the specifics in question.

For my understanding of what it took to transport large bodies of soldiers by sea I am indebted to Jorit Wintjes for sharing his paper 'Hauling a Legion across the Ocean: Roman Military Sealift Capabilities beyond the Mediterranean' so generously. I had no idea that many legions had an officer on the staff who was expert on the methodology of legion maritime transport, testament to the ubiquity of these military juggernauts.

And my grasp of the sheer complexity of the Parthian empire's military capability – which was until then limited to what I'd read about Carrhae – was abruptly and amusingly improved by a Skype session with three students of Persian history whose intelligence, wit and humour was both entertaining and highly informative. Nadeem Ahmad, Amir Yahyavi and Patryk Skupniewicz provided me with an insight into the varied capabilities of the kingdoms that made up Parthia's ability to face off to Rome's more or less constant encroachment.

With the manuscript written I fell back upon my usual team of beta readers – David Mooney, Vivienne Maxwell and John Prigent – whose varied styles of feedback provided me with their usual valuable perspectives on what I'd got right and wrong when it came to writing an informative and entertaining story.

And domestically, from the moment I typed the first word in

Thunder of the Gods, all the way through the usual elation and despondency of a novel's sometimes painful gestation, right up to that moment when the book lies steaming and complete, and the usual celebratory bottle is opened, my wife Helen's usual no-nonsense tolerance and encouragement was invaluable. My editor Carolyn was as patient as ever.

And one more thank you. When the title of this book was first debated, and I wasn't quite sure what it ought to be, I put it out there for discussion. The brief: Parthian heavy cavalry, lots of noise, very scary, and so on. My good friend (and occasional partner in hedonistic food and wine excess) Robyn Young came to the party with the killer title – *Thunder of the Gods*. Let's hope book nine has a title that works as well.

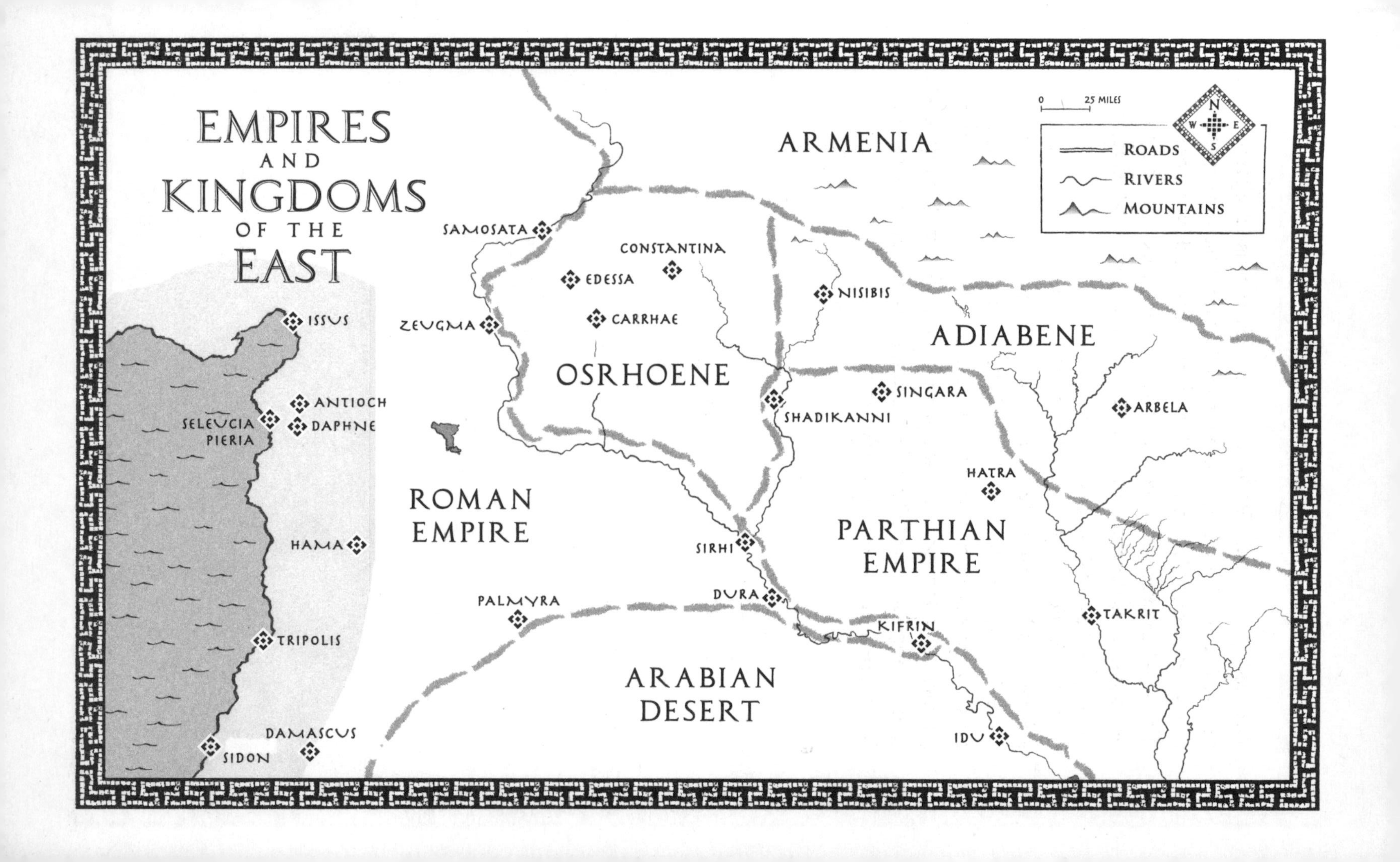
EMPIRES AND KINGDOMS OF THE EAST
0
25 MILES
N
W
E
S
ROADS
RIVERS
MOUNTAINS
ARMENIA
ADIABENE
OSRHOENE
ROMAN EMPIRE
PARTHIAN EMPIRE
ARABIAN DESERT
SAMOSATA
CONSTANTINA
EDESSA
CARRHAE
NISIBIS
ZEUGMA
ISSUS
ANTIOCH
SELEUCIA PIERIA
DAPHNE
SINGARA
SHADIKANNI
ARBELA
HATRA
HAMA
SIRHI
PALMYRA
DURA
TAKRIT
KIFRIN
TRIPOLIS
DAMASCUS
SIDON
IDU

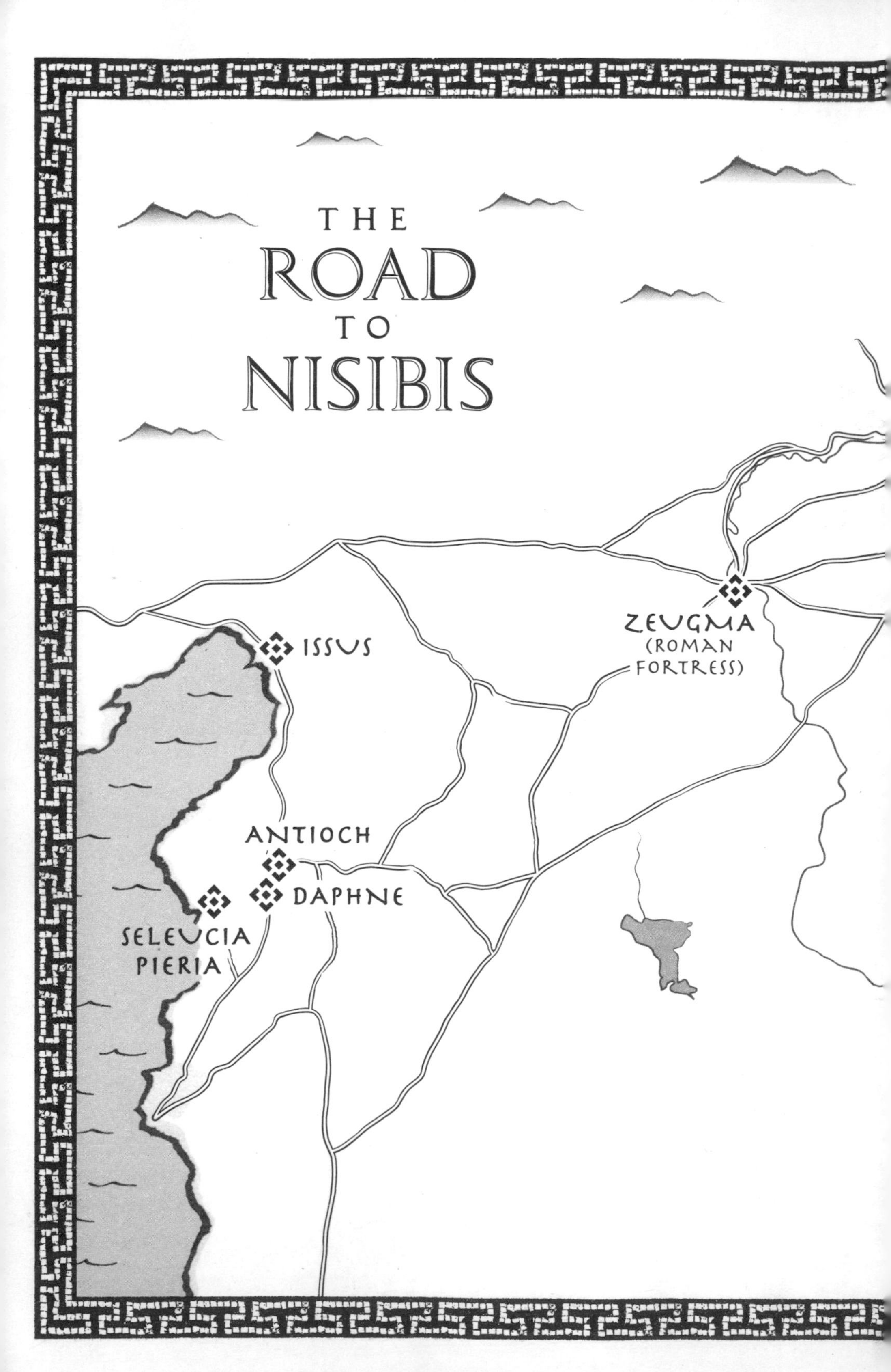
THE
ROAD
TO
NISIBIS
ISSUS
ZEUGMA
(ROMAN
FORTRESS)
ANTIOCH
DAPHNE
SELEUCIA
PIERIA

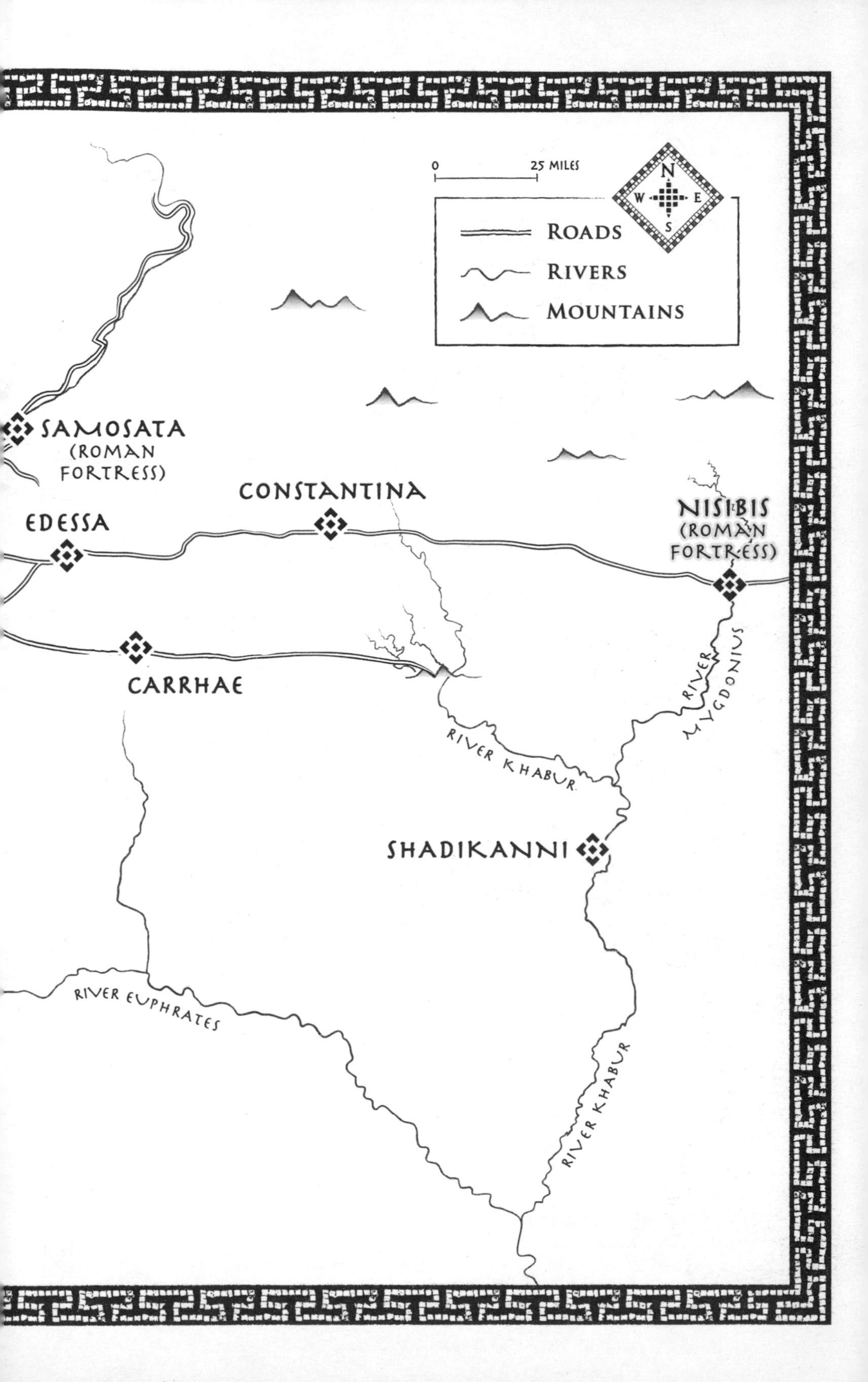

0
25 MILES
N
W
E
S
Roads
Rivers
Mountains
SAMOSATA
(ROMAN FORTRESS)
CONSTANTINA
EDESSA
NISIBIS
(ROMAN FORTRESS)
CARRHAE
RIVER MYGDONIUS
RIVER KHABUR
SHADIKANNI
RIVER EUPHRATES
RIVER KHABUR

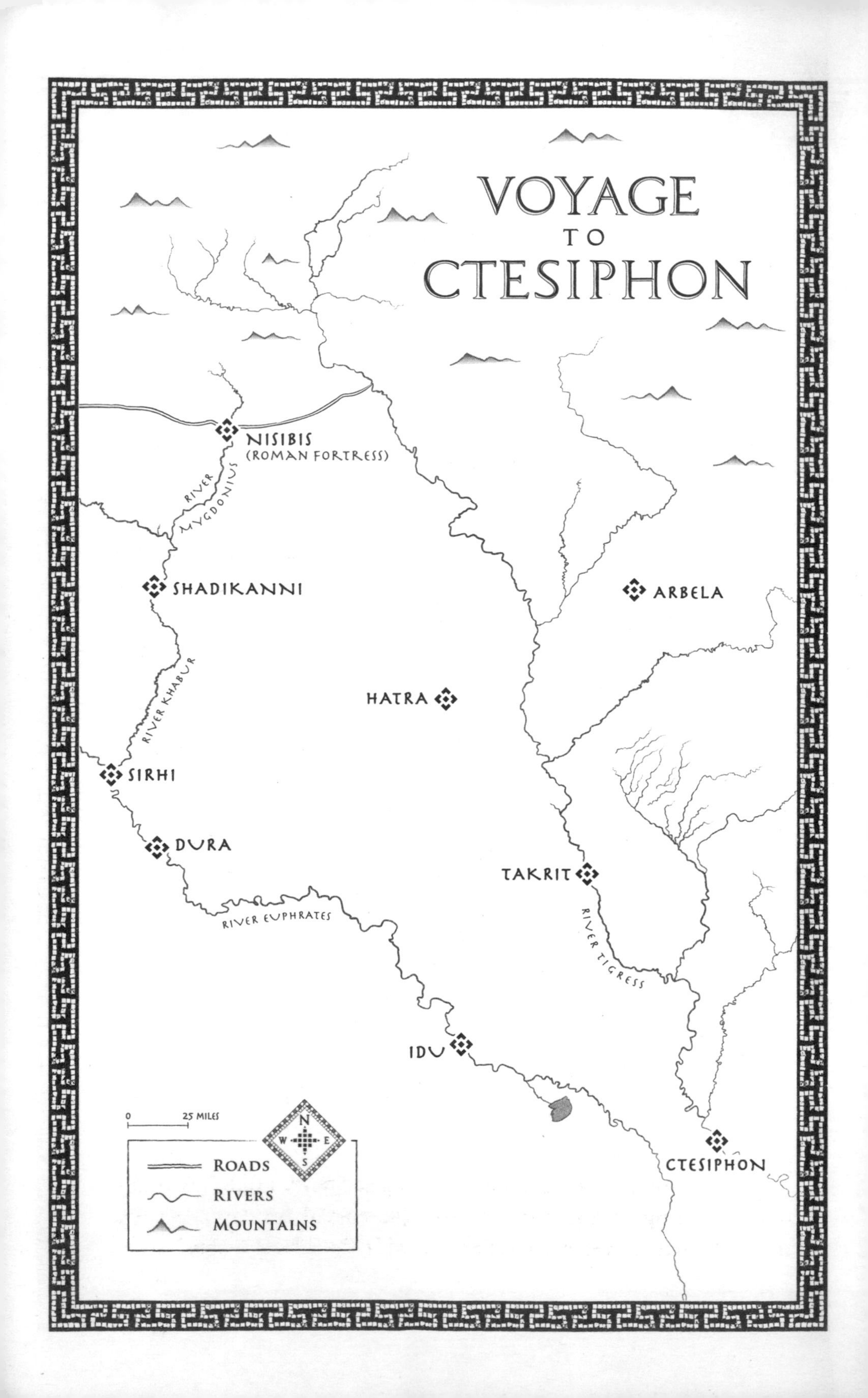
VOYAGE TO CTESIPHON
NISIBIS
(ROMAN FORTRESS)
RIVER MYGDONIUS
SHADIKANNI
ARBELA
RIVER KHABUR
HATRA
SIRHI
DURA
TAKRIT
RIVER EUPHRATES
RIVER TIGRESS
IDU
CTESIPHON
0
25 MILES
N
W
E
S
ROADS
RIVERS
MOUNTAINS

Prologue

September AD 184

'Well now Tribune, are you still sure you wouldn't rather be back in Antioch with your young friends?'

Gaius Vibius Varus looked down from his horse at the centurion marching alongside him with a quick smile, easy in his relationship with the older man despite their twenty-year age difference and the social gulf between them.

'It's a difficult choice you pose, First Spear. On the one hand, I could be lounging around drinking wine and watching exquisite young ladies oil each other up for my entertainment. On the other, here I am, breathing in the fart-laden dust of five hundred men's boots.'

He paused for a moment, looking up at the sky and pursing his lips as if in thought. The cohort's senior centurion grinned up at him, flicking away a vicious-looking fly that was hovering over his head with a practised sweep of his vine stick.

'You forgot to mention the heat, the insects, the constant moaning of soldiers on the march, the occasional screams of abuse from my more vigorous centurions . . .'

He winked at the younger man.

'Which is to say all of them. That and the fact that any "young ladies" you encounter in Nisibis will have bandier legs than most cavalrymen you've ever met.'

Varus shrugged.

'Surprising though it might seem, First Spear, I didn't actually have whoring on my mind when I persuaded my father to use his influence to get me a tribunate with the Third Gallic.'

The older man, technically his subordinate but very much the master of all he surveyed, and happy enough to indulge a tribune whose apparent disdain for the differences between them was in pleasant contrast to the usual attitudes of sons of the aristocracy towards the soldiers they commanded, snorted gentle derision.

'Which is quite unlike most of your colleagues, if I might be so bold. Antioch sees a good sight more of you young gentlemen than the fortress at Zeugma ever will, and as for Nisibis . . .'

Varus barked out a harsh laugh, his mimicry of the legion's senior tribune uncannily accurate.

'Only a bloody fool ever makes the march to Nisibis without direct orders, young Vibius Varus! The whole town positively *stinks* of unwashed Arabs.'

The centurion smirked at the precision of his tribune's imitation of their mutual superior.

'And the *women*! Dear gods, the women are fit for nothing better than servicing the common soldiery!'

The senior centurion shrugged, conceding the point.

'Tribune Umbrius has something of a point, as it happens. You'll see the wisdom of his words soon enough, once you've spent a few days with nothing more entertaining to fill them than walking the city's walls and staring out into the emptiness that surrounds the place. You mark my words, young Tribune, you'll be yearning for the delights of Antioch soon enough . . .'

He fell silent, his sharp eyes narrowing at the sight of a half-dozen horsemen galloping back down the road that led away into the east.

'What's got *them* moving so fast, I wonder? Trumpeter, sound the halt!'

The long column of soldiers stopped marching at the horn's signal, their officers watching with calculating expressions as the cohort's scouts came down their line at a fast trot. The horsemen's leader jumped down from his mount and saluted the centurion with the look of a hunted man, belatedly turning to repeat the gesture towards Varus. His face was seamed from a lifetime spent in the saddle under desert skies, although he was little more than a decade older than the tribune.

'What is it Abbas? Did that pretty little mare of yours get stung on the arse?'

The officer's tone was light, but there was no mistaking the look on his face. The scout pointed down the road to the cohort's front as he replied, his words a near gabble.

'Horsemen! More horsemen than I can count!'

The first spear nodded slowly, as if deliberately refusing to allow himself to be infected by the panic that was clearly gripping the man before him.

'What sort of horsemen?'

The scout gestured again, looking back over his shoulder as if he expected whatever it was he'd seen to come over the horizon at any moment.

'Archers. Many archers. And *cataphracti* . . .'

Varus started at the word, drummed into him years before by his Greek tutor. One of the riders waiting behind him muttered something unintelligible in their own language, clearly keen to be gone, and the scout gestured angrily for silence without turning from the officers, bowing to the centurion before speaking again. His voice was quiet, and to Varus's ears carried the solemnity of a funeral orator.

'First Spear, you are a good man. I have enjoyed marching with you, and I will pray to my god for you.'

The centurion reached out a hand, gripping the other man's arm as he turned to remount.

'And where do you think *you're* fucking going?'

The scout looked down at the hand, then raised his gaze to the Roman's face.

'To stay here is to *die* here, Centurion. I choose to live. And you need word of this to reach the city of the bridge, no?'

The Roman released his grip, nodding slowly at the scout's logic.

'How many *cataphracti*? Could they be local troops or some sort of bandit gang?'

The scout shook his head quickly.

'So many armoured men, the land shines like polished silver. These are not bandits. There are too many of them.'

He leapt into his horse's saddle, threw the two men a hasty salute and led his compatriots away at a fast trot.

'You're letting them go, First Spear?'

The older man nodded, grinning grimly at Varus's bemusement.

'It was either that or I'd have had to order them killed. And he's right. If these horsemen are what he believes them to be, then the legion at Zeugma needs to know that the treacherous bastards have invaded Osrhoene. If we're lucky, they'll have seen our scouts and decided not to pick a fight today. After all, it's been a long time since the Parthians were any real threat to the frontier—'

A chorus of shouts from the front of the column gave the lie to his hopes, and Varus straightened his body in the saddle to gaze out to the east, over the heads of the stationary column of soldiers, as a solid mass of cavalry began to rise into view from a fold in the landscape. He shook his head in disbelief as the Parthian army continued to emerge into view, hundreds upon hundreds of horsemen with a mass of armoured warriors at their core, whose polished armour made the sun's reflections from the iron plates almost painful.

'What can you see lad?'

The younger man was silent for a moment more, until a tap on the shoulder from the centurion's stick wrenched his attention from the oncoming enemy.

'It's like something out of the history books . . .'

He glanced down at the centurion apologetically.

'Sorry First Spear, just not what I was expecting to see when I climbed out from under my blanket this morning. We seem to be standing in the way of several thousand rather unfriendly looking cavalry . . .'

The centurion was already running for the column's head with his trumpeter hot on his heels, and after a moment's consideration of the options, the young tribune dismounted, handing the horse's reins to a soldier, and ran after him.

Stopping alongside the foremost century, the first spear looked out across the mile of flat, dusty ground that lay between his men and a thick line of horsemen who were trotting their mounts towards the Romans.

'Form square! Deploy to the left on me! *Double time!*'

He pulled the tribune to one side as the leading century's men trotted out to the left of the road, leading the cohort's change of formation from the column of march to a hollow square, nodding in quiet satisfaction as the manoeuvre's near faultless execution.

'See that? There are enough horsemen out there to kill the lot of us half a dozen times over, but I give these lads a bit of drill to perform, something they've practised a thousand times, and they jump to it like veterans.'

His voice was suddenly gruff, and Varus realised that the older man's eyes were shining with barely suppressed emotion as he stared at the advancing cavalry, speaking without taking his eyes off the oncoming threat.

'And now I need you to do something for me that will stick in your throat. Get back on your horse, Tribune, and ride for Zeugma as if your life depended on it!'

He turned to face his superior, raising a hand to forestall the protest that was on the tribune's lips, his face twisting with anger that set the younger man back an involuntary half pace.

'*No!* You may be my superior, but you will fucking well do what you're told by a subordinate just this *one* time!'

Shaking his head, he waved his vine stick at the line of soldiers forming behind him.

'These men and me, we've no choice in the matter. If the Parthians have decided that this is our day to fight for our lives, well then that's just our luck. We can't outrun them, and we don't have the weapons to give them back the pain they'll start heaping on us soon enough. But there's no reason for you to go throwing your life away alongside us.'

Varus opened his mouth to protest, but the centurion shook his head sadly, his expression choking off the younger man's retort.

'You know the worst thing about this for me? It ain't dying, if it's my day to die. Every man dies, young 'un, *every* man. Rich or poor, we're all dust on the wind sooner or later. It's just a question of when, and more importantly *how*. And it ain't just *how* we die that matters, but how we're *seen* to die. It's whether my brother officers shake their heads in disgust at the loss of a good cohort . . .'

His voice hardened.

'Or if they can nod with pride when they hear how many of these cock-sucking eastern cunts we took with us!'

He pointed back down the road at the man holding onto Varus's horse.

'So, Tribune, in a moment you're going to get back on that beast and ride away, far enough that you can see what happens here without getting an arrow stuck through you. Because the only way we get to die with some self-respect is if you watch us fight it out, right to the end, and then you take the story back to the legion. If you want to throw your life away after that, then by all means take the first chance you get, but *not* before you've given these men the reputation they'll be earning once those bow-waving tosspots get their shit in a pile and come for us.'

He stared wordlessly at the young officer, holding eye contact until Varus dropped his gaze and looked at his boots for a moment. When he looked up again the centurion was smiling at him, his face split in a taut, humourless grin.

'I know. This don't feel *honourable* to you, does it? Like I say, you'll have plenty more opportunities to die gloriously, but me and these men – this is our only chance. And you won't take that from us, not a decent man like you.'

The tribune nodded reluctantly, holding out a hand, but the older man wrapped an arm around him, slapping him on the back.

'It's not like I'm at any risk of being demoted for overfamiliar behaviour to a senior officer, is it? Go well, young 'un, and choose your time for glory carefully, eh? Don't go sending yourself to meet Hades too quickly; make sure you make an exit that'll make men nod their heads when they hear your name. Now, shall we get these apes into the mood for a fight?'

He turned away with a wink, walking into the square with the tribune at his heels as the last man marched into position and closed the formation.

'Sixth Cohort, face inward!'

The soldiers pivoted to look into the space enclosed by their ranks, and the centurion took a deep breath before speaking again. 'You *lucky* bastards! No bugger on this frontier's seen any action for thirty years, and now the gods have seen fit to grant us the honour, the sheer fucking privilege of getting the chance to show these Parthian animals the way that *real* men fight. And better than that, the tribune here is going to watch us make a stand against them, and take an accurate account back to the rest of the legion. Does any man here want him to have to tell them that the Sixth Cohort lacked the balls to give a decent account of itself?'

One of the soldiers in his own first century raised a hand and opened his mouth as if to speak, but the stupid grin plastered across his face raised a titter across the formation, and broke the tension in an instant. The first spear raised a knowing eyebrow, his lips twitching in a slight smile even as he raised his vine stick in admonishment.

'Yes, there's always one!'

His expression hardened.

'I won't lie to you lads, this is a tough spot. Worse than tough, this is shit so deep that we're already up to our nuts in it. We either fight these arse punchers to a standstill here and now, or else we go to meet our gods, either with dignity or with our pride in tatters.'

He looked around at them, swelling his chest out and raising his head defiantly.

'And if it comes to dying, I know which way *I'm* going! I'll face whatever's coming to me and meet it head on. After all, we know what they do to their prisoners, don't we?'

He looked about him in silence for a moment, then bellowed out a challenge.

'So, are we going to face these fuckers like men?!'

The soldiers roared back at him, waving their spears and shields. He nodded to the tribune, slapping the younger man on the shoulder.

'Good enough. Right then, get yourself away, Tribune, before the trap closes on you as well as us.'

Varus nodded mutely, saluting the centurion and then turning away, pushing his way through the soldiers and hurrying to the mare. Mounting, he looked over the square to find that the Parthian archers had reined in their horses just outside bow shot of the Romans, pausing to order their ranks and ready themselves for the battle. The cohort was still turned inward, their attention fixed on the first spear as he paced around inside the square, exhorting his men to sell their lives dearly. The tribune shook his head, raising a hand to his face to wipe away the tears trickling down his cheeks, then turned the horse to the west and spurred it away at a canter, back down the road that led past Osrhoene's capital Edessa, and on towards the legion fortress at Zeugma. Reaching a rise in the road he reined the mare in, turning in the saddle to look back at the battle that was unfolding across the arid plain. The legionaries had turned to face their enemy, their shields raised in defence against the steady rain of arrows that the horse archers were now dropping into their ranks, each man trotting his mount forward, loosing a shot and then reversing his course to ride back a few dozen paces while another archer took his turn. A score and more dead and wounded soldiers had already been dragged into the shelter of the square's raised shields, struck by arrows that had found the inevitable gaps in their defences, or whose shields had failed to stop the plummeting missiles.

His gaze shifted back across the plain behind the bowmen, to where a force of armoured horsemen gleaming with the sun's reflected light stood beside horses bearing coats of the same shining metal scales, patiently waiting while the Romans stood beneath the iron rain that was slowly, inevitably, picking apart their formation. The time would come, he knew, when the defenders would be too weak to resist the final killing blow that would fall upon them from behind the archers. Horns would sound, and the bowmen would ride away to either side, making room for the *cataphracts* to sweep into the attack. He briefly considered riding away, at the same time knowing all too well that he could never break the promise he'd made to the centurion. Dry-eyed now, his emotions wrung out by the slaughter playing out before him, he raised a hand to salute the single figure still standing at the cohort's heart.

'I won't turn away from you, First Spear, not unless they chase me away. I'll watch you and your men die, and I'll take your story back to the legion. I will find my own path to glory, when the time is right. And I will see you again. In Hades.'

I

February AD 185

'You're confident that's our landfall, Navarchus?'

The hard-faced officer acknowledged his superior's question with a look of disbelief and a curt nod, his voice harsh from years of barking commands at his crew before his promotion from ship's trierarchus to commander of the fleet.

'Yes, Procurator. Completely confident.'

The equestrian official turned back to the soldier standing alongside him, his grey-flecked hair ruffled by the wind as he raised a hand and pointed out over the ship's bow.

'As I said, there it is, Legatus. Seleucia.'

Legatus Gaius Rutilius Scaurus stared out over the warship's prow as it sliced through the ocean under the urging of the massive vessel's banked oars, looking past the massive bolt thrower that dominated the vessel's bow, raising a hand to shield his grey eyes from the winter sun's glare. A line of mountains was just visible on the eastern horizon, seemingly rising from the sea to block their course, their bases almost invisible in the sea's haze.

'The gateway to the east. Well done, Cassius Ravilla, you and your men have performed your task admirably, given the circumstances.'

The fleet's navarchus turned his bearded frown from procurator to legatus for a moment, then shook his head and walked slowly away from the two men, his face taking on the look of a man hunting for someone on whom to exercise his considerable irritation. The vessel's trierarchus and his centurion turned and walked away towards the *Victoria*'s stern with the look of men earnestly discussing the finer points of ship handling, prompting a knowing smile from Scaurus.

'He's still not the happiest of men, is he?'

Ravilla shook his head, the wind ruffling his thick black hair.

'He swears that if he'd not made sure we made a decent sacrifice to Neptune every time we made land safely, we'd all have been at the bottom of the ocean a month ago. Apparently the weather at this end of the Middle Sea hasn't been this quiet in the winter closed season for all the years he's served in the navy.'

Scaurus grinned at the grizzled sailor's back as he stooped to berate one of the flagship's oarsmen for some small infringement.

'Has he considered that he might simply be terrifying the waves into submission?'

He looked back over the vessel's stern at the line of ships following in their wake at precise four-hundred-pace intervals.

'After all, he seems to have your fleet's trierarchi drilled to within an inch of their collective lives.'

The procurator shook his head ruefully.

'I know. I sometimes wonder which one of us is really in command of the fleet.'

His answer was a hollow laugh.

'Welcome to my world. Have you ever seen your man there and my first spear talking to each other? They're like two fighting dogs sniffing each other's backsides and trying to work out which of them would win if it came to blows. And trust me, when Julius decides that my cohorts are to do a thing in a certain way, that's the way in which that thing will be done, with no ifs or buts. I'm allowed the luxury of determining our strategy, and after that . . .'

'You're in the hands of the professionals?'

'Exactly.'

Ravilla looked at him in silence for a moment.

'You said *cohorts*, legatus, rather than *legion*. And while my father told me at great length never to pry into another man's business when I was a child . . .'

He left the question hanging in the crisp sea air rather than asking it directly.

'You'd like to know exactly how it is that a man wearing the same thin stripe as the one on your tunic ends up in command of one of the emperor's legions.'

Ravilla shrugged.

'You'll admit that it is something of a curiosity? Of course I've heard the stories of how Marcus Aurelius sometimes gave command of his legions to legion first spears who'd been promoted to the equestrian class during the German War, but I thought that such egalitarianism had been quietly forgotten once Commodus had made peace with the tribes after his father's death. The status quo has been restored, and to command a legion anywhere other than Egypt, a man must once again be of the senatorial class, if not already actually in possession of his father's ring and death mask. And suddenly here you are, quite obviously an equestrian like me, and yet blessed with a legion!'

Scaurus smiled tightly.

'And you'd like to know the secret. How does a man make that impossible leap to fame and fortune without first putting a thick stripe on his tunic?'

'Of course.'

The legatus shook his head.

'First you'd have to provide a man close to the throne a service that would show him how valuable you could be to him in the future. Like giving him the opportunity to take the place of the emperor's most trusted adviser, that kind of thing.'

Ravilla raised his eyebrows.

'You were part of *that*?'

Scaurus shrugged in his turn.

'It's not something I'll readily admit to having participated in, but let's say, just for the sake of the discussion, that I was.'

'Then the man who replaced the Praetorian Prefect must owe you a huge debt.'

'And you think that's it? The gift of a legion as the reward for the chance to take ultimate power?'

'Wasn't it?'

The legatus shook his head.

'Who could be more dangerous than a man ruthless enough to engineer the death of the man he seeks to supplant? Why would he leave anyone who was part of the act alive to tell the story?'

Ravilla nodded slowly.

'I take your point. Unless he wanted more from the men in question?'

'Indeed. It seems that our particular capabilities were too valuable to be discarded, once we'd served our initial purposes. See my tribune there?'

The procurator frowned at the change in conversational focus, glancing down the ship's length at the tall, well-muscled figure of a military tribune clad in a shining bronze breast plate and bearing his usual two swords, one an infantry gladius with a magnificent eagle's head pommel. Alongside him stood an older soldier wearing the scaled armour and cross-crested helmet of a legion centurion; the two officers engaged in the routine inspection of the centurion's men.

'Yes. He seems a good enough man, if a little . . . taciturn. The centurion with him though, now *there's* a dangerous man.'

'Cotta? He's sudden death with any weapon you could mention, but the tribune?'

Scaurus grinned at Ravilla.

'Tribune Corvus could take Cotta to pieces, literally, in the span of a dozen heartbeats. His men call him *"Two Knives"*, because he fights in the style of an old-fashioned dimachaerus. He was taught by a champion gladiator of some fame, a big man who, like Corvus there, always fought with two swords. You might have seen the man's recent and rather spectacular comeback appearance in the Flavian arena?'

'You don't mean . . .'

Ravilla whispered the gladiator's name in an awed tone, and when Scaurus nodded in reply, his face took on a fresh expression of amazement. The legatus smiled at his colleague's genuine astonishment.

'Indeed. And while his pupil may lack the big man's sheer

brute power, he has a speed with the blade that you might call divine, were you to believe that the gods occasionally bestow their gifts on us mere mortals. He wears a quiet enough demeanour for the most part, but when he's roused . . .'

The procurator mused for a moment.

'So the new man behind the throne must have wanted something more from you? Something that involved your tribune?'

'He did, and in a roundabout sort of way he got exactly what he wanted from us.'

'And then?'

Scaurus raised his hands and gestured about him.

'And then . . . here we are. Apparently we're too valuable to be quietly murdered and forgotten about, and so instead we find ourselves sent east to deal with a problem on the empire's frontier instead. And that feeling of envy you were expressing before?'

Ravilla looked at him for a moment.

'Has somewhat diminished, I'll wager, and has been replaced by one rather large question.'

The legatus smiled knowingly.

'Which, I would imagine, is that given the rather dangerous nature of the information I've just shared with you, why in the name of Mithras didn't I just fabricate some rather more anodyne story to tell you?'

'Exactly.'

'And you're right to be concerned.'

He passed the procurator a scroll, the paper still sealed into a tight tube with wax bearing the imperial mark. Ravilla took it from his hand, grimaced at the seal and then snapped it, opening the message and reading swiftly. After a moment he handed it back to the legatus with a single word.

'Shit.'

'Indeed.'

Word spread quickly through the port city of Seleucia, as the flagship and the fleet of warships that followed in her wake appeared over the western horizon in swift and efficient succession, each fresh sighting whipping up the collective state of excitement until the entire port was alive with the news that a fleet of twenty-five warships was approaching. The men tasked with the harbour's defence ran for their bolt throwers, pulling off heavy waxed canvas covers and going through the motions of winding the weapons' massive bowstrings back ready to fire, while above them in the lower city's main tower, the port's procurator stared out at the oncoming vessels. He looked to his chief pilot, the man who did most of the actual work involved in his role, raising an eyebrow in question. The older man, approaching his sixtieth year with no sign of any urge to retire, took another long look at the line of ships advancing towards the walls of the outer port and then turned back to him with an expression that was as much of perplexity as recognition.

'If I didn't know better, I could swear that's the old *Victoria* leading them in. I remember her from the time she escorted the imperial flagship into harbour back at the start of the last war with the Parthians. But what would the Praetorian fleet be doing this far east at this time of year?'

His superior's eyebrows arched in surprise.

'The *Praetorian* fleet?'

'I know, it's not likely, is it? But I could swear that's the old *Victoria* . . .'

The procurator goggled at him for a moment before turning to his secretary.

'Have a messenger ready to ride to the governor's office in Antioch at my command!'

The slave inclined his head respectfully.

'As you order, sir. And the message?'

'I'll know that when I see who walks off that leading ship.'

Ravilla's navarchus had waved away the offer of a pilot with a grim shake of his head, leaving the cutter wallowing in the quadrireme's wake.

'No fucking easterner's going to scrape my flagship down a

harbour wall and then tell me he hadn't realised she answered her rudder so slowly! Trierarchus, get the sail furled!'

He took the warship out in a wide arc to the west of the port, then straightened her course and guided her towards the opening in the outer harbour's walls where the two massive moles came within fifty paces of one another, a gap seemingly barely wide enough to admit the vessel. The deck crew had furled the massive sail with their usual practised speed, leaving the oarsmen as the *Victoria*'s only means of propulsion. Scaurus and his officers watched with interest as the walls of the outer harbour loomed on either side of the warship, while the navarchus called out small changes to the men controlling the steering oars and bellowed for the rowers to back water, reducing the big ship's speed to walking pace. As the gap between the two walls that enfolded the outer harbour enveloped them, he barked out a terse order, his voice raised to carry along the ship's entire length.

'Raise oars!'

As one man the rowers pushed the long shafts of their oars forward and downwards, elevating their blades like the furled wings of a swan, and the *Victoria* eased through the gap with no more than twenty paces to either side. The stub end of the wall to their left passed with a gurgle of water racing between stone and ship, while that to their right presented a smooth, unbroken surface that curled around to form the outer harbour's southern mole.

'Steering oars, hard left turn! Lower oars! Left-hand side – back water!'

The rowers on the flagship's left-hand side heaved at their shafts, pulling the *Victoria* round to her left in a graceful turn.

'Both sides . . . back water!'

The warship slowed to an imperceptible drift with three swift strokes from the oarsmen, while the navarchus stared about him at the berths available along the northern and southern moles, half of them empty, the others occupied by a variety of vessels. Making a swift decision, he pointed to a vacant section of the northern mole to their left, returning command of the ship to its captain.

'There! Trierarchus, put us against the wall there!'

The ship cruised slowly up to the mole, sailors on bow and stern throwing ropes to the waiting dock slaves while the rowers pulled their oars inboard to avoid them being trapped between ship and quayside. As the gangplank was dropped into place, Cassius Ravilla walked up its length and stepped onto the mole's flat stone surface, looking about him with a calculating expression as a group of men hurried out along the wall from the lower city. A middle-aged official who appeared to be their leader bowed deeply, waving an arm at the *Victoria* with an ingratiating smile.

'Greetings, and welcome to—'

Ravilla raised a hand to silence him, pointing out to the north at the next ship in his squadron, which was bearing down on the harbour's entrance.

'My name is Praetorian Fleet Procurator Titus Cassius Ravilla. And do you see that ship? There are another twenty-three just the same in her wake, each one carrying a century of legion infantry. I need twenty-five unloading berths, and I need them now.'

The port official bowed his head again, respectfully acknowledging Ravilla's seniority as a member of the group of senior equestrians known as the 'best of men', those given the empire's most prestigious commands.

'You're carrying soldiers?'

A new voice interjected into their conversation.

'The Praetorian fleet has been directed to deliver two cohorts of legionaries and myself to Antioch with all possible speed, Procurator. I'm taking command of the Third Gallic, and since I have urgent business with the governor I'll need my horses unloaded as a matter of priority.'

The official turned to look at Scaurus, who had strolled up the plank behind Ravilla unnoticed, bowing even deeper as the splendour of his uniform sank in.

'My apologies, Legatus, I didn't see you there.' He turned to his assistant. 'Have the warships berth on the mole, unload their cargo and then pass them on into the inner harbour. We've all the facilities you'll need there, Cassius Ravilla, the port was built for a far larger fleet than we maintain these days. You'll be able to run your ships ashore and perform any maintenance with the assistance of the port's carpenters. You do intend docking for the rest of the closed season, I presume?'

Ravilla shot Scaurus a resigned look.

'It seems that we do.'

Walking up the plank that connected the ship and the mole's stone surface, laden down by the weight of his weapons, shield and equipment, Sanga spat into the water below, stepping out onto the quay's flat surface with a smile of satisfaction. His comrade Saratos followed him down the quayside in the long procession of men making their way along the mole under the direction of their officers, looking curiously up at the mountains that loomed over the port.

'So, is end of voyage.'

Sanga grunted his appreciation of the sentiment.

'Thank fuck for that.'

The Dacian behind him shook his head.

'I happy on ship. No war to fight on ship. Now we here, war come soon.'

Sanga laughed tersely.

'It's what we do mate. All them ships did was get us to the scene of the next fight quicker. That and empty my guts out every now and then.'

Their century's line ran into the back of other men disembarking from ships further down the mole, and without need to be told both men grounded their shields and leaned on them, waiting for the route to clear.

'Is true. You not make good sailor.'

Sanga snorted derisively.

'Is true alright. My guts wouldn't stand for it, and nor would my arse. That lot have been too long away from women if you ask me. It ain't healthy living like that.'

'Not like you big tough men, eh?'

A marine standing guard on the vessel alongside which they were halted shook his head at the two men in disgust, and Sanga shrugged back at him.

'What do you want me to say? You're at sea half the year, without even the sight of a woman, never mind the chance to get your leg over. It's no wonder you're all cuddling up to each other at night, is it?'

The blue-tunicked soldier shook his head, adopting a sad expression.

'Well now friend, that's true enough. We do spend a lot of time at sea alright, and that's lonely for a man that likes the company of women.'

Sanga smirked at him and opened his mouth to push home the advantage, but closed it again as the other man raised a finger, his doleful face suddenly brightening.

'On the other hand, look at our situations now, eh? Off you go to pick a fight with whoever feels like sticking it up the empire's arse. The next few months are going to be all marching, getting shouted at and, if you're really lucky, having some mob of dirty eastern bastards trying you on for size as their new bed warmers. But me . . .'

He paused, smiling brightly.

'We're going to be stuck here for the rest of the winter, aren't we? Stuck in a great big port full of taverns, with nothing better to do but drink and wait for the seas to open again. And let me tell you boys, if there's one thing that a port like this has in large numbers, it's whores. There'll be whores everywhere, in the taverns, on the docks, even down by the ships once we've dragged them up onto the beach.'

He winked at Sanga.

'Spare me a thought lads, while you're slogging your way through the wind and the rain, and when the arrows are flying past your ears like hail. I'll most likely be knocking back a cup of wine and wondering which of the girls to favour next . . .'

Sanga spat into the water again, lifting his shield as the line of soldiers ahead of them started moving again. Saratos followed suit, grinning at his comrade's back.

'He tell you, eh?'

The veteran shook his head in disgust.

'Fucking navy. Come on then you Dacian halfwit, let's go and find out what it is we're doing here in the arse end of nowhere.'

An hour later, with the last of his men in the process of being chivvied ashore to form up beneath the towering walls of the upper city, and with all of the two cohorts' centurions having made their reports, their first spear snapped a crisp salute at his legatus. Scaurus turned from his discussion with his companions, his German slave Arminius, and the Britons Martos and Lugos, originally captives of the war in Britannia but now free men who had chosen to accompany the Tungrians first to Rome and then onward to the east.

'Yes, First Spear?'

'First and second Tungrian cohorts ready for duty, Trib— Legatus. Fourteen hundred and thirty-seven men present and fit, seven recovering from injuries sustained at sea and two men missing. Presumed drowned.'

Scaurus inclined his head in acknowledgement of the report.

'Thank you, First Spear. It won't be very long before you'll have to stop calling them Tungrians, for a time at least. These men will shortly be legionaries in the Third Gallic legion.'

His senior centurion's face was impassive.

'Those that survived the journey in one piece and didn't go over the side. Legatus.'

The senior officer raised an eyebrow.

'You may not have enjoyed the journey, Julius, but consider the alternative - if we were marching from Rome to Antioch we'd still be sailing down the Danubius, with eight hundred miles of slogging it through Thrace and Asia Minor waiting for us at the end of the voyage. My distaste for our new sponsor notwithstanding, I can't deny that he makes things happen. Who else could have ordered the entire Praetorian fleet on the west coast to concentrate at Misenum and sail for the east at ten days' notice? Twenty-five ships sent two thousand miles at the click of one man's fingers – now *that's* power.' He tapped the centurion's scale-armour shirt with a knowing smile. 'And who else could have ordered up fourteen hundred sets of legionary equipment with the stroke of a stylus?'

The first spear, a heavily built man with a dark and brooding bearded face, smoothed back his grey-streaked hair and nodded reluctantly.

'I won't deny the man's ability to make his subordinates jump. Not that I'm used to this stuff yet.'

He tapped his own chest morosely, looking down at the scaled armour that had replaced his mail shirt, lifting one of the thumbnail-sized tinned iron plates that were fixed to the linen shirt in overlapping ranks with wire fasteners.

'Why I couldn't just have had a shirt of that segmented armour like the men all got is beyond me. This just doesn't *feel* right . . .'

He pulled a face, looking down at his booted feet.

'I can't get used to these boots that are more hole than leather either, or having my legs bare.'

The tribune's German servant smirked at him, tilting his head back to emphasise his height advantage over the senior centurion.

'I think the problem is that you've had your delicate little cucumber hidden away in leggings for so long that when it's exposed to cold air it shrivels up to the size of a mushroom.'

Scaurus pursed his lips, darting a glance at the long-haired barbarian standing alongside him as he fought the desire to laugh at his subordinate's gloomy disdain for his new equipment. Julius's scowl set harder. The two Tungrian cohorts had been processed through the Misenum armoury with impressive speed, a succession of counter staff issuing each man with replacement armour, helmet, sword, dagger, tunics and boots to replace equipment long past its best days. Having already asked in an aggrieved tone why there were no leggings being provided, Julius had raised his hands in disbelief on seeing his replacement armour.

'I'm not wearing that!'

Scaurus, having expected the protest, had carefully positioned himself alongside his senior centurion, waiting for the moment when his new equipment hit the counter's scarred wooden surface.

'First Spear, whether we like it or not, we are, for the time being at least, a legion cohort. Two cohorts, if we include the Second Tungrians. And in the legions, let me assure you, centurions simply do not wear the same armour as their men unless in absolute extremis. You're gaining membership of a proud elite, Julius, there are less than two thousand men like you in the whole army, and your new colleagues will be expecting you to look the part. Come on, let's try it all on, shall we?'

In truth, the big man still looked as ill at ease in his finery a month and a half later, as if he'd been dressed in equipment that, whilst it all fitted perfectly, still had the appearance of having been borrowed for the day.

Ignoring the German's witticism, Julius turned to look out over the docked ships again.

'Forced to wear armour that makes me look like the emperor's favourite bum boy, with my woman held as a hostage in Rome while I sail thousands of miles to a place I've never even heard of . . .'

His look of disgust deepened, and Scaurus nodded his agreement.

'And why us, eh Julius? After all, there are plenty of other troops who could have been sent to Syria? Dozens of eager men of the senatorial class who would have jumped at the chance of the legion command that I've been granted, all of whom would be spitting blood to know that an equestrian like me has been chosen over them. You know the answer as well as I do . . .'

'Cleander.'

Julius spat the name out, shaking his head in combined disgust and anger, and Scaurus nodded, his eyes fixed on the ship behind them.

'Indeed. Marcus Aurelius Cleander, former slave, arch schemer and, in consequence, the current imperial chamberlain. The man who controls the empire on behalf of a man with much better things to be doing, and therefore the man with absolute power of life and death over me, you, my man Arminius here, your woman, and anyone else that either of us hold dear. When Cleander invites the most exalted men in the empire to jump, those of them with any sense, which is to say just about all of them, will only pause to enquire as to the height he expects them to achieve. And we've no one to blame but ourselves, Julius, you know that just as well as I do.'

The first spear shrugged.

'What were we to do, wrap the man in chains to stop him going after the bastards who killed his father, slaughtered his family and forced him to abandon the name he was born with?'

Scaurus looked across the parade ground's wide open space, to where the man in question was making his rounds of the troops waiting to march, in the company of Cotta and a hulking centurion carrying a pioneer's axe over his shoulder.

'I doubt that would have worked too well. Tribune *Corvus* isn't the type to take no for an answer, is he?'

All three men contemplated their comrade for a moment, Scaurus's lips creasing in a quiet smile.

'And unfortunately for us, he was rather too effective in his quest for justice. The chamberlain now sees us as a means to an end, dangerous men whose obedience must be guaranteed by a simple and direct threat to those we love.'

His eyes hardened with the words, the line of his jaw tautening with anger.

'And he's right.'

Legatus and first spear fell silent, both reflecting on the overt threats Cleander had made to the former on the day that their transports had sailed from the Praetorian fleet's base at Misenum. Staring out over the huge harbour's glittering waters at the assembled Praetorian fleet, waiting to carry the two cohorts away to the east in defiance of the lateness of the season and the imminence of the seas' closure for the winter, he had spoken with his usual amused candour.

'You have your orders, Rutilius Scaurus, you simply have to

carry them out to the letter. Succeed, and your status as a legion legatus may last longer than the time required for this simple task. Not to mention the equestrian status I've granted to your man Corvus, or rather Marcus Valerius Aquila, the son of a disgraced and executed traitor, as the events of the last few days have so conclusively proven to be his true identity. Fail, on the other hand, and you'll find the welcome on your return more than a little chilly . . .'

The object of their discussion of a moment before walked steadily back across the wide open square towards them, the centurions strolling half a pace behind their tribune. Scaurus looked at the three of them for a moment, resisting the temptation to smile at the fact that while his newly promoted tribune wore his usual thoughtful expression, and his friend Dubnus was pulling at the collar of his armour with the frown of a man unaccustomed to such warmth in the middle of winter, Centurion Cotta's demeanour was more that of a man enjoying an extended and leisurely holiday.

'Your men will be pleased to have their feet back on solid land for more than a night, I presume, gentlemen?'

Cotta shook his head briskly.

'On the contrary, Legatus, I think I've adapted to the ocean-going life, especially seeing as we had the biggest ship in the whole of the ocean for a private yacht. Now we're ashore again it'll be back to shouting at idiots and trying to get the sand out of my arse crack again.'

Julius raised an eyebrow at Scaurus.

'I've said it before—'

The veteran centurion nodded with a soft snort of laughter, seemingly unconcerned by the big man's superior rank.

'And you'll say it again, First Spear?'

'And I'll say it *again*. Bringing this insolent, worn out and *retired* officer along for the ride might have seemed like a bright idea back in Rome, when all he had to do was walk around behind the women and tell his men when to carry their shopping, but—'

A rare smile creased Marcus's face, and the first spear turned a hard stare on his former centurion.

'Is there something amusing you, *Tribune*?'

The younger man shook his head, bowing slightly in recognition of both Julius's irritation and his own temporary status as superior officer to the man from whom he'd been taking orders only two months before.

'Nothing, First Spear. Please do continue.'

'Thank you, *sir*. Where was I . . . ?'

'Carrying the shopping.'

'Thank you, Martos . . .'

The first spear attempted to skewer the one-eyed barbarian warrior who had joined the discussion with the same glare he'd used on Marcus, but the Briton simply raised a knowing eyebrow until Julius turned back to the object of his ire.

'Do you *really* think you'll be able to keep up on the march? At your age?'

Cotta shrugged.

'We'll know soon enough, won't we First Spear? After all, given that I joined up at fourteen, I'm still younger than a good few of *your* old sweats.'

Julius opened his mouth to retort, but Scaurus raised a hand, his face set in the expression that every man in the group had learned to recognise as meaning the discussion was over.

'The main reason that Centurion Cotta has been recruited to our ranks is obvious enough. I have been directed to take control of the Third Gallic, and the centurion here ended his service as a centurion with the very same legion.'

He opened his mouth to continue, only to close it again as Cotta beat him to it, his tone suddenly deadly earnest.

'There are one or two other reasons, although the legatus here is trying to spare you your blushes, First Spear. Shall I name them?'

Julius looked at the veteran centurion from beneath lowered brows, and Marcus wondered if he'd detected a hint of a twitch in his friend's lips.

'Go on then.'

Cotta straightened his back.

'Not that you'll recognise any of them, given you've spent most of your life chasing blue-nosed tribesmen round some small wet island, but here they are. Zeugma, Edessa, Nisibis, Singara, Hatra, Ctesiphon . . .'

He paused, looking at Julius with a questioning expression, but the first spear's shrug was eloquent.

'None of which means anything to me.'

The veteran smiled grimly.

'They all mean something to me. Garrison duty, skirmishes, pitched battles, even a burning city with the legion turned loose to do its worst, may the spirits of the dead forgive us. What it means, First Spear, is that I've been this way before, and with the very legion your legatus here has been sent to take a grip of. I fought all the way down the Euphrates to the Parthian capital twenty years ago under the emperor Verus, and then I watched the Third fall to pieces when the plague took hold, and we retreated back up the river with half of the lads either dead or on their last legs. I know that legion inside out, Julius, and all of the current crop of centurions were no better than chosen men when I left.'

He gestured to Scaurus.

'The legatus here needs an edge, a man who knows where the bodies are buried. And that means me.'

'The centurion's experience will be of enormous value, if we're to take a grip of the legion and shake it into some sort of order. So, as long as Cotta here can do a meaningful imitation of a legion centurion, he will remain just that. This is unfamiliar territory for all of us, First Spear, and I have the suspicion that we're going to need every little advantage we can get.'

Julius fixed the veteran soldier with a dark gaze.

'I'll be watching you, Centurion. I suggest you work hard on not attracting my attention. *Very* hard.'

Scaurus turned away with a beckoning nod to Marcus.

'March the cohorts up the road to Antioch once they're ready to move, will you First Spear? I think the port's procurator has had long enough to get word up to the governor's residence, so

Tribune Corvus and I had better go and show our respects, and give him the bad news. I'll take Silus and his horsemen with me as well; I've a small but rather important job in mind for them.'

Cotta and Julius turned to look at him, and the veteran centurion raised a questioning eyebrow.

'Bad news, Legatus?'

Pursing his thin lips, Scaurus shrugged at them both, tapping the sealed leather document case that Arminius had guarded closely throughout the six weeks of their journey from Rome.

'I might be wrong, of course, but the look on the Chamberlain's face when the discussion turned to Governor Dexter wasn't the happiest of expressions. And, I should point out, before his untimely demise with the blunt end of a guardsman's spear thrust straight though him, Praetorian Prefect Perennis did oversee the appointment of several well-placed provincial governors, including one Gaius Domitius Dexter. All of them were given control of provinces whose opportunities for the generation of private wealth go hand in hand with significant military commands, two or three legions apiece. And all of them were, I gather, men likely to show their gratitude for being awarded such lucrative and influential positions by . . .'

He paused, his lips twisting into another wry smile.

'Let us simply say that their happiness at being granted opportunities to generate considerable personal wealth would probably have been expressed in the most practical of manners, involving the loyalty of their legions, in the event that Perennis had been forced to take the purple by some cruel circumstance such as the emperor's assassination.'

Cotta inclined his head with due respect to his legatus's point.

'So now that Perennis is dead, it's probably not good news for the governors he appointed?'

The legatus shook his head.

'No, Centurion Cotta. Probably not good news at all.'

'Leave? You want me to leave the city? *Now?*'

Imperial Governor Gaius Domitius Dexter, sat forward in his chair, leaning his arms on the wide, polished wooden desk in front of him and stared at the suddenly discomfited legion commander who was sitting bolt upright on the other side with a face set in lines of shocked distress.

'In point of fact, I want you to leave the *province*, Magius Lateranus. And most certainly now! You have been replaced, unscheduled, unannounced, and quite astonishingly, by a man who's been delivered here by means of the Praetorian fleet, which sends us a message in itself. Your replacement disembarked from the flagship less than two hours ago, and will doubtless be up the road and knocking on your legion's gates before sunset. And I have to say that a man who arrives courtesy of the emperor's private navy is likely to be a man with a fairly well-defined agenda. Not to mention a man in something of a hurry. So I don't think it would be good for either of us if you were on hand once he gets a good look at the Third Gallic, do you?'

The legatus nodded slowly.

'But to leave so suddenly?'

Dexter waved a hand to dismiss his concerns.

'A death in the family. Your father, perhaps? That would be more than sufficient reason for you to leave for Rome, would it not? And in the absence of any ship's master being willing to risk such a voyage at this time of the year, you'll have the perfect reason to travel overland, thereby avoiding the risk of meeting your replacement since you will leave the city to the north while he arrives from the south.'

'But my personal belongings—'

Another wave of the hand.

'Can be sent after you. Whereas if this man Scaurus lays hands on you, given what we both know you've been doing over the last three years . . .'

The words hung in the air while the officer's face slowly drained of blood.

'What *I've* been doing?'

The governor leaned back in his chair.

'Come now Legatus, it's a well-known fact that what I know about the military could be captured in very large letters on a very small scroll. It's a mystery to most of my peers how I was ever appointed to command a province with such a strong complement of legions, although I think we both know why Perennis favoured me over the better-qualified candidates. Whereas you have all the right experience, don't you? After all, *you* were a tribune with one of the Rhine legions, were you not? *You* know how a legion works.'

He leaned forward.

'And so does this man Scaurus. Have you ever met him?'

The soldier shook his head, sniffing in disdain.

'He's not one of us, I know that much.'

Dexter nodded, steepling his fingers under his chin.

'Indeed he isn't! He's an equestrian, which makes the whole thing that little bit more puzzling. His family used to be senatorial, but his ancestor managed to get on the wrong side of Vespasian, back in the Year of the Four Emperors, and was reduced to a thin stripe as his punishment. The family have scraped along ever since, but they've never lost their patrician sense of duty and honour. The man's father fell on his own sword twenty years or so ago, accepting the blame for some disaster or other on the Rhenus it seems, whereas the legatus who was actually responsible walked out from under that particular falling tree without a blemish on his honour. The younger Scaurus was at an impressionable age, it seems, and he promptly swore to avenge his father.'

He smiled up at the legatus.

'And, in consequence, he's something of an animal when matters of military propriety are under consideration. He shipped out here with the last governor as a tribune on the man's staff. It seems that Helvius Pertinax has become something of a sponsor to him, and he certainly gave Scaurus free licence to go wherever and do whatever he liked while he was governor of the province. He made the man his inspector of troops, and woe betide any legatus or prefect whose manpower wasn't what it ought to be, or whose soldiers weren't properly trained. I met him just the once, during the official handover from Pertinax to myself, and he was never anything less than polite and respectful.'

He shook his head at the memory.

'And yet I had the impression that he could have bitten my throat out without a change of expression. How the young bastard's ended up commanding a legion, I can only imagine. Anyway . . .'

Standing, he reached into a desk drawer and pulled out a small but heavy bag.

'Gold. Enough to get you back to Rome, if you spend it sensibly. Go now, unless you still want to be standing there with your mouth open when the man makes his appearance. I'll have your affairs tidied up and send the rest of the money on after you.'

Lateranus looked at him for a moment with a nonplussed expression, then nodded wearily.

'I'll go. But what about our co-conspirators?'

Dexter shook his head dismissively.

'They'll keep their heads well down until I find a way to deal with Gaius Rutilius Scaurus. And having them close to him will be the best way to ensure that when that opportunity comes I'm ready to ram it home with both hands, so to speak.'

'There it is. Antioch.'

Scaurus reined his horse in and raised a hand to halt the men behind him. From their vantage point at the top of the mountain that towered over Seleucia, the city was spread out before them, still five miles away but with its magnificence undiluted by the distance.

'Make the most of it, gentlemen. Up close it's the usual mix of poor hygiene, inadequate sewerage and public indecency. Half a million people crammed into a city fit to house no more than half of them.'

'Sounds good to me.'

Tribune Corvus raised an eyebrow at the cavalry detachment's decurion.

'I presume that your enthusiasm is mainly in anticipation of the public indecency aspect of the legatus's description.'

Silus nodded happily, patting the purse hanging from his belt.

'I've a mind to go riding, Tribune. And I may ride them two or three at a time.'

'And you didn't get enough *riding* practice, while you were sat around the transit barracks in Rome with nothing better to do?'

The decurion grinned back at him.

'I won't deny it was good of you to spend as long as you did on that private business of yours in Rome, Tribune, and gave us all a nice rest from galloping round pulling your chestnuts out of the fire. But after all that time on a boat with nothing better to screw than Old Lady Palm and her five daughters, the prospect of a city that's known for its professional women is enough to have me nudging my saddle horns.'

Scaurus shook his head.

There won't be any professional women where we're going, Decurion. Take a good look at the city, and tell me what you see.'

Silus leaned over his horse's neck, his eyes narrowing as he stared at the city nestled beneath the mountain that loomed over it.

'A lot of buildings beneath a mountain, with a wall around the whole thing and a river running past it.'

And further out?'

'Fewer buildings . . . farms . . . ah.'

'Yes. A fortress. And it's a big one, big enough for a legion in fact. They're usually based on the frontier, or in known centres of potential trouble, but the governors of Syria have always kept a base of operations ready here, in case of a defeat on the Parthian frontier and the need to pull back to defend the city. Although quite how one might go about defending a city with a damned great mountain towering over it always rather baffled me. The policy with regard to this province has been one of forward defence for as long as I can remember, but all that seems to have changed from what the harbour master told me.'

He put his heels into the horse's ribs, encouraging the animal to a swift trot, and the rest of the party followed suit.

'Oh, and Decurion . . .'

Silus trotted his beast up alongside the legatus's animal.

'Sir?'

'I've a job for you, something perfectly suited to your diplomatic skills. Take Centurion Cotta along with you, I think you'll find his prior experience with this legion both valuable in opening doors and entertaining, when the men behind them see who it was knocking.'

Silus raised a jaundiced eyebrow at the veteran.

'I was wondering why you'd brought him along. The horse'll certainly be grateful to be out from under him, given he's got all the riding ability of a sack of badly trained shit.'

'Gentlemen, Governor Dexter.'

The governor's secretary withdrew, leaving Scaurus and Marcus standing in the middle of a wide expanse of spotlessly clean marble across which their dusty boots had left faint ochre tracks. The governor was sitting behind his desk when the two men entered the light, airy office, his face turned towards the window that looked out over the city that sprawled away to the east before washing up against Mount Silpius's western flank. Standing a pace behind his legatus, Marcus studied the senator's appearance with an eye long accustomed to picking out the subtleties of fashion among the empire's ruling class. The man sitting opposite them, deliberately turning his profile to them in an arrogant display of his superiority, had evidently cultivated the bushy, combed-out beard that had become the norm as Rome's elite carefully aped the emperor's chosen look. The beard's fluffy hair disguised a jowly chin, and the governor had the look of a man unaccustomed to physical exercise. Turning theatrically, he stood, smoothing out his toga before striding round the desk with an outstretched hand and a broad smile.

'Legatus Scaurus, greetings. Welcome back to Antioch.'

Scaurus stepped forward and took his hand, presenting a composed face to match the governor's inscrutability.

'Greetings, Governor Dexter! I have sailed from Rome to take command of the Third Gallic legion at the express command of the emperor, and to bring you this.'

He held out the message scroll that the imperial chamberlain had given him on the day of the Tungrian cohorts' sailing, his face fixed in neutral lines as he recalled Cleander's wry advice: 'I can assure you that Domitius Dexter isn't going to be a happy man when he opens that scroll, so you'd probably be well advised to make sure you look appropriately innocent when he does so.'

Dexter took the scroll, still staring fixedly at the man standing before him with a look that combined curiosity with something harder.

'Thank you . . . *Legatus*.'

In the governor's mouth the last word was more question than title, and Marcus saw signs of a growing incredulity spreading across his face despite his obvious efforts to compose himself. Scaurus offered him a second scroll, already unsealed and with its edges foxed from repeated reading.

'Just for the sake of formality, Governor, you might like to read *my* orders . . .'

His tone was light, but the edge of steel in his voice caused Dexter's eyes to narrow as he reached for the scroll. Reading swiftly, his head shook slightly from side to side with apparent amazement.

'If I wasn't reading it with my own eyes then I simply wouldn't have believed it. You are appointed to command the Third Gallic, to gather whatever forces can be spared, and then to march to our outpost at Nisibis, defeating any enemy forces that may be threatening the integrity of Rome's rightful frontiers.' He looked up at Scaurus with a bemused expression. 'You. An *equestrian*. In all my years I can honestly say I've never once been as genuinely amazed as I am now. An equestrian legatus? What next?'

'A freedman as imperial chamberlain, perhaps, Governor?'

Dexter's head snapped up, his face suddenly dark with anger.

'If you're trying to make fun of me then I'll warn you that I'm not a man who reacts well to humour at my expense.'

Scaurus shook his head.

'I'm deadly serious, Governor. There is a freedman currently occupying the role of imperial chamberlain, and running the empire in all but name.'

Dexter leaned back in his seat with the look of a man who saw the walls around him starting to topple inward.

'Cleander?'

Scaurus nodded, and the governor ran a hand through his hair.

'Gods below, the empire's fate has slipped into the hands of the most venal individual in the palace. What happened to Perennis?'

'The praetorian prefect managed to incur the displeasure of the emperor. I believe it had something to do with his putting his own image on a large number of coins, which then found their way into the emperor's hands. As you might imagine, the matter didn't end well for him.'

Dexter leaned forward, his eyes suddenly hard.

'And this happened when exactly?'

Scaurus delivered his reply with a deadpan expression, although the words were subtly barbed.

'Three months or so.'

He paused for a moment, then twisted the knife.

'Clearly I must apologise for being the bearer of bad news. I would have expected you to have heard of the change before this.'

'Fetch the centurion of the guard would you lads?'

The two soldiers guarding the legion barracks main gate dithered for a brief moment, each of them looking at the other in consternation, and Cotta shook his head in amusement.

'I see the quality of the average recruit out here hasn't got any better while I've been away.'

'You! Stay here and make sure I don't try anything underhand. And you!'

The other man snapped to attention.

'Very nicely done, soldier. You go and fetch the duty officer, right?'

The soldier in question darted back in through the gate, leaving his mate to stare at the two officers before him in bemusement. Cotta grinned back at him, clearly enjoying the legionary's discomfiture.

'I know, it's not every day that two strange officers turn up and tell you to go and find an adult for them to talk to, is it? And Silas here smells of horses, just to make it even stranger. Back in my day, you know, you wouldn't have—'

His monologue was interrupted by the curt interjection of a centurion who appeared behind the soldier with a glowering stare.

'Yes?'

Cotta smiled.

'Good afternoon. We are officers of Legatus Scaurus's personal staff, and we're here to see the camp prefect.'

The centurion shook his head in obvious incomprehension.

'Who the fuck—'

'Is Legatus Scaurus? He's your new commanding officer, you dozy bastard.'

The centurion bristled, but Cotta was faster to the punch, raising his vine stick to point at the clearly irritated officer.

'And don't go thinking you can just fuck me off and go back to your nap. I knew you when you were a snotty-nosed recruit, so all that chin jutting isn't going to work with me!'

The duty officer's eyes narrowed, and his response was little more than a whisper.

'Cotta?'

'Yes. And yes, I am that evil-minded bastard you never thought you'd see again, you halfwit.'

The veteran centurion stepped forward.

'Your new legatus has sent me here on a mission of the highest importance. So point me at the camp prefect's office and I'll be on my way.'

Coming out of his momentary shock, the duty officer shook his head.

'I can't.'

Cotta grinned back at him.

'You don't have any choice, sonny. My *legatus* has given me this. And my legatus outranks your first spear quite nicely.'

He unfurled the scroll that had been waiting in his right hand:

'You will proceed to the headquarters of the Third Gallic Legion and take possession, on my behalf, of any and all legion records, in order to ensure an orderly handover from the previous legatus to myself. Any officer who obstructs this lawful order will answer directly to myself as legatus of the legion, as appointed by the emperor himself.'

He grinned at the centurion.

'You quite literally have no choice. Get in my way and my legatus will tear you a new arsehole, one so generously sized that you'll fall into it and disappear.'

The other man shook his head.

'No, I mean you literally can't see the camp prefect. There isn't a camp prefect.'

While Cotta frowned, the man beside him grinned happily.

'I remember a joke someone told me . . .' Silus pondered for a moment. 'Oh yes. Why is a camp prefect like an arsehole?'

Cotta turned to Silus with a raised eyebrow.

'Go on then, it seems we have time for your joke.'

The decurion shrugged.

'Well, he does some really important shit, but nobody wants to spend any more time with him than they really have to.'

Cotta nodded equably.

'That's actually not bad. Well done, Silus.'

He turned back to the legion officer.

'So, in the absence of a camp prefect . . .' He shook his head in disbelief. 'We'll just have to go for the next best thing. Is your first spear in camp?'

The centurion shook his head again.

'He's in the city. He went in last night and isn't back yet.'

The veteran pulled a face.

'Well I'm not going anywhere near the tribunes. Where's your legatus?'

'He went into Antioch in a hurry this morning and hasn't come back.'

Cotta pointed at the man with a triumphant expression.

'So as duty centurion you're the most senior man left in the barracks! Come on then!'

He brushed past the man with a gesture for Silus to follow him.

'Here, you can't—'

Turning back to the centurion, Cotta tilted his head to one side.

'Well in truth it does rather look as if I can, doesn't it? I have orders from the legion's new commander telling me to do so, the legion's old legatus seems to have made himself scarce by the looks of things. Someone's been careless enough not to bother replacing whoever the last camp prefect was, and your first spear seems to like it in the town a lot better than out here with the soldiers. So I'm just going to do what every good soldier should and follow my orders, which means going for a look at the legion records to see what's what. You can either arrest me – which will be interesting given that Silus here has a pathological hatred of being confined and could punch the head off a statue – or you can come with me to make sure I don't try to make off with the legion's pay. Oh, and you might want to send a runner into the city, to tip the first spear off to the fact that he's going to have a very bad-tempered legatus here within the hour. It seems only fair to give the poor man some warning, eh?'

Governor Dexter looked down at the scroll on the desk before him with the expression of a man contemplating a live scorpion, and the two men waited in silence while he broke the parchment's wax seal and unrolled the message.

'Do you know the contents of this message, Legatus?'

Dexter's voice was suddenly quiet, his former bombast replaced with a softer, more menacing tone, and Scaurus simply shook his head.

'Then for your information I am hereby relieved of my duties as governor of the province of Syria, and instructed only to conduct essential duties of state while I await my successor.'

He shook his head bitterly.

'A successor who will doubtless have been hand-picked from among the emperor's extensive collection of arse-lickers and catamites!'

He sat back in the chair and looked up at Scaurus through narrowed eyes.

'Essential duties of state. The term covers a multitude of potential activities, does it not?'

Leaning forward, his voice took on a conspiratorial tone.

'I'll tell you what it does include, Legatus. Matters of the empire's defence against its foreign enemies. After all, the province of Syria Palestina can hardly be left rudderless, drifting aimlessly at the mercy of the whim of our enemies, can it?'

Scaurus nodded briskly.

'I understand, Governor, and I laud your commitment to your province's security. You wish to march on Nisibis at the head of the Third Legion.'

His answer was a spluttering laugh.

'At the head of the legion? Of course not! My place is here, ensuring that the entirety of my province is protected from the rapacity of those who would seek to exploit any weakness. You only have Nisibis to consider, Legatus, but my responsibilities are far more broad than one scruffy little desert town that isn't even part of my province. No, I shall stay here in Antioch, and ensure that the potential disaster of Rome losing this pearl of a city does not come to pass. You may march on Nisibis, Legatus, but you may take no more than half of the legion's strength with you. The remainder will stay here, under my command.'

Scaurus raised an eyebrow.

'Stay here, Governor? Surely the Third Gallic should be based at Raphanaea, or up at Zeugma, strengthening the watch on the border with Osrhoene?'

Dexter waved a dismissive hand.

'Osrhoene, Legatus, is a client of Rome. The risk that King Abgar might invade the province is only slightly greater than that of a revival of the Republic, which is to say none at all! I decided at the start of my tenure that Antioch would be best protected by the presence of its own legion, permanently available to safeguard the city. A detachment from the Third Parthian more than suffices to keep watch on the Euphrates at Zeugma, and in time of need my Gauls could be marched to reinforce them quickly enough. After all, we'll have plenty of warning from Abgar's scouts, should the King of Kings make the unlikely decision to move against us.'

'But the city can only be attacked if an enemy manages to cross the Euphrates, which is why the fortress at Zeugma—'

Dexter shook his head briskly.

'Your predecessor Legatus Lateranus and I decided that the position at Zeugma is far too easily bypassed by an enemy as cunning as the Parthians, so we centred our defence of the province's north on Antioch instead.'

Dexter turned away to look out over the city again.

'You can discuss the military ins and outs of the matter with Lateranus when he returns from leave, if you're still here, of course.'

Scaurus stared back at him for a moment before answering.

'Leave? When do you expect his return?'

Dexter shrugged, his face professionally expressionless.

'I have no idea. We received word of his father's death only yesterday, and so of course I sent him back to Rome immediately. He'll be gone for months, I'd imagine.'

The legatus stared levelly at his superior for a moment.

'I see.'

'I'm sure you do. After all, you're no less a gentleman for only being an equestrian. So serious a family matter must take precedence.'

Scaurus nodded.

'I think I understand the urgency of my predecessor's departure only too well, Governor. With your permission I'll go and take command of my legion, since it's here?'

Dexter nodded, turning back to his view across the city.

'By all means, Legatus. I'm sure you'll find your deputy Gabinus Umbrius has a firm grip of matters. I'll have your orders written up and sent over to you this afternoon.'

The two men bowed and left him staring over the rooftops, making their way out of the palace in silence. Scaurus stopped at the top of the steps and looked out at the city with a small shake of his head.

'Half the legion. Five cohorts against a Parthian army. We'll all be dead before we get within sight of Nisibis if that order stands. Let's go and break the good news to Julius.'

2

Legatus and tribune found Cotta standing outside the Third Gallic's fortress, alongside a tall, thin man who was equipped in an almost identical version of his centurion's uniform. His long faced was heavily lined, and his hair completely grey, but his demeanour seemed steady enough at first glance. The legion officer seemed to be remonstrating with their colleague in a lively manner, but both men snapped to attention on noticing the approach of senior officers.

Cotta strode forward, speaking quickly to Scaurus in low tones calculated not to carry to the legion officer.

'The legion's records are as they should be, Legatus, properly maintained and fully detailed. Apart from the fact that there's a lot of men away on leave, it looks clean enough.'

He extended a hand to introduce his colleague.

'Legatus, this is First Spear Quintinus. We served together in the last war with Parthia.'

The legion man snapped to attention and saluted.

'Legatus! First Spear Gaius Quintinus at your disposal! We will do what is ordered and at every command we will be ready!'

Scaurus and Marcus returned the salute, the legatus choosing to acknowledge the first spear's obvious look of disgruntlement when it was suggested that Cotta might be best employed finding barracks to accommodate the Tungrian cohorts, waiting until the veteran officer was out of earshot before turning to his new senior centurion.

'Is there a problem, First Spear Quintinus?'

Quintinus shook his head.

'It's not right, Legatus, not when we didn't even know that

Legatus Lateranus was being replaced. Cotta and your Decurion simply barged into the camp and made their way to the headquarters building, and when they were challenged by the duty centurion they simply handed him your written orders and refused to take any more notice of him. You're lucky that none of my officers decided to push the issue.'

Scaurus considered him levelly for a moment before replying.

'But they didn't, did they? Which speaks volumes for both my men and your officers. But it's just as well.'

He lowered his voice, forcing the first spear to lean closer to hear his words.

'Any man who chooses to disregard my orders can expect to find himself roped to a post with his back hanging off. *Any* man. It would have made for an interesting fight though. I believe Centurion Cotta's famously short temper would have gone up like a signal fire doused with naphtha if he'd felt that his long service with this very legion wasn't being accorded the right degree of respect.'

The first spear nodded angrily, clearly holding onto his own temper by a narrow margin.

'And that's another thing, sir. In this legion appointments to the rank of centurion are approved by a committee of centurions. Cotta may well have done his time wielding a vine stick, but he left the Gauls ten years ago, and under a cloud of suspicion to do with the death of an emperor. An *emperor*, Legatus. Under the circumstances I don't think that the centurions will—'

Scaurus shook his head, his eyes narrowing with anger, raising a finger to forestall any further complaint.

'Two points, First Spear. Firstly, the *emperor* you're talking about was no more an emperor than you are. This legion acclaimed Gaius Avidius Cassius as ruler for the simple reason that the officers of the day expected to be handsomely rewarded for their loyalty. In removing Cassius's threat to the legitimate emperor, Centurion Cotta did no more than was his duty, and he did it under the command of a tribune who had been placed in his role by Marcus Aurelius himself, and for precisely that purpose.

A wise emperor knows where threats to his rule will come from, and positions the right men in the right places to deal with them as required. And Marcus Aurelius was no fool.

'Furthermore, First Spear, Cotta's *suspected* role in Cassius's death will remain no more than suspicion, if you're still keen to be carrying your vine stick for the rest of your career.'

He stared at Quintinus for a moment before continuing. 'And secondly, First Spear, to whom exactly do you imagine that this legion belongs? To you and your brother officers, or to the people and the senate of Rome?'

Quintinus looked at his superior for a moment before replying. 'To the people and the senate of Rome, Legatus.'

Scaurus nodded.

'Exactly, First Spear. The people's will is enacted by the senate, among whom the emperor is *primus inter pares*, First Spear, very much the first among equals. And when the emperor awarded me the singular privilege of commanding this legion, he made no mention of having to run any of my decisions past *committees of centurions*!'

He spat the words out with a vehemence that made the first spear flinch minutely despite his attempt at portraying iron self-control.

'Centurion Cotta is an experienced officer who, as you know all too well, has seen combat on numerous occasions in the course of his career. On top of which, he's already commanded men of this legion, and in consequence he will be of great value to me as I get to grips with my new command. If you and your fellow centurions have any complaint with that decision I will be happy to hear that concern, and any recommendations you may have for me, in due course and in the time-honoured manner. I will not, to be very clear, be setting any store by an informal and highly irregular decision-making process that only serves to illustrate the sort of man my predecessor here seems to have been.'

He looked about him, staring with apparent curiosity at the rows of barrack buildings on either side of the street that ran to the headquarters building.

'Now, to business. How many men do you have here in Antioch?'

Quintinus opened the tablet that had been sitting in his left hand.

'Nine cohorts, Legatus. We've a large number of men on leave and on detached duties of various sorts, but this is the heart of the Third Gallic, with two thousand, nine hundred and sixty-four men available for duty.'

'*Nine* cohorts, First Spear?'

Quintinus turned to Marcus, who had stepped forward alongside Scaurus with a look of incomprehension.

'Yes Tribune . . .'

'My name is Corvus. Marcus Tribulus Corvus. Where is the tenth cohort?'

Quintinus looked at Marcus for a moment before answering, a shadow of pain creasing his face.

'We lost the Sixth on the other side of the Euphrates months ago, Tribune. They were killed to the last man, except for a few local scouts and a tribune who managed to evade the Parthians to bring the story of their deaths back.'

The younger man frowned.

'He ran, rather than facing the enemy with his men?'

Quintinus shook his head.

'Not really sir. I'd suggest you meet the young gentleman and draw your conclusions once you've looked into his eyes.'

Marcus nodded.

'Fair enough, First Spear. And where might I find this man?'

The senior centurion pursed his lips.

'In Daphne, Tribune, with the rest of the legion's senior officers, yourself and the legatus here accepted. The legatus, Legatus Lateranus that is, arranged for himself and his young gentlemen to be quartered there when the legion's not in the field.'

'Daphne. I see. The place does have a certain . . . reputation.'

Scaurus smiled at Quintinus's almost imperceptible flinch as a look of disgust crossed his tribune's face.

'Why don't you take yourself off to Daphne, Tribune Corvus, and deliver an invitation to a briefing with their new legatus on my behalf? I'm sure you'll find a way to make the point to them that any failure to attend this evening will result in their new legatus taking a positively violent exception to their continued occupation of their current positions.'

Marcus saluted and turned away. Quintinus was silent until he was out of earshot.

'I can't see our officers being all that happy to have their evening spoilt, Legatus. I believe they've recently become rather fond of dinner parties . . .'

He fell silent as Scaurus smiled and shook his head.

'And just how many *young gentlemen* does my new legion have on its books, First Spear?'

Quintinus sighed.

'Nine, Legatus. Two broad stripe tribunes and seven of the equestrian class.'

'*Nine*. I see. And we are supposed to have how many exactly?'

'Six, Legatus. One broad stripe tribune who has the role of your deputy, and five narrow stripe tribunes who are—'

'Who *should* be competent military men, respected equestrian officers each with a cohort command under their belts and therefore respected by the legion's centurions. They should be capable of performing the full range of administration for a pair of cohorts, and providing leadership in battle. Is that what they are, First Spear?'

Quintinus shook his head.

'Our narrow stripe tribunes are for the most part serving for the first time. As, to be fair, are both of the broad stripe men.'

Scaurus looked at him.

'Two senior tribunes?'

'The legatus believes – *believed* – that a backup for his deputy would be a positive thing.'

The legatus shot him a derisive look.

'So, they should be experienced soldiers, instead of which they all seem to be neophytes. We should have six, and instead we have nine of them. They are the sons of rich men, I presume, sent here purely because Antioch is something of a backwater where they will be at little risk of anything as vulgar as actually having to go to war. After all, the Parthians haven't threatened the border for twenty years after the battering we gave them the last time they tried it on, so why not send their boys to Syria, and let them spend their time chasing girls in Daphne, eh?'

He stretched.

'And now, First Spear, I think I'll go and inspect my quarters. After that I'll be going to my office to examine the Third's records, and see what sort of legion it is that I've been bequeathed by Legatus Lateranus. You, no doubt, will be keen to greet my cohorts into camp; they should be here soon enough now under the command of my first spear. You'll know him easily enough, he's a little older than me, black hair and beard with more than a little grey, and spectacularly bad tempered even for a centurion. He's in command of two full cohorts of Tungrian auxiliaries who the emperor has seen fit to second to this legion while it's under my command. You might want to warn your officers that my Tungrians are battle hardened, and won't take kindly to any of the usual games that tend to get played when new units arrive in a camp. So don't say I didn't warn you!'

He turned away, then spun on his heel.

'I almost forgot. Doubtless you'll also want to arrange for the traditional demonstration of your men's abilities? Let me know what time tomorrow morning you'll be parading the men, I'm looking forward to seeing if my new command has the skills to deal with what it's going to be facing a few weeks from now.'

He walked away up the street, leaving the first spear staring at his back with a disquieted expression.

Marcus walked his horse through Antioch's teeming crowds with a watchful group of legionaries detailed to escort him through the busy streets by Quintinus, men well accustomed to the variety of tricks and ruses employed by the city's thieves and pickpockets. Hemmed in by the mass of humanity brought so close together by the lure of the city's sophistication, he allowed himself to progress at the pace of the street, his senses still reeling at the rich smells of the taverns and spice shops after so long at sea, exotic scents underlaid by the deeper, richer stench of too many men and beasts packed into a confined space.

As the group of soldiers neared the southern wall, the city's magnificent agora opened out to his left with the gaudily painted bulk of an amphitheatre rising behind it, the wide open space thronged with men gathered around a troupe of gladiators who were demonstrating their abilities to the admiring crowd. Halting his escort, Marcus mounted the horse so as to get a better view of the scene, watching through the colonnade that lined the street as matched pairs of fighters went through their mock-antagonistic routines to enthusiastic applause from the watching multitude. Most of them were no better than average, but among them were a few men who moved with crisp purpose, the arena killers against whom their hapless fellows were dead meat.

'You like the games, do you, sir?'

The question broke his reverie, and the young tribune looked down at the soldier holding his horse's bridle with a faint smile.

'I was trained to fight by a man like that.'

The man's eyebrows raised in surprise.

'Gladiator, was he, sir?'

Marcus nodded, feeling an almost physical pain at the sudden, brutal reminder of the events that had led to the Tungrians being posted to Syria.

'He was the finest gladiator ever to fight in the Flavian Arena, some say. To me he was more like a second father . . .'

He dismounted, gesturing to the gate rising over the crowd, two blocks distant.

'Shall we?'

The soldier nodded, turning to the people nearest to them with a sudden flash of anger as a man stretched out a finger to touch Marcus's sculpted breastplate with a look of awe.

'Oi, get your fucking hands off the officer, unless you want me to cut them off and stuff them up your arse!'

The man looked at him uncomprehendingly, and with a sigh of irritation the soldier switched from Greek to Aramaic, backing up the threat with the highly polished blade of his dagger. 'Fucking peasants. Anyone'd think you was Achilles himself from the looks they're giving you.' The soldier shot him a swift apologetic glance. 'Not that you don't look proper hard, Tribune. Be nice to have some men with scars and hard faces leading the legion for a change.'

The young tribune reflexively put a hand to the freshly healed cut across the bridge of his nose, the legacy of a frantic escape from the heart of a barbarian fortress, and the ensuing hunt across northern Britannia's lethally treacherous marshes. At the Daphne Gate he ordered the men to wait for him, smiling as they immediately gathered around in the wall's shadow and started a game of dice. Trotting the beast down the road to the south, he mused on the contrast between the teeming city thoroughfares and the lightly trafficked street that ran along the mountain's shoulder. After five miles or so, the reason for the road's relative emptiness became apparent, as he rode around a bend to find his way barred by a wooden gate, a military checkpoint manned by legionaries.

Seeing his lavishly decorated equipment, the soldiers jumped to attention, saluting at the detachment commander's barked order while Marcus climbed down from the horse's saddle.

'Tribune Sir! We will do what is ordered and at every command we will be ready!'

Marcus looked round at the men of the detachment.

'Good afternoon, gentlemen. I'm looking for the Third Legion's officers. Do you know where I might find them?'

The detachment's chosen man, a heavily built man with the look of a pugilist, stepped forward and nodded vigorously.

'Yes Tribune, I'll have one of the men walk you up there.'

'Up?'

The big man smiled.

'Nothing but the best for our young gentlemen, sir. They've rented a villa on the mountain slopes, high up, with a view for miles around.'

The soldier gestured to one of his men.

'You, take the officer here up to the Honeypot.'

Marcus raised an eyebrow in question.

'Honeypot?'

The chosen man smiled knowingly.

'You'll see why we call it that soon enough sir. I presume you'll be moving in with the other gentlemen?'

Marcus held his gaze for a moment, reading the man's barely hidden cynicism as to the legion officers' professionalism, and by association his own.

'Thank you, Chosen.'

He turned away, leaving the soldiers staring after him, and followed his guide along the road's path as it ran through a further belt of forest until it branched into three, one running straight on, a second climbing gently away to its left, and another taking the steepest path up into the foothills.

'This way sir.'

The soldier indicated the steepest of the three roads, and after a moment's walk Marcus found his calves aching at the sudden and unaccustomed exercise after so long at sea. The soldier turned back, and, seeing the pained expression on the officer's face, slowed his pace.

'Keep walking,' said Marcus. 'I'm just unfit from too long on a ship coming here from Rome.'

The road ran out of the forest and on up the slope into a wide open area in which a dozen or so palatial villas had been built on the hillside, high above the groves of bay laurels that had given the city's richest and most decadent suburb its name.

'Are these the largest houses in Daphne?'

The soldier shook his head.

'No sir. Some of the villas lower down the hill are bigger, but the young gentlemen say they like to be above the town, for the privacy.'

Marcus nodded, turning to take in the view over the ranks of trees across the valley, the mountains five miles distant on the far side a misty grey in the afternoon's haze. When they reached the house in question he dismissed the man to rejoin his fellows, striding through the open gate into a well-maintained garden clearly designed around several mature trees, which had been left in place when others around them had been felled to make way for the house's construction. A lone red-haired figure in a sweat-soaked tunic was exercising with sword and shield in one corner, repetitively cutting and stabbing at a wooden post with a blunt practice weapon, stepping back into a defensive shield brace after every strike, before stamping forward to repeat the attack. As Marcus strolled towards him the man spotted him from the corner of his eye and nodded, but continued his exercise with undiminished vigour.

'You're opening your body up for too long when you lunge.'

The labouring man, clearly no older than Marcus himself, shot him a sideways glance.

'You speak from experience?'

His voice was taut, that of a driven man, as he stabbed the sword at the post again. Marcus shrugged.

'Enough not to have any strong desire to see any more. Britannia, mostly, plus enough experience in Germania and Dacia to make me appreciate the protection to be had from a well-made shield. You must be Varus?'

The exercising man stopped in mid-thrust, slowly straightening out of the lunge with a look of resignation.

'You mean I must be the man who rode away when his cohort was ambushed and massacred by the Parthians?'

Marcus nodded.

'Why else would you be pushing yourself so hard in the heat of the day, when your fellow officers are probably all indulging in rather more relaxed pastimes given the stories the soldiers at the road gate told me?'

Varus propped the shield against the wooden post, crossing his arms with the blunt sword blade pointing back over one shoulder.

'I know what you're thinking. I see it in every man's face, when they realise who I am. I'm the officer who ran from battle, and left his men to die. The man who saved his own life on the pretext of bringing the news of the Parthian attack back to the legion.'

'Whereas . . . ?'

Varus snorted.

'Whereas *what*? You want to hear my side of the story? You want me to tell you how my senior centurion implored me to bring the story of their glorious fight to the death back to the legion? I'm tired of the sound of my own voice, and of trying to convince myself that I didn't just run for my life.'

He stared at Marcus, his expression close to pleading.

'That I didn't agree to his request simply because I'm a coward. So why would I waste my time on you, when you're not going to believe it either?'

Marcus shrugged again.

'So what's the truth of it?'

Varus stared back at him.

'The *truth* of it? The truth of it is that I was ready to die, friend, ready in an instant. And yes, I know it would have been a hard death if they'd managed to take me alive, but I would have fallen on my own sword if it came to that. And then the first spear asked me to leave, and showed me a way to avoid that ignominious death, and I took it, like a . . . like a *fucking* coward! I grabbed it and I ran for my life. Can you imagine that, you with your scars, and your two swords, and your Britannia, Germania and Dacia?'

Marcus smiled wryly.

'Of course I can. Any soldier who says he hasn't considered running at some point or other is nothing more than a liar. So now you wish you'd stayed and shared that glorious death with your fellow soldiers, do you?'

Varus nodded mutely, and Marcus smiled at him without humour.

'In that case, Tribune, you may have your wish granted soon enough.'

He turned away and walked towards the house with Varus following. In the villa's airy atrium a servant hurried up with a bowl of water.

'He wants to take your equipment, and wash your feet.'

Marcus waved the man away with a reassuring smile.

'I'm not staying that long, thank you.'

He followed the sound of voices into the house's central courtyard, stopping at the sight of a swimming pool with seven men in their twenties reclining on benches around the edge, their attention fixed on a trio of naked women floating in the pool's crystal-clear water.

'What's this, Varus? Have you found yet another new pair of ears for your story of how you ran away when the Parthians came knocking? And who's this oaf without the good manners even to disarm himself before coming into the house, never mind take his boots off?'

The speaker had risen to a sitting position and was eying Marcus with a look of disparagement. The man reclining to his left, his tunic marked with an identical broad purple stripe to his comrade's, spoke without looking up from his study of the girls' naked bodies as the pool's rippling water caressed their pale flesh.

'Control yourself, Flamininus. Whoever you are, state your business and be on your way.'

Marcus looked at them each in turn, unconsciously taking stock of each man with a swift, ruthless assessment, as his gladiator mentor had taught him a decade before:

'Some men will fight, young Marcus, and some men won't. Some will fight just for the hell of it, while others will have to be looking down the blade of a sword before they'll raise their own weapons. And the secret to knowing which is which, who'll come at you and who'll run from you, is all in the eyes. Oh yes, a man's willingness to offer you violence can sometimes be understood by the set of his body, or the way that he moves, but the truth is always there to be seen in an instant, there in the middle of his face. Just look in a man's eyes, and you'll see everything you need to know about him, when you've looked at enough men and done enough fighting.'

The man called Flamininus was on the verge of springing to his feet, his stare filled with hostility and the need to do harm.

'Tribune Umbrius told you to state your business! And you can salute, while you're at it!'

Marcus looked back at him with a face set in hard lines, unable to control his reaction to the man's arrogance and need for violence.

'I'll salute, when I see someone worthy of the respect.'

The eyes fixed on him around the pool snapped wide with shock at the flat statement, and Flamininus surged to his feet.

'*Hold!*'

The broad stripe tribune had raised his head to look at Marcus with a calculating gaze, the female bather momentarily forgotten. He waved a hand at his colleague, and Flamininus slowly sank back onto his bench with the look of a man whose grip on his temper was tenuous at best.

'Who are you, stranger? It might be useful to know your name before I turn this animal loose on you.'

Flamininus grinned at him with his teeth bared in a half-snarl.

'You'd be well advised to keep him restrained, unless you want blood in your swimming pool. My name is Tribulus Corvus, Tribune, Third Gallic.'

The broad stripe shook his head in obvious amusement.

'Oh no you're not. These men around this swimming pool represent the entire senior officer strength of the Third, us and the legatus.'

Marcus allowed the smile to spread slowly across his face.

'Then I seem to be the bearer of news, gentlemen. Legatus Lateranus has been replaced with immediate effect. We arrived together by ship from Rome this morning to take up our positions, your new legatus and I, with orders to take the legion north to deal with the threat to the empire's frontier with Parthia. And on behalf of your new commanding officer, since the last man to hold the position seems to have made a very swift exit, I have been sent to summon you to a command meeting this evening. You will attend the legion's headquarters building in Antioch by the time the lamps have been lit, and any man failing to do so will be making a prompt return to Rome, dismissed from his position.'

He turned to leave, weighed the moment for an instant, and then turned back.

'Speaking personally, I think it might well be for the best if none of you were to attend.'

With a growl of anger Flamininus leapt to his feet and strode around the pool, raising one big fist with the clear intention of knocking the newcomer to the floor. Marcus waited for him, stepping forward while his opponent stormed around the pool's narrow side, moving so close to the water's edge that his would-be assailant was forced to turn step around the pool's corner to confront him, momentarily throwing out an arm to retain his balance.

'I'll have your f—'

He staggered back as Marcus struck a lightning-fast jab into his face, using the heel of his hand to deliver a crushing blow to the tribune's nose and then, as his victim's momentum made him stagger forward another pace, kicked his feet from under him and swept him into the pool, sending a wave of sparkling droplets over the reclining tribunes. The naked women squealed in horror, flinching away from the flailing tribune.

'Anybody else?'

Marcus waited for a moment, then shook his head with a look of disappointment, as Flamininus dragged himself from the water with a stream of blood dripping from his broken nose.

'Do you want to try again?'

The soaked, bleeding man shook his head with a look of venomous hatred.

'I thought not. As I said, all you have to do if you want to avoid facing battle against the Parthians is to stay here and give your new legatus a reason to dismiss you. Then again, it might be entertaining for Varus here to see how you react to facing the enemy, rather than being forced to tolerate your jibes on a subject he understands a good deal better than you.'

He turned and left, leaving the group staring after him. At length one of them spoke.

'Who the fuck was *that*?'

Varus turned back to face them with a hard smile, patting his practice sword and turning away.

'That, you bastards, was Britannia, Germania and Dacia. And unless I'm much mistaken, he'll very shortly be Parthia too. As will we all.'

The tent party, of which Sanga was the defacto leader, found their new quarters much as expected, given that barracks buildings were constructed to the same pattern all over the empire. Four bunk beds for the eight men more or less filled the space, while a smaller room was walled off from the living space to allow for the storage of weapons. The veteran soldier looked around the cramped room, then pointed at the closed wooden shutters.

'Different province, same shitty barracks. Get that fucking window open, it smells like a donkey took a shit in here.'

Daylight did little to improve the picture.

'Not donkey shit. Look more like soldier.'

Sanga shook his head.

'Dirty bastards. You, get your spade out and carry that turd down to the latrines. You, fetch a bucket of water and wash away whatever's left.' He stuck his head through the open window, drawing in a lungful of clean air before bellowing his anger into the afternoon's comparative warmth.

'You bastards had better watch out or you won't see me coming!'

Saratos shook his head.

'You waste breathe. Local soldier no speak Latin, he speak Greek. And you no speak Greek.'

His friend wrinkled his nose again, as the freshly laid faeces assaulted his sense of smell with renewed vigour.

'I'll teach the bastards some fucking Latin. Starting with the words "good", "fucking" and "kicking".'

He turned to the rest of the tent party.

'Right, we've all seen a turd before, so stop looking like you want to honk up your biscuits. Get your fucking kit stowed and we'll go for a look around and see if we can't scare up something to drink or screw. Except for you . . .'

He pointed at the tent party's newest recruit.

'You can stay here and make sure the locals don't take a shine to our kit. Don't wash that shit off that spade once you've dumped it in the log cabin, and if anyone comes poking round just wipe it down their face as hard as you like. That ought to do the trick.'

The legion's tribunes gathered late that afternoon, Flamininus among them with his face bruised and his eyes boring into Marcus at every opportunity. The object of his ire, for his part, chose to ignore the challenging stare, smiling quietly to himself at some private joke, or so it seemed. After a few moments, Scaurus swept into the room, looking around the gathering with apparent surprise.

'All nine of you? That's gratifying. I had wondered if a few of you might have chosen to ignore my message.'

'Legatus, if I might make some intro—'

'Introductions? Not just now, thank you Tribune Umbrius. There'll be plenty of time for getting to know each other later, when we've worked out which of you will be staying with the legion.'

He looked around at them, waiting for someone to break the silence.

'Staying with the legion, Legatus?'

The broad stripe tribune had spoken again, clearly intent on playing to his role as the most senior of the group, and his legatus's deputy.

'Indeed, Tribune. Which of you will be considered fit to remain in your positions, and which of you I will be forced to dismiss from imperial service. As of now this legion is under wartime conditions. We will be marching for the border within a few weeks, with the intention of finding, challenging and destroying the Parthian force that has been harassing our outposts in Adiabene.'

'But surely it's too early in the year for a campaign of any duration. The weather . . .'

Scaurus shook his head at the attempted intervention.

'The worst of the winter is over, Tribune. The weather from this point onwards, from my previous experience of the province, won't ever get cold enough to freeze water. Compared to northern Britannia, or Dacia, that's positively comfortable for a well-equipped infantryman kept warm by sufficient food, thick clothing and plenty of exercise. I think we'll be safe enough making a swift march from the Euphrates to Nisibis. And when I say swift, gentlemen, you should take my words at face value.'

They looked at him uncomprehendingly.

'The route I plan to take is, I'll admit, a little risky. There will be times when we have no option but to double pace the legion for ten or twenty miles at a time.'

He waited for a moment for the real meaning of his words to dawn upon the officers gathered around him, but none of them showed any sign of comprehension.

'I see that I shall have to make this very clear indeed. When I say that the legion will be forced to march at the double pace, I was speaking literally. Every man in the Third is going to have to learn to cover twenty miles in five hours with full equipment.'

Still the officers failed to react with any sign of understanding.

'*Every* man, gentlemen. Including all of you.'

'But . . .'

'Yes, Tribune?'

Umbrius's face was creased in a frown.

'Legatus, the legion's gentlemen *ride* to war. We do not march like the common soldiery.'

Scaurus raised an eyebrow, apparently intrigued by the idea.

'I see. How very . . . *gentlemanly*. And tell me, Tribune, what will you do if your horse goes lame?'

'I'll get on my spare, Legatus.'

Scaurus nodded, conceding the point with a knowing smile.

'And if a Parthian raid makes off with your horses – all three of them, obviously – what then?'

Umbrius looked back at his commanding officer with dawning horror.

'I'll . . . march?'

Scaurus nodded slowly.

'Indeed you will. The purposes of an officer's horse, gentlemen, are several. The horse provides a vantage point over the heads of the men around the officer, allowing him to see and be seen. The horse provides its rider with speed over the ground for the swift delivery of messages, and allows him to move quickly to points where his presence is essential. It provides a means of following up behind a retreating enemy, in order to guide in the pursuers and be sure that no ambush has been set by the rear-guard. It is most emphatically not intended to enable him to avoid undertaking the same hardships we expect of our men. And gentlemen, I expect every man in this room to be capable of matching our soldiers stride for stride over any distance and at any speed of *march*. While we train for war you will therefore march alongside your men, all of whom will be carrying a good deal more weight than you since your possessions are carried in carts while they have to hoist everything they own onto a pack pole.'

He looked around at their horrified faces.

'You may not like it, but there it is. You all volunteered to be officers, and in *my* legion officers don't sit around all day allowing their centurions to run the show. Your days of indolent luxury in Daphne are over, as from the moment you walked into this office. This legion needs officers. Your soldiers need leaders, men they can see sharing their hardships, living alongside them, fighting alongside them and if necessary, dying alongside them too. You will all, every one of you, learn to march very quickly indeed, and brush up on your weapons skills too, if you don't want to be left behind when the legion marches.'

He looked about him again with a hard smile.

'Oh yes, there's a threat that some of you will be considering with an inner smirk, isn't there? To be left behind in Antioch, while the rest of us march off to provide the Parthians with a little light target practice, doomed to die in the desert at the hands of eastern barbarians? That doesn't sound so bad an alternative, I'd imagine. Except, gentlemen, consider this.'

He pinched the wool of his tunic, emphasising the garment's thin stripe.

'I'm sure you noticed it the moment I walked in. I'm just an equestrian! An upstart! A man with everything to prove, which is probably why the freedman who's currently running the empire gave me command of this legion. He knows that I'll beat you all into prime condition, and give the enemy more to think about than they're expecting, given just how dissolute their spies will have been telling them *you* are.'

He grinned at them without a trace of humour.

'But while I may only be an equestrian, I'm nobody's fool, gentlemen. I accepted this command from the imperial chamberlain in return for one simple promise. He guaranteed me that any man I choose to send home, any of you judged to be unfit to hold the position of tribune in my legion for the reason of failing to make sufficient effort in his training, would have his family's affairs investigated most thoroughly.'

He smiled at them knowingly.

'It was a promise he was delighted to make. You're all the sons of rich men, by comparison with the poor bastards you're supposed to be leading. Can you all say with absolute certainty that your fathers came by that wealth fairly? That they've all paid their taxes on time and in full? That none of them has ever bribed an imperial official? I wouldn't have thought that even the most scrupulous of men would relish Cleander's investigators picking apart the seams of their lives, looking for hidden gold. And that, I promise you, would be the least of it.'

'I have nothing to fear. My family's wealth is honestly come by, and so vast that fraud really isn't necessary.'

Scaurus smiled back at Umbrius.

'On the contrary. The empire, by which of course I mean the emperor, has an insatiable thirst for gold. Anyone's gold, whether fairly taken or not. I'd imagine that the prospect of turning his men loose on your father's great fortune would make Cleander's mouth water. Even the smallest of financial irregularities, the most innocent of mistakes by a scribe, would be enough to redouble their interest in your father's doings. Few men's affairs can stand up to such thorough scrutiny.'

He smiled at them, seeing the realisation that their lives were about to change irrevocably dawning upon the brighter among them.

'So here it is, gentlemen. If you're invalided out of the legion while genuinely trying to prove your fitness to come with us, then I'll allow you to take passage back to Rome by merchant ship, after the winter, when the seas are open again. But if you fail to display the zeal I'm looking for, or try to count yourself out with some imagined ailment, then I'll put you on a praetorian warship that's waiting in the harbour at Seleucia for just the purpose, ready to sail immediately. Cleander's waiting for that ship, gentlemen, and the men that walk off it in Misenum can be assured that their families' lives are about to get a good deal more interesting than might be considered healthy. You choose. It's really all the same to me.'

'So, Vibius Varus, tell us about the destruction of the Sixth cohort.'

The tribune looked about him, uncertainly, and Scaurus smiled reassuringly.

'I know, you've told the tale a hundred times already, I've read the record. Your previous legatus called you a coward for not dying with your command, despite not having set foot over the Euphrates in all his time in command of this legion.'

Varus nodded warily.

'I hear the insult a dozen times a day. They call me coward behind my back, loudly enough to be sure I'll hear, men with no idea what it was that we faced.'

Scaurus spread his hands in agreement.

'Exactly. But *we* understand. We've all seen the same terrible face that battle wears.'

He gestured to the men gathered around his desk. Marcus, Julius, Dubnus, and Cotta.

'Varus, it's clear to me that your First Spear sent you away to make sure that the manner of his cohort's destruction reached his legatus. None of us is going to judge you, and if your failure to have died alongside the men of the Sixth Cohort troubles you, then you'll have the chance to prove yourself soon enough, if that's what you want.'

Varus nodded slowly.

'When the cohort's first spear sent me away, I rode far enough to see the whole thing without becoming a target. I took refuge in a fold in the land, a slightly elevated position from which to watch the battle, as the first spear had requested.'

He shook his head at the memory.

'It was like a scene from one of the arches in the forum, our men in a four-deep line and crouching behind their shields, with the rear two ranks protecting their heads.'

Scaurus shook his head grimly.

'All very well in the assault, but not the best choice if you find yourself trapped under the bows of the Parthians with no cover to be had. How many archers were there?'

'At least five thousand, Legatus, all mounted. Once the cohort had formed a square they rode around it, just shooting volley after volley of arrows in from all sides. When their arrows were spent they rode to meet men on camels laden with spares, then came back and started the whole horrible thing again. Some of the legionaries died instantly, hit by arrows that found a gap in the shields, or simply punched straight through the wood at close range.'

He grimaced at the memory.

'They were the lucky ones. Others were only wounded, unable to hold their shields up against the constant rain of arrows. I saw one man crawl out into the middle of the square, to get out from under his comrades' feet, I suppose. I watched him jerk as each successive arrow hit him, until he just stopped moving.'

'How long did they keep this up?'

Varus turned to face Marcus.

'Two hours? Perhaps three . . .'

'And then?'

The tribune shook his head.

'I thought that watching five hundred legionaries being picked apart one man at a time was the worst thing I'd ever seen. But then, as the afternoon heat really started to tell on the men left standing—'

'How many were still able to fight?'

The tribune pursed his lips in thought.

'Perhaps two hundred. They were still huddled together around the dead and wounded in the double line, facing both ways. Their shields were black with the shafts of arrows by this point, and many of them were already wounded. I knew their time had come when the cataphracts mounted their horses. They had sat on the ground watching as the archers killed our men, talking amongst themselves and waiting for the right moment to make their attack. I remember one man losing his wits under that unrelenting rain of death, and charging out of the line with his spear ready to throw. He only managed twenty paces, of course, before they shot him down with half a dozen arrows clean through his shield, and the cataphracts stood up and applauded his bravery. But eventually they mounted their horses and rode forward to finish the job.'

The men sitting around him waited patiently while he took a deep breath.

'Even now the thought of it terrifies me. The archers rode back to either side, leaving those men that were still alive to stand and stare as the heavy cavalry formed up. They mounted without any noise or shouting, seemingly without urgency, as if they were simply parading for inspection. Their leader rode out in front of them, spoke a few words of encouragement, then started trotting his horse towards what was left of our men with the rest of them following him.'

'How many where they?'

'A thousand, all fully armoured. The horses too.'

Dubnus shook his head in disbelief.

'Armoured *horses*?'

Varus nodded grimly.

'Scale armour, hundreds of pieces of iron plate the size of a small child's palm sewn onto heavy coats, and overlapped until the resulting defence is thick enough to stop a thrown spear. The plates were silvered, to make them shine like the sun itself, and when they started to move it was like a wall of light crossing the desert. They went from a trot to a canter when they were two hundred paces or so from our line, and the *noise* . . .

'My family has an estate on Sicily, on the slopes of Etna, and when I was young the volcano erupted for several days before the gods saw fit to calm its anger. I've never forgotten the grinding, bone-shaking fury of the mountain's rage, and the sound of their hoofs was the closest thing to it I've heard in all those years, a constant growling thunder even from a mile away, as if the gods themselves were fighting. What it must have been like for the men standing helplessly waiting for them to attack is beyond my imagination, but only two of them ran. How they can have imagined they were going to escape from an army of mounted men baffles me, but I don't suppose they were thinking all that clearly. The rest of the legionaries just stood and waited while the cataphracts rode up to them and started into them with their lances, stabbing down from out of sword reach. A few men threw their spears in reply, but they didn't seem to have much effect. Then a horn sounded, and the riders dropped their spears and rode in closer with what looked like maces.'

Varus put his face into his hands, his next words muffled but still distinguishable.

'It was a slaughter. Every time a cataphract's arm rose and fell, one of our men went down. It was that simple. The fight was over within fifty heartbeats, and all that was left were the two men who had run. The cataphracts played with them for a short time, riding at them and turning away at the last moment, and then a man wearing black armour trotted his horse up and killed them both with two sweeps of his mace, as quick as it takes to tell you.'

'What did they do with the bodies?'

Varus looked at Cotta with blank eyes.

'Left them where they lay. They will not defile the purity of the fire they worship with human flesh, and I doubt enough wood could have been found in any case. For all I know their bodies still rot where they fell.'

'And that was it?'

The young tribune shook his head at Dubnus.

'Not quite. The man in the black armour climbed down from his horse and made sure that both of the soldiers he had killed were truly dead, then raised the mace in his hand and shouted up at the hills, as if he knew I was watching. His Latin was perfect, but his voice was a cold as the dagger at your belt.'

'What did he say, Tribune?'

The young man turned to Scaurus.

'He said "*Let this be a warning to all whose boots disturb the blessed soil of our motherland! Rome's presence will no longer be tolerated! I, Narsai of Adiabene swear this!*" And then he mounted, turned his horse and rode away without once looking back.'

Scaurus nodded.

'Thank you, Tribune, for your honesty. A lesser man would have been more bombastic, whereas your humility in the face of such a trial does you great honour. I look forward to marching to confront this enemy with you at my side.'

Varus saluted and left the friends in silence. Once the door was shut, Scaurus looked around at his officers.

'As I feared, the enemy we will be facing is indeed Parthian, almost certainly drawn from the provinces that abut Adiabene and Osrhoene. The action he describes is straight out of the history books too, clouds of horse archers pinning an enemy where they stand, shooting their arrows and then running away faster than any infantryman can pursue, gradually weakening their enemy to the point of collapse. And then they unleash the finest heavy cavalry in the world, their cataphracts. Armed with lances, swords and maces, the mere sound and threat of their advance can be enough to break an already demoralised army before any contact, while in combat their armour makes them almost impervious to any attack. They are dangerous beyond belief, gentlemen, and I doubt very much that the numbers described by our colleague Varus represent their full strength, given that he made no mention of the infantry I'm sure they will have levied from their peasantry. Fighting our way past them to relieve Nisibis is going to prove difficult, especially with only half a legion.'

'Why bother, Legatus?'

The men turned to look at Dubnus, but the big man simply shrugged.

'What's so important about a town in the middle of the desert? It seems to me that the only reason for caring about the place is to be able to draw a line on a map.'

Scaurus raised an eyebrow at Cotta, who nodded back at him and turned to address the question.

'I had much the same point of view until the first time I marched east from Zeugma. Why cross three hundred miles of desolate, barren ground to go and stand garrison duty on a city in the middle of nowhere? Why go to the bother of taking it from Adiabene in the first place, and holding it in the face of the locals' anger at our boots dishonouring their soil? It's only when you get there that you realise why such a city should have come into being in that place, where there's nothing much of any value apart from the timber from the mountains to the north and whatever can be grown on the margins of the river that runs past it to the south, eventually flowing into the Euphrates but navigable only in the spring, when the mountain snows melt.'

He fell silent, and Dubnus raised an eyebrow.

'And . . . ?'

'The secret, my friend, lies in the city's placement, almost equidistant between the Parthian capital of Ctesiphon and the borders of the empire. You see, there is a place very faraway to the east of Parthia, across a desert of enormous size, where a race of people quite different to us live. I saw some of them in Nisibis once, a trading party on their way to Rome. They have different-coloured skin to us, more yellow than pink, and their eyes are different too, less round than ours. And in this faraway place they grow and make things that the rich citizens of Rome want to buy, expensive fabrics so fine and smooth to the hand that a woman dressed in them might as well be naked, and exotic spices found nowhere in the empire. They bring these goods across the desert to Parthia, and then barter some of their cargo for the right to cross the empire and sell their goods to our merchants.'

'Who in turn add their own markup when they get the stuff to Rome?'

'Exactly. It's a long road from this distant land in the east, and at every stop the traders must give up some small part of their profit in order to be allowed to progress which, of course, means that the price to the end customer in Rome is that little bit higher.'

Dubnus nodded knowingly.

'So Nisibis is owned by the emperor, right?'

Marcus nodded.

'As my Greek tutors laboured long and hard to make me understand, the history of this part of the world is both long and complex. Rome has been fighting Parthia for control of the region for at least two hundred years, and the lines on this particular map have moved around quite vigorously, depending on who has had the upper hand in the constant battle of wills. The current Parthian king attacked us, back in the joint reign of Marcus Aurelius and Lucius Verus, and was so soundly beaten by a general by the name of Avidius Cassius . . .'

He raised an eyebrow at Cotta, who gave him an emotionless return stare.

'. . . that he hasn't moved against us in all of the thirty years since. Rome established a client kingdom adjoining Syria, Osrhoene, and pursued the usual policy of putting a forward base right in the middle of Adiabene, the next-door kingdom. Nisibis was the natural choice, the main trading city in Adiabene, the perfect place for a customs post out past the empire's edge, where goods can be taxed before they get into the hands of men who are rather better skilled at avoiding payment.'

'So when these eastern traders reach Nisibis, they have to pay a toll, which goes straight to Commodus?'

Marcus nodded at his friend's question.

'Exactly. If we lose Nisibis then we lose a source of wealth to whoever it is that has decided to take it off our hands. Wealth which will then be used to bolster their ability to repel any attempt to recapture the place.'

Cotta raised a hand.

'If I might comment on the odds of taking the city back, once we've lost it?'

Scaurus nodded, staring hard at the map painted onto the office's wall.

'A tour of duty in Nisibis was the most boring tour of duty you can imagine, but if that place was one thing above all, it was *strong*. Two circular walls, a mile long, both over thirty feet tall, with a twenty-five foot-wide dry moat between them. In time of peace the moat is bridged, but when there's a threat to the city the bridges are dismantled. The Parthians don't have any siege machinery, so all they can hope to achieve is to take the outer wall, at a huge cost in dead and wounded, after which they have precisely nothing because there's no way across to the other wall until the moat is filled in, with bowmen and bolt throwers on the inner wall – which is taller, of course – busy killing anyone foolish enough to venture out onto the outer wall. Oh, and the city has its own fresh water springs, and grain stores big enough to feed the population and a legion for six months if need be. If they manage to starve the garrison out we'll never take it back again without a full-scale war like the one thirty years ago. Nisibis can be taken by defeating the Parthians in battle and humiliating them into surrendering the fortress, but not by direct assault.'

The legatus nodded.

'Quite so. The legatus who manages to rescue the city from this threat will be judged to have done his job effectively, while the man who presides over its loss will return to Rome in disgrace. No wonder the governor's reaction to my thin stripe was to starve my command of men, he knows enough to understand that it's the simplest way he can see off Cleander's little experiment in allowing a man of my class to command a legion.'

Julius cleared his throat, looking at Scaurus with a questioning expression.

'First Spear?'

'I'm less interested in why they want to take this desert city and rather more in how you think we're going to stop them. And how you think we'll even be able to reach the place, given you think that the force that destroyed Varus's cohort was only part of their strength.'

Scaurus nodded with a knowing look.

'I thought you might be, so I prepared a list of the things that we're going to need if we're to stand a chance of putting them back in their place.'

He opened a tablet.

'I'll take you all through them tomorrow, since you're going to be doing most of the work to procure them, in some cases by means of subterfuge and probably even theft. Some of them are simple enough, and merely require the expenditure of gold, albeit that we might have to exercise a little wit to avoid overpaying. Others will require the exercise of a little of that senatorial authority we've heard so much about. And one, gentlemen, the most important factor of all if we have to face the Parthians in battle, will cost us nothing whatsoever – but only if we're in the right place at the right time.'

Marcus came out of the headquarters building to find the two Britons who had travelled with the Tungrians from Rome waiting for him, the giant Lugos looming over his one-eyed companion with whom a fierce initial enmity, born of their different tribal origins, had evolved into firm friendship over the years of their service with the Tungrians.

'Tribune. We find ourselves with nowhere to sleep, unless we . . .'

Martos fell silent as Marcus put his hands on his hips and stared back at him with a jaundiced eye.

'This was Dubnus's idea, wasn't it?'

The Briton shrugged.

'He might have mentioned it. It seems that all you important men will sleep in a barracks block, with one tent party room apiece.'

The Roman nodded, unable to resist a smile at his memory of tribune Umbrius's horrified reaction to the revised billeting.

'We have to sleep in a barracks? Like the soldiers?'

Scaurus had been unmoved by his officers' collective amazement.

'Give me one good reason why not? But make it a good one, Tribune, or my admittedly generous offer might just slide off the table to be replaced by something less luxurious.'

'*Less . . .*'

'Luxurious. I'm offering you young gentlemen as much space as is usually occupied by an eight-man tent party, with an additional room for your equipment and space enough for your servant to sleep in besides. If I were you I'd take me up on the offer, or you might find yourselves sharing.'

Umbrius had stared at him for a moment.

'You want to tell me that I can't do this. You want to go to the governor and have him overrule me. But you're worried as to what I might do if you were to do so. And you're right to be concerned.'

Umbrius had nodded, reluctantly agreeing to the drastic revision of their living arrangements, and the tribunes had trooped out to discover just how appalling their new quarters were.

'Dubnus think you make enemy. Ask we to sleep with you.'

Marcus sighed at Lugos's blunt statement of the facts.

'He may be right. And the company might help me to stop brooding about my wife and child. Come on.'

They found the barrack easily enough, grinning at the loud complaints issuing from within several of the rooms as the sons of Rome's aristocracy discovered their new living conditions. Flamininus was standing outside his room with a cup of wine, and his bemused expression became a sneer when he saw Marcus approaching.

'Here he is. This was your idea, wasn't it, Thin Stripe? And what are these, your barbarian catamites?'

Martos, who had removed his eye patch during the walk from the headquarters building, grinned evilly and stepped in front of the nonplussed tribune.

'This barbarian speaks your language, so mind just how hard you push or you might find that I oblige your apparent need to fight. I only have one eye, boy, but I can recognise a fool when I see one.'

'He can't speak to me like that!'

Marcus nodded, his face lit up with amusement.

'I think you'll find that he can. That, Flamininus, is a genuine example of British tribal aristocracy. He's a king, and kings speak to anyone they like, any way they like.'

'And yet he's following you round like a—'

He flinched back as the Briton leaned forward.

'Say the word, Roman. Give me a reason to stop your wind.'

He stepped back, looking the tribune up and down.

'I was captured in battle by this Roman, as was my companion here.'

He waved a hand at Lugos, who stepped forward, forcing Flamininus to incline his head to look at him as he stared down at the tribune dispassionately.

'We could both have been executed, but Tribune Corvus not only treated us both fairly, he refused to enslave us. And so we follow him, in the hope of repaying our life debts. And beware, Roman . . .'

He leaned close to Flamininus again, lowering his voice.

'Lugos here makes me look like a priest when he decides that the time to fight has come. If he catches any of you people in the Tribune's quarters I imagine he will tear that man's arms off.'

Marcus walked on, and the two Britons made to follow, but Flamininus fired a parting jibe at Martos's back.

'If you're such a great warrior, how do you come to be missing an eye?'

The Briton turned to stare back at him, and Marcus stepped between them.

'He lost the eye storming his tribal capital, after he was betrayed by an ally who sought to take his kingdom. By the time we were in control of the fortress he'd killed a score of the enemy tribesmen, most of them by the simple but direct method of cutting off their genitals. Think on that before you provoke him again, because this is the last time I'll stand between you.'

They found the barrack much as expected, but the floor was dry, and Lugos made swift work of the detritus that littered the room once Martos had taken a lamp from his pack and lit it, bringing a glow of warmth to the room.

'Have sleep in worse.'

Martos nodded at the giant's observation.

'Not in these beds you haven't. I doubt they'll hold your weight.'

Lugos shrugged.

'I sleep floor. Is dry.'

Marcus untied the ribbon around his chest that denoted his rank and took off the heavy front and back plates, stretching luxuriously before rolling himself into his blanket in one of the four bunks that filled the room.

'We'll get rid of two of these beds tomorrow, but all I want now is to enjoy the feeling of not carrying all that bronze around on my back.'

Martos, having shrugged out of his chain mail, chose another bed and emulated the tribune's example.

'You're lucky. You might think that a man of my age would be used to the weight, but it only gets worse as the years go by.'

A note of curiosity crept into the Roman's sleepy voice.

'So why didn't you return to your own people when the cohorts marched for Rome last year? You could have chosen to live quietly, filling your days with hunting, instead of accompanying us to this distant part of the world to fight for an emperor you can only despise?

The Briton was silent for a moment.

'I could never have returned to the Dinpaladyr for any longer than a few days. Even during my brief return I was aware of the tensions building around me. I gave the throne up, Marcus, and named my nephew as my successor. My presence anywhere in his kingdom would have been a provocation, one way or another. The young king's advisers would have seen me as a threat, and those who were unhappy with their rule would have sought to make me their champion. No good could have come of it. And . . .'

He fell quiet, wrestling with memories of his time as king. Lugos's voice growled a single word from where he lay on the floor.

'Family.'

Martos was silent for a moment.

'Yes. My family.'

His voice had sunk to a whisper.

'My wife and children died as the result of my stupidity in believing Calgus when he told me that we would share power, once you Romans had been driven off our land. My home holds memories that I do not wish to recall. My life as a king is finished, and now I am simply a man. Wherever you go, my friends, I will go too.'

He laughed softly in the near darkness.

'And after all, without your companionship how else would I have travelled so far, and in such luxury?'

'Legionary Sanga! Get your lazy arse out here now and bring your mate Saratos with you!'

Having only just laid down on his bed after a fruitless hunt for either alcohol or female company, the veteran soldier groaned, rolled to his feet and stepped out of the barrack into the cool night air wearing nothing but a fixed grin, followed a moment later by his friend who had yet to strip off his tunic.

'Evening, Centurion.'

Quintus shook his head with an expression of disgust.

'Put something on, you ape!'

Rolling his eyes at the change in his orders, the veteran stepped back into the stone room, pulled a sock from his boot and rolled it over his genitals before stepping out into the chill again, snapping to attention in front of the two centurions who stood waiting for him. Quintus thrust his vine stick up under Sanga's scrotum, forcing the soldier up onto his toes.

'Think you're funny, do you Sanga?'

Knowing that any answer he could make would only worsen his officer's already volatile temper, the soldier stared at the wall of the barrack opposite until the furious centurion pulled the stick away and paced around him.

'Are you sure this is the soldier you want, Qadir? Surely there are men with more discipline and better attitudes that you could use instead?'

The Hamian centurion facing the two men shook his head with a slight smile.

'Much as I hate to disappoint you, I am obliged to disagree. My need is for a man with exactly the blend of guile, sly wits and, when the need arises, ruthlessness that this man possesses in such abundance. Not to mention the equally important abilities with which Saratos compensates for his shortcomings.'

Outlining what it was that was required of the two men, he handed Sanga a sack, ignoring the veteran's wounded expression.

'Tunics. One for each of you. You'll need them tomorrow if you're going to blend in.'

Knowing better than to ask the question as to exactly what it was that would be expected of them in front of their own centurion, Sanga went straight for the practicalities.

'This is a street job, right Centurion?'

Qadir nodded.

'In that case sir, we'll need—'

'The money is in the bag. A leather purse.'

The veteran's smile broadened.

'Thank you Centurion. We won't let you down.'

Quintus shook his head wearily.

'Only I could get promoted to Centurion to a century that was home to both you *and* Morban. It's either him fleecing my soldiers by getting them to gamble on which horse has the bigger dick, or you vanishing off for days at a time to drink and whore at the legatus's expense. If I didn't know better I'd ask what the—'

'But you do know better, colleague.'

Qadir leaned close to Quintus.

'That's the reason why the first spear selected you to replace Tribune Corvus upon his promotion. He knows that you can be counted on not to ask that question, or to speculate as to the answer when, really and truly, you know you're much better knowing as little as possible.'

Quintus nodded glumly, then turned his ire on the waiting soldiers.

'Get out of my sight Sanga, you revolting animal. And don't come back pissed up or I'll take the greatest of pleasure in beasting you round this camp until your legs are so short that you'll need a sock over your prick to stop it rubbing on the fucking ground! Dismissed!'

3

Scaurus looked over the parade ground with an appraising stare as the Third Gallic marched out into the wide open space, his eyes roaming over the marching ranks from the vantage point of his horse. With the benefit of a night in which to prepare for the parade, their equipment was every bit as well presented as he had expected, their armour and helmets gleaming in the winter sunlight. The legion's centurions would have had a busy night of it.

'Tidy drill, First Spear.'

The senior centurion nodded his head respectfully at the compliment.

'We drill the men every day, Legatus. They practise battlefield manoeuvres for the first hour, just to get them warmed up, then we put them through all the usual practice: sword work, spear throwing, working on both distance and accuracy, defensive and offensive shield fighting, wrestling—'

'Wrestling?'

The first spear nodded.

'Wrestling, Legatus. For one thing, there's a strong tradition of the sport in these parts, as you can imagine, and for another, I won't have a man reduced to impotence when his shield's been wrecked and his sword blade breaks.'

He shrugged at Julius's raised eyebrow.

'Yes, I know, if one hundred unarmed men face an enemy with a sword then perhaps only one of those one hundred has any hope of winning, and then only if he has divine providence on his side, but while they fight on they're not running and making men who are still equipped look to their rear rather than engaging the enemy. We have regular competitions at all levels of the legion, from the centuries upwards.'

'Perhaps your Tungrians would like to take part, Legatus?'

Scaurus turned in his saddle to address Tribune Umbrius, resplendent as ever in his gleaming breastplate and impeccably polished boots.

'Indeed, perhaps they would, Tribune. Although *we* tend more towards simple bare-knuckle fighting. Tell me First Spear, how often do your men exercise their legs in the country?'

Quintinus looked back at him in bafflement.

'I'm sorry, I ought to have been clearer. How often do they march any distance?'

Quintinus took on a regretful expression.

'We don't march in winter, Legatus. Legatus Lateranus said there was no point, since we were committed to the defence of the city. He wasn't much for anything that would take him away from Antioch.'

The legion had paraded in its standard formation, the First Cohort at the right-hand end of the line with each succeeding cohort arrayed to its left. The soldiers appeared strong and well fed, and their equipment, while just as non-uniform as he had expected, with both mail and laminated armour in evidence, was well maintained to judge from the dull shine of oiled metal. Every man carried a shield protected by a leather cover in his left hand and a pair of practice javelins in his right, their swords having been replaced by heavy wooden practice weapons. Scaurus looked out across the open space, pursing his lips at the thinness of the ranks of men facing him.

'How many men do you have available for duty today, First Spear?'

Quintinus consulted a writing tablet.

'Two thousand, nine hundred and fifty-two, Legatus.'

'I see. And the other two thousand soldiers?'

Another glance down at the tablet.

'The majority of them are on leave in their hometowns and villages, Legatus. I took the opportunity of this period of relative quiet to send them away, as it was their turn.'

'And the rest?'

'Detached duty for the most part, although we do have a fair number hunting wild beasts.'

'I see. So each of these centuries has fifty or so men on parade?'

The first spear nodded, and Scaurus held his gaze for a moment.

'Carry on then, let's see what the remaining two thousand, nine hundred and fifty-two are capable of, shall we?'

Quintinus waved his hand at the trumpeters to his left, and a blare of sound set the legion's centurions into action. At their shouted commands, the odd-numbered centuries marched forward out of the line towards the review stand until they were thirty paces from their remaining comrades. Halting with a clatter of hobnailed boots they performed an impressively co-ordinated about-face that hinted at their foot drill being well practised. The even-numbered centuries had not been idle, each of them having quickly formed a protective testudo, their shields raised to provide them with the protection to their front and flanks, while the men inside the formation overlapped their shields to form a roof overhead.

The front ranks of the odd-numbered centuries stamped forward, a shower of practice javelins arcing from their line to hammer at the testudos' shields with a rattle like hail on roof tiles. In one of the target centuries, a man in the front rank was unlucky enough to be hit on the foot by a lucky throw, hopping out of the formation in evident agony just as the second volley arrived. The wooden tip of another javelin thumped into his thigh, and as he started back in fresh agony a second weapon hit him squarely in the face, felling him with a boneless slump that told its own story. Quintinus looked at Scaurus, but the legatus shook his head solemnly.

'Continue. The men will see much worse soon enough.'

With another peal of horns the opposing centuries reversed their roles, the odd numbers forming testudo with practised ease, while their counterparts hurled their own practice weapons across the gap between them, the rattle of their wooden heads testament to the shields' robust defence. With all of their javelins thrown, the two lines reformed, still facing each other with the casualty lying between them, and the soldiers waited while a bandage carrier and his mates ran across the parade ground to where the comatose soldier lay. They gathered around the man for a moment, the stretcher bearers waiting while their leader knelt beside the man. After a moment, one of them staggered away from the huddle of men and vomited onto the parade ground's surface, clearly unable to stomach the nature of the man's injuries. Rolling his body onto the stretcher so that he was lying face down, the medical party carried him away, while the legion's soldiers maintained a respectful silence. The first spear signalled again, and the two lines drew their practice swords.

'I do so enjoy this part of the exercise!'

Scaurus nodded at his senior tribune's enthusiasm, watching as the opposing centuries started their barritus, the war cry building slowly until they were bellowing at each other at the tops of their voices. Then, with a swift sweep of their vine sticks, the centurions on either side unleashed their men, the centuries dashing forward into a pitched mock battle that seemed to the legatus almost recklessly enthusiastic.

'You trust your men to pull their blows, First Spear?'

Quintinus spoke without taking his eyes off the melee.

'For the most part, Legatus. And I'll admit that this scale of mock battle is a special treat for the Third, as a means of showing you that our men aren't quite as effeminate as some commentators would have you believe.'

Scaurus shook his head brusquely.

'You forget that I was the previous governor's inspector of troops for two years. I wouldn't have thought for a moment that your men were anything less than professional soldiers. And I suppose this sort of mass brawl does allow them to get rid of their excess energy . . .'

Scaurus paused, giving the senior centurion a knowing glance.

'And a chance to even out any scores that might have been festering. Very well, I've seen enough.'

The horns sounded again, and the two sides separated and reformed their individual centuries, half a dozen men limping away from either side at the command of their centurions, some clutching their sides and one staggering, supported by another man. Tribune Umbrius leaned forward in his saddle, raising an eyebrow at Scaurus.

'What a fine display! Don't you think so, Legatus? Roman military prowess at its most impressive, and a fine advertisement for the superiority of the legion! Do your auxiliaries perform their drill that well, First Spear?'

Julius, who had watched the display in silence, replied with a commendably straight face.

'I very much doubt it, Tribune. My men have been a little too preoccupied with fighting actual battles to spend much time working on the finer points of drill and hitting each other with bits of wood, sir.'

Umbrius frowned, taken aback by the subtle rebuttal.

'You didn't tell us that your men had combat experience, Legatus?'

Scaurus smiled thinly.

'I don't recall you asking the question, Tribune, but since the matter of my men's combat experience has finally arisen, I'll allow my first spear to list the Tungrian cohorts' recent battle honours.'

Julius spoke without taking his eyes off the legion's ranks.

'We fought off ten thousand barbarians at the start of the recent revolt in Britannia . . .' He nodded at his colleague Quintinus's raised eyebrows. 'We had some luck, and after that it was mostly down to carefully chosen ground, sound motivation . . .'

He smiled grimly.

'That and the fact that there was nowhere to run. We've fought four other major engagements in Britannia, and a number of other skirmishes, sieges of barbarian fortresses, that sort of thing.'

He paused for a moment, and Umbrius drew breath to speak.

'Then there was Germania, hunting bandits, dirty fighting for the most part although we did kill a few hundred of them once we got down to it. And Dacia, putting a Sarmatae tribe back in their place. And a small army of German auxiliaries too, when they decided to mutiny and take over a gold mine which the legatus here had been detailed to secure.'

He paused, pointing out across the parade ground.

'It seems your horsemen are ready to perform.'

The legion first spear stared at him for a moment before turning to the trumpeter. At the signal the legion's one-hundred-and-twenty-strong horsemen cantered proudly into the open space in front of the legion's line of cohorts, and Julius grinned at the sight of half a dozen centurions wielding their vine sticks at men they suspected to be the source of clearly audible ribald comments aimed at the cavalry.

'Your squadrons of horses seem to be pretty much up to strength.'

Tribune Umbrius nodded in silence, doing his best to ignore his new legatus's questioning look. Julius stared out at the horsemen, nodding appreciatively.

'And well drilled, from the look of things.'

Umbrius leaned forward again.

'Indeed so, First Spear. They routinely train with our resident Phrygian cavalry wing, the governor's own bodyguard. Their prefect is a proper Roman gentleman, and a master horseman to boot.'

'And the governor has taken them under his wing, so to speak?'

Umbrius laughed at Scaurus's joke.

'Very good, Legatus, a wing under his wing. Yes indeed, and he takes a close interest in their being fully manned and equipped.'

Scaurus smiled back at him.

'I'm sure he does.'

The cavalrymen were performing a flawless demonstration of horsemanship. Having expended their spears at a row of man-sized targets, with an accuracy that had Julius nodding appreciatively, they drew bows from the cases strapped to their saddles and proceeded to ride at the targets, one squadron at a time, loosing one arrow before turning their horses about, another shot loosed over each rider's shoulder demonstrating the same expertise as the previous arrow.

'The Phrygian's prefect has had his men practising shooting from the saddle for most of the year. That last little trick is called—'

Scaurus spoke without taking his eyes off the cavalrymen.

'A Parthian shot. The Phrygian's wing's prefect and I have clearly been reading the same books. Ah, it seems that the display is complete. Shall we go and inspect the men?'

Quintinus raised an eyebrow.

'It's more usual for the legatus simply to address them from his horse, Legatus.'

Scaurus shrugged.

'Everything changes, First Spear. And I'm not much of a man for following rules whose point I struggle to comprehend.'

He dismounted and strode out onto the hard, sandy surface, heading straight for the cavalrymen in their place on the line's right. Dismounted, each man stood by his beast's head, their weapons and equipment as carefully presented as their infantry colleagues.

'You put on an impressive show, Decurion.'

The senior squadron commander saluted crisply.

'Thank you Sir. We practise daily with—'

'The Phrygian wing. Yes, First Spear Quintinus mentioned it. I'll have to meet with their prefect, he sounds like a good man.'

'He is, sir, a real soldier if you take my meaning . . .'

He dried up under Quintinus's scrutiny, but Scaurus nodded.

'I take your meaning well enough, Decurion. My congratulations on your turnout.'

He walked along the line of infantrymen, looking hard at each cohort in turn with Quintinus following him in bemused silence. Once he had reached the Tenth Cohort's place at the far end, he turned about without a word and made his way back to the point where the men of the missing Sixth Cohort would have stood, glancing at the First Spear.

'Here will do.'

Clearing his throat, he raised his voice to be heard across the silent parade ground.

'Soldiers of the Third Gallic! You have presented a flawless display of your martial prowess! Your testudo was swiftly formed, and resisted the attacks of the forces opposing you. Your formation-keeping was precise, and the manner in which you went about your mock battle was fearless and decisive. You are to be commended for living up to the high standards that have been set by your legion since it was formed by the Divine Julius Caesar himself, serving under such inspired generals as Marcus Antonius, Gnaeus Domitius Corbulo and the divine Titus Flavius Vespasian! Indeed it was this legion's decisive role at the battle of Bedriacum that assured that most august emperor's claim on the imperial throne!'

He paused, looking up and down the ranks of solemn-faced soldiers.

'The Third Gallic has been an essential part of Roman rule in this province for almost two hundred years, and I have every expectation that you will continue to show our enemies that Rome is not to be treated with anything other than the greatest respect! Soon we will be marching east, tasked by our emperor with the responsibility to teach some uppity Parthian king or other that while our empire's rule is beneficent, our anger when roused is truly a thing of terror. You men and I will put right a wrong that has been done to our brother soldiers, and in doing so make our borders safe for another hundred years! But for now . . .'

He paused again, forcing himself to grin wolfishly.

'For now, you have earned a little free time!'

Men were nudging each other in the cohort's front ranks in anticipation of the words they so badly wanted to hear.

'The rest of the day will be treated as free time for anyone without essential duties to perform. Make sure that you're in a fit state for sunrise tomorrow, but make the most of this reward for your excellent performance!'

He turned to Quintinus.

'Dismiss your men, First Spear. And take the afternoon off

yourself, along with your centurions. First Spear Julius and I will look after the guard rota.'

Julius walked across to join his superior officer once Quintinus had saluted and marched away, raising an inquisitive eyebrow.

'The Tungrian cohorts aren't included in your generosity, Legatus?'

Scaurus nodded with a crooked smile.

'I don't think that would be wise. Antioch may be a big place, but the odds are good that our boys would end up nose to nose with those soldiers, and given that they know the city and our men don't, it might very well get ugly. I don't want to risk putting them together in the presence of drink and women until they all know each other a little better. And you might want to warn your men that tomorrow morning's parade is likely to be followed by something a bit more strenuous than a morning's sword drill and *wrestling*.'

Julius saluted and turned away to supervise the Tungrians back to their morning exercise, his place promptly being taken by the senior tribune who had been waiting behind him.

'Well said, Legatus, if I might be allowed to offer a congratulation on your oration? I had no idea the legion's reputation was so strong—'

Umbrius's eyes narrowed with surprise as Scaurus shook an exasperated head.

'Reading, Tribune, is a powerful way to find out things you don't know. And the Third Gallic, for your more complete information, were indeed formed by the blessed Julius, in Gaul, logically enough, but they ended up on the wrong side in the wars that followed his death. Once Marcus Antonius had killed himself after Actium they were sent here by the emperor Augustus as punishment for taking the wrong side in the civil war. And the reason the legion was so instrumental at Bedriacum was that, being an eastern legion, they stopped fighting to greet the sunrise with a salute, which Vitellius's men mistook as a signal to reinforcements from the east, causing them to lose the will to fight. The history of the Third Gallic, Tribune, is the same mixture of bravery, disaster, stupid mistakes and blind luck that every other legion parades as its claim to eternal glory. Including, on occasion, that old favourite . . .'

He turned away, barking his last words over his shoulder.

'Pernicious fraud!'

'Does everyone have a cup?' Scaurus looked around his officers, raising his wine in salute. 'Here's to audacity, gentlemen.'

With the legion busy enjoying itself in the wine shops and brothels of the city, the legatus had gracefully accorded his senior officers the same privilege, knowing that he could count on them to indulge themselves in similar fashion to their men, thereby giving him the opportunity to meet with a select group of men he knew he could trust to plan their next steps. The officers sitting around him lifted their drinks and echoed the toast.

'Audacity!'

Cotta sipped at his wine appreciatively.

'Two of the reasons that I like you, Legatus, are because you serve damned good wine and because you know when to take risks. I presume our toast means that you have a little more risk taking in mind?'

Scaurus nodded, looking around him at the faces of his men.

'It's clear enough that the governor intends to thwart me in any way that presents itself to him. And if he knew the contents of the report I'm intending to send back to Rome regarding the state of the province's defences, he would promptly redouble those efforts. If he has his way then we will march east with no hope other than that our deaths will be swift and honourable.' He looked around at the gathered officers.

'And speaking for myself, I have no plans to meet my ancestors for a good while yet. So, each of you is here for a reason, each man with a role to play in ensuring that when we march east we go equipped to conquer whatever it is that's waiting for us beyond the Euphrates. Julius.'

'Legatus?'

'We don't have time to turn the legion's men into thirty-mile-a-day marching animals, but we do have time to find out which of them have the potential. And you don't have the time to make them very much more proficient with their weapons, but you can assess who'll be confident enough to use their spears and swords when the time comes. You've got a week, no more, and then we'll make the decision as to who we take east and who we leave here for the governor to play at soldiers with.'

The first spear nodded, and Scaurus switched his gaze to Cotta.

'You, Centurion, I need to find out which of the legion's centurions can be trusted when the going turns nasty. I want a list, no more than a week from now, of who you believe we can trust to keep their nerve when the arrows start flying. And who we can trust, full stop. I've no intention of taking any of Domitius Dexter's men with me, if I can avoid it.'

Cotta smiled back at him.

'As you wish, Legatus. Although First Spear Quintinus isn't going to like you picking and choosing from his officers.'

The legatus shrugged.

'First Spear Quintinus isn't going to have any choice in the matter. Dubnus . . .'

The hulking centurion stiffened in his seat.

'Legatus.'

'You, Centurion, I need for the sheer brute force possessed by your axe men. The Tenth Century will be the muscle power that drives our most effective weapons. And you, Qadir . . .'

'Legatus?'

Where Dubnus's voice was a bass growl, the Hamian's lightly accented response was smooth, almost cultured.

'You, and your archers, will take that muscle power and deliver it to the places where it will have the maximum impact.'

Qadir inclined his head in respectful acknowledgement.

'Avidus.'

The African engineer nodded briskly.

'You and your men are our experts at making things, or at least that was the story you told me when I was debating whether to agree to Julius's brazen plan to bribe you and your century out of the transit barracks at Rome.'

He passed the centurion a wooden writing tablet, which Avidus opened and perused, his eyebrows rising at the list's contents.

'I need you to get me all of these items. Make them, or have them made in the city's workshops, borrow them or steal them, I care little as long as they're ready on time.'

'In a *week*, Legatus?'

'In a week, Centurion.'

The pioneer officer pursed his lips.

'Ox hides by the thousand, linen by the mile, iron – a *lot* of iron – enough wood to build a battleship. It won't be cheap, sir, and getting it done that quickly will just make the merchants and smiths greedier than they usually are.'

Scaurus pointed a hand at the chest that occupied one corner of his office, the reason why the Tungrians mounted a heavy guard around and inside the building both night and day.

'I know. You'll have all the gold you need.'

Avidus nodded and turned his attention back to the tablet, his mind clearly already preoccupied with how to meet his legatus's requirements.

'Tribune Corvus.'

Marcus looked up.

'Legatus.'

'You, Tribune, have two men with key roles to play, and I have a particular task in mind for you as well. This is what I need . . .'

Marcus rode his horse down the hill into Seleucia the next morning at the head of a long train of empty carts, looking out across the port at the praetorian warships that had been beached on the inner harbour's shingle. Half a dozen remained afloat within the protection of the outer harbour's thick walls, moored stem to stern along the northern mole. The morning guard directed him to the better of the port's official guest houses so, ordering the carts to wait for him, and tethering the horse under their watchful eye, he walked the last few hundred paces to find the fleet's procurator taking the morning air, leaning back in a wooden chair with the look of a man at his ease. The expression fled Ravilla's face the instant he saw the younger man approaching.

'I've been waiting for you to come back down that hill, Tribune. Not with any keen sense of anticipation, mind you.'

Marcus inclined his head in recognition of the naval officer's irritation, having fully expected his appearance to confirm the man's worst fears. Scaurus had warned him what to expect before he'd climbed into the saddle for the short ride to the port earlier that morning: 'He's not going to like it, Tribune. You'll have to find a way to make it clear to him what's going to happen if he doesn't cooperate.'

He bowed respectfully.

'I completely understand, Procurator. The Legatus asked me to convey to you his regret at having to make the request . . .'

'But unfortunately he has no choice in the matter?'

'Something very much like that, yes sir.'

The procurator scratched at his beard, shaking his head unhappily as he accepted the scroll that Marcus had produced from his belt, opening it to read Scaurus's orders.

'So he proposes to take my marines away with him into Parthia, where he will almost certainly get them all killed? I suppose I ought to be grateful he's not ordering me to bring him a few cohorts of sailors as well?'

The younger man shook his head.

'In the years I've known him it's been my observation that while Legatus Scaurus can at times be pragmatic to the point of ruthlessness, I've never found him to be a sadist. And arming your crews would be sadism of the lowest type, given the enemy we're marching to face. He believes that your marines will suffice.'

The procurator glowered at him in silence for a moment.

'And what's he going to do if I refuse, eh? March his legion down here and drag my men away? Tell me that, Tribune. What's he going to do if I send you away with the hard word?'

'Nothing, sir. But then it's not what the legatus will do that should be troubling you.'

Ravilla looked at him, seeing the shadow of pain cross his face. 'I was wondering why he sent you, rather than coming down here in person. I'd put it down to his not wanting to have to face me while he stripped my fleet of its men, but that's not the reason, is it?'

Marcus shook his head impassively.

'No, Procurator.'

'Then why? Why you, and not Rutilius Scaurus in person.'

'Because the legatus has no one to lose, sir. Whereas I do.'

Ravilla nodded slowly.

'Wife? Children? Parents?'

'My wife and child. They assure my complete commitment to the emperor's cause, and my eventual return to Rome. And yourself, Prefect? Do you have family in the capital?'

The prefect looked back at him for a moment before replying.

'I have children, and a wife I still love. My father lives with my family, to keep them from harm.'

'Could your father fight off a dozen hardened killers? Imperial justice takes as violent a form these days as it did towards the end of the civil war, Prefect. Men of substance are torn from their families and murdered on the slightest pretext, their estates and property confiscated. All the men behind the throne need is a reason to come after you . . .'

'And?'

'Prefect, my legatus is an honourable man who has been put into a corner, and under such circumstances all he knows how to do is fight. If you fail to assist him then you will leave him no alternative but to report your non-compliance with the valid and rightful order of a superior officer. As a consequence you are likely to find yourself on the wrong end of imperial justice, I'd imagine, with all that implies. But then *your* death wouldn't really be the worst of your problems, I'd imagine.'

First Spear Quintinus led the Third Gallic onto the parade ground the next morning with the air of a man compelled to hand his daughter over in marriage to a bridegroom with a known taste for domestic violence. The soldiers were quiet for the most part, their half-day off having for the most part been spent in pursuit of alcohol and Antioch's notoriously large population of whores.

'Fucking look at them, every one of them hanging from his chinstrap like the shithouse dogs they are!'

Saratos grinned at his comrade's disgusted opinion.

'Not every day Legatus tell soldier he part of proud tradition that go back to blessed Julius. Is funny.'

Sanga shook his head.

'Problem is, you dozy Dacian prick puller, they'll be honking up all that wine before they've done more than a mile. And given that we're their new Sixth Cohort, we're going to be ankle deep in last night's pork before you know it.'

He wisely chose to fall silent before the vine-stick-wielding wrath of their new centurion reached them, spittle flying from the newly promoted officer's lips as he raged theatrically at his men.

'Shut the fuck up! The legatus is about to address the legion!'

Scaurus strolled out in front of his command, his uniform as impeccably turned out as the previous day, although the more astute of the Tungrians had already noted the fact that his best boots had been exchanged for the standard-issue infantry footwear, their soles studded with hobnails.

'Here we go again.'

Quintus spun round from his fond contemplation of the man who had so recently fulfilled his life's only remaining ambition, by promoting him from the rank of chosen man where, he had become convinced, he was doomed to languish for the remainder of his twenty-five years of service. Legatus Scaurus had made Quintus a centurion, and in turn Quintus was determined to spend the rest of those years living up to the trust placed in him. Faced with four ranks of impassive faces, none of whom showed the slightest sign of any guilt, he drew the inevitable conclusion, swinging his vine stick to land an expert blow into the space where the standard-issue helmet was deliberately cut away to allow its wearer to hear commands in the nightmarish din of battle.

'Shut the fuck up, Sanga! And don't try looking innocent on me, soldier, I'm too experienced to fall for your attempts at indig—'

'Soldiers of the Third Gallic!'

The legatus was speaking, his voice floating across the parade round and echoing faintly from the distant barracks as he repeated each sentence in Greek.

'I hear you did yourselves proud last night. No drop of wine left unconsumed! No whore left unpleasured! No song left unsung!'

The legionaries grinned smugly, a good number of those closest to the Tungrians cheering up sufficiently to nod and make obscene gestures that they knew would leave the northern barbarians in no doubt as to the prodigious nature of their evening's entertainment, while others pointed and mimicked the only sexual release that their new fellow legionaries would have been enjoying.

'And now, having demonstrated that you know how to put on a decent show on the parade ground, you will now demonstrate your prowess at the most essential skill a soldier must possess!'

The Tungrians waited with broadening smiles while Scaurus repeated the statement in Greek, nodding back at the Third's men knowingly as the easterners frowned, trying to work out what this new challenge might be.

'Your founder, the blessed Julius Caesar, was famed for his ability to appear out of nowhere at the head of his men, this proud legion included, and to seek battle where his presence was least expected! And do you know how he used to achieve that feat?'

'Here it comes, you smug bastards!'

Scaurus glanced down the legion's line to where the Tungrians stood impassively for the most part, his lips twitching in a slight smile at the shouted comment. Close enough to the man to see his lack of concern at the comment, Quintus, whilst clearly aware that Sanga had once more been unable to resist the urge to express his indignation, did no more than shrug and nod his head at the outburst.

'Your forebears of two hundred years ago were men of iron! They could march twenty-five or thirty miles in a day and then offer their

enemies battle, as fresh as if they had covered half the distance at a gentle stroll! You and I, legionaries, will soon take pride in just that same ability, for we will need to cover ground at a prodigious rate once we have crossed the Euphrates!'

The Tungrians were grinning back at their Syrian comrades now, nodding and smiling at the sick looks that were spreading across their ranks.

'Today, soldiers, we will start gently, to allow the men who have recently sailed from Rome the chance to recover their fitness, and not to be embarrassed by your greater abilities!'

Scaurus's grin was now open, as he laid down a challenge he knew full well would have his men straining at their collars.

'Today we will march no more than fifteen miles! Not even a full day's march at the standard pace!'

He turned to find Quintinus and the assembled tribunes staring at him with expressions ranging from discomfort to outright horror, while Julius stood to one side with an impassive face.

'Ready gentlemen? Since there are nine of you, I suggest you each take a cohort. First Spear Quintinus, please lead the legion for me today. I intend to march with my Tungrians, and to ensure by my example that they don't shame themselves too badly after such a long time on board ship.'

He strode away to the Tungrians, nodding to Julius as the Tungrian first spear shook his head in dark amusement.

'Ready for a run, Julius?'

The older man nodded.

'A good deal better prepared than these poor bastards.'

Scaurus shrugged.

'War has a way of teaching bloody lessons to the unprepared. And I need soldiers who can cover ground when needed, not barrack-room slugs.'

He waved to Quintinus in his position at the head of the legion's long column.

'Ready, First Spear!'

The legion jerked into motion one cohort at a time, each of the divisions obeying the command of their senior centurions and striding out bravely enough while their wind was still fresh. Quintinus led them out of the fortress and onto the road to the north, setting a brisk pace in the fresh breeze that was blowing from the west.

'Bloody winter, and it's still warmer than most summer days back at The Hill!'

Saratos nodded at his comrade's comment, putting his head back to gulp down the cool air.

'Is no rain neither. I like.'

'When we going to start running, sir?'

Sanga ignored both the muttered curses from the men around him and the hard looks that his centurion was shooting at him, grinning broadly at the legatus to indicate that his question was genuine.

'Soon enough, soldier. I thought a gentle pace might be better for the first two miles, to give you time to stretch out those muscles before we start to speed up.'

He led them along the broad road in pursuit of the cohort ahead of them, quickly closing the hundred-pace gap that had separated the two units, until the Fifth Cohort's rear rankers were looking over their shoulders in dismay at the grim-faced northerners hard on their heels. After a short while the legion trumpeters blew their horns at the column's head, and, cohort by cohort, the Syrians upped their pace to the quick march. Already sweating heavily, as their exertions of the previous evening began to take their toll, the legionaries quickly began to labour as the increased pace began to punish their legs and lungs. The Fifth Cohort were soon barely managing to keep up the pace, and Scaurus exchanged a glance with Julius, who simply nodded.

'Tungrians! Follow me!'

The legatus stepped smartly to his right and began to lengthen his stride, pulling his men along behind him, all sweating freely despite the cooling breeze, but not a single man failed to keep up.

'Does nobody have a song to offer us?'

Sanga laughed at his legatus's challenge, putting back his head to bellow out the first line.

'Our centurion's got a bigger stick than yours!'

The whole cohort followed his cue, roaring out the verse with sufficient gusto to turn heads up and down the column.

'Our centurion's got a bigger stick than yours!

Our centurion's got a bigger stick than yours!

And he's going to ram the bastard where the sun don't shine!'

To the dismay of the men alongside them, the Tungrians were slowly accelerating, gradually progressing up the Fifth Cohort's six-century length as the northerners found their stride, grinning across at the struggling legionaries as they passed despite their own pain.

'Our centurion's got a bigger dick than yours!'

Our centurion's got a bigger dick than yours!

Our centurion's got a bigger dick than yours!

And he's going to ram the bastard where the sun don't shine!'

As if on cue, the trumpets blared again, and the legion's column lurched from a quick march that was slower than it could have been to a run that was no better than a shambling trot. Scaurus turned momentarily to face his men, raising his hand and then pointing it forward in a sweeping gesture.

'Tungrians . . . at the run . . . RUN!'

When the Tungrians staggered back onto the legion's parade ground later that morning, they were surprised to find a cohort's strength of armed and armoured men waiting for them, their dark-blue tunics the only clue the soldiers needed as to their identity. While the exhausted soldiers mustered their energy, Scaurus walked across to where Marcus stood talking to Procurator Ravilla, offering his hand to the fleet's commander.

'Greetings, Cassius Ravilla, and my thanks for your quick response to my request for assistance.'

The other man looked down at his hand pointedly before saluting with a punctilious precision that raised the legatus's eyebrows.

'I had no choice but to do my duty, Legatus. That was made very clear to me.'

Scaurus nodded his understanding gravely.

'And for all your understandable reluctance, your marines may be the difference between success and failure. I promise you they won't be misused.'

He stopped speaking as the procurator put a finger on his breastplate.

'I know. Because wherever you take them you'll find me at their head. Legatus you may be, but we're men of the same class, so if you want these men in your ranks you'll have to settle for me leading them.'

Scaurus smiled slowly, his eyes stonelike.

'You commanded a cohort before taking to the sea, I presume.'

Ravilla nodded, his lips tight.

'In Germania. At the tail end of the war with the Marcomanni. I saw a little fighting.'

'I see. Very well, Cassius Ravilla, you'll lead your cohort as a tribune. Which means that the the legion has ten such men where I'm supposed to have six. Did you bring the equipment I detailed in my message?'

Ravilla nodded.

'I did. Although quite how you expect them to work without a deck to bolt them to is beyond me.'

The legatus grinned wolfishly.

'Let me worry about that. I know a man who'll put that right in no time.'

After a frugal lunch, taken in the open under the shade of their shields, the legion paraded again, and Scaurus walked down the line of cohorts with pursed lips, looking closely at the condition of his men and clearly finding himself unimpressed by what he saw.

'Our men took over five hours to cover fifteen miles, First Spear Quintinus, and yet despite posting that rather mediocre time for a distance which is somewhat less than the usual daily march, half of them look as if they've gone a dozen rounds with the legion's champion wrestler. You may have been teaching them to fight, but their marching skills are sadly underdeveloped. Nothing that can't be rectified by a week or two of hard training though, is it?'

Quintinus inclined his head respectfully.

'Indeed not, Legatus.'

'Indeed not. I'm half tempted to send them around the circuit again, to accelerate the process of hardening them up, but that might be a little much for the first day, so I think we'll concentrate on the further development of their fighting skills, shall we? Sword drills, I think.'

The senior centurion saluted and turned to his officers, who swiftly set about putting the men to work with wooden swords and heavy practice shields while the tribunes watched with expressions that in a few cases were little better than idle curiosity.

'You too, gentlemen. Doubtless there are some well-trained swords among you who can teach the remainder a thing or two about the finer points of wielding a blade?'

Calling for practice weapons, they paired off at Umbrius's suggestion.

'Let's have some sport from this, shall we? There are a dozen of us, so we'll fight in pairs until we're down to the last three and then they can fight each other in turn for the title of best sword. I'll put up a jar of wine for the winner to share among us and toast his victory.'

Pairing up with his first opponent, a man barely out of his teens who had completely failed to make any impression on him until that moment, Marcus waved away the offer of a shield and picked up a second sword instead.

'You do fight like a dimachaerus then?'

He nodded, raising the twin weapons.

'Ready?'

The younger man nodded and stepped forward to fight with an almost comical look of determination. A simple feint low and to his right put him off balance sufficiently for Marcus to spring onto his other foot and snake the point of his right-hand sword over the top of the tribune's shield, accommodatingly lowered to deal with the initial attack. The rough wooden weapon's tip puckered the man's neck at the point where the veins that ran to his brain were closest to the surface, making him jump back with a surprised expression. He dropped his sword to rub furiously at the sore spot, and Marcus turned away, shaking his head at the ease with which he had taken the victory.

'You're dead. When you fight a man with two swords you need to watch his weapons, not his eyes.'

He stood and watched while Umbrius and Flamininus both won their bouts effortlessly, and smiled quietly as Ravilla, theoretically at a disadvantage given he was ten years older than his opponent, dismantled the younger man's defences with swift and economic ease. Barely breathing hard, he strolled away from his victim, left sprawling on the parade ground's hard surface by a trip which he had instantly followed up with a sword jab to his exposed thigh. He raised the weapon in ironic salute to Marcus.

'I'll see you in the next round, perhaps?'

It was not to be. When the lots were drawn for the last six, Ravilla found himself paired off against Umbrius, while Flamininus grinned evilly at his man, one of the better-trained tribunes. Marcus was matched against Varus, and the two were soon facing each other with their weapons raised while the other officers gathered around them to watch. Varus raised his shield to the textbook position, staring at Marcus over the brass rim with a grim smile.

'So, Britannia, Germania and Dacia, I've been practising what you told me—'

He lunged forward without warning, the attack so swift that Marcus had to step back sharply and parry the sword thrust away from his face. He spun away from the brutal swing that followed rather than block it, then avoided the weapon's blurred arc again, content to evade the tribune's strikes rather than parry them, while Varus came after him with the speed and determination of a man who knew that nothing less would have any chance of success. Flamininus folded his arms with a sneer, calling to Umbrius loudly enough for everyone in the group to hear his words.

'I told you the man was a fraud. Look at him ducking away from poor little Varus's attacks!'

Marcus looked across at Flamininus briefly, noting the man's twisted smile. He swayed back to allow Varus's sword to hiss past his nose with an inch to spare, then stepped in to attack with an abrupt violence that put him face-to-face with the young tribune, pushing his right sword out wide to pin the other man's blade against his shoulder and putting out a knee to prevent him from punching out with his shield.

'That was better, Tribune. Good aggression with the blade, tidy defence with the shield. Now let's see how well you cope with an attack. Ready?'

Varus nodded and fell back, waiting with his sword and shield positioned in readiness for his opponent's attack. Flamininus snorted his disgust behind Marcus.

'Gods below, this isn't some sort of glorified training session! Either fight or get the fuck out of the ring and let some real men have a go!'

Marcus replied without turning his gaze from Varus.

'Let me know when you find a real man, Tribune Flamininus, and I'll be delighted to spar with him. Until then I suggest you keep your mouth shut unless you want it shutting for you . . .'

He waited a beat for the insult to sink in.

'Again.'

The evil-tempered tribune stormed forward, raising his sword and shield.

'Get out of the way, Varus, I'm going to teach this upstart bastard a lesson!'

Varus straightened up from his defensive pose with a look of confusion, and Umbrius beckoned him over.

'There's no reasoning with the man in this mood. He won't be happy until he's faced this man and proved himself to be the better of them.'

'Prove myself the better of him?'

Flamininus raised a disgusted eyebrow.

'I do that simply by standing here. I'm going to teach this fool what it means to face a trained swordsman. By the time I left Rome there wasn't an instructor in the city I couldn't beat.'

He sprang forward, lunging with his wooden sword's point, repeating the move twice more as Marcus calmly stepped back with his swords held ready, not deigning to block or parry.

'You fucking coward! You're no better than Varus!'

Abandoning his fencing style, Flamininus attacked again with a swing of his sword, the blade skating harmlessly down a sloping sword raised in effortless defence. Stamping forward to punch at his opponent with his shield's heavy iron boss, his strike found only empty air as Marcus span away to the left, jabbing his sword's blunt and splintered point into the bicep of Flamininus's right arm.

'Fuck!'

Stepping back, Marcus waited while his opponent grimaced at the pain, barely managing to maintain his trembling grip of the heavy practice sword's hilt.

'You're too slow. Too predictable. And you make threats that your skill can't deliver.'

The tribune's face twisted in anger, the pain in his arm forgotten as he squared up to his tormentor.

'I'll have you, you f—'

Marcus was upon him in a whirl of blades, forcing his hapless opponent back half a dozen steps before Flamininus's mind had caught up with the havoc that the Tungrian was playing with his defence. A wooden sword point snaked through his guard to jab into his thigh, and while he was still reeling, another smashed the shield from his hand. Umbrius nodded decisively.

'That's enough! Give it up, Flamininus, he has you at his mercy!'

The tribune recovered himself enough to look down the length of the wooden sword point only inches from his face.

'Nothing to say, Flamininus?'

The response was growled between gritted teeth.

'This isn't over.'

Marcus smiled equably back at him.

'I'm afraid it is. Your skill at arms is no better than average, no matter how many instructors took your gold and told you that you were a second Achilles. This bout *is* over.'

He turned away, tossing the wooden swords aside for the next man, only to stiffen in pain as Flamininus slammed his weapon's wooden blade into his right thigh with enough force to leave a line of blood oozing where the sword's ragged wooden edge had pierced the flesh. The enraged Flamininus drew his sword back again, his eyes pinned wide with the need to do harm, and as Marcus turned to face him, he whipped the weapon in at head height in a vicious swing clearly intended to strike him in the face.

Ducking under the attack, Marcus fell back, twisting sideways to evade a furious lunge.

'Stop this idiocy, or I'll—'

The sword swung high into the air, his assailant clearly aiming to deliver a knockout blow, and Marcus stepped swiftly in, butting his opponent hard with the brow guard of his helmet and sending him staggering backwards with blood running down his face, clearly dazed.

'Umbrius, call this fool off before I'm forced to put him down hard!'

The senior tribune shrugged with a half-smile.

'You've enraged him past the point that I can control him, Tribune Corvus. I suggest you make yourself scarce before he regains his wits.'

Flamininus shook his head and roared back into the fight, swinging the wooden sword extravagantly and forcing Marcus to retreat in the face of its whistling arcs.

'*This* is how a Roman gentleman deals with a piece of shit like you!'

He raised the sword and stepped in fast, once more clearly going for the blow that would finish Marcus, but in the split second that the blade was raised to its highest point the Tungrian stopped retreating and stood his ground, suddenly face-to-face with the enraged tribune. Stabbing out with a half-fisted punch, he lunged at Flamininus, twisting to put the full strength of his body behind the blow. Seeing the punch coming, and with no way to avoid it, Flamininus instinctively reared back, taking the full force of Marcus's knuckles not in his face, as had been the intention, but squarely in the throat. He staggered back, his eyes bulging as he fought for breath that would not come through his traumatised windpipe. An attempt to speak resulted in nothing more than a strangled grunt, his gestures becoming increasingly frantic as he beckoned for help with imploring eyes.

Umbrius stepped forward with a look of concern.

'Very well, you've stopped him, now help him—'

Flamininus fell to his knees, his lips turning blue as he stared helplessly at the men around him. Marcus shook his head as he looked down at his stricken colleague.

'I've seen this before, I'm afraid. He's already dead.'

Umbrius turned to stare at Marcus, his face suddenly aghast as the Tungrian's words sank in. Before he could speak, the tribune toppled full length into the parade ground's dust, writhing as his body contorted in its death throes.

'You've killed him.'

Umbrius dragged his gaze away from the twitching corpse, shaking his head in amazement.

'You've killed a brother officer!'

Scaurus sat back in his chair, looking at his senior tribune with an expression of disbelief.

'You want what?'

Umbrius's face was set hard.

'Justice, Legatus.'

'Justice? And what measure of justice am I supposed to indulge you in, when a man who was clearly a lunatic provokes another who is far more skilled, and then through his own ineptitude suffers the consequences?'

Umbrius nodded, his face hard.

'There! You say it yourself! Your man Corvus has fought in a dozen battles! He is a consummate killer, and when poor

Flamininus provoked him he responded with immediate deadly retaliation. No warning, no attempt to disarm his opponent, just a straight punch to the throat. A punch he knew would kill Flamininus.'

He folded his arms, his face set in lines of defiance. Scaurus pursed his lips, his expression a combination of amusement and irritation.

'Don't think I don't know the game you're playing, Tribune.'

The silence stretched out until Umbrius decided to ask the inevitable question.

'Game, Legatus? A Roman gentleman is dead, murdered in cold blood by your man. Why would I be playing *games* under such a circumstance?'

'Please, give me credit for a little intelligence. I'd imagine you're delighted to have Flamininus off your back, given that he was little better than a mad dog. But you know that the governor has taken a violent dislike to me, mainly because I was the messenger of his removal from the post from which he's made so much money. You know that if you make a formal complaint to Domitius Dexter then he'll be delighted to overrule me, and declare a formal investigation into Flamininus's death. Doubtless he'll call in one of his cronies from another legion, and between them they'll manage to find Tribune Corvus guilty of murder. So let me make this very clear to you, Tribune, you can go running to higher authority if it pleases you, but if you do you'll be inviting him to victimise a man who is guilty of nothing more than defending himself against a lunatic.'

Umbrius shrugged.

'I can only ask for the justice I feel—'

Scaurus rode over him in a tone that brooked no argument.

'But if you do seek to take advantage of my strained relationship with the governor then I warn you, beware of the consequences.'

Umbrius gaped at him.

'Are you *threatening* me, Legatus?'

Scaurus shook his head with a tight smile.

'I would never do any such thing, Tribune, not given our respective social statuses. But I warn you, Tribune Corvus has been to war with my Tungrians, and they feel a fierce affinity with him. If you challenge him then you challenge them. And my Tungrians, Tribune, are not the sort of men to take a challenge lying down.'

'You can't do this.'

Scaurus looked up at Marcus, turning his attention from the paper on his desk to the incredulous tribune.

'I most certainly can. And I will. And you, Tribune, will obey my lawfully issued orders.'

'The governor will hold you responsible! He'll—'

'Not immediately he won't. The first thing he'll do is send men to bring you back. Which will take time.'

'But that—'

'Will be days from now. Whereas if I don't send you away immediately you'll be arrested within hours and dead soon after. So stop arguing and start listening.'

He folded the paper, securing it with thin ribbon and then dripping a thick blob of candle wax onto the spot where the fabric strips crossed, pressing a waiting seal into the hot globule.

'There.'

He passed it to Marcus.

'You have your orders. Execute them, Tribune, and leave the worrying about the consequences to me.'

The younger man saluted and turned on his heel, leaving the headquarters to find Martos waiting for him.

'Who told you?'

The Briton's one eye was bright with the joy of the moment.

'Your first spear. He thinks you might appreciate some company. I have horses saddled and ready, your cloak, provisions for a week. I even found your socks and packed them. Lugos will stay and look after the rest of your gear.'

Marcus smiled, despite the seriousness of what they were about to do.

'I doubt there's a horse in the stables that could bear his weight.'

Martos grinned back at him.

'I doubt such a beast exists in the whole of this city. So, Tribune, where is it that we're headed?'

Governor Dexter swept into the fortress in his full pomp the next morning, his ceremonial escort of six lictors preceding him into Scaurus's office, their leader announcing Dexter's presence while he lurked in the corridor.

'Gaius Domitius Dexter, Proconsul Legatus of his imperial majesty's province of Syria Palestina, commander of the imperial legions!'

The governor stalked into the office, looking about him with an air of dissatisfaction before fixing his attention on Scaurus, who now stood to attention awaiting his superior's command.

'Legatus.'

Scaurus saluted.

'Governor. If I'd known we were to be honoured by your presence I would have arranged for some refreshment.'

Dexter shook his head, waving the lictors from the room now that their intimidatory purpose was done with.

'No need, Rutilius Scaurus. As you may have guessed from my official escort, this is no social visit. I am here to transact official state business in my role as commander in chief of the Syrian legions.'

Scaurus bowed, gesturing to one of the chairs set out before his desk, but the governor shook his head with a thunderous expression.

'I'll stand. I have received word from within your legion that a crime has been committed against a senior military tribune, a man of the senatorial class. A crime of murder.'

He stared intently at his junior, but Scaurus wasn't prepared to be intimidated.

'I'm aware of the source of your information, Governor. Tribune Umbrius made it perfectly clear that he intended to report Tribune Flamininus's death.'

'I should think so!'

The governor's brow lowered over his eyes, an apparent sign of his fury over the matter.

'Young Flamininus was the son of a close friend, and was serving here at the express request of his father, in the hope that he would return a better man. Instead of which he lies rotting in the earth . . .'

He paused, shaking his head at Scaurus.

'How am I to explain this to his father? Tell me that!'

The legatus waited a moment to be sure that the outburst was over before replying.

'I suggest you tell Flamininus senior that his son was a bully, with the twin curses of delusions as to his own competence with weapons and a temper that should have been dealt with in the nursery.'

'What?!'

'Further, Governor, I suggest that you tell him his son was foolish enough to attempt serious harm to a fellow officer who also happened to be a veteran of several bloody campaigns, and who was recently appointed to his tribunate by the emperor himself.'

Dexter shook his head, refusing to be put off his indignant stride.

'Your man Corvus killed him!'

'Indeed so, in a freak accident of the type which will happen when one man attempts to physically damage another who is by far his master with the weapons to hand. Flamininus had already attempted one physical attack upon his colleague, with nothing better to show for it than a badly bruised face. He tried the same trick with a practice sword, forcing Corvus to put him down, made a mess of his defence and took Corvus's blow in the throat. I have several witnesses to the event, officers who—'

'Who will retract, when they realise the seriousness of the charges facing your man.'

'Charges, Governor?'

'Charges, Legatus. Murder, for the most part. I will not tolerate such a thing. Have him delivered to my presence for judgement. Today.'

Scaurus stared at him for a moment before speaking again.

'Unfortunately, Governor, I sent him away last night.'

Dexter stared back, his eyes narrowing.

'You . . . *sent him away*?'

'Indeed. I have many and varied needs if I am to take my legion, my mistake, my *half*-legion, into Parthia, some of which I cannot satisfy with purely local resources. Tribune Corvus has travelled south to Hama, in order to procure some of that province's excellent archers to serve alongside my legionaries.'

'Has he indeed? In that case, Legatus, I shall detail a man of impeccable character to fetch him back!'

He turned on his heel, calling over his shoulder as he exited the room in high dudgeon.

'I'll have your man Corvus in front of me before the week's out! This transparent attempt to delay imperial justice won't save him from the fate that's waiting for him!'

'Gentlemen, my apologies for not receiving your debrief from the night of the legion's festivities in the city a little earlier. I've been somewhat preoccupied. I've now had time to read Centurion Qadir's written report, which makes for interesting reading.'

Scaurus looked up from the scroll, raising his eyebrows at the two soldiers who were standing to attention before him.

'You're *quite* sure about this?'

Sanga nodded confidently, while Saratos stared at the wall behind the legatus and let his comrade do the talking.

'There's no doubt about it, Legatus.'

Leaning back in his chair, the legatus looked at the two men thoughtfully.

'And you've shared this information with whom exactly?'

Sanga shook his head.

'No one outside this room, sir. I ain't that stupid, and Saratos here tends not to say much at the best of times.'

'Good. In which case you're both dismissed to get on with that other matter we discussed. I don't know how you're going to find him, but doing so is of the greatest importance. I have a description of the man . . .'

He handed Sanga a tablet, then looked down at the papers on his desk, and Julius tipped his head to the door.

'Dismissed. Back to work with the pair of you.'

Once the two soldiers had marched from the room, Scaurus's clerk entered.

'Sir, there's a prefect to see you from the Phrygian cavalry wing. Says he's on the governor's business.'

Scaurus pulled a face.

'I'm sure he is. On your way, First Spear, I don't want you involved in this.'

The prefect walked into Scaurus's office and saluted briskly, his masked helmet dangling from its chinstrap as the two men looked at each other for a moment before the visitor spoke, apologetically waving a hand at the thick film of dust on his otherwise spotless armour.

'Greetings Legatus. I was planning to come across and pay my respects to you this afternoon in any case, although as you can see from the state of my bronze, I was still on the training field when the order from Governor Dexter to take a certain matter in hand arrived.'

His accent was pure Roman aristocrat, but the tone in which the statement was delivered was suitably respectful of the two men's ranks, and Scaurus waved the cavalry officer to a seat with an encouraging smile.

'And I've been intending to send you an invitation to dinner with my officers, Prefect. It's a pity we couldn't have had this meeting under happier circumstances.'

The younger man grimaced.

'I can concur with that sentiment, sir. You'll have to forgive me for the formality of this meeting, but I'm left with little choice.'

'I understand, Prefect. Shall we get down to business?'

'Thank you, sir.' The officer straightened in his chair. 'You will be aware, Legatus, that I am ordered to ride for Hama, and to apprehend and return to Antioch a narrow stripe tribune by the name of . . .'

He made a show of consulting his tablet.

'Marcus Tribulus Corvus. Apparently this man Corvus is guilty of the murder of your broad stripe Tribune Lucius Quinctius Flamininus?'

Scaurus shook his head.

'The governor and my senior tribune both call it murder. I'm more inclined to the term "self-defence".'

He smiled thinly.

'But then I would be, wouldn't I?'

The prefect nodded, his face set hard.

'Nevertheless, Legatus, as a loyal officer of Rome you are, I presume, willing to assist me in the pursuance of my orders?'

'Of course.'

'Thank you, sir. So, is this man Corvus accompanied?'

Scaurus smiled.

'Yes. He has with him a one-eyed Briton of the Votadini tribe who should be considered extremely dangerous.'

The cavalryman nodded.

'I see. And they've ridden for Hama?'

'He left via the Oriental gate late yesterday afternoon.'

'So there's no point my despatching riders to any other of the province's forts?'

Scaurus shook his head.

'I know my duty, Tribune. And I am only a loyal servant of the emperor. Tribune Corvus is to be found in Hama, I can assure you of that.'

4

When Julius reported to the headquarters building the next morning he found Scaurus waiting for him on the steps.

'Make your report as we walk, First Spear, your officers are perfectly capable of running morning training without you breathing down their necks this once. I think it's time we found out how well your man Avidus is doing with those manufacturing jobs I asked him to sort out.'

They walked briskly through the camp to the armourer's workshops, finding the pioneer centurion waiting for them at the door.

'Legatus, First Spear, come inside. I've got something to show you both.'

They followed him into the armoury, but where the first spear had expected to find trained soldiers working to repair the usual broken armour hinges and lost strap rivets, he was surprised to find the workshop in relative silence. Looking around he took in the neatly stacked bales of linen in one corner, the pile of ox hides in another, and the rack of shields awaiting the skilled tradesmen's attention. Raising an eyebrow, he looked at Scaurus with a questioning expression.

'You really think we can make these shields arrowproof with linen and leather, Legatus?'

His superior nodded equably.

'It'll work. Centurion?'

Avidus gestured to the shield before him, its red painted wooden surface as yet unadorned.

'We glue a layer of linen to the wood, give it time to dry and then add another layer, and so on until we've laid on a dozen or so. Then we top it off with a layer of ox hide to protect the linen against any rain, and paint the hide with melted beeswax as waterproofing before nailing the rim back into place.' He grinned at Julius. 'Given that your boys will be looking for a way to make the bloody things lighter again, the leather also acts as a form of protection against tampering. Anyway . . .'

He gestured to a soldier who carried forward a modified shield, its painted wood now completely concealed by the linen and leather that had been fixed to the curved surface. Julius took it from him, hefting its weight with a grunt.

'It's heavy.'

Avidus nodded.

'The additional protection weighs about six pounds. But come and see this before you tell me it's not worth the extra load on our men.'

He led them across the workshop, gesturing to one of his men.

'Fetch the shields we were using earlier.'

He turned to Julius while the man disappeared.

'I was more than a bit doubtful that the legatus's idea would work, so I got one of the Hamians to put a few arrows into a pair of shields at thirty paces. Ah, here's the first of them, before we glued on all that linen and leather.'

Julius stared darkly at the damage the arrows had done to the painted wooden surface. One of them was lodged halfway through the shield's wooden boards, but the other three had punched cleanly through. Avidus lifted the shield to allow daylight to shine through the holes.

'Whichever one of your grunts was carrying that is out of the fight, I'd say.'

The first spear nodded gloomily at his words, turning his attention to the leather-faced shield that had been carried in while his attention had been distracted.

'That's . . .'

The pioneer centurion grinned at him.

'Hard to believe, isn't it? I wouldn't have credited it myself, if I hadn't seen it with my own eyes.'

Where the first shield had been wrecked by the arrows' destructive impacts, its leather-covered companion was relatively undamaged, with the missiles' iron points wedged in its surface rather than having punched through it.

'Three of them haven't even fully pierced the wood.'

Julius nodded.

'And the one that has is only a third of the way through the board. This man's still fighting.'

Scaurus tapped the waxy leather surface with his finger.

'So it's not pretty, it weighs a good deal more than the usual shield, but it stops arrows shot at it from close range. What do you think, First Spear?'

Julius looked at him with a disgusted expression.

'I think, Legatus, that you knew very well what was going to happen when our man loosed those arrows at this. Let it never be said that you lack any flair for showmanship. Perhaps you should have taken up acting as a career.'

His superior winced at the insult.

'That's harsh, Julius, but I take your point. Although considering the effect that our colleague's demonstration has had on you, imagine the sense of amazement and consternation that will be experienced by the Parthians when their fearsome volleys of arrows fail to make much of an impression on our ranks?'

Julius looked at the protected shield again.

'How quickly can we have every man in the legion protected like this?'

Avidus pursed his lips.

'I can convert five hundred shields a day given fifty men to work with. After all, it's just cutting and gluing for the most part. Dirty work, but not difficult, and the raw materials are already in hand. Eight days?'

Scaurus slapped a clenched fist into his palm.

'I can't give you eight days. You'll just have to go faster. I want a thousand shields a day converting, and I don't care how you make it happen.'

He grimaced at Julius.

'There must be that many men in the legion cells after last night's rather vigorous celebrations. Tell them that their punishment is five days of gluing linen to wood, and that the sooner they get done the quicker they'll be freed.'

He turned back to Avidus.

'That's a good start, Centurion. Now let's talk about the rest of that list I gave you, shall we.'

The African nodded.

'Yes Legatus. Now firstly, about these other shields you wanted making? I'm still struggling to see what use they're going to be when they're so big they can barely be lifted.'

'Mules, Dubnus?'

'Mules, Morban. Four legs, big ears, nasty kick on them?'

The veteran standard bearer looked up at the man who had once been his colleague with an expression of disgust, putting down his spoon and resting his elbows on the taverna's dining table.

'I should have known there was more to the offer of a feed in the city with you two than met the eye.' Dubnus smirked at him from his place alongside his colleague Otho, chewing hard at a piece of gristle. 'And I do know, *Your Highness*, what a mule is. I was simply expressing my lack of understanding as to why you should need so many of them.'

Otho, a famously pugilistic officer with a reputation for punching first and then not asking any questions before punching again just to be sure, leaned forward and bared his gaped teeth at the standard bearer in a fearsome smile, his voice permanently hoarse from a lifetime of bellowing at recruits.

'But if we told you, it wouldn't be much of a secret, would it, what with your constant hunt for inside information? Before we knew it, the legion would be taking bets on what all the new mules will be carrying.'

'I can be hurt, Centurion! You may see me as a bluff, hard-faced soldier, but—'

Dubnus laughed, tapping Morban on the chest.

'Don't forget I was Chosen Man to Tribune Corvus, back when he was a centurion and you were his statue waver. Which means that what *I* see you as, Standard Bearer, is a venal bastard with an eye to his own enrichment and an unending thirst for other people's gold. But while you're all those things, you're also the best man I can think of when it comes to buying three hundred mules for the legion.'

He watched as the standard bearer's eyes narrowed in calculation. Morban took another mouthful of his meal, clearly thoughtful as he chewed energetically and swallowed before speaking again.

'Three *hundred* mules? *Really?*'

'Three hundred. All to be capable of carrying a heavy load, with plenty of life left in them. If you think you'll be able to make a profit by buying animals bound for the slaughterhouse, you're missing one critical factor from your calculations.'

Dubnus hooked a thumb at the man sitting next to him.

'Him.'

Otho grinned at the standard bearer, ostentatiously raising his vine stick in a fist that was more scar tissue than knuckles, and Morban nodded slowly.

'I can see the merit in your argument, Centurions. So, you want to buy these beasts of burden without the sheer size of your requirement forcing prices up?'

The veteran centurion raised an eyebrow at Dubnus.

'You see? I told you he still possesses enough wit to see sense.'

He turned back to the standard bearer.

'You've got it. That's why if the fact we're buying mules leaks out I'll be forced to beat you until that's not all that's leaking out.'

His colleague reached out and took a handful of the standard bearer's tunic.

'Or to put it another way, if it gets out that the legion wants to buy that many animals, the price going through the roof will only be part of our problems. So, if by any mysterious means that should happen, once Otho here has broken your nose for what will clearly be the twentieth time, I'll confiscate not only your profits but every coin in your purse, those held for you by your various employees, and in your various *secret* hiding places.'

Morban shook his head in irritated bafflement.

'I can take a hint. But if it's that important to get these beasts bought, why not just gather the city's donkey dealers and show them the colour of your gold and the edge of your dagger? Since when did the army ever negotiate with a pack of mule mongers?'

Dubnus smirked.

'You may know how many beans make three, Morban, but you're not the sharpest sword in the armoury when it comes to outwitting senior officers, are you?'

He shook his head at the older man's bemusement.

'The governor has forbidden the legatus to take more than half the legion with him over the Euphrates.'

The standard bearer shrugged.

'I knew that.'

The centurion turned away, looking about him at the taverna's other clients and making sure that their conversation could not be overheard.

'You would have been hard put not to have heard it. The governor has made a point of making it clear to one and all that he intends to protect the city with the other half of the legion. So, what do you think he might make of the news that the legatus is in the market for such a very large number of mules?'

'Ah . . .'

'Indeed, ah. So here's the bargain, Morban. You will receive enough gold to purchase three hundred mules at the current market price. You will find those mules, you and whoever you choose to join you in the venture, and you will buy them, quietly and without a fuss, within the next two days. You will not pay other men to steal them, which will inevitably attract both attention to our preparations, and Otho's vine stick to your nether regions.'

Otho smiled evilly, holding up his vine stick again and pointing to a knot on one side.

'And when you've managed to put three hundred more beasts

into the legion stables, you can share whatever money you have left with the men you chose to help you.'

The standard bearer nodded swiftly.

'I'm your man, Centurion.' He grinned across the table with a conspiratorial wink.

'And just between us three . . . say the legatus does manage to smuggle another cohort or two out from under the governor's nose. It still doesn't take three hundred mules to carry that much equipment. So what's the real need for that many animals, eh?

Dubnus beckoned Morban with a crooked finger. The burly centurion leaned closer, his voice so quiet that the veteran could barely hear the whispered words.

'I can tell you something. Something the legatus said to me . . .'

The standard bearer leaned closer, his eyes narrowing in concentration.

'Yes?'

Dubnus nodded, and his battle-scarred colleague whipped his vine stick into Morban's crotch beneath the table, the standard bearer's eyes suddenly bulging at its hard intrusion.

'He specifically told me to bring Otho to this discussion because he knows that you and I go back a long way, which could well reduce the credibility of any threat I might make if you were stupid enough to think in the wrong way. Whereas Otho here would be only too happy to use you for a punchbag.'

The veteran officer withdrew the stick, repeating his horrible grin as he leaned back and picked up his wine cup.

'Buy the mules, Morban. Leave the rest of it to the grown-ups.'

The next morning saw a repeat of the previous day's training march, with much the same result once the Tungrians hit their stride. After the lunch break, the legion was sent to weapons practice, thousands of men settling into the mind-numbing routines intended to make the use of their swords, shields and spears second nature when the time came to fight in earnest, but two centuries of the First Tungrian Cohort followed their officers away to a quiet spot between two barrack blocks. Scaurus and his first spear watched in silence as Qadir's Hamians and Dubnus's hulking axe men paraded on either side of him, each of the two centuries considering the other with expressions of disparagement. The Tungrians of the Tenth Century loomed over the Syrian archers, every one of them taller and more muscular than the biggest of the Hamians, and Dubnus shared an amused smile with Qadir before barking out an order.

'Attention!'

The Tenth Century stamped to attention in perfect synchronisation, chests and jaws thrust out pugnaciously, while the Hamians stiffened into the brace with less drama, but equal speed and precision. Julius nodded at Dubnus, and the big man strolled forward, looking up and down the double line of his men.

'Very good, Tenth Century! The Bear would have been proud of you! You're still the biggest, nastiest and proudest century in the First Tungrians, but now you've got an entire legion to dominate!'

The soldiers stared fixedly ahead, their eyes shining with pride and the memory of their former centurion. Dubnus swept his gaze up and down their ranks with a knowing smile before speaking again.

'And now, my brothers, you have the opportunity to wield a power so great that it will strike a mortal fear into the hearts of all who oppose the legion's will. You will be responsible for striking blows into the ranks of our enemies that will demand every ounce of strength in your bodies. And you will perform this duty in combination with our Hamian brothers here.'

He pointed at the archers with his vine stick, fighting to restrain a smile as the eyes of the men closest to him widened with surprise. Scaurus walked forward, beckoning to Avidus, who was waiting with several of his pioneers beside something the size of a small altar that had been shrouded in thick cloth to disguise its purpose. The grizzled centurion nodded to the men waiting around whatever it was that was concealed, and they picked it up, carrying the mystery object forward and placing it between the two centuries. Dubnus grinned at his men.

'You won't be needing to lift any more weights to build up your arm strength from now on, my lads!'

The legatus nodded to Avidus, who pulled away the cloth to reveal a machine of wood and metal mounted on a wooden frame. The seam-faced African gestured to the weapon.

'We have thirty of these beauties, the single most deadly weapon on any battlefield. This, gentlemen, is a Scorpion. It is a lightweight two-man model of the big bolt throwers carried by the navy's ships and used to protect our legion fortresses. It can throw one of these . . .'

He took a bolt from Avidus, holding it up to display the missile's sharp iron point.

'Out to a range of four hundred paces. It is so powerful that when this bolt hits a man – or a horse – protected by armour at close range, it will tear through that armour and kill the target, quickly and without fail. And this is how it works.'

He pointed at the Scorpion.

'Load!'

A pair of his men stepped up to the weapon, swinging it to point at three wooden posts joined by a crosspiece one hundred paces distant, the middle post rising above its fellows. Taking a whistle from his belt pouch Avidus blew a single note, and a pair of men hurried out from behind the barrack block closest to the target point. They were carrying between them a shirt of laminated armour and a standard-issue helmet, placing the armour onto the crosspiece and balancing the helmet on the nub of the middle post that rose above it before running for cover. The bigger of the two men standing by the Scorpion had grabbed a pair of winding handles, and was working vigorously to crank a ratcheted slide back down the channel that ran the weapon's length, his biceps bulging with the effort as he laboured over the mechanism.

'The Scorpion stores its user's strength in these . . .'

Avidus pointed to the machine's innards.

'Torsion springs made from animal sinew. As you can see, the bow arms are inserted through them, and are gradually being forced back against the springs' resistance. When the springs are stretched to the maximum safe extent, the bolt is placed into the channel.'

The soldier working the weapon's crank stepped back, nodding to his comrade and shaking his aching arms. The other man placed a bolt gingerly into the channel that ran down the machine's length, sighting carefully on the target.

'Shoot!'

The waiting soldier pulled a trigger, loosing the bolt in a whip-crack explosion of motion. In an instant the missile was gone, spat across the gap between weapon and target faster than the eye could follow. It struck the armour with a metallic thump, drawing a chorus of appreciative mutterings from the Tungrians.

'Reload!'

The big man bent to his task again, grunting with the effort as he turned the twin cranks as fast as he could. Sneaking a sideways glance at the Tenth Century's men, Scaurus smiled to himself at the sight of their massive biceps twitching in sympathy as they imagined themselves working to wind the terrifying weapon. The Scorpion's operator placed a second bolt into the mechanism, bending to crouch over the weapon, and a hush fell across the parade ground as the watching Tungrians realised what he was attempting to do. With a twang and a thump the bolt smashed the helmet from its resting place on the central post, throwing it back thirty paces to clatter off the wall of a barrack.

'Cease shooting!'

Avidus blew the whistle again, and the same pair of men re-emerged from their cover of the barrack block, hurrying to collect the battered targets and carry them across to where legatus and first spear were waiting.

'Look closely, gentlemen.'

The laminated armour was wrecked, a hole the size of a man's thumb having been punched in the overlapping plates that would have been protecting the wearer's stomach and back. The helmet was horribly deformed, the bolt that had smashed it almost flat stuck halfway through its thicker iron plate. The soldiers stared at it with expressions of fascination and horror as Scaurus held it up for them to see.

'The man who was wearing this armour is dead. And so is the man behind him, most likely. The officer who was wearing this helmet is no more than a maimed corpse, with his head burst like a melon that's fallen off the farmer's cart. His fellow officers will be terrified to raise their heads for fear of stopping a bolt in the same manner once they see the state of him!'

He strolled across to the bolt thrower.

'As I said, we have thirty of these beauties, which means we can kill between twenty-five and fifty of the enemy with every shot. But to make the most of this power we need two different types of men.'

He pointed at the Tenth Century's hulking axe men.

'Giants, like you, with the strength to make your weapon ready to fire in less than a dozen heartbeats, time after time.'

His gaze turned to the waiting Hamians.

'And men like you, with the skill to put your shot where it will do the most damage, time after time.'

He grinned at their faces.

'I know, it's not what either of you would have expected. But believe me, soldiers, the combination of your brute strength and skill with the bow is going to make the sight of you the most terrifying thing our enemies have ever seen. And quite possibly the last . . .'

Timon was, by his own admission, having one of his less effective days. It was mid-afternoon, and not one of his half-dozen mules had set a hoof outside the small stable in which they were quartered while waiting for customers. Not so much as the shadow of a buyer had darkened the threshold, and the boy who kept the animals clean and well groomed was lying asleep in the hay, having brushed them so many times for the lack of anything more interesting to do that Timon had told him to stop for fear that he would wear the brush out and turn the day's disappointment into a full-blooded commercial disaster.

Hearing voices in the street, the trader's phenomenally sensitive hearing, attuned to the slightest sound of a customer, plucked the word 'mule' from the rumble of men's voices. Darting for the door, he was just in time to find a group of three men, obviously military to judge from their haircuts, turning away from his shop front. One of them was speaking in Roman, a language in which any self-respecting Antioch mule trader made a point of being fluent.

'No, let's go back to the one round the corner. He seemed much keener to—'

Timon launched himself into the street with a hearty cry of welcome, taking the nearest man firmly by his arm, his tried and tested means of preventing potential customers from even considering leaving without at least perusing his stock.

'My friends—'

His practised sales patter dried up abruptly as the man whose arm he was holding turned to stare at him with an expression that promised great pain were he not to release the limb promptly, an impression made all the more forbidding by the two deep scars that adorned his face, one running from his right cheekbone to the point of his chin, the other, shorter but deeper, scoring his nose and running across the first as it ran halfway to his earlobe. Raising his hands in apology, Timon bowed deeply, raising his gaze to find all three men staring at him.

'We're not your friends, mule man, although we might well be your customers, now that you've bothered to come out onto the street.'

The oldest of them, a stocky man with the face of someone who had tended to fight and lose in his younger days, waved a dismissive hand.

'Come on lads, let's go back to the dealer on the main street. He had some healthy-looking animals, and . . .'

Timon's eyes widened in horror.

'Honoured customers, I can only entreat you not to indulge in such an unwise course of action. Whilst it ill behoves me to speak ill of a member of my own profession, the honesty to which my father raised me – for my name is Timon, which in Greek means “honour” – forces me to warn you that my competitor of whom you speak offers a selection of animals which, compared to my own beasts, should hang their heads for shame.’

The three men stared back at him, their expressions dead pan.

‘And besides, I am offering a special discount today.’

The scar-faced man leaned forward.

‘Discount? How much discount?’

Timon groped for a number, and in that instant the oldest of the soldiers took the opening.

‘Ten per cent. Make it ten per cent and we might be interested. Otherwise we’ll be off round the corner.’

Wincing with the pain of having been taken halfway to his bottom price without so much as a protest that he was taking the bread from his children’s mouths, the trader swallowed his pride and smiled broadly.

‘Ten per cent it is! Come in, my fr— no, honoured customers, and feast your eyes on the best mules to be found in all of Antioch! Boy, the wine!’

A swift kick at the sleeping boy sent him scuttling for the cups and flask with a look of surprise that Timon chose to ignore. The three men raised their cups in salute and drained the wine in swift gulps, grinning at Timon’s poorly hidden discomfort as he poured them refills.

‘You’re a gentleman, Timon!’

He laughed nervously at the scar-faced soldier’s praise as the second cup went the way of the first.

‘I am always happy to share a drink with the men who protect us from the eastern barbarians.’

‘But you’re not drinking!’

He nodded weakly at the scarred man, wondering why it was that the soldier’s disfigured face worried him.

‘I do not drink when I am working. It would be . . .’

‘Fucking unwise!’

The burly man who had introduced himself as Morban slapped his comrade on the shoulder.

'Leave him alone Jesus, and let's have a proper look at these mules!'

Timon frowned.

'You call your friend "Jesus"? He is a follower of the Nazarene?'

Morban laughed.

'No mate, we call him Jesus because some nasty hairy men got lucky and carved a cross into his face, just like the one your god was killed on!'

Timon managed to keep a straight face.

'The Christ was not a god, but the son of *the* God, Our Lord, the only God.'

Morban smiled tolerantly.

'We follow Mithras my friend, but we're not against other men's beliefs. Now, do you want to sell us some mules or not?'

The salesman's eyes narrowed.

'More than one? How many?'

The soldier looked around the stable, nodding with pursed lips.

'Your stock seems sound enough. How badly would you like to empty the stable? We've a long way to march, now that we're retired and heading back north, and we'll have a lot to carry. So tell me, Timon old son, how about you give us another five per cent discount to take them *all* off your hands?'

Fighting to avoid the stutter that afflicted him at moments of the greatest stress, Timon pulled at his lower lip.

'Well . . .'

The soldiers turned to leave, and with a sudden flash of panic he found himself agreeing to the deal, despite the obvious damage that it would be doing to his reputation.

'Don't worry, friend. We won't be telling anyone what we paid, and in return you can keep this sale to yourself. We're not the only men taking their diplomas and saying goodbye to the legion, so if the price is right you can do some more business with us, just as long as it stays between us. Ourselves and some of our mates have got it in mind to try some trading between the border and here, make a nice little profit to retire properly on, but we don't want anyone else stealing the idea, so if you want to sell more mules, you'll keep it to yourself, right?'

'Yes indeed. You can be assured of my discretion, noble sirs.'

Never one to beat around the bush where a potential sale might be staring him in the face, Timon felt sufficiently emboldened to enquire as to the sort of numbers the soldiers might be looking for, were more beasts to be required.

'Forty? Fifty? Of course if you can't deal with that sort of volume, no problem, we'll just be on our way, but we'd need them by—'

'You have assuredly come to the right place, my esteemed customers. I am more than capable of procuring you this volume of mules, and of the same high quality you see here!'

'By tomorrow night.'

Timon swallowed, considering the lengths to which he might have to go to satisfy such a large order, pondered the potential illegality and then, considering the amount of money involved, put out his hand.

'Fifty mules, at the price we have agreed for these six prime specimens, to be delivered to . . .'

'The Third Legion's fortress.'

'I know it well. To be delivered to your fortress by dusk tomorrow evening.'

Assured at length that Timon was a man who could indeed cope with such an order, the soldiers enjoyed the remainder of his wine while precise arrangements were made to deliver the mules. They then made their way into the street a good deal more cheerfully than they had entered his premises. The trader leaned back against the door and wiped the sweat from his brow.

'You see, boy? Was I not magnificent? I still have the gift . . .'

The boy shrugged, happy that his day was clearly about to end early given his master's propensity for celebrating sales with wine and female company, but realised that the trader had fallen uncharacteristically silent.

'And now I must leave you to close the shop, and feed and

water the soldiers' mules. I have to see a friend of mine with a business proposition.'

'We're looking for a man.'

The man to whom the statement had been addressed shrugged, staring back at the two men before him with knowing eyes. They had been waiting outside his premises when the doors were opened for business, which, given he owned a brothel whose staff routinely worked late into the night, was at a rather more relaxed time than the city's more mundane businesses who raised their shutters soon after dawn. Their entry to his place of business had been respectful enough, but he was nonetheless grateful that his customary bodyguard was close to hand, the cold-eyed Syrian staring at them with just enough menace to make clear that they were tolerated rather than welcomed.

'One man. In this city? I wish you joy with your search.'

He turned away, but the older of the two men spoke to his back, his tone unchanged despite the obvious brusque dismissal.

'We already worked that one out, after a day spent drinking watery wine all over this city and getting precisely nowhere. So my Dacian mate here had the one and only good idea I've ever heard out of him, which brings us to you. See, this man only has one skill – he knows the roads to the east of the frontier as well as he knows the lines on his palm. And you're known as a trader who employs men with that skill.'

'You are soldiers. Am I right?'

Sanga nodded.

'It's that obvious?'

'To a man with my experience. I have been trading in the lands beyond Rome's borders for most of my life, and it has been a long life. I have seen many soldiers in my time, and they have a certain appearance. You have the haircuts, you have the muscles . . .'

He looked them up and down, staring intently at both men's faces.

'And you have the eyes. So this man you seek, he is a scout?'

'Was. He left the empire's service all of a sudden like, and he's not been seen since he left the fortress at some place called Zeugma, heading for the city.'

The trader smiled.

'That would make sense. He was part of your lost cohort? The news was never official, but *karawan* masters who have trodden the northern route to the Sea of the Persians speak of coming upon the site of a massacre, of hundreds of Roman corpses picked clean with their remains strewn across the desert.'

Sanga nodded silently.

'So, this man made his escape before the Parthians fell upon your comrades, reported the matter to the men who hold the bridge over the Euphrates and then . . . ?'

'Rode south.'

'And you believe he came here?'

'What do you think?'

The trader shrugged.

'Why would I care?'

Sanga reached into his purse, pulling out a freshly minted gold aureus and dropping it into the trader's open hand. The Arab looked at the coin, frowning at the head depicted in profile.

'Which emperor is this?'

Sanga shrugged.

'Who gives a fuck? I've got four more like that, if you help me to find the man in question. I believe his name was Abbas. Here's his description.'

The trader thought for a moment.

'It does seem logical for a man seeking to hide from vengeful people like you – and the gods know that your empire has a solid reputation for taking revenge on those who betray it – would seek shelter among the teeming masses of the city. But how do you propose that I might find this man?'

Sanga gave him a pitying look.

'For five gold pieces I'd say you can do your own thinking. But I'd have thought that if anyone can persuade a man like that to come out of hiding, a trader who routinely uses the roads between here and the east to make his money would be the favourite.'

The Arab looked at him appraisingly, lifting the coin to the tavern's lamplight.

'Four more of these?'

The soldier nodded.

'Five in gold for this man Abbas – that and a night with the pick of the girls upstairs for the two of us. And wine.' He winked at the bodyguard. 'Plenty of wine.'

It was dark when Scaurus's clerk ushered an unexpected visitor into the legatus's office, taking the man's travel-stained cloak and helmet.

'Prefect. I wasn't expecting to see you again quite this quickly.'

Scaurus shook the Phrygian officer's hand, calling for cold drinks and directing him to a chair, taking his own seat.

'Am I to presume from your rather dusty appearance that you've ridden here from Hama?'

The younger man nodded, gratefully taking a long drink from the jug of cold water offered to him by the legatus's German slave.

'You presume correctly. I left yesterday at dawn and reached the city late in the day, to discover that your man Corvus has not been seen, at least not by the military authorities.'

Scaurus raised an eyebrow.

'Which is most unlikely. The arrival of a senior officer would have been noted by the men on duty, at whichever gate he entered, for a start.'

The Phrygian nodded with an unhappy expression.

'Which can only lead me to conclude that he didn't actually ride for Hama in the first place.'

Scaurus looked back at him, his face expressionless.

'Those were his orders. But who knows what lengths a man unjustly accused of murder will go to if he fears a show trial and prompt execution, solely to satisfy the spite of a man who should know better?'

The uncomfortable silence was broken by the prefect, who picked up his helmet and stood up.

'Legatus, you realise that I have no choice but to take this news to the governor?'

Scaurus nodded equably.

'It was good of you to bring it to me first. Of course, you must report back to your superior, who will in turn doubtless summon me to his palace for a discussion without wine. That is the way of things.'

'Legatus . . .'

'I know. The governor's most likely reaction will be to assume that I've sent Tribune Corvus away to somewhere very far from Hama. Not only will he rail at me for this assumed act of defiance, but he will almost certainly declare that I am to be held responsible for Quinctius Flamininus's murder in Corvus's place. He will have me arrested and conduct a quickly convened trial, declare my guilt and oversee my execution which, if I am fortunate, will be conducted in a swift and merciful manner to avoid any stain on his character.'

The prefect shook his head unhappily.

'And I can see no way to avoid bringing this fate about. I cannot fail to report my findings to the Governor, and when I do . . .'

'The summons will be immediate.'

The prefect leaned forward, lowering his voice.

'I cannot fail to report to the governor. But I can fail to report *tonight*.'

Scaurus inclined his head.

'That would be generous of you, Prefect.'

'What will you do?'

The legatus smiled wanly.

'Leave the city, obviously. What other choice do I have?'

Timon drove the mules that he had collected from his business partner earlier in the day up the road from Antioch to the barracks' gates, where a weary-looking sentry took one look and hooked a thumb at the nervous salesman.

'Up the road to the corner of the wall and turn right. You'll find the stables easy enough, just head for the sound of your mates and all *their* mules. Not to mention the fucking smell.'

Making his way round the perimeter of the legion's base, it didn't take him long to realise that he wasn't the only vendor on whom the soldiers had called the previous day. Recognising the faces of several of his competitors from across the city, he exchanged mutually wary greetings with the man he considered to be his closest rival.

'Three soldiers, one with a cross carved into his cheek and going by the blasphemous name of "Jesus"?'

Timon nodded unhappily.

'And not that either of us will admit as much to another living soul, but a large number of mules to be delivered in only a day, at a price which despite its keenness left a fair profit for yourself? Such a large number that I have made undertakings to certain people in order to find the money required to procure the animals, procurement that may well not have been of a legal nature. And undertakings that will prove painful to me should I fail to repay them. And now I discover that I am not supplying these mules to retired soldiers, but to the army itself.'

He nodded again, and his competitor sighed in apparent relief.

'You cannot know how pleased I am to see you here. I was thinking that you had been spared the ignominy of having been deceived by these . . .'

The other mule dealer fell silent, as the soldier who had conducted negotiations the previous day stepped onto a box to address them.

'Greetings gentlemen! My name is Morban, as most of you probably remember! I see you're all here, with the mules you promised to supply!'

A hard-faced officer and a pair of cavalrymen stood beside him, while a legion clerk known to all of the dealers had taken a seat at a desk behind them, and was fussing with his abacus and writing materials.

'Well done my friends! You're all busy men, so we're going to get you all sorted out and paid as quickly as we can. When your name is called, bring your mules forward. They will be examined by my colleague Silus here and his men, passed as fit and entered into the record as having been purchased from you. When all your beasts havc been either passed into the stables or rejected as inadequate for service, then the clerk here will record the details . . .'

He paused to clear his throat, and Timon's fellow vendor muttered a curse.

'I don't like the sound of this.'

'Will record the details in the legion's records and then write you a syngrapha.'

Half a dozen angry voices were immediately raised in protest, and the soldier waited with a patient expression until they gradually ran out of steam.

'The sooner we get on with this the sooner you'll be able to get away and start planning how to spend the money!'

The man standing next to Timon waved his clenched fist in the air.

'A fucking syngrapha? A piece of paper promising to pay us at some point in the future? You promised me payment in gold!'

The soldier shrugged.

'You didn't ask. You just took the gold I offered for what you had in your stables, and then assumed that we'd pay the same way for the rest of the beasts.'

'This is robbery!'

He turned to the new protester.

'There's nothing making you do business with us. Just take your mules and leave, if you're that unhappy.'

Silence fell, as each man present reflected on the risks they had each taken in pursuit of the profit they had expected. Theft, loans, and in Timon's case not only the questionable means by which he had acquired his mules, but also a formidable wife who was yet to be told exactly how their savings had been reinvested and who, he fervently hoped, would never find out.

'And besides, these syngraphas will be dated for tomorrow. All you have to do is go down to the governor's palace first thing and the provincial treasury will honour them on the spot. After all, you can't expect the legion to have that sort of money lying around, can you? A syngrapha with the legatus's official stamp on it is as good as gold, my friends. You'll all be paid, you'll just have to wait a few hours.'

He looked at each of them in turn, and Timon realised with a sinking heart that neither he nor any of his competitors could afford to walk away from the deal.

'Excellent! Let's get started then, shall we?'

Passing unnoticed through the quiet pre-dawn streets of the city, the Arab known as Abbas slipped into the brothel by its seldom used side door. Unlike the ornate main entrance, guarded by a quartet of hard-faced former soldiers who job was to keep order and ensure that any legionary who got out of hand left the establishment with a permanent reminder of the event, the side door was used only by men known to the owner. They came not to use the services of the establishment, but simply to frequent the small and exclusive tavern he maintained for the use of men either willing to spend their money in greater amounts than the average customer, and who wanted to avoid the inevitable crowding when the legion came into town with sex on its collective mind, or to provide him with the investment opportunities to best utilise the substantial revenue that flowed in from his various business activities. After waiting for a short time, the Arab was shown into the owner's presence, bowing deeply to show his respect for a man famed for the size and profitability of his camel trains, which routinely travelled the various routes from the Persian Sea through Parthia to the province's borders. At such an early hour the only other men in the tavern were a pair of Romans who, having clearly used the brothel's services well, if not wisely, were recuperating after a hard night with a cup of wine apiece, their eyes barely open as they laid back on their couches. Swiftly laying out his experience, and his desire to find employment in the near future, he was delighted when, after a moment's thought, the trader nodded acceptance of his proposal.

'You are well informed. I do indeed have need of experienced men such as yourself.'

'You'll take me as an outrider?'

The other man nodded.

'One of my *karawan* masters will begin the journey from Antioch to the Gulf of the Persians in three days' time, bearing enough Roman gold to purchase a two-hundred-camel load of silk and spices. I need a man with extensive knowledge of the roads through Mesopotamia, and one is not afraid to stand behind a sword in the event of attempted robbery.'

The scout nodded eagerly.

'I have ridden the road of silk for most of my life. I know every pace of every path and goat track between Zeugma and the ocean, and I also have a nose for trouble.'

'But you *can* fight? We carry no passengers.'

'I can fight. As long as you do not expect to be making war on the Parthian empire.'

The merchant sat back in his cushioned chair.

'The empire does not seek to rob us. Far from it, in fact, for they know that the tax they will take from our *karawans* over the years will far outweigh any benefit to be had from the short-term gain of theft. And you speak as if the King of Kings has declared war upon Rome, although I think we would have heard of this, were it to be true.'

The scout acknowledged the point with a respectful inclination of his head.

'Indeed you are right. But I have seen armed men of the army of Parthia take the field against Rome in recent times.'

His potential employer regarded him levelly for a moment.

'These are interesting times, that I will grant you. But have no fear, no Parthian king would countenance the use of violence against the men who provide the bulk of his income. So, will you join us?'

The Arab nodded.

'I will be pleased to. I have had the unnatural smell of this city in my nostrils for long enough.'

'Good. Then meet me at the Oriental gate, at dawn three days from now, and you will have a place in this trading expedition, and at the rate you named.'

The scout bowed deeply.

'Thank you. In three days.'

He was halfway to the door when the trader spoke again, his question couched in a deceptively light tone, seemingly an after-thought.

'And how shall we contact you in the event that our departure plans change?'

The Arab turned, meeting the trader's eyes for a moment and then turned swiftly for the door, only to find himself looking down a long knife blade whose design, he noted with a sinking heart, was distinctly Roman. He reached for his own blade, only to find himself on the floor looking up as the second Roman kicked his feet from beneath him and followed up with a swift knuckle jab into his sternum, briskly relieving him of the weapon while he curled up in agony. Recovering some of his wits, he spat an imprecation at the trader.

'I'll make you bleed for this!'

The Syrian shrugged.

'In truth, I expect not. Given the amount of gold that the Romans have promised to pay me for finding you, you'll either very shortly be underground with your throat cut or going away with them for a holiday to Nisibis. And we all know that since Governor Dexter is only allowing half the legion to march north, neither they nor yourself are likely to be coming back.'

He held up his hands in a semblance of apology.

'No offence intended, gentlemen, I have to state the facts as I see them. And now, I believe, there is a matter of payment to be completed, given you have your man?'

The older of the two Romans tapped his belt purse and shot the trader a hard grin as he knotted a fist in the protesting Arab's hair and dragged him onto his feet.

'You've had one coin. And since you think I'm already a dead man I'm suddenly feeling no need to pay you the rest. After all, you'll find it hard to collect unless you've got a trading route into the underworld.'

His younger comrade wagged a disapproving finger that, combined with the threat of the scout's confiscated knife, made the trader's bodyguard settle back into his seat before his attempt to challenge the Romans had progressed far beyond the thinking stage. The Arab raised the single gold coin that he'd received earlier.

'But this is—'

'Barely enough to cover the women we've spent the night with and the wine we've drunk? In truth, the women weren't up to much, I'd say you're working them too hard. And I've drunk better wine. So that's all you're getting, friend. Make the most of it, unless you'd like your teeth putting down your throat as well. No offence intended, I'm just stating the facts as *I* see them.'

The lamps had long since been lit in the legion's headquarters by the time Scaurus's officers gathered to discuss the plan for the next morning.

'Matters are progressing a little faster than we might have preferred. Before I outline my intentions, I think we ought to review our progress with the various items of equipment and . . .'

Scaurus fell silent as his clerk stepped into the room, listening as the man spoke quietly in his ear.

'Really? What excellent timing. By all means have him brought in.'

The gathered officers turned to the door, watching as the duty centurion came through it followed by two soldiers who had a third man between them, his hands tied behind his back and a black hood over his head.

'Greetings gentlemen! What do you have for me under there?'

Scaurus watched as Sanga pulled off the captive's hood to leave him blinking in the lamplight.

'This is the man, Legatus. He was stupid enough to start quacking on about having seen the Parthians having a go at our lads over the border.'

He dropped a purse onto the desk in front of Scaurus.

'We was going to pay five in gold for him, but the man we used to find him made the mistake of thinking he could piss on us without getting some of it back when the wind changed direction. So we only paid him one.'

Scaurus nodded, looking at his men with a wry smile.

'Which, speaking of urine, seems mostly to have been spent on entertainment, from the look of you both. Well done once more, gentlemen. You'd better go and sleep it off. I think there are enough officers in the room that this man would deeply regret any attempt to run.'

The captive said nothing, but as he looked about him he seemed to sag slightly. Scaurus stood, walking over to him and looking him over in silence for a moment before speaking in Greek.

'So you were present when my cohort was destroyed, were you? Or rather you were doing your very best not to be present, eh? You're the scout who went east of the Euphrates with my men and came back without them?'

The leather-faced Arab stared back at him without speaking, and Julius tapped the vine stick resting on the table beside his wine cup with a questioning expression.

'I may not speak Greek, but I can recognise an uncooperative bastard when I see one. Should I beat it out of him?'

The legatus shook his head.

'No, thank you, Julius. I think this one will respond better to a little psychology.'

Fixing the scout with a knowing smile, he sat back in his chair and addressed the man in Greek again.

'You think I'm going to punish you for my men's loss. So you think that if you stay silent and play dumb I'll be forced to let you go.' The scout's look of incomprehension remained fixed. 'I see. That's a shame. I'd hoped not to have to resort to anything so crude, but if you're not going to admit to your near perfect command of Greek, I shall simply be forced to pass you on to my legion's centurions. They're still more than a little unhappy about the way you made such a swift exit when the Parthians came for their comrades. They tend to frown on that sort of thing in a way I doubt you'd understand, although I'm sure you'll get the point once they get to work on you. Presumably that's why you've been hiding in the city's slums all this time?'

The man looked down at him for a moment more before sighing deeply.

'And if I admit to being the man you take me for, then you'll execute me, yes?'

'No.'

Shaking his head in disbelief, the scout folded his hands across his chest, but Scaurus simply looked up at him with a raised eyebrow.

'Why would I kill you? You were out there with the Sixth Cohort because you know that ground as well as you know the village in which you grew up, right? And you knew they were doomed from the moment you saw the enemy cavalry, not because of their numbers but simply because of the precise place in which the battle was to take place. That's why you rode away and left them to it, because you saw no way that they could win the battle, given that ground.'

The scout nodded reluctantly.

'And after you rode away, that entire cohort was massacred, just as you knew would happen.'

He stared up at the Arab with dispassionate eyes, watching the trickle of sweat that was running down the man's neck until it sank below the line of his rough tunic, then leaned forward suddenly, making the man flinch at the speed of the movement.

'I plan to take revenge for my men, and to do so I will need every one of the dice to be loaded in my favour when I throw them. I need the right men, with the best weapons, and I need them all to be arrayed on the best possible ground. And you, my friend, are my best chance to put their boots on that fated patch of earth. Whether *you* like it or not.'

He sat again, his gaze still locked onto the scout's face.

'I was going to offer you the choice, either to accompany my legion to the east or to suffer a death every bit as ignominious as theirs, but I'm not much of a man for cold-blooded murder. And besides, any promise you made under such a threat would be meaningless, wouldn't it? You would promise me anything I asked for, and then the second my back was turned you'd be away like a rabbit, burying yourself back into the city so deep that we'd never find you. So I have a better idea.'

He pointed to Julius.

'That is my first spear. The centurions you served with have been hard men, but fair. When you ran from the battle that destroyed my Sixth Cohort, their first spear allowed you to make your escape rather than put a spear in your back. Whereas Julius here is somewhat less forgiving.'

Julius growled something in the language of the Romans, his tone clearly uncomplimentary, and the legatus translated with a smile.

'He says that he's going to have you crucified if you so much as twitch in the wrong direction.'

He shook his head with a smile at the expression that had crossed the Arab's face.

'I know what you're thinking. The first opportunity you get, you'll just ride away from us, laughing as you once again show what fools we are. Except you should also meet this man. His name is Silus.'

The officer indicated simply smiled broadly.

'He commands a squadron of cavalry whose only responsibility once we're in the field will be to shadow you, night and day. And if you attempt to run, they'll stake you out, open your guts and leave you for the carrion birds. There are thirty of them, more than enough for there to be a dozen or so of them around you all day. When you sleep they will watch you, and when you squat to empty your bowels they will be there to tell you just how badly your shit smells. Let us hope that you are a man capable of exercising self-restraint when it comes to . . .'

He made a circle of thumb and forefinger, moving it to and fro to the amusement of the officers.

'Yes, you'll be better protected than the emperor himself, with a dozen watchful men like Silus around you at all times. There will never be a moment when you run the slightest risk of harm. Isn't that good to know?'

5

'So, Legatus. Will it be the usual this morning? Weapons drill followed by a march?'

Scaurus shook his head, looking out across the parade ground at the legion's assembled ranks as the soldiers reordered themselves after the customary prayer to greet the sun's rebirth for another day. The legion's senior officers were gathered to one side as usual, under the aegis of Tribune Umbrius, although he noted with a quiet smile that Varus was standing as far from the broad stripe tribune as he could without actually detaching himself from the group.

'No, First Spear, this morning I have something different in mind. This morning I plan to march for Zeugma with my entire force, once the extra equipment I've had manufactured has been distributed to the men and loaded onto our carts.'

Quintinus gaped at him.

'You intend to march . . . this morning?'

The legatus smiled beneficently.

'It's either that or wait for the governor to come down here and arrest me on a charge of deliberately acting to conceal the location of a fugitive from justice which, as I'm sure you can imagine, isn't really a desirable outcome. Not desirable for me, and for that matter most certainly not desirable for the man who ordered me to relieve Nisibis. You may have seen his head on the coinage you're paid with.'

'But . . .'

Scaurus patted him on the shoulder.

'No need to trouble yourself, First Spear, *you* won't be coming with us. My own first spear is more than capable of running a half-strength legion, and one of his centurions can step into his shoes for the time being. Your place will be here, commanding the defence of what the governor has pointed out is a vital imperial trading city. All that remains for you to do, before I march my men out to battle on the emperor's behalf, is to make some organisational changes.'

He motioned to Julius, who stepped forward and gestured to the waiting cohorts.

'After yesterday's weapons drills, we marked every man who my officers felt capable of standing up for themselves in a proper fight with a circle drawn in henna. And after the practice march, we marked every man who finished under a certain time with a cross, having allowed them to march at their own best speed rather than in cohorts.'

Quintinus nodded. The exercise had excited much comment among his men, with the strong rumour that anyone who gained both marks being granted a day's holiday from duty resulting in a significant improvement in the numbers of men pushing themselves to keep up the marching pace.

'Indeed. The men with both symbols on their hands have been strutting around like peacocks ever since.'

The legatus smiled.

'I'm glad to hear it. If you'll be so good, order every man who doesn't have either mark to leave the parade ground.'

Quintinus frowned in incomprehension.

'But what—'

'All will become clear, First Spear. In the meantime, please just make it happen. Send the unmarked men back into their barracks if you like, but make sure any of them with the new shields leave them behind, will you?'

Still baffled, Quintinus strode out across the parade ground's wide expanse, shouting commands to his cohort commanders. The men who had failed to meet Julius's expectations in either regard walked away with grins at those who had performed better, while the remaining soldiers looked at each other with trepidation as to what might be happening. Quintinus made his way back to the legatus with a hard face, clearly having realised what was happening.

'Thank you, First Spear. Now I need you to reorder all of the cohorts with the exception of my Tungrians and marines, retaining the First, Third, Eighth and Tenth, and feeding the remaining men into them to make up their numbers. Array them in four ranks, with the front two ranks to contain as many men with both marks as possible.'

'Legatus, I—'

'Now, First Spear.'

Quintinus stared at his superior for a moment and then stalked away to obey the command.

'He's not happy.'

Scaurus laughed softly, shooting a surreptitious glance at the increasingly perplexed Umbrius.

'He's going to be a lot less amused by the time I'm done. And he's not the only one.'

With the remnant of the legion reshuffled into four more or less full-strength cohorts, Quintinus returned once more, his face now set in angry lines.

'I see from your thoughtful expression that you've discerned my purpose, First Spear Quintinus. And yes, I am indeed moving a considerable number of men into the four best cohorts in the legion, those which traditionally contain the strongest and best soldiers. What I'm doing, Quintinus, is bringing all four of those cohorts as near to their full strength as possible. Each of them will have something close to the number of men that they would have had they not been reduced to half the manpower due to leave and other duties. I shall march north with those four cohorts, plus my own Tungrians as my legion's new Fourth and Fifth Cohorts, and the marines as the new Second. Since they fall under the command of the emperor rather than the governor, I do not consider them to be under the constraints of his order.'

He waited with an imperturbable expression while Quintinus stared back at him with a look of angry consternation.

'You plan to march with *seven* cohorts, Legatus?'

The first spear shook his head in apparent fury.

'Including my best four cohorts?'

'It's really quite simple,' Scaurus replied levelly. 'I'm taking just about anyone from the remaining cohorts who actually knows how to handle a sword or has enough stamina to cover twenty miles in a day, and I'm putting them into the cohorts that are marching east, not just to bring them up to full strength, but to give them a fighting chance when we meet the Parthians in battle. Those men who will struggle on the march will be encouraged by their centurions and chosen men. Vine sticks and fists can be quite remarkable for helping a man to find stamina he didn't know he possessed. And those men who have stamina, but who are yet to fully master their weapons, will have their opportunity for some intensive practice under battle conditions quite shortly, I expect. Do you have a problem with that?'

'But your written orders from the governor—'

'Say that I am permitted to march for Nisibis with half of the legion's strength. There are ten cohorts in the legion, First Spear, and I'm marching from here on my way to Nisibis with four of them. It seems like a fairly basic piece of arithmetic. I'd say I'm exceeding the governor's instructions. I expect he'll be appropriately appreciative.'

Quintinus shook his head.

'But—'

'*No.*'

The legatus's voice cut him off with an abrupt force of personality that he'd chosen not to display since arriving in the city.

'The trick with orders, First Spear, lies in the way that they are written and the way in which they can therefore be *interpreted*. I am ordered to march from here with, in terms I have committed to memory, "No more than half of the legion's strength". And so I shall, taking four full-strength cohorts to make up less than half of the legion's theoretical manpower. After all, my orders made no mention of the words *actual strength*, did they? And I'm leaving you to defend the city with the Second, Fourth, Fifth and the Seventh cohorts. With the transfers I've just effected, you'll be left with eight hundred men or thereabouts, more than enough to keep order in a civilised city like Antioch, I would have thought?'

Quintinus shook his head, unsure how he should present his objections to the orders scratched into the tablets' waxy brown surfaces.

'Legatus?'

Scaurus waved a dismissive hand at his broad stripe tribune.

'A moment, Gabinus Umbrius. The first spear and I will conclude this discussion very shortly.'

Quintinus shook his head unhappily.

'Legatus, with all due respect, this will leave me with only the youngest recruits and the oldest veterans to defend Antioch. That hardly seems fair to—'

'To the people of the city? Or to you, First Spear? What precisely was it that you expected? That I'd be stupid enough to obey the orders of a vindictive and corrupt fool like Domitius Dexter? That I would happily march out of here with just enough men to raise a decent dust trail once I'm across the Euphrates, and bring the enemy down on me? After all, half of the legion's actual spear count is barely fifteen hundred men.'

The senior attempted to interject a second time, his voice beginning to sound as much petulant as concerned.

'Legatus?'

Scaurus waved his hand again without turning to look at the tribune, a smile twitching at his lips.

'Indulge me a little longer, Gabinus Umbrius.'

Quintinus shook his head, his face a picture of bafflement.

'But what if the Parthians get around you, cross the Euphrates and attack the city? Surely you can't simply ignore the governor's orders?'

'Legatus!'

Scaurus turned to look at his deputy, his face suddenly dark with anger at the attempted note of command in his subordinate's voice.

'My patience with you, Tribune Umbrius, is at an end. First Spear Julius!'

Julius stepped forward with a grim face.

'Legatus?'

'Draw your sword. And if this young *gentleman* speaks just one more time without being invited to open his mouth, use it to behead him, here and now. The charge on which he will have been executed will become clear soon enough.'

Julius swept his sword from its scabbard with a hiss of oiled metal, raising the brightly polished iron to show the tribune the weapon's edge, and Umbrius took a step backwards when he saw the absolute certainty in the first spear's eyes that he would obey his legatus's command. Scaurus turned back to Quintinus with a questioning look.

'Now, you were saying? Ah yes, what if the Parthians get around my admittedly small force and attack the city? Surely the answer to that one is clear enough?'

He laughed hollowly.

'All you have to do is order your men back from leave. Pull your detached units back into the city. And call back the soldiers you've set to making the countryside safe by hunting wild animals. That will more than double your manpower.'

He fell silent, staring implacably at Quintinus while the older man struggled for words. When he spoke again his voice was deceptively soft.

'Except you can't, can you? Because, First Spear, as we both know all too well, not very many of those men actually *exist*, do they?'

Silenced reigned for a long moment before he continued in the face of the first spear's dumbstruck silence.

'It has been evident to me from the first day of my command, First Spear, that something was deeply wrong with a legion that had so many men recorded as absent, especially as Quintus Magius Lateranus was careful enough to take his secretary with him when he left so suddenly, along with the set of legion records that would have exposed your fraud, leaving only the official version of the records for me to examine. It didn't take me long to work out what was going on, of course, but I saw no value in accusing you of being responsible for the scheme since I was also pretty much convinced that it probably wasn't directly of your making. To be brutally honest with you, First Spear, you're neither brave enough nor stupid enough to have been the man responsible. You were clearly involved, but more by way of tolerating what was being done to your legion than an active participant. There had to be bigger men than you behind the whole thing.'

He turned and stared pitilessly at the tribune, nodding grimly as the man's face went red.

'Men like you, Gabinus Umbrius. Well-connected men with that sense of entitlement that seems to permeate so many of your class.'

He turned back to Quintinus.

'But now it's time for the truth. If I catch you lying to me one more time, First Spear, I'll have you flogged to ribbons and executed on the parade ground this morning, with your legion watching you. You will die as a disgraced private soldier, your savings and property will be sequestered by the state in compensation for your theft, and your family, who you will never see again, will be thrown out onto the street.'

The first spear started, and Scaurus shrugged wearily.

'Did you imagine that nobody knew about your little secret? Since it was clear to me that Lateranus and his cronies must have had some hold over you, I set a couple of my men to follow you on the day that I gave the legion a half-day's holiday. They tracked you into the city, as a result of which I know enough about your illegal wife and child to understand how it was that you were forced to remain silent as your legion was bled dry. After all, Lateranus could have seen you dismissed in disgrace, with your property confiscated in its entirety, down to the last coin in your purse. You knew only too well what would happen to your family if you were suddenly rendered destitute, here in Antioch of all places. But now, of course, your loved ones pose you a different problem, not one of keeping silent, but rather one of speaking the truth, here and now. Because if you continue to keep the truth from me, I will have no option but to exact the punishment I've already described. I won't take any pleasure in doing so, First Spear, but trust me, I *will* do what I have to.'

Quintinus had gone deathly pale, and could do no more than stare mutely at Scaurus, as the legatus rammed home his advantage.

'So, First Spear, you have just one chance to tell the truth. Were you involved in the fraud I have uncovered?'

Quintinus straightened his back.

'Yes, Legatus.'

'How wise of you to admit it. So, how many men are genuinely absent with permission?'

'No more than five hundred.'

Scaurus stared at him in disgust.

'And how does this fraud work exactly?'

'Two hundred men or so leave the legion every year, as they take their retirement. And Legatus Lateranus was a strict officer, dishonourably dismissing men from imperial service at any opportunity. And with every man's retirement or dismissal, new names have been entered into the legion records as fresh recruits.'

'False names?'

'Yes, Legatus.'

The legatus looked across at Umbrius, who was now staring at the floor.

'And their pay, the cost of equipping them and their rations goes straight into a few select purses. Did neither of you really think this would never come to light? You may speak, Tribune.'

The patrician's voice had utterly lost its former superiority.

'It was Legatus Lateranus's idea. He believed that the Parthians are a broken enemy, commanded by a king so old and lacking in power that all of his attention will be given to simply holding onto his throne. He believed that we would get so much notice of any threat that recruiting and replacing the fictitious men with new recruits would be easy enough.'

Scaurus bellowed an order at the patrician, his voice snapping out with unaccustomed ferocity.

'Stand to attention, Tribune!'

After a moment's hesitation, Umbrius drew himself up into the brace position, and Scaurus walked across to stand behind his deputy, speaking quietly in his ear with an edge of menace whose barely controlled ferocity chilled even the men who knew him.

'It was all Quintus Magius Lateranus's idea? He's to be the sacrifice on this particular altar is he? When my formal report goes to Rome, it's to place the blame on Lateranus, is it? With you and the first spear here as his victims, unable to resist his authority, and no mention of Domitius Dexter.'

'The governor had nothing—'

'I grow weary of your lies, Tribune. The governor, as we both know only too well, had everything to do with it.'

The tribune's eyes widened, and Scaurus shook his head in amused contempt.

'You fool. You see a thin stripe on a man and immediately jump to the conclusion that he won't understand your cosy little closed world, or comprehend you people and the less than endearing habit of a small proportion of you who always find a way to skim the cream off the top of whatever you're given to manage, no matter how wealthy you might already be. Well here's the shock news, Tribune – my family was senatorial until a century ago, and I can assure you that even in the depths of disgrace we never quite lost those links. My sponsor was the governor of this province before Gaius Domitius Dexter replaced him, and he knows *all* about your family. He told me how your appointment to the Third Gallic so soon after Domitius Dexter took over the province might have been mildly surprising were it not for the fact that your father also happens to be his best friend. So if the governor was here now, I'd be threatening him with exactly the fate that hangs over you.'

The tribune swallowed, suddenly pale.

'You mean . . .'

'I mean that you have two choices.'

Scaurus smiled thinly.

'Two choices which are really only one, of course. You can of course return to Rome. I could try, convict and execute you myself, but I find the prospect of leaving you to take a ship back to the capital rather more amusing. You see, by the time you get there, you'll find that the man who stands behind the throne will already have received my report on the matter of the legion's woeful undermanning. I had Tribune Corvus dispatch it while he was on his way to Hama. The imperial chamberlain will in all probability already have started uprooting your family, and in a rather vigorous manner, if his track record is any indication. After all, and as I warned you, it is the chamberlain's job to hate treason and love gold in equal proportions, so what better opportunity to exercise both of those responsibilities than to take the throne's revenge for your crimes, and those of your uncle?'

'And my other choice?'

'I think you already know the answer. You have a sword, so fall on it. Or if you can't raise the nerve to use a blade, buy yourself some poison or a venomous snake. This is, after all, Antioch, so I doubt the means of a more elegant suicide are in short supply. And now, Umbrius, you can get out of my sight. You'll remain under arrest until after I've marched from this barracks, just to make sure you don't go running to Domitius Dexter. After that, it really is up to you, although if I ever see you again I'll take my own sword to you. Get out of my sight.'

He waited until the tribune had left the parade ground under the guard of a tent party of Tungrians led by Otho.

'Let's hope for his sake that he doesn't try to use his authority on Otho, given that I've told the centurion that he's to consider any such idiocy as an attempt to resist arrest. As for you, Quintinus, you've falsified the existence of over a thousand men. You do realise that the imperial authorities reserve some very special punishments for men who perpetrate fraud on this scale?'

The first spear hung his head.

'I inherited the whole thing from my predecessor. Legatus Lateranus told me that I'd be very sorry indeed if I were to be foolish enough to cause any problems.'

'I see.'

He stared at the senior centurion with a scowl.

'You've been complicit with a fraud that has endangered the security of Rome's frontier with the Parthians, and quite possibly condemned to death the men who have to march out tomorrow to confront the enemy. Since that includes both myself and First Spear Julius, I'd say that the idea of your treatment for this crime being a lenient one is not one that's very much in favour with either of us.'

He turned and walked away a few paces, looking at the mountain that towered over the city.

'I do, however, owe some small duty to the people of Antioch. You will continue in your role for the time being. You will commence a recruitment and training drive aimed at bringing your remaining four cohorts up to full strength, and raising at least one more with which to replace the Sixth. If I'm satisfied by your efforts on my return, I will consider some degree of extenuating circumstances for your crime. After all, it's not as if you were the ring leader, or even given much of a choice in your complicity. Let me down in this and it'll be the last mistake you make. Now go and muster your men, First Spear, you've got a job to do.'

The final change that Scaurus had ordered to the four cohorts' organisation was enacted swiftly and without ceremony. Julius strode out before his new command and barked out a swift address.

'My name is Julius, and for those of you who've been asleep for the last hour, I am your new First Spear! If you march and fight like men then you and I will get on well enough. If you fail to do either then you will find me at your back, with my boot, my vine stick or, if need be, with a fucking scourge. I expect some of you to disappoint me, but I only expect you to make that mistake once!'

He paused, looking up and down his cohorts with a grim face before pulling a tablet from his belt.

'The following centurions, step forward!'

He read out half a dozen names, waiting until the men in question were standing in front him before pronouncing on their fate.

'Following the advice of one of my centurions who knows most of you rather better than I do, I've decided that you're better suited to assisting First Spear Quintinus here in Antioch than marching into Parthia with the legion. Dismissed.'

Unsure whether to be elated or dejected, the officers followed his pointing arm and walked away towards the barracks, while Julius addressed the remaining officers.

'There are now precisely enough of you left to command every century in the four cohorts we're taking with us, but none of you who are left in command have any reason to feel smug. Those were the men I judged least likely to cope with what we're going to do in the next few weeks, but if I'd had another five good officers up my sleeve, another five of you would have been walking. Bear that in mind before you start relaxing. I'm watching you, and I will deal with any man who lets me down with the harshness you'd expect, given your importance to our effectiveness in battle.'

'None of them look relax to me. All look like need good shit.'

Sanga nodded at his mate's whisper, watching as a line of mule carts squeaked onto the parade ground.

'This ain't looking good.'

Julius walked over to the closest of the waggons, pulling back the canvas cover to reveal its load, and the veteran craned his neck to see what lay beneath.

'It's a pile of long wooden poles. What the fuck we going to do with those, fend the fuckers off?'

'Silence!'

The growing rumble of muttered comments died away, and Julius lifted one of the poles from the cart to reveal the truth of the matter. Amazed, Sanga was unable to restrain himself.

'I've already got to carry a shield that's twice as heavy as it should be, and now they want me to prance about with a ten-foot spear! How the fuck am I supposed to throw that bastard thi—'

'Silence! The next men to open his mouth without being asked to comment will receive five lashes, here and now! Today of all days you do not want to get on the wrong side of me!'

Julius composed himself before speaking again.

'Front and centre, Legionary Sanga!'

His face reddening, the soldier marched forward and stamped to attention, knowing what was expected of him.

'First Spear!'

Julius walked towards him with the outsized weapon held in both hands across his body.

'You were saying, Legionary?'

Sanga swallowed, feeling a trickle of sweat running down the middle of his back.

'I was—'

'Louder, Sanga, let's all hear what was on your mind.'

'I was wondering, First Spear, how I could throw such a thing, but now you've brought it closer it looks a lot easier.'

The senior centurion looked at him with a pitying expression for a moment.

'It's not a throwing spear, you donkey, it's a thrusting spear! Back in ranks!'

'If I might have a word with the legion, First Spear?'

Scaurus waited for Sanga to return to his place before addressing his men.

'Legionaries of the Third Gallic, this is a design of spear that goes back to the days before there was anyone with the leisure to sit and write down all of the battles and wars that are now only remembered in a handful of legends! It was used by the ancient Greeks in their successful wars with Persia . . .'

'And when we kicked the shit out of them.'

'And, as some of you are apparently speculating, when we overran Greece!'

Julius glared at Sanga so fiercely that Quintus turned round and flicked his vine stick out, rapping the hapless soldier on the side of his knee.

'I won't bore you with the reasons why a weapon will work

under some circumstances and not others, but let me assure you, these spears are going to be a large part of the difference between life and death for all of us when we meet the Parthians on the field of battle! These spears and one or two other ideas I've learned from my studies.'

He turned back to Julius with a nod of thanks.

'Carry on, First Spear.'

'The first two ranks of every century will give one of their two spears to the two men behind them. They will advance smartly to the closest cart and each man will take one long spear. They will then return to their position with both their long and short spears held in an upright position. *Move!*'

'He told you what, exactly?'

'That he has no idea where Tribune Corvus might be if he's not to be found in Hama, Governor.'

Domitius Dexter stared at the Phrygian, a slow smile spreading across his face.

'And there was no word of Corvus in Hama?'

'Not in the city or the fortress, Governor.'

'Do you believe that the tribune was ordered to travel to the city?'

After a long pause the younger man answered, clearly sickened by the implication of his words.

'No, sir. I believe he was sent elsewhere.'

'And did Legatus Scaurus manage to convince you otherwise?'

The Phrygian opened his mouth, then closed it again.

'Come now, Prefect, I understand your desire not to implicate a fellow military man, but the issues here are bigger than simple loyalty. Did he convince you otherwise?'

'No, Governor. He did not.'

Dexter smiled triumphantly.

'As I expected. You are dismissed with my thanks, Prefect. Secretary!'

The prefect saluted, turned and walked towards the huge office's door, only partially aware of the hubbub behind him.

'Secretary! Where is that bloody man? Ah, there you are. Fetch my lictors immediately!'

The front two ranks of the legion had retaken their places with their new spears, as the carts raised clouds of dust in their wake as they rumbled off the parade ground. Unable to help themselves, the legionaries holding the new weapons were looking up at the long iron spearheads ten feet above their heads.

'Nobody likes change, it seems.'

Standing next to Julius, Scaurus grinned broadly.

'I know. Although the rest of the legion seems to be enjoying the spectacle well enough.'

Muttering and quiet laughter was spreading across the legion's line, only the forbidding presence of their officers preventing more widespread mirth from the men not tasked with carrying the new spears. Julius strode forward, bellowing a command at the top of his voice.

'As you were!'

Waiting until silence had fallen, the legatus stepped forward.

'Soldiers of the Imperial Third Legion, I have orders to advance into the Parthian kingdom of Adiabene, and to secure our outpost fortress of Nisibis from the siege to which we believe it has been subjected! As many of you know, Nisibis is a mighty fortress, a stronghold whose walls will stand for many months against the most determined of foes. But without our intervention, it will surely eventually fall. Our emperor is a wise man, and he knows that Nisibis will not satisfy this enemy, but will only serve to encourage him to march on our ally, Osrhoene. And when Osrhoene falls, the next natural step for Parthia will be to cross the Euphrates into Syria, with their eyes firmly set on the great city of Antioch! To wait for the Parthian to come to us is to allow him the luxury of more conquest, and to grow in confidence and strength, and so my orders are to cross the river at the first opportunity, seek battle and defeat this aggression before it has the chance to take advantage of that opportunity!'

Complete silence now gripped the thousands of men paraded

before him, and Scaurus stalked towards them until he could see the individual hairs in their beards.

'You heard me! We will be across the Euphrates within a week, and in Nisibis ten days after that, unless we bring this Parthian army to battle . . .' He paused theatrically. 'In which case it will take us ten days and an hour!'

The men closest to him smiled weakly at the joke.

'I know you're troubled by the loss of your fellow soldiers in the Sixth Cohort, and in truth you wouldn't be human if you weren't! The gods know it troubles me! That a single cohort should be sent to its doom in such an amateur way is beyond belief! But we're not amateurs, you men and I! We are professional soldiers, and we will make those eastern goat worshippers pay a high price for their fleeting moment of inglorious revenge on Rome!'

He turned to Julius.

'Get them ready to march.'

The first spear nodded, taking his legatus's place in front of the legion.

'Prepare to move! Pack poles, spears, helmets and shields! Any man that leaves anything behind will be pulling double guard duty all the way from here to the river! On your toes, you animals!'

'Tell me what we're supposed to do when we get to the barracks again?'

The most senior of Governor Dexter's lictors scowled without turning to look at his subordinate as they hurried down the road from the city's western gate towards the Third Legion's barracks.

'You heard well enough the last time I told you.'

The man walking beside him shook his head, hefting the bundle of rods that he was carrying onto his other shoulder with careful respect for the axe blade protruding from its middle.

'I heard it, I just didn't believe it.'

His superior gritted his teeth before speaking again.

'Our orders from the governor are clear. We arrest the legion's legatus, we take him back to the palace and we hand him over to the governor's men.'

'And why didn't he send one of his procurators to make the arrest?'

'Because, you idiot, it's more than likely that the soldiers wouldn't have recognised the man's authority.'

The other man laughed bitterly.

'So it's better for us to have our authority flouted than them?'

The group's leader stopped walking, turning to his subordinate with a raised finger.

'Look, as far as I'm concerned—'

A blare of trumpets interrupted him, as the gates of the fortress swung open and, after a moment's pause, the head of a marching column of men emerged onto the road.

'We're too late!'

The senior lictor shook his head angrily.

'No we're bloody not. All that's happened is that this Scaurus has got the shit scared out of him and decided to make a run for it with his men. Come on!'

Leading his reluctant comrade towards the barrack, he ignored the shower of catcalls that rained down on them as the column's first centuries marched past. Squeezing in through the gateway, he looked around for a moment before his eyes alighted on a group of figures, the junior man's lips moving as he counted the men still waiting to join the line of march.

'I thought he was only allowed to take half the legion.'

'He *is* only allowed to take half the bloody legion.'

The two men strode across the parade ground under the eyes of thousands of men, stopping a few paces from their intended target as Scaurus turned around and smiled at them.

'Ah, gentlemen. You both look somewhat hot and bothered, but that's what happens when you go rushing around in a full-weight toga carrying a big bundle of rods and an axe, I suppose. Can I ask someone to get you a cup of water?'

Shaking his head, the chief lictor drew himself up, drawing a breath ready to pronounce the legatus's arrest, only to find himself silenced by a raised hand.

'Before you say whatever it is that you've come to say, I suggest that you save yourself some wasted breath by reading this.'

He passed the man a scroll, which he unrolled and started to read.

'Those are my orders, which direct me to take command of the legion and proceed across the frontier into Osrhoene at my earliest opportunity. Once I've paid my respects to King Abgar, I am to head straight for Nisibis, defeating any Parthian forces I meet on the way, overcome any siege of the fortress, and then return to the province to await further orders. Note the seal, by the way. It's not every day that you'll see the imperial seal on a document. The last time the governor saw it was when I delivered him the paper telling him that he'd been officially relieved of his duties.'

He smiled at the two men again as they looked at him aghast.

'No, I suspected that hadn't been communicated very widely. Anyway, read on chief lictor.'

After a moment, the toga-clad official looked up from the scroll in his hands.

'But this—'

'Gives me absolute authority over any and all of the emperor's subjects that I need to further my mission. Including, since you've doubtless been sent here to arrest me and therefore significantly impede my mission, *you*. So I suggest you turn around and go back to the governor with that as an explanation for the fact that you don't have me in your custody.'

'But *my* authority—'

'Is granted to you by the emperor, is it not?'

Seeing where Scaurus's line of argument was taking him, the chief lictor rallied his arguments.

'Yes, but—'

'Read the scroll again. Look for the words "obstruction of this officer will be considered grounds for immediate execution". And consider whether you really want to obstruct me, given that I'm quite possibly marching to my own death in any case, and therefore might not be in the most tolerant frame of mind. If you take my meaning . . .'

'If you're trying to threaten me, Legatus . . .'

The legion commander laughed softly.

'Trying to threaten you? Of course I'm not *trying* to threaten you. Consider my threat overt, consider it blatant, consider it bloody handed if you like, given the number of men my orders have killed in the last few years. But consider it quickly, because if you're still here by the time I've counted to fifty, I'm going to take that small but very important sentence in my orders very, very seriously indeed.'

He turned away, and his hard-faced senior centurion stepped forward and whispered in the lictor's ear.

'I think what the legatus is trying to say is this . . .'

He drew a deep breath, narrowed his eyes and bellowed a single word.

'RUN!'

'Shouldn't people be cheering? Throwing flower petals? Kissing soldiers?'

Sanga laughed at his mate with a distinctly sardonic tone, adjusting the hang of the shield on his shoulder for what seemed like the twentieth time since they had marched from the fortress.

'This fucking shield is going to cut me in half, it's so bloody heavy. And no, in my experience the people of any city, town, or village do not turn out to send the boys on their way with loud cheers and tits hanging out. Tits only hang out when we march *into* town, and that's only because the whores they belong to are looking forward to getting paid for letting us nuzzle up to them for a while. Perhaps when we march back again . . .'

'You won't be marching back again if you don't pick the pace up Sanga!'

The veteran turned his head with a weary sigh.

'It's this shield, Centurion. All the stuff the bloody armourers have glued onto it has made it heavier than a soldiers' balls after a month in the field.'

Quintus shrugged, waving his vine stick under the soldier's nose.

'Deal with it. And pick the pace up before I'm forced to use this.'

Sanga squared his shoulders and lengthened his stride, muttering under his breath.

'Before he's *forced* to it . . .'

He fell silent, then snorted with laughter at the sight of two men arguing at the city's Oriental gate as the Tungrians swept towards the northern wall and the road beyond it. A man in the uniform of the city watch was remonstrating with the legion's senior centurion, waving his arms for emphasis.

'. . . and my orders are to close the gate! Orders from the gov—'

Sanga grinned again as Julius stepped forward, raising his vine stick.

'And my orders come from my legatus, so you can kiss my hairy wrinkled arsehole . . .'

They passed out of earshot, the two men's voices lost in the racket of thousands of pairs of hobnailed boots crashing onto the road's stone surface.

'He too late. We last cohort.'

'That's as maybe. You know Julius never steps back from a fight.'

Sanga cranked his head round to stare back at the two men, then raised his voice to shout a question at the century's standard bearer.

'Hey Morban, what do you reckon the odds are on Julius taking his vine—'

After a moment's pause he shrugged and turned back to the direction of march.

'Never mind! Question answered.'

'The governor told me to send you in immediately.'

Dexter's secretary and the Phrygian prefect exchanged knowing glances, it being routine for the governor's appointments to begin with the usual lengthy wait in the anteroom that adjoined his office. He walked past half a dozen would-be supplicants, their irritation at his taking of their turn in the queue somewhat diluted by the rage-filled shouts that leaked into the room as the office door was opened. Setting his face into a professional mask, the tribune entered, to find a pair of lictors standing in front of Dexter's desk beside the prefect who headed the city watch. While the former looked more than a little dishevelled, the prefect had clearly been in an altercation, a substantial bruise adorning his jaw.

'First you two incompetents fail to arrest a man who clearly intends to flout my authority for all the world to see, and then you, supposedly the controller of everything that happens in the city, can't even stop him from marching his legion across the bridge and onto this island, into the city and out through the Oriental gate! Between the three of you you've managed to make the office of the governor a laughing stock!'

The prefect waited for his turn, looking around at the office's lavish wall hangings while Dexter heaped yet more anger onto his hapless functionaries. The story, the secretary had told him as they climbed the long staircase together, was already flying around the city, of how the lictors had run back to the city and ordered the gates closed only to find themselves and those members of the watch who had attempted to obey their orders forcibly restrained by armed soldiers.

'And now he's marching east with my bloody legion!'

His tirade exhausted, Dexter turned his attention to the prefect.

'You took your time answering my summons.'

The Phrygian ignored his superior's acid tone.

'Apologies, Governor, I was on the practice ground with my men when your message arrived.'

The older man glowered at him for a moment.

'Well you can go straight back again, muster your wing and get after my legion! I want Gaius Rutilius Scaurus back here, in chains, and I want the Third Gallic back in barracks! *Now!*'

The Phrygian nodded his understanding.

'As you wish, Governor. And what are my orders if the legatus refuses to surrender himself into my custody?'

Dexter's rage exploded again.

'I don't care what you have to do! Bring him back in one piece or carve him into mince if that's thc only way to do it! Just don't come back here without the man! Is that understood?'

The prefect saluted crisply.

'Perfectly, Governor.'

'This better than ship. Even with stupid spear and shield made from stone, I having good day.'

Sanga snorted his disgust, looking up at the point of his own weapon and rolling his eyes as a bead of sweat fell from the end of his nose. The legion was slogging up a narrow valley ten miles to the north of Antioch, and the lack of any shelter from the sun was making the legionaries suffer from more than just the exertion of the road's remorseless incline.

'You're off your head, boy. It's too fucking hot now, it'll be too fucking cold when the sun goes down, there'll be nothing to drink, nothing to screw, and probably not much to eat either. And this Nisibis place we're marching for is four hundred miles away, across a bloody great desert full of snakes and scorpions. And just to make the whole thing perfect, at some point in the march a bunch of maniacs on horses are going to have a fair old go at recreating the battle of . . . what was it again?'

'Carrhae. That what tribune call it.'

'Well he might just as well have called it "goat fuck", 'cause that's what it'll be. Add in the fact that the legatus has made us the rearguard cohort, so we'll be last to get into our blankets and I reckon—'

Saratos turned his head, waving a hand at Sanga to silence him.

'Quiet! I hear horses!'

A swift blast of the trumpeter's horn brought Scaurus and Julius back down the column, the latter ordering the legion to halt.

'Stand easy!'

Reaching the rearmost cohort, he barked a swift order to Dubnus that made it clear he expected trouble.

'This may just be Silus and his scouts rejoining but I don't intend getting caught with my dick hanging out. Fourth Cohort, battle order! Dubnus, give me a double line across the valley, long spears in the front four ranks!'

Throwing their packs aside, the soldiers scrambled to fulfil his instructions while the sound of horses' hoofs grew steadily louder, so that by the time the leading rider appeared around the valley's bend, the ground to either side of the road was blocked by a determined defence bristling with spears. Sanga and Saratos found themselves in the front rank, angling their spears out to join with their comrades in offering a thicket of iron spearpoints to whoever was approaching along the road that led back to Antioch.

'Mind you, what I'm supposed to do with this fucking thing if it comes to a fight beats me. Swing the fucker around and hope to take some bastard's eye out?'

The horsemen rode into view, half a dozen of them climbing the valley's slope at a fast trot, and Silus led them through the gap that Dubnus had opened in the wall of spears, grinning as the hedge of iron spikes closed behind his last man.

'They may look a bit stupid on the march, but they'll give any of us donkey wallopers a creaky backside when he sees that lot pointing at him.'

He climbed down from the saddle and took a swig from his water skin.

'There's a full cavalry wing overtaking us from the south. I'd guess they'll overhaul your mules before you've gone much further.'

'In which case, we might as well wait here for them. It *is* the Phrygians, I presume?'

The sweat had barely dried on the soldiers' scalps before their pursuers caught up with the waiting legion, the growing swell of noise from their hoofs abruptly doubling as the leading riders came into view around the valley's bend, the officer at their head raising a hand to halt his men and coming forward at a trot. The cavalrymen waiting behind him were fully armed and equipped, their shields held ready to use rather than slung across their backs. Julius looked down at them from his vantage point on the valley's side with a dour expression.

'It's the Phrygians alright, and they're not out for a pleasure ride, that's obvious. And I think it's fairly clear what their orders are.'

The cavalry prefect reined his horse in just short of the forest of spears, looking up and down the Tungrian line with an approving smile before shouting a greeting to the waiting officers.

'If I hadn't seen it with my own eyes I wouldn't have believed it, Legatus. You actually plan to take the fight to the Parthians.'

Scaurus pushed his way through the line and stepped out in front of the cavalryman.

'My men are still at the stage of wondering just how their new spears are supposed to be used, but yes, I'm under no illusions that we'll have to give battle, and I'm damned if I'm going to make it easy for them.'

He looked up at the Phrygian with a grim smile.

'And so you, Prefect, I presume, are under orders to take me back to Antioch?'

The horseman nodded sombrely.

'In chains.'

'In chains? I'd imagine nothing less would satisfy the governor's need to restore face. And if you can't achieve this act of submission on my part?'

The cavalryman shrugged.

'Domitius Dexter was completely unambiguous on the subject; I'm to take you back to Antioch, intact or in pieces. He went as far as to tell me that if I can't bring you back to Antioch, and *his* legion as well, then I'm not to come back at *all*. Which puts me in something of a difficult position, as I'm sure you'll appreciate.'

Scaurus pursed his lips, then waved a hand back at his waiting spear men.

'My orders aren't exactly open to misinterpretation either, and they certainly don't leave room for me to do anything other than march for Zeugma and then on into Osrhoene. Which leaves us both with a dilemma that there may only be one way to resolve. So, if that's the way it has to be, Prefect Felix, and if your men are as ready as they seem, then shall we get on with it?'

Marcus marched into Zeugma two days after the legion's arrival, leading a long column of lightly armoured soldiers, each man with a bow over his shoulder and a quiver of arrows at his thigh. Behind them marched five hundred slightly built men clad only in thick woollen tunics. Sanga, watching from his sentry position on the earth wall of the legion's marching camp, turned to Saratos in bemusement.

'Some bow benders and a cohort of little boys. What fucking use are they going to be?'

Scaurus and Julius greeted the auxiliary cohorts' prefects at the fortress's main gate, the legatus grinning broadly at the sight of another part of his plan coming to fruition.

'Well now, Tribune Corvus, what have we here?'

The biggest of the three men stepped forward and clasped the legatus's arm, slapping his shoulder in the manner of a man greeting an old friend.

'What we have here, Legatus, are three prefects wondering how in Mithras's name an equestrian gets to command a legion! If a bad-tempered young hothead such as yourself can make make it to the peak of our profession, there's hope for the rest of us yet!'

They clapped his shoulders in congratulation while Julius walked out through the gates to get a closer look at his new archers.

'You're lucky to find us all still here you know, another six months and we'd all have been replaced by new men.'

Scaurus nodded at the speaker, the tallest of the three.

'And I'm more grateful for that turn of fortune than you can imagine. Without some form of missile threat, my legion would have been at something of a disadvantage against the Parthians, even with the modifications that we've been making to weapons and tactics.'

'Your man Corvus has been telling us all about it, but I'd like to go through the way you plan to take them on once we're over the frontier. Without cavalry you'll still be at a disadvantage when it comes to . . .'

He frowned at the legatus's slight smile.

'You have cavalry? How did you pull *that* one off? As far as I'm aware there's no one left in command of a wing from the days when you were last here.'

'And you're right. But the Lightbringer has shown me one last small piece of favour. Prefect Felix?'

A man stepped forward from the group of officers behind him, and with a laugh Marcus strode forward to meet him, taking him by the hand.

'Gaius Cornelius Felix! Of all the men I expected to have found their way here, I'd have put you close to the bottom of the list. Surely stopping a Selgovae arrow in Britannia entitled you to a position with a little less risk attached to it? Shouldn't you be commanding an auxiliary cohort somewhere nice and quiet, rather than riding to war again?'

The cavalryman saluted him briskly.

'Something of that nature was offered, Tribune, after my rather lengthy convalescence. I couldn't have condemned any other man to the risk of having to ride that bad-tempered bastard Hades though.'

'He still bites?'

Felix nodded with a weary smile.

'Yes, And when the bastard's not biting, he kicks like a bolt thrower. But gods below, he's still the best horse in the empire. Give that nasty-tempered creature his head and it's like riding one of Zeus's thunderbolts! And my wound is fully recovered.'

He raised his arm to show a knot of scar tissue in his left armpit.

'It healed perfectly, thanks to your wife's expert care, so I'm as good as I ever was apart from some stiffness in the joint.'

He looked over at the waiting auxiliaries, then shook his head in disgust.

'Hamians. You were in Hama after all, weren't you?'

Marcus laughed.

'One of my centurions was born and raised in the city, so it wasn't hard for him to ride into the city and bring out civilian clothing for myself and Martos to wear. We entered Hama as merchants looking for silk at a better price than we'd have to pay in Antioch, and made contact with the prefects once you'd been and gone, to save them the embarrassment of having to lie to you. But what are you doing here? Surely the governor issued you with strict orders to apprehend the legatus?'

Felix smiled beatifically.

'He told me not to come back without Rutilius Scaurus. So I ordered my men to load their horses with everything they would need for a march to the Euphrates and took them after the Gauls. Once I'd overtaken the legion, and it was apparent that the legatus wasn't going to turn his men around, I decided to accompany him on his way, obviously making sure to point out to him that he's acting in defiance of an order from his superior officer.'

He shrugged easily.

'If the legion's not for turning, and I'm expressly forbidden to return to Antioch without its legatus, then all I can do is tag along, and hope that he'll eventually see sense. Of course, by the time we return to Antioch, if we survive whatever's waiting for us over the border with Parthia, Domitius Dexter may have left his post.'

'But nobody will be able to say that you didn't execute your orders to the letter.'

Marcus thought for a moment.

'Although I would have expected the governor to send further orders, when you didn't return that evening?'

Felix nodded.

'I expect he did. But there seems to be some sort of bandit gang operating on the road north from Antioch, deserters from a legion cavalry squadron. Two messengers have walked into the fortress already, stripped of their horses and indeed their messages, although interestingly they were allowed to keep possession of all their personal possessions and weapons. The Fourth Parthian's legatus is expressing sympathy, but had declined to provide them with replacement mounts until these bandits have been dealt with, for their own safety. It seems he's taking a fairly dim view of the governor's fraudulent scheming, since he was already harbouring some fairly strong suspicions of his own. And he wasn't the only one, it seems, since someone appears to have communicated their concerns to Rome, to judge from your swift means of transport out to the province . . .'

He smiled again, and Marcus shook his head with a knowing smile.

'It was *you*, wasn't it?'

Felix sniffed disdainfully.

'No true gentleman would stoop to such a grubby scheme. I expect my father was only too happy to pass on my musings on why it was that the Gauls were so short of numbers. Although without evidence I've no doubt that the ghastly man will manage to slip off the hook. Come along, I'll show you to the officers' quarters and then to the bathhouse. You look like a man in need of a sweat and a shave. Oh, and don't worry if you think you can hear shouting from the parade ground. First Spear Julius seems to be determined to drill some semblance of order into his new command, and he's approaching the task in, shall we say, a somewhat brutalist manner?'

The legion marched east from Zeugma the next day, crossing the long pontoon bridge that gave the city its Greek name and using the road that ran straight for Edessa, capital of the client kingdom of Osrhoene. Moving in strict battle order, with scouts riding ahead, behind and to both flanks, the soldiers were for the most part now covering twenty miles a day without their former discomfort, but if the issue of their stamina had been resolved, it seemed that some among their ranks would never meet their first spear's expectations in terms of either drill or weapons handling.

'We'll do it again tonight, gentlemen, and we'll keep doing it until the entire legion can get out of its blankets and into formation to defend the camp in less time than it takes for a new recruit to blow his load the first time his mates take him into a brothel to get his fucking cherry popped!'

The legion's centurions looked at each other in disgust at the prospect of yet another night's sleep being rudely disturbed, and Julius shrugged, shaking his head at them.

'Don't be giving me the cow's eyes, because one of these nights you might owe your life to these drills. If you want me to stop them then persuade your fucking halfwits to get it right.'

Scaurus had instructed his senior officers to take their share of the duties expected of the cohorts' senior centurions, and Marcus took command of the night watch that evening with a wry smile at the duty centurions as they trooped away from the briefing.

'You're really convinced that the enemy are going to attempt a night attack at some point?'

Julius shook his head.

'Far from it, Tribune . . .'

The emphasis that Julius had initially placed on his former subordinate's title had vanished in an instant the moment that he'd been appointed as the legion's first spear, a reflection on his own professionalism, but he was unable to resist speaking to the younger man in the same brisk manner that he used with his centurions.

'But you know as well as I do that the one means of coming after us that we don't prepare for will be the one they use to stick a big one right up us. So the scouts are out all day and in all directions, the legatus keeps drawing his maps with his Arab, the men practise formation manoeuvres two hours a day and they'll keep on practising night camp defence until I think they've got it. And now, sir, I'll go and see how the latest picture of the ground between here and Edessa is shaping up, and leave you to your rounds.'

Smiling at his friend's back as he left the command tent, Marcus stepped out into the dusk's faint light to find Martos waiting for him.

'What is it now? Orders from the legatus to ride back to Zeugma in the hope of sneaking one of the Fourth Legion's cohorts away while nobody's looking?'

The Briton grinned at his acerbic humour.

'No, Roman. I am simply bored and in need of entertainment. And what could be more entertaining than watching you inspecting the camp's sentries. We'll take this one along with us . . .'

He jerked a thumb back over his shoulder at the giant in the shadows behind him.

'Just in case anyone needs a taste of discipline a little more effective than those silly sticks your centurions carry.'

The three men made a leisurely tour of the camp's earth walls, checking that each cohort's section of the defences was manned by the appropriate number of sentries and that none of them had succumbed to sleep. Reaching the Tungrian's section of the perimeter, Marcus returned Quintus's salute with a smile, the expression broadening as Sanga and Saratos stamped to attention.

'Good evening, Centurion. All's well?'

'All's well, Tribune sir.'

He'd turned to leave, only to look back when Sanga had blurted out a request.

'Tribune sir, permission to ask you a question?'

Raising a hand to forestall Quintus's inevitable outburst, Marcus raised an eyebrow at the soldier.

'Yes, Soldier Sanga. I presume this is a military question, and not simply an enquiry as to the number and quality of the whores in Hama?'

'No, sir. It's just that Saratos here heard you telling one of your colleagues about a battle near here? A battle that didn't go well for the legions?'

Marcus nodded.

'The battle of Carrhae. Forty thousand legionaries commanded by a politician called Crassus confronted ten thousand Parthians led by a general called Surena. Twenty thousand of our men were killed on the battlefield, mostly killed by arrow wounds, and another ten thousand were taken prisoner. Rumour has it they were sold to the Parthians' trading partners in the east. Not the brightest day in our military history.'

'What happen to Crassus, Tribune?'

'Crassus? He attempted to negotiate a retreat from Parthia the day after the battle, and was murdered by the enemy under a flag of truce. And just to prove there's no justice, the Parthian general was also murdered, but by his own king, for being too successful and thereby threatening the man's position. And, as my tutor used to tell me, we learn two things from all of this: never trust a Parthian general to keep his word, and never let yourself be seen as a threat to an insecure king! Good night gentlemen!'

He walked away into the darkness with the Britons following behind him. The sentries watched them leave in silence until Sanga snorted derisively.

'The lesson I take from that little story has nothing to do with generals and kings, and a lot more to do with arrows.'

6

The days that followed soon settled into the same mind-numbing routine of marching, drilling, night exercises and exhausted sleep. In the evenings, as the shattered legionaries cleaned and mended their equipment under the watchful eyes of their centurions, Scaurus would sit in his tent with the Arab scout and plan the next day's march with particular attention to the nature of the terrain across which they would be passing. The first three days' march, covered at the standard pace to allow those men who still lacked stamina a chance to build their strength for the trials to come, took them from Zeugma to the Osrhoene capital Edessa, a way station on their route to Nisibis that the legatus considered a necessary evil.

'King Abgar will be happy enough to replenish our rations, and will doubtless entertain the officers to a most excellent banquet in our honour, but I'll be amazed if he has any more assistance to offer than his hearty good wishes. And we can be assured that the enemy will have enough spies in the city to ensure that their generals know all about us within days. We'll camp outside the gates, far enough from the walls that even the keenest sighted watcher won't be able to see the toys we've brought along.'

The single night spent outside the city was both a blessing and a curse for the men of the legion. On the one hand, they enjoyed a blissful night of uninterrupted sleep, as Julius elected not to provide any hint as to their growing abilities at the very particular drills to which they were usually subjected at the end of each day's march. Conversely, however, the proximity of a city that, if the older legionaries were to be believed, contained enough taverns and brothels to entertain several cohorts at a time, was sheer torture for men confined to camp, with armed guards posted to keep the city from the legion and the legion from the city's wine and women. They broke camp and marched away the next morning, their supply waggons refilled and the various implements, over which the craftsmen and smiths of Antioch had laboured mightily for Centurion Avidus, carefully concealed under sheets of rough canvas. Scaurus watched the preparations with quiet satisfaction, complimenting Julius on the changes that were starting to become evident in his command.

'They're looking more like soldiers, and less like a collection of whore mongers and idlers, which is to your credit. Please pass my congratulations to your centurions. You can also tell them that we're going to need a faster pace from here, First Spear. It's sixty miles to the next settlement, and I want to cover it as quickly as we can. Abbas tells me it's as flat as a table ten miles to each side of the road all the way, and you know what that would mean if the Parthians were to take us by surprise. Can we do it in two days?'

To the dismay of all concerned, the next two days' travel was indeed carried out at the quick march, and by dusk on the second day the legion was settling into a freshly dug camp outside the desert town of Constantina, with guards once more posted to ensure that legion and populace were kept well separated. Scaurus gathered his officers for a conference that night, showing them a map that the scout had drawn for him and pointing to a spot at its right-hand side.

'That, gentlemen, is Nisibis. It's four days' march from here, so with fresh supplies and a good knowledge of the watering places between here and the city, we're going all the way as quickly as we can. But . . .'

He looked around the tent, his face set hard.

'There can be no doubt that the enemy know we're coming. If there weren't spies in Edessa, then it's a certainty that there'll be spies here, so close to the border with Adiabene. And the Parthians aren't going to let us march into Nisibis, they'll be determined to stop us somewhere between here and the city, with the certain intention of bringing us to battle on their ground, and on their terms. I, on the other hand, have other ideas. So from here on we march with cavalry scouts out in strength to the front and both flanks. And when our scouts find the enemy, the first spear and I will choose a course of action that will be dependent on exactly where we find ourselves at that point in time.'

He gestured to the map, largely bare of any notable terrain.

'The secret of success in battle, gentlemen, is very often rooted in the general's choice of ground. And this particular piece of the world is so well suited to the style of war that the Parthians have evolved that we're going to have to be exceptionally light on our feet to even the odds up.'

The march resumed the next day, the soldiers' usual grumbling redoubled by each man being required to carry a piece of equipment that had until then been stacked in carts in the legion's baggage train, exchanging their pack poles for long wooden stakes topped with a pointed iron head, an iron square having been nailed to the wood halfway down its length to enable it to be hammered into the ground.

Ten miles into the march, the leading cohort halted without warning, and on reaching the column's head Julius found Procurator Ravilla staring out over the desert before his men with a bleak expression, his marines unusually quiet as they surveyed the scene of carnage laid out before them.

'If I'd known we were going to stumble over this, I'd have asked to take the rearguard for the day. My lads aren't as used to this sort of thing as your legionaries.'

Julius shook his head.

'Seeing men die in battle's one thing, but this . . .'

The human remains of a battle were strewn across the desert before them, hundreds of what had been dead bodies months before now reduced to scattered bones and what little was left of their equipment.

'Get your men digging, Procurator, and I'll have the rest of the legion collect up everything we can find ready for burial.'

Ravilla nodded gratefully, turning away to get his cohort organised as Scaurus reached the spot and stared out across the scene.

'In all the months that these men have lain here, left to rot and as prey to the carrion birds and animals, not one of the passing trade caravans has thought to bury their remains. What does that tell you?'

Julius turned away from the grisly view.

'It tells me that the traders who've passed this way either hated Rome enough to be happy to leave dead men unburied or didn't want to be taken for sympathisers.'

The legatus nodded.

'Which means that the men who did this haven't gone very far. They know we have to react to this, and they want to be ready when we do.'

The two men looked at each other in shared understanding.

'Do we have time to get what's left of them underground?'

Scaurus nodded slowly.

'Prefect Felix's scouts will give us plenty of warning if the enemy are at hand. And these men need to see their fellow soldiers laid to rest as well as can be managed under the circumstances. Take the time you need . . .'

The Tungrians stood guard while the legion's remaining cohorts stacked their shields and spears, formed a line and crossed the battlefield at a slow pace, the soldiers gathering together their dead comrades' bones and broken equipment for burial. Tribune Varus stood with Marcus and watched as the collected remains were gathered close to where the marines were working away at a pit deep enough to take them. A soldier walked up with a helmet that had evidently been stoved in by a heavy blow, the remnant of a centurion's crest holder bent over almost at a right angle.

'That's the first spear's helmet.'

Varus walked over to the man and took the damaged helmet from him almost reverentially, turning back to Marcus. The iron bowl's interior was black with dried blood, and the heavy iron brow guard was notched in three places.

'He went down fighting.'

Varus nodded.

'I never doubted it. He used to say that if he was going to the underworld he'd be taking a few men with him on the boat ride.'

'Will you keep the helmet?'

The younger man shook his head.

'It belongs here with the rest of him.'

He placed it down onto the pile of iron and bone, stepping back and bowing his head in a moment of silence.

'I'll come back this way when we're done and tell him what happened. If we're not all dead . . .'

The remainder of the day's march was conducted in a sombre silence broken only by the rattling jingle of the legionaries' equipment and their officers' shouted commands. When Julius drove his men through a fresh series of drills incorporating the iron-tipped stakes, there was little of the usual complaint from men sobered by the day's discovery. The same routine ensued the following night, each cohort competing to be the first to have all of their stakes set in the ground, and their legionaries set in a defensive line in front of the pointed iron heads. Called upon to judge the competition, Scaurus declared the result too close to call, and rewarded the legion with the promise of a day's holiday once they reached Nisibis. He strolled back to the command tent with Julius and Marcus, musing thoughtfully on the likelihood of their seeing action the next day.

'I thought they'd be on us the moment we left Constantina, given enough notice from their men in Edessa, but perhaps King Abgar was right when he told us that he's killed every spy in the city. Whoever it is that's commanding the opposition isn't going to want to let us get much closer though, or he risks our slipping past him in the night and reaching Nisibis unchallenged. It has to be tomorrow, if it's going to happen at all.'

'Perhaps they've packed up and gone home, rather than face the might of Rome's retribution?'

Scaurus laughed softly at Julius's grim jest.

'Perhaps.'

* * *

The legion marched at dawn, a brisk, cold wind out of the north ruffling the centurions' crests and blowing the dust from the soldiers' booted feet away, preventing it from rising in the usual choking cloud that frequently forced men to tie scarves across their faces. Felix's Phrygians ranged forward to the east, tasked with seeing how far they could ride towards the city before encountering the enemy. He returned at the canter two hours later, his horses sweating heavily at their exertions. Reining his mount in alongside Scaurus, he pointed back the way he'd come.

'Those friends you were expecting are somewhere close to hand. We ambushed a party of their scouts about ten miles further on.'

The legatus looked up at him, taking in the blood spattered across the prefect's armour.

'Did any of them get away?'

The cavalryman shook his head.

'No, Legatus. I lost a dozen men, but we ran them all down. By the time we were done there was dust on the horizon. A lot of dust.'

Scaurus turned to his scout.

'You know where we are. Does our plan still work, given this ground?'

The man answered without hesitation.

'Yes. But we must move swiftly.'

Scaurus turned to Julius.

'As we planned it last night then.'

The senior centurion saluted and turned away, beckoning his trumpeter to his side, while Scaurus looked back up at prefect Felix.

'Lucky by name, lucky by nature, eh Felix?'

The younger man grinned down at him.

'Sometimes, Legatus, sometimes. At least this time I managed not to get an arrow in my armpit.'

'Just as well. Tribune Corvus's wife won't be there to perform miracles if you should manage to get yourself perforated this time.'

The legatus paused for a moment, looking down at his dusty boots as the trumpeter's call rang out across the legion's length.

'You know what I need from you now, don't you Prefect?'

His eyes narrowed at the sudden bray of Julius's trumpeters, and both men watched as the column's head abruptly turned left, leaving the road and heading north across the open landscape. Felix looked along the legion's snakelike length with a fresh grin and raised an eyebrow at his commander.

'I suspect I can guess, Legatus. Many of those unfriendly men over there . . .'

He waved a vague hand in the direction from which he had ridden.

'Are mounted on horses, which makes them at least twice as fast as your soldiers. You need me to go back over there and get in their way for a while, don't you?'

The trumpets blared again, and the legion's column lurched into motion back the way they had come with a mass grinding rasp of hobnails on the road's grit. Scaurus looked up at him for a moment, crooking a beckoning finger, and Felix bent over his horse's neck as the legatus stepped in close, apparently not worried by the beast's fearsome reputation.

'I'd be careful if I were you, sir, the bastard'll have your blasted ear off if you give him half a chance.'

The legatus shook his head, matching his prefect's grin with a hard smile.

'I think not. If your fucking horse so much as nibbles me I'll geld him. Now . . .'

He looked up at the young prefect with an expression that was in some small part almost pleading.

'Cornelius Felix, I know how you stupid bloody aristocrats think.'

Felix smiled knowingly.

'Because in reality you're a stupid bloody aristocrat yourself, sir?'

Scaurus shook his head in mock irritation.

'Yes, Prefect, most likely that's the reason I know that you're currently in that "expendable" frame of mind that overcomes you lot when you see an opportunity to do your "Horatius on the bridge" act. *Dulce et decorum est pro patria mori*, eh, Cornelius Felix?'

The prefect shrugged, and Scaurus shook his head in irritation, his voice a vehement snarl.

'Well not today, you young prick! Today you take your command, all five hundred of these precious horsemen, and you do *not* engage, Prefect, do you understand?'

Felix tilted his head, as if the instruction simply failed to make any sense to him.

'If we're not to engage . . . ?'

'You *display*, Prefect Felix.'

The look of incomprehension on the younger man's face became simple confusion.

'*Display*, Legatus?'

'Display, Prefect. Pretend you're on parade, with the dragon banner whistling like the scream of a harpie and your ceremonial armour making the women wet with excitement. Get their attention and hold it. Distract them from my legion, Prefect, and give me time to get to the ground I need if I'm going to beat them.'

He paused for a moment, eyeing Felix with a look that brooked no argument.

'Bring me that cavalry wing back intact, Prefect, because when I've taught those men what it really means to take on Rome, and sent what's left of them back east with their arses stoved in, I'll be needing you to lead the pursuit and keep them running.'

Felix smiled and the legatus nodded knowingly.

'I thought you'd like the sound of that.'

The prefect shrugged, straightening up in his saddle.

'Never fear, Legatus! I'll be back in good time if there's a chance to witness some sort of military miracle!'

He turned Hades away, tugging at the fearsome stallion's reins as the beast pranced with the desire to be away.

'Come on then, Seventh Phrygians! Today, my lads, we go forth with a noble objective!'

He paused, and the horsemen to either side of him grinned at their prefect, clearly in love with his approach to their craft.

'Today we go forth not to die for Rome, but to make a fine display on her behalf!'

He led the horsemen away towards the rest of his men, and Scaurus rejoined the column alongside Julius, who had stood waiting while he'd briefed Felix.

'You really think we can hold off thousands of horse archers?'

The legatus shrugged.

'At least our understanding of the landscape means that we won't be fighting them on level ground. And in any case, it's too late to be worrying now. The die, as the Divine Julius so succinctly put it, is well and truly cast.'

His first spear nodded grimly.

'So all we can do now is pray to Cocidius and look to our weapons.'

Scaurus marched in silence for a moment, looking down the column's length to its head, from where the sound of braying mules was issuing as their keepers drove the animals on without regard for their protests.

'You pray to your gods for strength in battle, First Spear, and I'll pray to mine that all those historians I've been taking lessons from weren't just pandering to their patrons when they told us how to beat the Parthians.'

'*Seventh Phrygians*,' Felix bellowed his command at the men of his cavalry wing. '*Form battle line! Decurions, to me!*'

His troopers obeyed with parade-ground precision, swiftly forming up into the formation he'd ordered, a battle line only two horses deep that stretched over half a mile in width, while their officers trotted their mounts to gather round the prefect, dismounting and waiting in disciplined silence for him to speak. When the last man was in position, he turned to his senior decurion, gesturing towards the distant dust cloud being raised by the oncoming Parthians.

'When you're ready, Decurion, I think we'll go over there for a look at those easterners. But let us all be very clear, gentlemen, our role today is to confuse the enemy, nothing more, nothing less, and there will be no glory hunting. Any man who breaks formation today, or who fails to obey the trumpet calls promptly, will be flogged in front of the legion tonight. *Any* man.'

The grizzled veteran nodded dourly, looking around the gathered officers.

'You heard the prefect! Legatus Scaurus has promised that we can ride those eastern goat nudgers down once they've been beaten, but until then all we're allowed to do is to dance around a bit and make them nervous for their flanks! Understood? Dismissed!'

With the officers dispersed back to their squadrons, Felix nodded to the decurion, who leapt into his saddle and pointed towards the dust cloud that was slowly growing larger on the eastern horizon.

'Shall we go, Prefect? If we wait any longer they'll be up in our faces and we'll have no room to manoeuvre.'

At the trumpet's signal, the five-hundred-strong cavalry wing started forward, first at the walk and then, with the gentle breeze keening through the dragon standard that flew proudly alongside Felix, the senior decurion ordered the horn to sound again. Accelerating to a canter, the horsemen stared grimly over their horses' necks at the enemy to their front still invisible bar the clouds of dust that were being kicked up by their horses.

'There must be ten thousand of them!'

Felix nodded at the man's shouted words, barely discernible over the rolling thunder of the cavalry wing's hoofs. As if on cue, they crested a gentle rise and there, spread out across the plain before them, was the enemy army. Two miles distant, the armoured heart of the enemy host, perhaps a thousand horsemen, glittered like a field of stars in the drab landscape. Fanned out across the plain ahead of them were several times their number of more lightly equipped horse archers, while the enemy army's rear was formed from a series of tightly ordered infantry columns, advancing at a brisk march in the wake of the horsemen. Felix and his subordinate exchanged glances, the prefect putting an involuntary hand to the hilt of his sword before he remembered the nature of Scaurus's orders.

'We need to turn now!'

Felix nodded his assent, and Quintus rose in his saddle, bellowing the command for a wheel to the left. The trumpeter blared out the order, and with a flurry of shouted commands the squadrons to their right speeded up their pace and pulled their mounts steadily around to their left, while the left-most squadron slowed until it was barely marking time.

'It's going to be close! Your legatus may get a cavalry action whether he wants it or not!'

The Parthian horse archers had already reacted, galloping forward towards the suddenly visible Romans with all the speed they could muster. Felix looked down the wheeling line of his wing with narrowed eyes, nodding slowly.

'Once the wing's in position, sound the gallop! We need to get out from under the threat of those archers!'

Quintus nodded, raising an arm ready to give the signal, and as the furthest right squadron wheeled through ninety degrees, he swept it forward, bellowing the order at the decurions who had already ridden their mounts forward of their men to better see him, anticipating the command.

'At the gallop . . . GO!'

The wing's horses leapt forward, eager to run, and with a hammering cacophony of hoofs, the squadrons accelerated away from the pursuing archers who fell away behind them, their mounts clearly blown from their impetuous charge. Looking over his left shoulder, Felix gauged the amount of progress that the fleeing wing had made, then turned in his saddle to stare back at the pursuing archers, who were now peeling away from their erstwhile prey to rejoin the main body in its remorseless advance towards the Roman main body.

'Slow them down to a canter and give the horses a chance to breathe!'

He waited while Quintus gave the order, watching as the archers fell in with the line of their army's advance.

'We haven't distracted them enough yet!'

His senior decurion looked back at the Parthians, then back at his prefect with a knowing expression.

'What are you thinking?'

The Phrygians were now riding out past the Parthian right flank, the closest of the enemy horsemen a good mile distant from the furthest right squadron in their line.

'As long as we just buzz around their line of advance like a sand fly, we're not going to distract them enough to give the legatus the time he needs!'

He looked back at his subordinate, his face hard with the certainty of what they were going to have to do.

The soldiers were sweating heavily now, working hard at the double march that was taking them north towards the distant mountains that formed the border with Armenia. Scaurus looked over his shoulder, seeing the Phrygians' dust moving slowly across what he presumed was the front of the Parthian advance.

'How far back do you think they are?'

Julius took a swift look back.

'Five miles?'

Scaurus nodded.

'No more than six. If they're trotting their horses to keep them fresh for the battle we might just beat them to the hills. But if they're cantering . . .'

Julius shrugged.

'Then we'll have to fight them on the plain. And we know from young Varus's account how well that's likely to go.'

'My orders from the Legatus were to distract the enemy from the legion for long enough to let him set up a defence, Quintus, and at the moment it's not working! We'll just have to try harder!'

The prefect grinned at his senior decurion, provoking a shake of the older man's head.

'Right wheel?'

Felix nodded back at him.

'Right wheel!'

Quintus shouted the order with a look of disbelief that was matched by the troopers around them as the wing began to pivot once more, turning gradually to the east, its path curving round to take the Roman cavalry around to the rear of the Parthian force and present a threat to the plodding infantrymen that he calculated the enemy general would be unable to ignore. Turning in his saddle, the young prefect watched the enemy host intently. Quintus shook his head.

'They're not reacting!'

'Just a little longer . . .'

The Phrygians had turned most of the way through ninety degrees, their course taking them past the right-hand side of the Parthian host with half a mile of empty desert between the two bodies of men. Quintus opened his mouth to argue with his prefect, closing it as Felix snapped out a terse command.

'Left wheel, canter pace!'

The Parthian host had abruptly wheeled to their right and accelerated to a headlong gallop, their commander heedless of his force's reserves of stamina as he drove them across the plain in pursuit of the Romans. For a moment even Felix was convinced that he had gambled and lost, as the leading Parthian horse archers galloped at his wing's rear with arrows ready to loose.

'Should we gallop them?'

The veteran shook his head with a scowl, looking back at the pursing archers.

'Their mounts will soon be blown at that speed, so they'll never catch us. Only question is whether they can get close enough to loose their—'

'Here it comes!'

One of the riders pointed at their pursuers with an urgent warning shout. Felix followed his pointing arm and cringed as the Parthian horsemen, knowing that the Romans would soon be out of range, loosed a volley of arrows at their maximum range.

'Shields!'

The first volley was swiftly followed by two more, the third flight of arrows leaving their bows before the first had fallen to earth, while each of the Phrygians raised his long oval shield to protect both horse and rider from the falling arrowheads. With an eerie whistle the first volley fell onto the very rearmost of the wing's riders, an iron rain that battered at their raised shields, hammering down into horses and riders alike. A score or more of the rearmost horses were hit on their unshielded hindquarters, most of them continuing on their way with no more reaction than a squeal of protest as the falling missiles drove the protective iron scales of their barding into the flesh below, but in four cases the arrows penetrated the armoured protection and drove deep into the flesh, causing the beasts unbearable pain and driving them to throw their riders in their kicking, screaming agony. The second and third volleys lanced down onto the fallen riders even as Felix hesitated, only one of them retaining sufficient of his wits to raise his shield and take shelter beneath its thick wooden protection. The other three troopers jerked under the arrows' impact, but as the Phrygians rode on, the last of their comrades threw aside his shield and stared after them in disbelief at his fate. Readying himself to turn and ride to the man's rescue, the prefect felt a hard grip clamp onto his right arm.

'No! No man breaks formation!'

Felix started at Quintus's barked command.

'And especially not you, Prefect!'

The prefect stared bleakly at his senior decurion.

'But . . .'

The decurion shook his head sadly, staring back at the solitary trooper as the Parthian archers rode towards the doomed man.

'You gave the order, no man to leave the formation, now you can honour it! He knows what to do . . . if he has the sense to use his dagger on himself before they get hold of him.'

The first cohort of legionaries marched wearily onto the hill's lowest slopes and were promptly turned from the line of march by the waiting Julius. He stalked alongside their senior centurion for a moment, barking out instructions and pointing out their intended position.

'Just as we practised it! Climb until you're a hundred paces from the crest, then turn to your left and take them along the hillside for three hundred paces, then stop! Make sure there's enough room behind you for the artillery to shoot over your heads! Face your men down slope and get your long spears to the front, then let them have a rest and a drink of water. I want a continuous line along the hill with no gaps, so make sure your boys and the next cohort have a seamless join! Right, get on with it!'

He turned away and walked down the cohort's column past rank after rank of grim-faced, sweating soldiers, ready to repeat his instructions to the next cohort's commander. The bulk of the legion was deploying across the hillside before Scaurus marched up with the rearguard, smiling when he saw the first spear waiting for him. The two men paused as the Tungrians marched on into the heart of the swiftly composed defence, taking their place in the central section of the line.

'Doesn't look like much, does it?'

Scaurus nodded, his gaze running along the line of men stretching across a mile or so of the ridge that ran from east to west, then turned to look out over the landscape below, the road they had left lost in the distance to the south. The legion's defensive positions were effectively at the top of a shallow climb of over a mile's length that steepened discernibly in its last two hundred paces, and Julius shook his head as he looked at the ground before them.

'I can't see how this gentle slope is going to make it any easier for us to beat them?'

His legatus turned and looked back to the cloud of dust that indicated the Parthian host's progress, already visibly closer.

'It looks just right to me.'

Julius raised an interrogatory eyebrow, and the younger man's lips twitched into a smile.

'I know you can't see it, but trust me, this is dangerous ground for an army that depends on horse archers and heavy cavalry.'

He pointed to the approaching enemy, now less than five miles away. 'That said, perhaps we'd be wise to put a legion between ourselves and those Parthians?'

The Parthian kings rode out before their men to see the Roman position for themselves, each of the three men escorted by a hundred of their respective household bodyguards, the knights surrounding them glorious in their shining magnificence.

'At least this time someone has had the sense to find some ground that does not insult us.'

The other two men regarded King Osroes of Media, the most senior of them by dint of the size of both his kingdom and his army, in an appropriately respectful silence.

'A good deployment too.'

He stared up the shallow slope with a keen gaze. A long line of infantry stretched along a half-mile of the ridge, their position apparently chosen with an eye to defence against cavalry.

'See how both ends of the line are anchored on breaks in the ridge line? We won't be able to take them in the flanks, and if we try to attack their rear I suspect we'll find the ground too difficult for our horses. Someone's been reading the histories.'

The young king of Hatra, barely a man and less experienced than the other two, stared up at the Romans with wide eyes.

'What will we do then, Osroes? How will we defeat them?'

The oldest man of the three, a black bearded thug of a man clad in black armour, in whose kingdom the Romans had chosen to make their statement of domination over the King of Kings' throne decades before by seizing his fortress city of Nisibis, growled the answer before the Median had a chance to answer.

'In the same way our ancestors dealt with them at Carrhae, Wolgash. With the flail of our archers to weaken their line until blood flows down that hill like water. And then . . .'

He slapped a heavy gold and silver decorated mace into his palm.

'Our knights will tear through them with the righteous rage of the Sun God's true followers! We will deal out the same fate to these men that we visited upon their brothers not far from here. And once they are scattered, Nisibis will surely fall to us.'

Osroes raised an eyebrow at his older cousin.

'But first, Narsai, given their numbers, we will exercise a little diplomacy.'

'Diplomacy! While their boots sully the earth on which my kingdom is founded?'

The Median smiled tolerantly.

'Our brother Narsai wishes to bathe in Roman blood once more, and paint himself from head to toe with the gore that will reaffirm his claim on the city.'

The king of Adiabene nodded his agreement.

'I do! And only their abject surrender will cure me of that need to put my foot on Rome's throat!'

'And yet . . .'

'And yet *what?*'

'And yet, Narsai, there may be a way to send them away, defeated and humiliated, without having to lose good Parthian warriors to their defence. It would be remiss of us not to enquire of them as to whether they would rather die in agony or live to recross the border with their skins intact.'

The older man snorted derisively.

'As you wish, Osroes. Perhaps your father's abject defeat at their hands has made you overly wary of these . . . *children.*'

The Median smiled slowly.

'Or perhaps you, Narsai, king of *half* a kingdom, are braver with my men at your back than you might be with only the force you can muster from your own land?'

His question was posed in the same light tone with which he had appraised the waiting Romans, but one hand had moved to rest on the handle of his own mace in its place at his belt.

'Whatever might be the truth, never forget that my father, his long life be blessed, sowed his seed in the most evil tempered of his wives to beget me. The patience he has bequeathed me wars with her implacable urge to cause damage during my every waking moment, and just once I might be tempted to unleash that darker side.'

Osroes met the older man's eyes and widened his own in challenge, the household knights around them fidgeting nervously at the threat of internecine bloodshed. He smiled suddenly, prompting an unconscious copy of the expression to break out across the younger king of Hatra's face in simple relief.

'And trust me, Narsai, one quick conversation with the leader of those walking dead men ought to suffice. He will surely realise that they will never be able to stand against five thousand of the finest archers in the world.'

'They seem to want to negotiate.'

Scaurus looked down at the party of knights approaching the legion's line up the hillside under a flag of truce, watching as the heavy horses' feet slipped and slid in the loose soil.

'Negotiate? The only thing they'll want to negotiate over is whether we get to keep our weapons, once we've marched under the yoke. And I'm not surprised. Someone down there has come to the unhappy realisation that this fight isn't one that he wants to risk, so he's willing to spend a few minutes finding out if we'd be good enough to abandon this rather impressive defensive position and slink off with our tails between our legs. And that's *before* he sees the surprises we have in store for them.'

He turned to Julius.

'The Parthians, First Spear, are well known for their habit of violating truces in order to win battles. Crassus was still more than likely to get away from Carrhae with most of his army intact until he was unwise enough to ride out to negotiate, and got himself decapitated. So, given I'm quite interested in what those men down there have to say for themselves, I'll take a century of your biggest, ugliest men with me, if you'll whistle up an appropriate escort?'

The black-bearded senior centurion nodded, turning away and bellowing an order at the legion arrayed across the hillside.

'Dubnus! I'll have your Tenth Century down here!

Scaurus watched with an amused smile as the recently promoted first spear led his axe men forward, bulling their way through the legion's line and reforming before the command group with impressive speed and precision. The Briton took his place before them and saluted with unexpected vigour, shouldering his massive axe.

'First Spear! The Tenth Century is at your command!'

'You can stop shouting, thank you, Dubnus.'

Scaurus stepped forward, looking the massive Briton up and down.

'Perfect. You and your men will do very nicely, Centurion, just as long as you can keep your temper in check.

Dubnus snapped to attention, and behind him his men followed suit.

'So gentlemen, you're going to escort me down to meet those horsemen. You *are* going to make sure nothing untoward happens to me, but you are *not* going to go starting any unwanted fights. There will be no hand gestures, no dirty looks and no fingering your weapons when I'm not looking. Is that understood, First Spear Dubnus?'

'Yes Legatus!'

'If any of you as much as twitches a muscle at these men, you most likely will be responsible for my death. And I won't bc the happiest of men under that circumstance. Is that understood, First Spear Dubnus?'

'Yes Legatus!'

'All I want from you and your men is to march down to meet those barbarians like you're the biggest, fastest, deadliest men in the entire empire. Make eye contact with a man, fix on him and hold the stare. Do not look away. I want those horsemen going back down the hill knowing that there's a race of fearless giants with axes waiting for them up here.'

'And you think the sight of The Prince and his men will stop them from attacking us?'

Scaurus turned back to Julius with a laugh.

'Stop them from attacking us? I very much doubt it. But it might give them pause for thought while they're toiling up that slope. You'd better stay here and take command in the event that anything happens to me. The negotiation will have to be conducted in Greek in any case. Come along then Tribune Corvus! Let's go and show these tribesmen some good old-fashioned patrician disdain, shall we?'

He turned to make his way down the slope, pulling tight the leather cord that secured his helmet's cheek guards.

'There is another reason for bringing you and your giants with me for this brief and doubtless disappointing meeting, First Spear.'

Dubnus puffed out his chest proudly.

'Legatus?'

Scaurus grinned at him, his features hardened by the helmet's harsh lines.

'Yes. While you and your bolt-thrower winders are down with me, there's much less risk of anyone being tempted to use a handful of Parthian kings for target practice.'

Ignoring the Briton's wounded expression, he marched down the slope, stopping ten paces from the three magnificently armoured men waiting for him in a half-circle of bodyguards. Bowing deeply, he straightened up and examined each of them in turn before speaking, noting the differences between their armour, equipment and bearing. At length, and with the equable tone of a man greeting visitors to his country estate, he raised his voice in greeting, switching to Greek in order to ensure that he was understood.

'Greetings, noble lords from the east. I always take pleasure in meeting men of high birth on the road with their bodyguards.'

Their apparent leader, standing in between the older and younger members of their party, stepped forward a pace with a look of amusement.

'And there was I, raised to believe that the Romans were a race of humourless murderers. It would be a shame to have to kill you, given that under different circumstances we might well have shared a jar of wine and told each other stories of our homelands. But kill you we will, unless—'

'Unless we agree to pass under the yoke and swear to pass back over the Euphrates, vowing never to return?'

The king nodded in silence, while his older companion stared at Scaurus with an intensity that made Dubnus's knuckles turn white on the handle of his axe. The legatus smiled tightly back at him.

'It would be helpful to know which august personages I'm addressing, Your Highness. Your names would make useful embroidery for my confession and death warrant, were I to accede to your request, I imagine.'

The king shook his head with a lopsided smile.

'You're an amusing man, Roman. But I will humour your request.'

He raised a hand to indicate the young man standing on his right.

'This is his imperial highness Wolgash the Second, king of the desert kingdom of Hatra.'

Scaurus nodded, bowing respectfully.

'Greetings, Your Highness.'

Wolgash inclined his head stiffly in reply, and his fellow monarch turned to the man on his left.

'And this is my cousin Narsai, King of Adiabene. He has sworn an oath to the Sun God that he will not wear any colour other than black until the day that his kingdom is free from the presence of your empire.'

Scaurus bowed again.

'Greetings, King Narsai.'

He turned back to the speaker.

'His armour will make him easy to pick out on the field of battle, I expect.'

'You will have no need to look for me, Roman. Stand still for long enough and you will find me in your face.'

The legatus inclined his head again, a slight smile the only indication of a reaction to the Parthian's bombast.

'And you, Your Magnificence. Might I know whom I have the honour of addressing?'

The king spread his hands.

'I am Osroes, son of King Arsaces the Forty-Fifth, the King of Kings, the Anointed, the Just, the Illustrious, Friend of the

Greeks. I rule the province of Media on behalf of my father, and it is with his blessing that I bring my army to the cause of my kinsman Narsai. And now that you know who it is that will deliver you to your gods, tell us your name so that we might decorate your grave appropriately.'

'My name, mighty kings, is Gaius Rutilius Scaurus. I am legatus of the imperial Third Gallic Legion, and I am sworn to my god, the Lightbringer, the Lord Mithras, to fight here and win a famous victory that will echo across the plains to the walls of your father's city Ctesiphon. Either that, or die in a manner that will bring pleasure to the spirits of my ancestors. And as to my grave . . .'

His face hardened.

'My only expectation, King Osroes, is that you will despoil my corpse in the same barbaric manner you did with my Sixth Cohort.'

He paused, playing a hard stare across all three men's faces.

'You may defeat my legion today—'

'We will bleed your legion with our arrows, then crush it flat with our maces!'

The Roman smiled again, showing his teeth.

'You *may* defeat us today, Narsai of Adiabene, but you will simply be postponing the day of your reckoning for these crimes. And beware, when you come up this hill seeking my head, because I will not be displaying my sense of humour.'

Osroes shook his head.

'You had better return to your command, Legatus, before you provoke my cousin here to an act that would dishonour him.'

Scaurus nodded.

'Sage advice, Your Highness. I wouldn't want to end up being murdered at a parlay, like my countryman Crassus, would I? An ignominious death is so bad for a man's reputation.'

He turned away and headed up the slope, the Tungrian axemen backing away in his wake, watched with angry eyes by the black-armoured monarch.

'I should have killed him.'

Osroes stared after the legatus.

'I could never permit such dishonour under a flag of truce. But if you're so certain that you have the beating of him, I suggest you seek him out once we have them at our mercy, and test your mettle against his. Come!'

He led the horsemen away, signalling to his general to begin the attack.

'Here they come.'

Julius pointed down at the plain below them, grimacing as thousands of Parthian horsemen began to move forward. Spreading out across the plain until their frontage was a good half-mile wide, they came forward at a deliberate pace and with unmistakable purpose. Julius stared down at the mass of men and horses, shaking his head in disgust.

'And not one of them wearing anything thicker than a felt cap.'

The different hued jackets worn by the three kings' men gave the scene a surreal look, their advance gradually flooding the ground with a riot of colour. Qadir nodded, a wry smile on his lips.

'These men do not face iron, First Spear, they only know how to deal it out by means of their bows. Threatened with attack, they only have one tactic – to run away and shoot as they do so, and as accurately as if they were going forward. Their record against Rome has tended to be the result not of their skills, which are undoubted, but upon the skills and preparedness of their opponents.'

He stared down at the horsemen riding towards them before speaking again.

'I suspect that this day may prove an unpleasant surprise for them.'

The legion stood wreathed in silence, the only sound that of the distant hoof beats as the Parthian horse archers trotted forward in a disciplined mass with their bows held ready for use. Scaurus's party threaded through the legion's line, and the legatus dismissed his escort back to their places before resuming his climb, shaking his head as he joined his officers.

'You'll have gathered from the enemy's advance that, much as expected, the kings in charge of that Parthian army aren't persuaded that they're making a mistake.'

'Kings?'

The legatus smiled knowingly at his First Spear.

'Yes. Three of them. Where we use imperial governors to administer the empire's provinces, the easterners use a system of minor kingdoms, each one ruled by its own king. There are three of them down there with their armies, one who rules a good-sized piece of the empire and two reasonably minor monarchs, and none of them was in much of a mood to compromise. As a consequence of which . . .'

He turned and looked down at the plain, waving a hand at the massed horse archers.

'This is what those poor bastards in the Sixth Cohort had to face before they died, except they were caught on flat ground with standard-issue shields that were little better protection than thin air, and with no means of fighting back. Those archers can put three arrows in the air before the first one falls to earth, and I suspect that my new friend King Osroes of Media has been reading the same books that I have. See the supply camels following the archers? They'll have enough arrows to keep showering them onto us until the legion's nothing but a shell, if we're stupid enough to let them.'

He smiled at Julius's expression.

'Which of course we're not.'

Julius shook his head.

'They have no idea what's coming, do they?'

Scaurus shrugged.

'Why would they? The Sixth Cohort rolled over and died in exactly the way they expected, in just the same way that twenty thousand men died at Carrhae for that matter, so why shouldn't we succumb to their rather thin bag of tricks in our turn? All it takes from their perspective is a barrage of arrows for an hour or two followed up by a glorious charge of their cataphracts to break what's left, a few minutes of bloody murder and the surrender and massacre of the survivors. Up until now the strongest requirement for a man serving in that army down there has been a capacity to tolerate spilt blood. The king in charge of that mass of men will regard this hill, and this legion, as no more than a minor hindrance, I'd imagine. And now, First Spear . . .'

He nodded decisively as the enemy horsemen approached the line of markers five hundred paces from the Roman line.

'Shall we see just how fast Dubnus's axemen can reload their bolt throwers?'

Julius turned to his trumpeter.

'Sound the Stand To.'

As the first notes of the command pealed out across the hill-side, the voices of dozens of centurions barked out over the trumpet's squeal, and with a sudden flurry of movement the legion's line lurched forward. Marching steadily down the hill, they advanced for a distance of thirty paces before stopping, centurions and watch officers swiftly dressing the line back into as near perfect straightness as could be achieved given the hill's undulating surface. On the ground near the hill's flat summit, a line of two-man bolt throwers stood revealed by the legion's advance. Behind each Scorpion crouched four men, two of them squatting beside one of the oversized shields faced with leather that had so mystified Centurion Avidus when he'd first seen them on the legatus's list of requirements. Julius raised his voice to bark a command that rang out over the distant noise of the advancing Parthians' hoof beats.

'Bolt throwers – load!'

With the screening infantry line no longer concealing them, the crews sprang into action, one of Dubnus's axemen gripping the winding handles of each weapon and cranking back the heavy bowstring of his allotted weapon with straining muscles, each of them shooting sidelong glances at the men on either side, determined not to be outdone in the race to complete his task. With the Scorpions ready to shoot, the operators, Hamian bowmen for the most part, carefully placed heavy armour-piercing bolts into their weapons' mechanisms and pointed the bolt throwers at the oncoming enemy.

'Bolt throwers – at maximum range . . .'

The Scorpions angled skywards, their operators looking to Julius for the order to shoot.

'Loose!'

In his place standing next to the legatus, the hairs rose on the back of Marcus's neck as, with a snapping twang, the Scorpions spat their deadly loads high into the cloudless sky. He watched, unconsciously holding his breath, as the salvo of missiles arced over their apogee and plunged down into the advancing horsemen. Along the Parthian line the impact was instantaneous and shocking, the bolts' impact punching men from their horses and, when a missile struck beast rather than rider, dropping the animals kicking and screaming to the ground in sprays of blood. Tearing his gaze away from the slaughter, Marcus shot a swift glance at the bolt throwers and the Tungrians already labouring to re-tension their strings, each man stepping away and raising his hand as the signal for the trigger man to load a bolt and elevate the weapon, ready to shoot once more.

'Bolt throwers – shoot when ready!'

Another salvo of bolts tore at the advancing horsemen as they passed the four-hundred-pace marker, and Scaurus smiled tightly down at the oncoming mass of men and beasts.

'So now the kings are looking at each other with *that* expression. We've all worn that face at some time or other, when something goes wrong without warning. After all, this isn't what's supposed to happen, is it? It's not enough to put them off the idea that their victory's predetermined, mind you . . .'

A third salvo of bolts hissed away from the Roman line, a little ragged this time as the faster crews loosed their bolts an instant before their comrades, and along the Parthian front more archers fell in bloody ruin or were thrown from their dying mounts.

'After all, their losses are only a pinprick to an army of that size, and once those horsemen get into arrow range they'll shower us with sharp iron in fine style. I doubt King Osroes is especially troubled at this point.'

He turned to Julius.

'Archers, First Spear?'

The first spear nodded, raising his hand again.

'Archers!'

From their places behind the legion's line, two full cohorts of Hamians stepped back up the slope ten paces, gaining sufficient elevation to see the Parthian light cavalry trotting towards them. Some men rotated their right arms in readiness for the exertion to come without any conscious thought, already lost to the drilled routine that made them so deadly to an unprepared foe.

'Archers . . . light targets!'

Each man reached his right hand back to the quiver of arrows waiting at his hip, using his thumb to find an arrow with a dimple drilled into the base of its shaft and delicately sliding it out of the press of its fellows. Some men kissed the missile's broad crescent heads as they lifted them to their weapons, others muttered quiet prayers to their goddess, but the majority, eyes stonelike with concentration, simply nocked the arrow to their bows and waited for the next command.

'At two hundred paces – draw!'

A thousand archers forced the perfectly trained strength of their upper bodies into their weapons, raising their arms until the arrows' heads were pointing high into the air and then holding the position, waiting for the order to kill their enemies.

Julius waited in silence until the trotting horses passed the two-hundred-pace marker.

'Loose!'

With a swishing sigh a thousand arrows flicked away from the Hamians' bows, the archers' previously slow, measured movements abruptly replaced by swift, merciless precision as they nocked their second arrows with hands that had been trained until the movements were simple muscle memory, mindless routine that they could repeat again and again until their quivers were empty.

'Loose!'

The first flight of arrows was high in the air above the Parthians as the second volley flew in their pursuit, and again the archers reached behind them with movements almost too fast to follow.

'Loose!'

The third volley was launched from the Roman line as the first struck, the isolated but crushing impact of Scorpion bolts suddenly augmented by something much deadlier to the men massed below the legion's line. Cowering beneath their hopelessly inadequate wicker shields, the leading enemy ranks shivered under the rain of iron, scores of men dropping from their mounts, their bodies spitted by the arrows' impacts, while some of the horses were hit by two or three of the broad-headed missiles. The screaming of men and animals rent the air, and the watching legionaries muttered to each other in genuine amazement as the Parthian advance slowed to no more than a walk, the ranks of horsemen following up behind obstructed by the dead and dying bodies of their comrades.

A horn blew, a clear and insistent command echoing out across the Parthian army, and the horsemen raised the bows that had been waiting for the command, arrows already nocked to their strings.

'Have they got the range to hit us from that far out, shooting uphill?'

Qadir pursed his lips at the first spear's question.

'Shooting uphill, First Spear, their arrows will be robbed of much of their power to pierce our defences. They won't be able to reach us here, and they won't trouble the Scorpions, but they'll be able to put their arrows into the infantry.'

Julius nodded to his trumpeter, and the horn sounded again.

'Third legion – cover!'

The command was echoed down the line by his centurions, each century's front rank promptly kneeling with their shields upright before them, while the second rank crouched behind them with their shields raised at an angle, the other two ranks standing with their boards held over their heads to provide protection against any arrows lofted high into the air above them.

'Archers – cover!'

Stepping in behind the legion's line, the Hamians ducked under the shield wall's roof, while the big men waiting to either side of each Scorpion lifted the massive shields that had lain on the ground before each of the bolt throwers, holding them together to form a wooden wall behind which the crews continued to work their weapons.

The Parthian horns sounded again, and the horsemen loosed a massed volley of arrows that arced up the hillside, seemingly hanging in the sky for a moment before hissing down into the legion's line, each heavy iron head smacking into the raised shields with a sharp thudding rattle that sounded like winter hail on a wooden roof.

'The shields are working!'

All along the legion's line the soldiers' shields were studded with arrows, but where the missiles would normally have ripped through the wooden boards and into the men behind them, they had for the most part utterly failed to penetrate the enhanced protection afforded by the layers of linen and leather so painstakingly applied in Antioch. Here and there a lucky shot would slip through the inevitable small gaps in the wall of leather-faced wood to find a target, but along the line the Third Gallica's cohorts were standing firm against the arrow storm. Scaurus grinned back at his genuinely amazed first spear.

'I wonder which one of the three kings is going to be the most unhappy when they realise what's happening!'

Few of the arrows had sufficient range to reach the legion's line of Scorpions, but those that did had no more effect on the giant shields than upon those wielded by the legionaries, protruding in lonely solitude from the protective screens. With a slapping twang the nearest Scorpion spat a bolt over the legionaries' heads, the missile vanishing into the mass of horsemen with unknown but deadly effect. Some of the Hamians were shooting arrows through small gaps in the line of shields, a rapidly swelling torrent of missiles raining down onto the Parthian archers and adding to the confusion on the plain below.

'We've stopped their advance! They can't perform their usual trot to within a hundred paces, loose and turn away, not with our Hamians shooting at them and dying horses struggling about the battlefield!'

Scaurus nodded, looking beyond the milling archers to where the Parthian heavy cavalry stood waiting for the moment that their monstrous power would be unleashed to deliver the legion's death blow.

'Indeed. I wonder what Osroes is making of this.'

'They're killing my archers! We have to *do* something!'

Narsai was bolt upright in his saddle, his thighs stiffened to raise his body higher for a better view. Ignoring the shouted imprecations of his fellow monarch, Osroes looked over the mass of the combined force of archers, their usual cycle of attack and retreat clearly reduced to a shambles by the growing number of horses and riders who were being killed and wounded by the Romans' unceasing shower of arrows and artillery bolts. On the slope above them, the enemy line was apparently untroubled by the volleys of arrows that were being launched at them by the remaining archers.

'There's something wrong here . . .'

Narsai leaned in close to him, almost climbing out of his gold- and jewel-encrusted saddle in his urge to be heard, bellowing at Osroes with such vehemence that his saliva spattered across the king's immaculate gilt armour.

'The only thing that's wrong is that we're sat here doing nothing while good men die at the hands of those fucking invaders!'

Osroes stared at him for a moment before replying, as curiously calm as he always was when the release of violence beckoned him.

'Show me that much disrespect just one more time, Cousin, and I'll consider a change of heart as to whether I'm best off fighting the Romans or bringing your toothless little kingdom to heel.'

Narsai jerked backwards as if he'd been stung, one hand straying towards the handle of his mace, but the movement stalled as he considered the threat of the bodyguard clustered around the royal party. Osroes nodded grimly, gesturing at the magnificently equipped heavy cavalry of his most intimate bodyguard.

'Wise, Narsai.'

He gestured towards the hill before them.

'Our enemy seems to have our measure, at least so far. By now I would have expected to see gaps starting to appear in their line as our archers thinned out their numbers, but all I see is the Romans standing firm on that slope, seemingly untroubled. They have bolt throwers and archers behind their line, and by some trickery or other, their shields are resisting our arrows.'

He pulled at his lip thoughtfully.

'And our archers are shooting uphill, at their longest range . . .'

Turning in his saddle he summoned his gundsalar, the general of his army, the bodyguard around him parting to make a path for the man's horse.

'Your counsel, Gundsalar.'

The cavalry commander bowed from the waist.

'The archers are failing, Highness. They will not break that line, and while they continue to try they will also continue to take casualties. They should be withdrawn, and used to threaten the Romans from another direction to make a shattering blow from our cataphracti possible!'

Narsai nodded violently, pointing at the legion and almost screaming his agreement.

'We must ride now, Osroes! *Now!* The honour of our nations depends upon it!'

The king of Media looked round to take the gauge of the third monarch's commitment, finding Wolgash white-faced with fear.

'Might a feigned retreat not lure them down from their positions?'

Osroes smiled despite himself, speaking kindly to the young man.

'Under normal circumstances, Cousin, that would be a most expedient tactic to use with the usual mindless barbarians thrown at the empire by the Romans, but in this case . . .'

He paused, looking up at the figures standing on the hill's crest.

'In this case it seems that someone with a little more subtlety has been placed in command of their attempt to relieve our siege of Nisibis. With this one, I suspect that only irresistible force will serve.'

'That's faster than I expected.'

Julius raised his vine stick to point at the Parthian archers, watching as they turned and pulled back away from the arrow-swept strip of ground across which the bodies of so many of their comrades was scattered. Scaurus nodded.

'It's the decision I'd make in his place. All they can achieve by persevering is to get a lot more of those poor bastards killed, whereas pulling them back now leaves most of them fit to fight another day.'

'So we've won?'

Scaurus turned to smile at Tribune Varus, who stood next to Marcus watching the battle.

'Not really, Tribune. At the moment I think the best we could claim is a draw, given that we're tied to this hill just as long as those archers are close enough to attack us on the march to the next one. If they were to catch us out in the open, I suspect that the balance would tip towards their side of the table. If I were the king of Media, I'd be considering sending for supplies and setting up camp to starve us out, although he probably suspects I'd make him regret the choice once the sun was down for the night. And he's right.'

The killing ground before them was now deserted, more or less, although the plaintive cries and whinnies of agony from wounded men and horses alike were clearly audible at two hundred paces. Beyond the corpse-strewn wreckage of the archers' attack, the enemy's heavy cavalry was on the move, hundreds of the powerfully built steeds necessary to carry both an armoured rider and their own body protection being marshalled into formation.

'They've going to attack us, aren't they?'

Scaurus smiled at Varus again, realising that tribune was in the grip of a powerful emotion.

'Yes, I suspect they are. They're going to come up this slope as fast as horses carrying that much iron can move, and they're going to try to tear a hole in our line one way or another, either by causing panic among our men or by using their lances to kill from outside the range of our spears. And then, Tribune, we'll find out if all that drill we've been doing has been a waste of time, won't we? Perhaps you young gentlemen had best go and join your cohorts? And remember, your ancestors are watching. Make them proud, gentlemen, show them that we still know what it is to be Roman.'

Marcus and Varus hurried down the hill towards the Fourth and Fifth Cohorts.

'I'll command both Tungrian cohorts to start with. They're more used to fighting as one unit in any case. If I go down, then you have command.'

The younger man nodded at Marcus, watching as he put on his helmet and drew the shorter of his two swords.

'And no heroics. If I do fall then these men will need you to command them. You're no good to them dead. That reunion with your ancestors you're planning will have to wait a while.'

Osroes watched with a wry smile as his cavalry commander arrayed the three kingdoms' cataphracts into their formation, the veteran soldier shouting and cursing as he laboured to make order out of their ranks, trotting his horse to and fro to deliver his commands in person rather than depend on messengers.

'I do believe that man won't be happy until we're as neatly paraded as those Romans up there. But, since we're not Romans . . .'

Encouraging his horse forward with no more than a touch of his heels, he rode out in front of the heavy cavalrymen, nodding his respect to the soldier who, recognising an unspoken command when he saw one, bowed at the waist once more and backed his horse into the body of his kinsmen, a pack of brooding killers with a fierce reputation for their valour in battle.

'Well now!'

The king's voice rang out across the horsemen's ranks, every man craning his neck to see and hear their king.

'Shall we spare our horses' strength while we talk?'

He dismounted, holding onto his mount's reins and stroking its scale-armoured head affectionately, waiting while his men followed his example. When every man was standing alongside his mount, the king took a step forward, looking to either side at the solid wall of armoured men and beasts in front of him before raising his voice to address them.

'Knights of Media! Honoured brothers of Adiabene! Desert warriors of Hatra! Our fight with the Romans has come down to one simple truth! We must dislodge them from that hillside, either that or we must retire from this place before nightfall, to avoid the risk of their attacking us in the darkness!'

He paused, silently revelling in the hard set of their faces.

'In truth, I have been waiting for this moment! This is our destiny! This is the moment in which we show these usurpers that they can never stand against Parthian nobility!'

Stepping away from the horse he gestured to it with his free hand.

'Those of you who are my kinsmen will know that when I first set eyes on this animal I knew I had to have the beast for my own.'

Men in the ranks before him were smiling, recalling the stories that were still told of the moment when Osroes had watched the horse as it had exercised under the command of a skilled rider. He recalled that moment when, despite his possession of a dozen such mounts, the animal's sheer speed across ground, and the graceful fluidity of its movement seemingly impossible given the weight of armour and rider, its barely controlled savagery in close fighting exercises, was enough to make him cry out in astonishment.

'You know that I was robbed like a blind man by this beast's owner, and you know that I would have paid three times as much to own this creature . . .'

He paused, smiling wryly.

'Although I would probably have flogged the man as the price of his impudence, if he hadn't been sweating like a young man on his wedding night.'

Laughter rippled across the ranks of horsemen, the assembled cavalrymen grinning as they recalled the story of how the horse's owner had walked a fine line between negotiating the sale of a treasured and valuable asset and the risk of incurring the wrath of the most powerful man in his world.

'So you can imagine just how delighted I am at the prospect of taking this magnificent creature up this hill to confront *that!*'

He pointed up at the Roman line.

'A single arrow could fell this, the best and most beloved of all the things I own. A bolt from one of their catapults could kill the noble creature in an instant – and if I am afraid for Storm Arrow here, how much more do I fear the loss of a single man from among you? No, my brothers, I do not wish to charge our enemy, up a slope and without the chance for our archers to reduce their numbers a little first!'

He paused for a moment, allowing the words to sink in.

'But, reluctant or not, Storm Arrow and I, and all of you, must take up arms against these trespassers! We must take that righteous fury that burns fiercely in our hearts at the sight of their boots fouling our homeland, and use it to inspire us to their slaughter!'

He strode forward, raising a fist to challenge the men before him.

'Ride with me, fellow knights, ride with me against these followers of false gods who sully our homelands! Ride with me, and we will have our revenge for their destruction of the King of Kings' city of Ctesiphon, a deed to make our fathers proud again! Ride with me, and we will show these ants in iron what it means to face the *hunar* of the *artestarih!*'

The knights arrayed before him erupted in a cacophony of shouts, echoing his last words.

'The honour of the warriors!'

Swinging his body into the saddle, he raised his kontos over his head.

'For Adiabene!'

The locally recruited men cheered in response, raising their own lances in salute. Narsai spurred his mount forward a few paces, bellowing something incoherent at the Roman line.

'For Hatra!'

Wolgash's knights added their voices to the swelling noise, raising their weapons high.

'For Media!'

His own men, by far the largest of the three factions present, drowned out their comrades from the smaller kingdoms with a roar that Osroes knew would be audible on the hill above them, and he grinned ferociously at them, his heart swelling with pride as he pulled lightly at the beast's reins to point it at the enemy.

'Ride with me!'

7

Julius nodded slowly as the loudest of the three cheers from the Parthian ranks echoed across the hillside.

'That's them ready to come up here then, I presume?'

Scaurus nodded.

'It does appear that way. And I see they have their archers following up behind to harass our line. I think we'll greet this attack in the way we agree, First Spear.'

The older man nodded brusquely, beckoning his trumpeter.

'Sound the Stand Fast.'

On the hill above the Tungrians a horn sounded, and Marcus stepped out of the shield wall to look up and down the line at the senior centurions on either side before raising his sword and shouting the first of the three commands that had been drilled into the legion over the previous weeks.

'Cohort! Ground and cover!'

The line of soldiers seemed to sink into the ground, each man kneeling to hug the hillside behind his shield, allowing the bolt throwers behind them to shoot with a flatter trajectory as the enemy cavalry drew closer. Turning back to face the oncoming horsemen and dropping into the cover of his shield, Marcus was struck by the sudden silence that had gripped the battlefield, the distant rumble of hoofs no more than a rumour of war compared with the sudden rattle of arrowheads on the line's shields as the enemy's first volley scattered across the defenders.

The Parthian cataphracts were moving, their horses striding easily across the last of the plain's flat surface as it slowly began to angle up towards the waiting legionaries.

'Archers! Hard targets – loose!'

As the enemy cavalry reached the two-hundred-pace marker, the legion's archers let fly from their positions behind the line of Scorpions, stringing and loosing arrows at their fastest possible rate. No longer consciously aiming, they were flinging their pointed armour-piercing arrows at the oncoming mass of horsemen as fast as they could, lofting the missiles high into the blue sky to let them fall onto the armoured cavalrymen and their mounts. The purpose-designed spiked arrowheads would strike with enough power to rock a man backwards and, if the missile's point of impact was favourable, to pierce the armour worn by their targets. Only a few of the oncoming horsemen were affected, but where a mount staggered at the shock of an arrow punching hard at its facial protection, the beasts following it were momentarily slowed, and where a man slid from his saddle with a shaft protruding from a chink in his armour, the chaos was that much greater.

With a massed snap of heavy bowstrings the Scorpions spat their deadly loads over the recumbent line of soldiers with almost horizontal trajectories, every one of the heavy bolts finding a target and piercing the layered armour plates that protected man and beast. All along the advancing line of gleaming iron, riders and their mounts died in searing agony, their bodies smashed by the catastrophic wounds inflicted by bolts as thick as a man's thumb, each one tipped with a pointed iron head that punched through their armour with ease. Horses simply died as they ran, ploughing head first into the dirt and throwing their masters onto the ground before them, too stunned to react before their fellows were upon them, trampling them into the battlefield's earth to die under a merciless succession of iron-shod hoofs. Where a rider was hit, the effect was less catastrophic, some of the dead merely lolling lifelessly in their saddles. Others were thrown from their mounts if the bolts that had taken their lives failed to penetrate the armour across their backs and instead spent their remaining energy lifting their victims bodily from their saddles, and pitching them into the equine maelstrom.

The legionaries watching from beneath their shields cheered loudly at the sudden carnage, their shouted abuse continuing as volley after volley of arrows arched down into the advancing mass of horsemen. One chance shot in a thousand caught a horse in the front rank squarely in the face, piercing the perforated eye cover that had been set in the lavishly gilded chamfron that covered the beast's face and skewering deep into the socket, sending the hapless creature into paroxysms of agonised, aimless rage. The legionaries cheered again as the beast gyrated out into the open in front of the advancing line, bucking and kicking in pain and shock as its helpless rider, unable to do anything more than cling on with his legs as his mount gyrated uncontrollably, was flung back and forth like a rag doll until his grip failed, then was catapulted into the path of his comrades. An instant after he struck the ground, the advancing mass of horsemen was on him, stamping him helplessly into the dirt to the loud enjoyment of the Tungrians. The noise was swelling as the armoured mass came on up the hill, the words that the soldiers were yelling at their foes indistinguishable from more than half a dozen paces, almost lost in the swelling roar of the cataphracts' approach.

Julius watched anxiously as the advancing cavalry swept imperiously past the one-hundred-pace marker, their progress perceptibly slowing as the effort of hauling five hundred pounds of rider and the armour that protected both man and beast up the long slope began to tell on the horses, massively built as they were. Knuckles white, as his fists clenched around his vine stick, he looked down at the bolt throwers as the exhausted Tungrians stepped back to allow the archers to load their final bolts.

'Come on . . .'

Scaurus grinned at him lopsidedly.

'Careful, First Spear. You don't want to go breaking that stick after all you've been through together. This is where all those drills bear fruit.'

The Scorpions spat death again, the range now so short that the collective snap of their release and the screams of dying men and horses were almost simultaneous. Julius swung to point his stick at the waiting trumpeter.

'Ready!'

Raising his head and peering back over the line's shields, Marcus saw the axemen step away from their Scorpions as the last volley whipped over his men's heads and hammered into the oncoming Parthians. The enemy arrows had stopped falling, and he stood, shouting at the soldiers staring out from beneath their shields as the legion's trumpets began to shriek again, unsheathing the eagle-pommelled gladius and raising it above his head, gesturing for his men to rise and reform their line.

'Ready, Third Legion!'

The oncoming mass of cavalry was close enough that Marcus, still standing half a dozen paces in front of his men, waiting for the command that he knew either had to be given swiftly now or not at all, could see their full, terrible glory rushing towards him. A horse's length ahead of his men rode the Parthian king, and the young tribune nodded quietly to himself as his noted the man's glittering armour and ornate helmet. Raising his lance high into the air, Osroes swept the tip down to point at the Roman line, and with marvellously disciplined precision, the advancing horsemen copied the move a heartbeat later. Their collective war cry reached his ears through the thunder of hoofs that was now shaking the very ground beneath his feet as they levelled their lances to form a shining line of polished iron rolling inexorably towards him. The noise of their passage over the ground was now an incessant grinding phenomenon the like of which he had never heard, almost suffocating in its intensity, its violence making his body tremble involuntarily, whether by vibration or simple primal fear, not clear even to Marcus himself.

'Now!'

The trumpeter took a swift breath and blew with all of his might, the peal taken up an instant later up and down the line by each cohort. Their collective single note split the air, the most basic and recognisable of signals, and legatus and first spear looked at each other wordlessly, unable to do anything more than wait for the legion to obey its command to do battle.

The harsh bray of trumpets sounded through the cavalry's tumult, and Marcus gathered his wits, sweeping his sword forward and bellowing a command that was lost in the all-consuming thunder of the oncoming host.

'Throw!'

A glittering shower arced out from the legion's line as the soldiers hurled the three precious objects that each of them had carried with them from Antioch, and Marcus grinned with anticipation as the riders bored in towards them without any clue as to the nature of the deadly seed with which the ground before them had been sown.

'Got you!'

Julius clenched his fist as the Parthian line abruptly disintegrated into chaos, dozens of horses suddenly pulling up in a cacophony of high-pitched screams as their horses' hoofs found the caltrops that had been thrown into their path a moment before. Riders with uninjured mounts swerved around their helpless comrades, bunching unavoidably and presenting the Hamian archers standing behind the legion's line with the targets they had been waiting for. While the advance faltered, they raised their bows and shot into the struggling horsemen at a range close enough for their arrows to fly almost horizontally across the short gap between the two lines of warriors, each impact marked by the thump of lethal pointed iron striking thick armour, snapping the horsemen back in their saddles and killing the unfortunate men whose layered scales failed to repel the arrows' brutal power.

Looking at his trumpeter once more, he raised a hand and, with a warning look that made clear what would befall the man if he blew too soon, waited as the oncoming wave of armoured horseflesh struggled through the chaos caused by their comrades' crippled mounts, brushing aside those men who had fallen from their beasts with the chilling, bloody reality of the battlefield. The Parthian line gradually reformed, presenting a solid face to the Romans once more, their lances now only fifty paces from the solid line of infantrymen waiting to receive their charge.

The thunder that had shaken the hillside was stilled within half a dozen breaths as the Parthian charge faltered on the sharp iron teeth of ten thousand caltrops. Marcus stood and watched as the horsemen fought to regain some semblance of order, as the unlucky men among them fought to control animals driven wild with pain, or slid from their saddles as their mounts staggered and fell. Their king was shouting again, some encouragement or other, Marcus supposed, and while the man goaded his riders with harsh words whose purpose rang clearly across the narrow gap separating the two armies, a fresh onslaught of arrows shrieked out from the Roman line in a cruel horizontal sleet of iron. Glancing back at the legionaries behind him he was met by expressions of astonishment for the most part, his soldiers clearly daunted as never before by the line of enormous armoured horses and their shining riders, looming huge in their vision even at fifty paces. He turned to face them, putting his back to the enemy.

'Tungrians!'

A thousand pairs of eyes snapped onto him, recognising in his shouted challenge the urge to kill that had his body taut with the need to fight.

'Do you see that man?!'

Pointing with his sword, he watched as the king realised that he was the subject of the Roman's ire.

'That man is *mine!* The soldier who kills him will face me

when this is done with, when whatever's left of these donkey fuckers has ridden away with their pride in tatters! He's *mine!*'

He turned back, knowing that the eyes hidden in the shadow of the man's helmet beneath the slim gold crown that encircled his armoured head were locked on him, the presence in their invisible stare almost palpable, and with a kick at his mount's flanks the king spurred his beast forward, lowering his lance to charge the lone figure waiting for him in front of the legion's line. With a roar his men followed his example and rode at the Romans with renewed purpose, spending the last of their war horses' wind in a trotting advance towards the waiting Romans.

The trumpets screamed for the last time, and with one final glance at the Parthian king, Marcus turned his back to the oncoming enemy, almost insolent in his leisure, casting the shield aside and raising both arms to point to the line's rear, ordering the cohort to carry out the manoeuvre that had so infuriated them with its incessant repetition over the previous days.

'Fall back!'

Obeying with unconscious skill, the legion stepped backwards up the gentle slope in one perfectly coordinated movement, washing back up the hill like a retreating tide to reveal the gifts that they had left for their enemy in their wake. Emerging from the receding line of legionaries was a row of iron-tipped wooden teeth, the stakes that had been set in place while the soldiers had waited for combat, each one three feet from the next. Jutting forward to face the oncoming Parthians in a mile-long rampart, they would offer an enemy on foot no more resistance than a moment's delay, but to a body of charging cavalry they represented a deadly threat. On the beat of the sixth pace, Marcus turned his hands outwards to display his palms, and the Tungrians before him halted their retreat. With the long spears still pointing to the rear over their shoulders, they stared over their tribune's shoulder at the oncoming Parthians, now barely twenty paces distant, as he strolled nonchalantly between a pair of stakes and turned to watch the enemy's final approach. A hand snaked out and gripped the collar of his bronze armour, gently but firmly pulling him back through the line of spear men as Dubnus's familiar voice chuckled in his ear.

'No you fucking don't. I saw you eyeing up their king, and you can just wait your turn with the rest of us!'

The trumpet blew for the last time, and Marcus bellowed the last of the commands that had been drilled to the point of perfection.

'Spears!'

As one man the legionaries swung their spears up and over in a ripple of movement that spanned the line's entire length, sharp iron flashing as the front two ranks levelled weapons twice the length of a man's body at the charging cavalry. Watching the king's oncoming horse intently, Marcus saw the man stiffen as he realised the nature of the trap into which he had led the pride of his kingdom's nobility.

'Brace!'

The horses were already starting to baulk at the solid line of men before them when the first rank of horsemen saw the deadly peril laid out before them. Reining in their mounts, they shouted warnings that the real threat wasn't the retreating Roman line but rather the iron-shod points of thousands of wooden stakes revealed by the legion's short retreat, but the men following up behind them neither heard nor heeded the warning. The simple remorseless weight of their continued advance was unstoppable, forcing the gesticulating riders in front of them inexorably onto the unforgiving barrier, behind which a glittering hedge of iron spearheads waited in their turn. Fighting to hold their mounts off the deadly iron spikes, the Parthian front rank ground to a halt, several horses being pushed onto the defences in a chorus of agonised screams as the waiting iron punched inexorably through their barding and tore into their bellies.

'Forward!'

The cohort's line advanced a single step, the front two ranks thrusting their spears out with a brutal lunge that brought the stranded riders face-to-face with their doom.

'Forward! Faces, armpits and balls!'

The men to either side of him advanced another pace and repeated the thrust, each man aiming for the points they had been instructed to seek out with their spear blades, and the screams of horrifically wounded men were added to the thrashing death throes of the stricken mounts. Marcus saw the Parthian king slide from the saddle of his maimed beast, tossing away his lance and pulling a heavy mace from its place on the transfixed animal's saddle. Half turning, Marcus nudged Dubnus, raising his gladius and staring at its eagle-headed pommel for a brief moment.

'Are you coming?'

'We have them! Now we close the back door before they realise they're dead men if they don't turn and run!'

Julius nodded at his legatus's command, gesturing to the big man waiting behind him.

'The black flag!'

Sprinting up the short stretch of hillside that separated them from the summit, the bull-like soldier wielded the flag with all of his strength, a nine-foot square of black linen snapping in the breeze of its passage through the air. A moment later an answering peal of trumpets signalled that the order had been received, and Scaurus nodded his satisfaction.

'That's going to come as a nasty surprise.'

On both flanks of the mass of horsemen, three centuries of tunic-clad slingers slipped through the legion's line, shaking out into a loose formation that gave them the space to swing their slings. Their lead bullets were innocuous enough in appearance, but when released from the whirling weapons they struck with sufficient power to punch through armour plate. As men and horses began to take casualties on either side of the cataphract's formation, riders turned their beasts and went after the lightly equipped skirmishers, only to watch in frustration as they scurried back into the legion's line, leaving their would be assailants dangerously exposed to the archers who were loosing arrows at them at no more than twenty paces. Julius nodded in satisfaction as the slingers darted out to loose their deadly missiles again, taunting the cumbersome cavalrymen as they pecked lethally at the Parthian flanks.

'And if that's bothering them then what's coming next will tear the arse right out of their day.'

Marcus stepped forward from the Tungrian cohort's line, smiling as the long spears to either side of him angled away to make room for his advance. Dubnus turned away from the press of battle for a moment, cupping his hands to bellow the only order he would need to issue to his men.

'Tenth Century, to me! For the Bear!'

Spurred by the reference to their former centurion's memory, his men were up and running from their places beside the Scorpions in an instant, each with his axe gripped in one hand and the other clenched into a fist, pumping their legs to cover the hillside at their best speed. Turning back and hefting his own weapon, he stepped in behind Marcus as the tribune crabbed forward towards the Parthian king with his gladius ready to parry, the longer spatha's lethally sharp blade waiting behind it.

'Osroes! Face me!'

The king's head snapped round at the sound of his name, his eyes visible in his gold-chased helmet's eye slits, locking stares with the Roman as he strode forward. Clad from head to foot in heavy armour, each scale edged with gold or silver in a glorious display of wealth, he paused for no more than a heartbeat before giving combat, raising his shield to match the threat from Marcus's gladius while the mace's many bladed head hovered at his shoulder, ready to strike. A sleet of arrows flew at the horsemen around him as the Hamian archers sought to protect their tribune, a rider behind Osroes falling backwards from his saddle as a well-aimed shot found the heavy chain mail that hung from his helmet to protect his face, brutally smashing the rings into the back of his throat.

'Media!'

The armoured figure stepped in quickly, dispensing with any

subtlety with his first sweeping strike, the mace's viciously sharpened ridges whistling through the air over Marcus's head as he flexed his knees to evade the strike. Lightning-fast despite the weight of his armour, Osroes snapped a foot out to catch the Roman while he was off balance, only to stagger as his intended victim sprang to one side, hammering the flat of his gladius at the outstretched leg hard enough to break the extended knee had it not been protected by overlapping iron scales. The Parthian staggered backwards, his eyes wide with the pain, then reeled as his attacker broke the blade of his spatha against the magnificent helmet with a brutal blow, sending the golden crown flying into the mud. Tossing the weapon's hilt aside he snatched up the king's fallen mace as a pair of unhorsed cataphracts struggled through the press, desperate to rescue their king.

The first of them had drawn his sword, but as he swung the blade back to strike Dubnus stepped in swiftly, hammering the heavy spike that backed his axe's blade hard into the Parthian's scaled chest and dropping him, writhing in agony. He stepped back as half a dozen lances stabbed out at him from the second and third ranks, but Marcus advanced to attack, parrying the other warrior's first sword stroke and then backhanding him with a sweeping mace strike that deformed his helmet, and bounced him off the armoured flank of a dying horse to fall limply into the blood-stained dust. With a savage cry, a rider in the second rank took his chance, jabbing his lance at the Roman while his attention was on the fallen man, catching him unawares and sinking the long spear's leaf-shaped head deep into his right bicep. His face contorting with the pain, Marcus wrenched his arm free, stepping back with his sword hanging limply from nerveless fingers, and the rider spurred his horse forward a precious foot, driving it into the mass of dead and dying animals as he raised the spear overarm, ready for the death stroke.

'For the Bear!'

The first of Dubnus's men to reach the scene thrust his way through the Roman line and leapt forward with utter disregard for his own safety, hacking his blade down into the horse's long face, the force of the blow sending armour scales flying as he killed the animal with a single blow. Collapsing into the churned and bloody dirt, the beast spilt its rider forward at the soldier's feet, and with a brutal economy of effort, the Tungrian wrenched his weapon's blade free, reversing his grip on the axe's handle as he raised it to strike before sinking the thick iron pick deep into the stunned Parthian's face through the mail that hung from his helmet, screaming the cohort's battlecry in his moment of triumph.

'Tungriaaaaa!'

More of Dubnus's Tenth Century were flooding into the fight, each man swinging his axe with a wide-eyed ferocity that had those cataphracts still in control of their mounts frantically seeking to back them out of the fray, knowing that their long lances were too unwieldy and their swords and maces too short to prevent the slaughter of their horses and their own inevitable defeat.

'Forward. Support them!'

With a roar the cohort stepped forward again, their long spears stabbing out at the riders stranded on their immobile horses.

Looking out to the legion's flanks, Scaurus saw the distant silhouettes of horsemen riding around the ends of his legion's line.

'Any moment now . . .'

With a sudden blare of horns the cataphracts were starting to disengage, those men who were able, turning their horses away from the fight and riding back down the hill, their mounts capable of little more than an exhausted trot after the exertion of their charge up the slope only moments before.

'Too late, I'm afraid. Far too late.'

The Roman cavalry bored in from either side of the legion's line, riders bent over their mount's necks to encourage them to their greatest speed as they raced across the hillside in pursuit of their shattered enemy. At their head the legatus could see Felix, his spear held high as he closed on the first of the fleeing cataphracts, Hades seeming to float across the ground such was the speed of his gallop. With a swift adjustment in his saddle, the young prefect lowered his weapon, leaning gracefully out of his saddle to thrust the long blade deep into the unarmoured anus of his target's mount. The horse went down in a flurry of limbs, throwing its rider heavily to the ground as Felix ripped the bloodied spear free and went after his next victim, while a man on his flank reined his horse in and jumped nimbly from the saddle, drawing his sword and standing over the fallen horseman.

Julius shook his head in horrified amazement.

'Is that usual?'

Scaurus shook his head.

'Hardly. But when your enemy has a weakness it's wise to exploit it, I feel. If we allow that many armoured cavalry to escape they'll soon enough regain their wits and come at us again. And all of those surprises we've sprung on them today won't catch them off guard the next time. Let's hope that our men remember that each of the enemy knights they take alive is worth his weight in gold.'

As the cataphractoi retreat quickened to a rout, a single man defied the tide of horseflesh washing back from the Roman line, stepping off his horse and striding forward to the place where his king lay stunned, drawing a long sword with his right hand even as he batted away an axe blade with the mace held in his left. Pivoting to kill the Tungrian behind the blade so quickly that the long sword was free in a shower of blood before his victim's lifeless body could slump into the gore-foamed mud beneath him, he planted his feet firmly over his ruler, snarling defiance at the Romans before him, ready to die in Osroes' defence.

'Hold!'

Marcus stepped forward, his gladius ready to fight but with the empty hand that had held his spatha half raised and covered in the blood running from his wound, the palm wide open. He bellowed at the warrior in Greek.

'Hold! Surrender and the king will live! Look around you!'

The cataphractoi were in full-scale retreat now, harried down the hillside by Phrygian cavalrymen who were taking a savage advantage of their unexpected vulnerability when attacked from the rear.

'You're alone! Throw down your sword, and live to protect your king in captivity!'

The nobleman looked about him again, seeing the spears levelled at him from all sides, then stared back at the tribune before him, clearly reckoning the odds. Marcus shook his head and sheathed his gladius, stepping forward with his right hand dripping blood from the wound to his arm. Face-to-face with the man, close enough to see the hatred in his eyes, he shrugged.

'You can kill me now. But you'll die here beside me, and what will become of your king without you to stand over him?'

The eyes held his own for a long moment before the helmeted head shook in brusque disgust. Sheathing his weapons, the warrior raised his arms and waited in silence for the inevitable. An axe man stepped in behind him, kicking hard at the back of the armoured giant's knee to drop him beside his king. Marcus nodded down at him, reaching down to pick up the king's mace and bellowing a challenge at the soldiers around him.

'*Alive!* The man that harms him pays the price with *me!*'

Narsai reached the safety of the Parthian infantry waiting at the slope's base with the dozen men who remained of his bodyguard trotting on either side.

'Gundsalar!'

The general hurried forward, looking to either side of the king with an expression of hope, but his only answer was a brusque head shake as Narsai pulled the helmet from his head.

'Osroes is fallen. Dead or captured, it makes little difference. Those honourless scum fought us from behind a wall of wood and iron!'

The older man looked up the hill with a calculating expression.

'We have suffered grievously, Your Highness . . .'

He looked at Narsai for guidance, but the king's gaze was locked on the ground.

'Your orders, Highness? In the absence of my king, your word is the army's command.'

The black-armoured monarch looked up.

'So it is . . .'

He sat straighter in his saddle, looking across the ranks of infantry waiting in silence, their faces set hard at the sight of so many dead men and horses scattered down the hill's bloody slope.

'Send our foot to dislodge them from their roost, Gundsalar.'

The general bowed.

'As you wish, Highness.'

He turned away, issuing a volley of orders to the waiting officers, and Narsai turned in his saddle to look back up at the Roman line with a calculating expression.

Scaurus walked across to the line of wooden stakes, shaking his head at the scene of devastation. The corpses of over a hundred magnificent horses were strewn in bloodied heaps across the churned, gore-covered ground, scores more studding the slope where the survivors had been harried back down the hill by Felix's cavalrymen. They were told to take prisoners.

'It worked. There was a part of me that wondered whether the histories were just so much nonsense made up to make the old generals look good, but it actually worked . . .'

He shook his head in bemused regret.

'If only we hadn't been forced to kill so many of these magnificent creatures.'

Julius shrugged.

'I would have been happy to have had a choice in the matter. I've given orders for them to be butchered. We've little enough food, if those bastards decide to keep us penned up here.'

Scaurus winced at the prospect, but gave no sign of countermanding his senior centurion's orders.

'As you decide, First Spear. But I doubt there's much risk of the Parthians trying to stop us leaving.'

He fell silent, and Julius looked up to find him staring down the hill.

'Well now . . .'

The Parthian infantry was marching forward, marshalling to

attack at the slope's foot, densely packed formations of spear men forming a fighting front barely half the width of the defenders' line. Julius stared down at them for a moment before voicing an opinion.

'Really? Are they mad?'

Scaurus shrugged.

'Probably not, but they seem brave enough to follow the orders some fool has given them.'

The two men watched the infantry's slow advance for a moment before Julius turned away, gesturing to his trumpeter.

'Sound the Stand To!'

Marcus had stood a close guard over the Parthian king as half a dozen Tungrians lifted the supine figure onto their shoulders and carried him with appropriate dignity to a spot high on the hill above the line of bolt throwers. The nobleman who had dismounted to protect Osroes had insisted on accompanying his ruler, surrendering his sword to Marcus with a flourish, holding the ornately decorated hilt out to the Roman while the Tungrians around him waited with their own blades ready to strike.

'This is the finest weapon in the whole of my *gund* . . .' He'd searched for the right Greek word for a moment. 'The word means *speira*.'

'Cohort?'

'Close enough. It has been edged with steel from the far south, and will cut cleanly through a silken scarf that is dropped upon the blade. A single blow will cleave an armoured man from his collarbone to his balls, if wielded by an expert.'

Marcus lifted the scabbard with a questioning expression.

'May I?'

The other man nodded, and the sword floated from the leather and gold sheath, perfectly balanced and as light as air.

'A fine weapon.'

Marcus handed the sword to Varus, who had joined him in the fight's aftermath, smiling as the younger man made a single hesitant cut with the weapon under its owner's disapproving eye before returning it to the scabbard. Marcus took the sword back, placing it beside the unconscious king.

'It will be kept safe until the time comes for your release, as will the crown your king was wearing.'

A sudden bray of trumpets pulled their attention back to the legion. The legionaries were hurrying for their positions, and three men looked down the hill over their heads while the Tungrian line reformed in front of them, centurions and chosen men pushing the exhausted soldiers back into their places with shouts and swift, urgent strikes with their sticks.

'An infantry attack. Perhaps your leaders would have done well to combine your foot soldiers with the cavalry, but to throw them in separately seems . . . unwise?'

The Parthian followed his captor's gaze.

'It is not the finest day for the empire, I'll grant you that.'

Marcus bowed.

'I'll leave you here with a few men to keep you safe from interference. My duty lies down there . . .'

He turned to find Dubnus striding up the hill with a forbidding look on his face.

'Orders from the legatus. He said to tell you that this fight's going to be no place for a man with one arm, and he's right. It'll be swords and shields that win this one, and you'll be no use to anyone face down in six inches of piss-foamed mud. Your orders, Tribune, are to stay here and make sure nobody takes a dagger to the king there while we're busy. Tribune Varus is ordered to take your place.'

Varus's face went pale as he absorbed the order. After a moment he looked at Marcus with an almost questioning expression, and the tribune nodded reluctantly, wearily waving his friends away.

'Go and do your duty. I'll watch over our guest. And you, Vibius Varus . . .'

His colleague turned back to look up at Marcus.

'No stupidity, Tribune. If you're going to sacrifice yourself then at least go to meet your ancestors with some style, not fighting a mob of half-trained peasants.'

The younger man nodded and was away down the slope, leaving Marcus staring at Dubnus with a raised eyebrow.

'Will you watch him for me?'

The big man nodded, his lips twisting in a mocking smile.

'Cocidius knows I've had enough practice.'

He winked at his friend and turned away down the slope to his men, shouting orders and spitting bombast as he strode back into their midst.

'Now *there's* a man who could give me a fight . . .'

The tribune turned to find the big Parthian at his shoulder, staring after Dubnus with a wistful look in his eye and unconsciously stroking his pointed beard.

'I could have taken you with one good arm.'

His prisoner guffawed at the suggestion.

'I would have bested you in a dozen heartbeats if you had three arms, but you had already earned your *hunar* by the time I faced you.'

He turned a level gaze on Marcus.

'The warrior, my friend, is the only member of society willing to sacrifice himself for the good of those men who sit at ease among their wives and children, and thus he learns to respect the *hunar* displayed by his brothers and those against whom he fights. And no true warrior could have shamed himself by taking his iron to a man who stopped fighting to preserve the life of a fallen king.'

'*Hunar?*'

The noble laughed curtly.

'You Romans may have heard of it, although your ways of fighting show little evidence of such a familiarity. *Hunar* is a man's most noble ornament, not simply his skill at arms but his willingness to use it, to risk a fitting death. His manliness, his—'

'Virtus. What you call "hunar", we call virtus.'

'Vir-toos.'

The big man rolled the word in his mouth.

'Well you, Roman, have vir-toos. I saw you challenge my king to single combat, and I saw you put him down as easily as if you were simply sparring on the training ground. And your men fight like uncaged beasts in your presence, each of them seeking to outdo your prowess.'

Marcus laughed.

'The Tungrians? That's just how they are. Experience has taught them that they are more likely to stay intact going forward than if they were to show an enemy their backs.'

The other man nodded sagely.

'Your words have the power to wound, given my men's defeat.'

He held out a hand.

'I am Gurgen, my king's *bidaxs*, first among his nobles, the fastest sword, the best saddle and the man with more vir-toos than any other knight of my king's court.'

Marcus made the clasp with him.

'And I am Marcus, a tribune of the Third Legion. Shall we watch the battle together and see which of our armies has the better of it?'

Sanga and Saratos obeyed the order to stand to with little more enthusiasm than their comrades, taking their places in the Ninth Century's front line beside each other and staring down the slope at the enemy infantry as they manoeuvred from column to line, spreading along the legion's frontage. The Dacian nudged Sanga, inclining his head to indicate the young tribune who had been keeping company with Marcus. Shorn of his friend, Varus was standing out before the cohort and watching the oncoming enemy infantry, one hand unconsciously fretting at the hilt of his sword.

'He looking for a fight to jump into, eh?'

Sanga shrugged, muttering a reply under his breath.

'Better him than me. And since that's the one who stood and watched the goat fuckers slaughter his cohort I won't be in any hurry to pull his nuts out of the fire . . .'

They watched the Parthian infantry for a moment, grinning at the distant shouts and screams of the enemy officers as they pushed and kicked their men into line. Sanga shook his head, his practised eye having already spotted a weakness in the formation facing them.

'Whoever ordered that lot to attack must be fucking insane. They're going to have open flanks on both sides.'

Saratos nodded at the observation. There were probably as many men facing the Third Legion as there were in the Roman line, but the spear men were arrayed four men deep.

'Why the fuck they have so short a line?'

Sanga shrugged, but the young tribune in front of them answered the question without turning.

'I saw them fight, on the day I stood and watched *the goat fuckers slaughter my cohort...*'

Sanga's ears reddened with embarrassment.

'They present four spearheads to every man facing them, the front ranker stabbing at any target in front of him. The men behind him use their spear in support, attacking any man who looks like presenting him with a threat.'

'Present with threat, Tribune?'

Varus turned to look at Saratos with a half-smile.

'If you look dangerous, Soldier, they will point their spears at you to keep their comrade safe. Wait until we're face-to-face with them, and then see if you fancy going in with your sword against that many long spears. It should be interesting.'

He turned back to his consideration of the Parthian line which, now more or less formed, had lurched into action to the sound of horns.

'Although I don't think they have any idea the size of the hornet's nest they're about to stick their spears into.'

Marcus and Gurgen watched in silence as the spear men advanced in near silence towards the legion waiting for them.

'Your men are battle hardened?'

The Roman shook his head.

'Not for the most part. My Tungrians though . . .'

The Parthian nodded.

'They are clearly used to the horror. The way they attacked

us was magnificent. But those spears coming for your men have all seen battle.'

Marcus frowned.

'Who have they fought against? Not Rome. Surely you can't believe that rolling over a single weakened cohort doesn't count for much experience?'

Gurgen grinned at him wolfishly.

'You will be aware that Armenia has recently allied itself with the King of Kings?'

'Of course. King Sohaemus was an old man, and when he . . .'

He fell silent, looking at the Parthian intently for a moment.

'Sohaemus didn't die of natural causes, did he?'

The big man shrugged.

'He was indeed an old man, at least as old as the King of Kings. My master Osroes was gifted the throne of Media in order to raise an army strong enough to invade Armenia and remove that old man from his throne. His brother Arsakes now rules Armenia.'

'And the threat of an Armenian invasion of Parthia in support of Rome is wiped from the board.'

Marcus nodded.

'A sound strategy, and one which explains why King Osroes' army is so strong in infantry.'

Gurgen nodded, smoothing his heavy moustache.

'Cavalry alone could never take a mountainous kingdom such as Armenia. And in the process of that swift subjugation the men behind those spears saw battle on more than one occasion. Those are well-trained men, hardened by their harsh way of life in the hills and mountains of Media. Men who have been blooded. Perhaps you will be my captive before the sun touches the horizon?'

The Roman shrugged in his turn.

'Perhaps. Either way we'll know soon enough.'

The enemy spear men advanced until they were fifty paces from the legion's line, halting at the sounding of a long horn blast to dress their ranks, made ragged by stepping over and around the dead men and horses strewn across their path. Silence fell across the battlefield, the only noise the isolated shouts and imprecations of individual officers on both sides of the space between the two armies as they corrected real or imagined faults in their men's positioning. Sanga looked across the gap between the two armies, seeing in the enemies' faces the same mix of fear, determination and pure bloody anticipation that he knew they would be seeing as they stared back at the Roman line. A voice was raised from somewhere close by, the shout drawing a chorus of dry chuckles from the men around him.

'Come on then, you fagots! We don't have all day for you to paint your fucking faces!'

The horn blew again, and with a collective battle cry the Parthians started forward at a fast walk, their spears still held aloft as they closed the gap between them and the waiting legionaries.

'Ready . . .'

Sanga nodded dourly at Varus's warning, his knuckles white around the shaft of his spear. The oncoming Parthians were forty paces distant, then thirty, their pace increasing as if they knew they were vulnerable in the last few moments before impact with the legion's line. The horn sounded again, and with perfect coordination, the oncoming Parthians swung their weapons down to point at the Romans, repeating the booming battle cry.

'Ready . . .'

The veteran soldier shot a quick glance at his tribune, but Varus's attention was utterly consumed by the Parthians. Looking back at the enemy, Sanga was just in time to see them reach the point where the fallen cavalry horses lay scattered in front of heavy wooden stakes, their immobile bulk forcing the spear men to break ranks to negotiate the twin barriers. A trumpet sounded from the hill's crest, and Varus bellowed the command every man in the cohort knew was coming.

'Front rank – throw!'

The cohort's front rank took a single step forward and launched their spears at the struggling Parthians, dropping to one knee to make room for the men behind them. Their weapons, deliberately thrown high to loft them over the enemy shields, arced down into the infantrymen to kill the unwary, and force those men who saw them coming to raise their shields in self-defence, and while they were still reeling from the first volley, Varus barked a fresh command.

'Second rank – throw!'

The rear rankers slung their spears with a flatter trajectory, razor-sharp iron heads flying into the enemy line with all the power they were capable of putting into the throw. Fresh carnage erupted along the Parthian line, as men with shields still raised against the initial attack received a volley delivered at waist height. Dozens of the men facing the Third Cohort fell in agony, clutching at their wounds as blood sprayed onto ground already soaked in the gore left by the previous attack.

'Swords!'

Varus had his own gladius free of its scabbard, and raised it over his head as he started forward, bellowing an incoherent battle cry.

'Fuck me!'

Sanga gaped at the sight of the lone tribune striding forward quickly at the enemy line, his pace accelerating to a trot. Suddenly Sanga was running in the officer's wake, his thighs pounding with the effort to overtake the younger man, knowing from the sound of running footsteps in the battlefield's blood- and urine-soaked mud that Saratos was a half-pace behind him. Behind them, barely audible over the screaming of the Parthian wounded, he heard Dubnus's gruff voice bark a harsh command from behind the cohort's line.

'Tungrians! Advance!'

A swift rearward glance confirmed the command. With a collective roar that seemed to pick the veteran soldier up and throw him headlong at the Parthian line, the cohort was on the attack, striding purposefully towards the halted enemy in a line of shields through which the blades of their swords flickered with every stride like shining iron teeth. The veteran soldier sprinted towards the ranks of spear men in the tribune's wake, leaping to hurdle a dead horse as Varus ran headlong into the enemy line. Using his shield more as a battering ram than for protection, the tribune burst through the first rank who were still struggling to reform from the impact of the Roman spears, scattering men in all directions, then took his sword to the Parthians with berserk fury. Curling his lips in an animal snarl, he buried the gladius's blade deep in a reeling spear man's neck, twisting the blade and tearing it free with a bestial howl of triumph before swinging to find a new target, the dying man's blood speckled across his face and chest.

The Parthians were trying to fight back, but their long spears were suddenly worse than unwieldy against a gore-spattered berserker within their own ranks. A desperate lunge by one of the rear rankers went wide of its target as the shaft was battered aside by the press of men recoiling from the sudden threat, spitting a front ranker through the back and leaving him tottering, staring in disbelief at the long blade protruding from his belly. Throwing down their spears, the men around Varus reached for their long knives, flashing the blades with a sudden yellow gleam of afternoon sunlight on polished metal, closing around the Roman with murderous intent.

Sanga smashed into the Parthian line's chaos, shield first, sending men preoccupied with killing Varus sprawling in all directions, while Saratos strode into the fight an instant later, systematically setting about the nearest of the enemy soldiers as they reeled from the fresh attack. The two men struck swiftly, both knowing that to stand still among so many of the enemy was to die, thrusting with fast, brutal stabbing stokes that sent them reeling back with blood spraying from their wounds, whipping their blades back to strike again. Sanga stepped forward to block a knife thrust aimed at his comrade's back with his shield, then killed the Parthian behind the blade with a swing of his sword that almost decapitated him, while Saratos, trusting his friend to guard his back, took his iron to a pair of men threatening Varus in his blood-soaked rampage.

Hamstringing the first, dropping him screaming into the bloody filth underfoot, he punched the point of his sword through the other's spine, kicking the nerveless corpse off the blade and turning to bellow his defiance at the men backing away from the bloody trio. As the rest of the Tungrians stormed into the Parthians, the lines of men staring in horror at the blood-soaked tribune and the two soldiers who had hacked their way to his side shivered and then scattered, hurling away their long spears and taking to their heels in the face of the ferocious Roman attack.

Staggering with exhaustion, Varus raised his sword at their fleeing backs, shaking his head in disgusted frustration before throwing the weapon blade first into the battlefield's foaming mud.

'Come back you cowards! You gutless bastards! Will none of you give me a proper fight?'

His own legs shaking with reaction to the sudden, bloody fight, Sanga grabbed at Saratos's arm to stop himself from falling, while the Dacian just stood and stared at the blood-soaked tribune as Varus bent, grasping his knees and vomiting into the battle-field's reeking mud.

Gurgen spat on the ground and turned away in disgust.

'This day will long be remembered in our history as a day of *margazan* . . .' He paused for a moment, looking at the ground. 'A day of infamy, marked by defeat and cowardice that has blackened the name of Media. To flee from the enemy twice in the same battle . . .'

'Your men were poorly used.'

The noble shrugged away Marcus's attempt to comfort him.

'It is true. And it matters little. For warriors, men sworn to die in the name of their king, to then run from the face of that death when it is before them? To die fulfilling the oath is to be blessed beyond compare, the finest fate a warrior of the empire can seek! Every man dies, Roman, from the greatest of kings to the meanest of beggars. The only true measure of a man is the way in which he dies. Or fails to live true to his word.'

He turned to face Marcus.

'You have taken prisoners.'

The Roman nodded.

'Then I ask you to take us to them. Let the men who have surrendered their warrior's virtue look upon the face of the king to whom they swore their oath of victory or death.'

Dubnus walked the bloodied tribune back up the hill to where Marcus had watched the battle, his face grim and a pair of blood-spattered soldiers following him, shaking his head at Varus's back as the young aristocrat stood staring blankly down at what remained of the Parthian infantry's failed assault.

'This young gentleman seems to have taken up where you left off, Tribune Corvus. He stormed the Parthian line single-handed, threw himself onto their spears and generally behaved more like a man seeking death than a senior officer.'

Marcus raised a wry eyebrow.

'I saw the whole thing. Who were the men who went in after him?'

'The usual suspects.'

He hooked a thumb over his shoulder at the soldiers waiting in silence behind him, and Marcus nodded his understanding.

'I see. To be expected, I suppose. Did they do so without being ordered?'

Dubnus nodded grimly.

'Half of their fucking century went in after them, which meant that the rest of the cohort was about two paces behind.'

'Which made the rest of the legion follow them in. It could have been a disaster.'

'So, what do you want me to do with them?'

Marcus stared hard at the two men, his face set hard.

'You two might have been responsible for the death of every man on this hillside, you do realise that? If the Parthians had managed to set themselves up properly and take their spears to you, the whole thing would have ended in a bloodbath.'

He walked away, gesturing for Dubnus to join him. His friend turned a hard stare on the two soldiers, gesturing at them with his vine stick.

'Wait here, you pair of cocksuckers. And I don't remember telling you to stand easy Sanga, so get your fucking chin tucked back in!'

Tribune and first spear shared a moment of silence for a moment, looking out over the battlefield's ruined terrain. Dozens of legionaries were carrying the dead and wounded into the legion's perimeter, stacking the Parthian and Roman dead in two separate rows.

'What were your casualties this time?'

The big man pulled a tablet from his belt pouch.

'Less than I'd expected. Thirteen dead and twice as many wounded.'

'Officers?

'None of the centurions, Cocidius be praised. One chosen man stopped a spear with his thigh, so he'll be out of action for a while.'

'You'll be promoting a watch officer to replace him?'

Dubnus looked at him for a moment.

'Really? You want to reward that act of idiocy with promotion?'

His friend shrugged.

'The man to blame here is Varus, and don't think that I won't be making that clear to him, once I think there's a chance he might actually hear what I've got to say. All those two did was exactly the same thing that other men have done for me on more than one occasion, when the blood rage has overcome me. And besides . . .'

The two men walked back to where Sanga and Saratos stood waiting to attention, Dubnus stopping in front of them with less than a foot between his face and Sanga's.

'You're a pair of lucky men. Left to my own judgement, I'd just have had you both beaten half to death, but my superior officer here has a different idea. And since, as we all know, superior officers exist for the sole purpose of never being wrong in any matter, his suggestion is my command. You will transfer to the Fourth Century, under Centurion Otho, as watch officers.'

He waited for the words to sink in, smirking as Sanga's eyes widened.

'That's right, no good deed goes unpunished. You pair of idiots can pay for this example of selfless heroism by helping Otho to keep a tight lead on his boys, not that he needs much help given that he put the last man to go against him in hospital with a broken jaw. I'd say you'll be less worried about keeping order and more concerned with making sure he doesn't have an excuse to do the same to you. Dismissed.'

Sanga opened his mouth to comment, closing it again as his first spear's eyes narrowed threateningly.

'Yes Centurion!'

The veteran frowned at his friend's prompt salute, then followed Saratos's example before they turned away down the hill. When the two men were out of earshot he whispered a furious protest, clenching his fist in anger.

'Cunt! Of all the bastards to end up soldiering for, it had to be that old fucker Otho!'

The big Dacian shrugged.

'You and me, we get more money, we get to say who clean out latrine. Is good for me.'

His comrade shook his head in disbelief.

'En't you been listening when the stories get told about our new centurion? He's—'

'Bastard fucker of mother, I know this. But I also know that me and you hard enough to make him happy. And me? I going to be centurion, you wait and see. You be my chosen, no?'

Sanga laughed despite himself.

'Fuck you! *You* can be *my* chosen!'

Saratos smiled inwardly as his friend shook his head and pointed at a section of the Tungrian line.

'Come on, let's go and present ourselves to the crusty old bastard.'

A party of Tungrians carried Osroes' unconscious body over the hill's shallow crest with Marcus and Gurgen following behind, the blood-spattered Varus walking quietly in their wake. The Parthian prisoners had been herded into a square encampment whose edges were delineated by a shallow ditch that had been hastily excavated by the century guarding them. As the two men watched, a fresh group of disarmed spear men were ushered in to join their fellows under the watchful spears of the sentries posted around them.

'We should be grateful that our prisoners have not been slaughtered on the spot? This is the usual Roman way of things, I believe?'

Marcus inclined his head in acceptance of the implied rebuke.

'It has happened. I have seen badly wounded captives given the mercy stroke to spare their suffering, and doubtless there have been occasions between our two peoples where men have been killed where they might have been made prisoner. The events that followed the battle of Carrhae are still a raw memory for many Romans.'

Gurgen nodded sombrely in turn.

'It is true. And the presence of so many disarmed men shames me further, for if we had fought with more conviction, perhaps more of these cowards would have been killed on the battlefield, rather than finding themselves stripped of their manhood.'

Marcus led the men carrying the king down the slope and through the ring of guards, greeting their centurion's crisp salute with a raised left hand.

'What state are these men in, Centurion?'

The older man grimaced, looking out over the prisoners, whose numbers had swollen to over five hundred with the additional infantrymen captured during their rout.

'Not good, Tribune. There are thirty or so we think are going to die, given the nature of their wounds, about a hundred who'll probably survive, for the most part, if they get some treatment, and the rest . . .'

'Yes?'

'The rest of them, Tribune, are just plain pissed off. *Badly* pissed off.'

Marcus looked at him, taking his gauge of the man and finding him both steady enough and at the same time clearly worried by the situation.

'Not the time to lighten the guard on them then?'

The centurion smiled wryly.

'Not unless we fancy five hundred angry warriors rampaging through the field hospital.'

He tipped his head at the medical tents beyond his men's cordon.

'I'd recommend that another century join us, but then I would, wouldn't I.'

'I see. And have they been given water?'

The centurion had the good grace to look sheepish.

'I thought not. Very well, send a runner to First Spear Julius, with the message that we need water and rations here, and quickly. Give them food and it'll give them something else to think about. And ask for another century to join the guard.'

The officer saluted with a look of relief and went about his instructions, and Dubnus took a hold of Marcus's wrist as he turned towards the Parthians.

'You can't go in there. What if they take you prisoner? Or just tear you limb from limb?'

The younger man grinned wolfishly at his friend.

'Why do you think I didn't send you to Julius with that message?'

He tapped the handle of the massive axe slung over his friend's shoulder.

'This is all the protection I need.'

He strode out into the space where the Parthians had been herded, knowing that every able-bodied man inside the ring of spears would kill a Roman tribune in an instant given the chance. Dubnus walked close behind him, muttering quietly under his breath.

'Walks into a pack of wolves and then tells me *I'm* responsible for his safety . . .'

Stopping in the middle of the impromptu encampment, Marcus stared around him, met on every side by hostile stares. Raising his voice to be heard by the prisoners, he called out in Greek to be sure that he was understood.

'You have been left without water! I apologise for that oversight! Water and food are being fetched! You will receive medical attention shortly! And to show our good intentions towards you, here is your king!'

He waited until his words had been translated into Pahlavi, then beckoned the party carrying Osroes forward, and the eyes of every man shifted from the Roman to the supine body of their king, many of them looking away as they met Gurgen's ferocious stare.

'You!'

A man in cavalry dress stepped out at the noble's barked command, his armour stripped away to reveal a padded tunic and leggings.

'Your king lives! Prostrate yourself before your king!'

The warrior fell to his knees, throwing himself full length in the act of proskynesis.

'All of you! The king lives!'

Marcus watched as every man within the ring of sentries repeated the gesture, nodding at the noble's brutal but effective tactic to take a grip of the situation.

'You seem to have this under control. I'm going to find some medical assistance.'

Gurgen inclined his head in thanks, then turned away barking out a string of orders at the captives while Marcus and Dubnus backed quietly out of the enclosure.

'Medical assistance? Where are you going to get that from?'

The young tribune smiled, peeling back the rough bandage that covered his wounded arm.

'Watch and learn. Come along Vibius Varus, we'll have you checked out as well.'

Nodding respectfully to the soldier being treated by the legion's senior doctor, Marcus squatted down to watch as the medicus extracted a barbed arrowhead from the soldier's leg with the aid of a pair of curved bronze blades, using the blunt metal probes to shield the flesh from the wicked iron barbs while he carefully extricated it from the sweating legionary's wounded limb.

'Neat work.'

Dubnus leaned in close, drawing an irritated glance from the doctor.

'I don't think your wife could have done it very much better.'

The soldier closed his eyes with relief as his thigh was bandaged tightly, a spoonful of honey having been coaxed into the bloody pocket in his flesh to the general approval of the men watching. Choosing to target his ire on the largest but most junior of the three officers, the harassed-looking medicus poked a finger into the Briton's chest, much to the bearded centurion's amusement.

'Are you two here to take the piss, or does he want that treating? Because if he does *you* can just—'

'Neither. What I want, doctor, is a *doctor*. For them.'

Raising his bandaged arm with a wince, he pointed at the enemy prisoners, now grouped together under the spears of two full centuries of legionaries. The doctor shook his head.

'Out of the question. We've still got hours of work to do to get our own men treated.'

He turned back to the next soldier in the queue, only to discover that Marcus had stepped in closer to him.

'You know as well as I do that there isn't any hurry to get most of these men treated. We won't be marching east any time before tomorrow morning. But half of those prisoners over there are likely to die if they go a night without treatment . . .'

He paused for a moment to allow the point to sink in.

'And believe me, they will recall very clearly the treatment they receive from us. If we allow their wounded to die untreated, then I doubt they'll handle us any better, should our luck run out between here and Nisibis. And let's face the facts here, Medicus, in the event that they do manage to roll over us, you're not likely to enjoy the luxury of a good death in combat, are you? I hear the Parthians aren't above skinning and salting men who arouse their particular enmity.'

The youngest of the legion's doctors stepped into the ring of sentries set to guard the prisoners, followed by half a dozen bandage carriers. Marcus looked behind him, but the medicus shook his head with a grimace.

'I'm all you're getting, I'm afraid. I'll sort out the treatable casualties from those whose time to greet their ancestors is upon them, and these gentlemen can visit their skills upon the least badly wounded. The rest of them we'll treat in the order of the likelihood of their recovery, shall we?'

Marcus nodded, turning away and speaking over his shoulder.

'Do the best you can with what you have.'

He strode deeper into the captives, Dubnus and Varus close behind.

'We have a doctor, and bandage carriers to stop the bleeding for those of you who look likely to live!'

An unarmoured cavalryman called out, his voice torn by anguish.

'And what if they look likely to die?'

The Roman paused, then turned and walked over to the bearded warrior. At his feet a younger man lay still, his breathing little better than a series of shallow panting gasps so slight that he seemed barely alive.

'This man behind me speaks no Greek, but he reads a man's face and body as well as anyone I know. Move swiftly at your peril.'

The Parthian nodded grimly.

'My son's wound . . . he will die, but slowly.'

'I see. This is a painful moment for you then. Do you wish to ease his death?'

The warrior nodded, swallowing painfully as his enemy became his confessor.

'Yes. If I can do so with honour.'

Without hesitation Marcus drew his dagger, passing it to the other man haft first, looking his enemy in the eye.

'Ease your son's path to the underworld. The blade has honour.'

The other man nodded, then bent to perform the mercy stroke, holding his son as the man's life left him. When there was nothing left in his arms but a corpse, he gently lowered the body to the bloodied grass, then stood, handing the weapon back to his captor.

'You are indeed a man of honour, Tribune Corvus . . . for a Roman.'

He turned to find Gurgen standing beside Dubnus.

'It was done well, and since the boy was one of my own, you have my thanks again, for that and for bringing your doctors to care for our wounded. The king is awake, although I doubt he knows very much of his whereabouts. His eyes are open, but he cannot speak and his body is limp.'

The Roman made his way to where Osroes lay, touching his head where the hair was matted with blood. The flesh beneath was taut, swollen with fluid, and hot; the king stiffened at the touch, his body shuddering with pain. Marcus stood, gesturing to the men clustered around their ruler.

'Bring him. He needs to be treated now.'

Looking at Gurgen, the warriors waited until he nodded his approval, then lifted their king's body from the ground with delicate care. The medicus took one look at their burden and pointed to the strip of ground where those men unlikely to survive were being placed to meet their fate.

'Put him over there. There are men here with more pressing needs.'

Marcus shook his head.

'Not unless any of them happen to be the king of a bigger kingdom than Media there aren't.'

The doctor frowned up at him.

'I fail to see—'

'Clearly you do. So let me make this a little clearer for your limited experience of this sort of situation. If this man dies then these others behind me will turn into a pack of wolves, and will almost certainly have to be put down to the last man. Which would be a waste of your handiwork, to say the least. On top of that, consider the implications for the likelihood of our being able to make it to Nisibis, if we allow this most important of hostages to slip through our fingers.'

The doctor nodded slowly, then gestured to the men bearing the king's body to lay him down for treatment.

'And if I can't save him?'

'Then you will have tried with all of your skill, and these gentlemen watching will doubtless be understanding . . .'

8

It was late in the day before a party rode up the hill, now bathed in the descending sun's soft, golden light, and demanded to speak with Scaurus, who quite properly made them wait while he finished a plate of freshly cooked horse meat before choosing to answer the peremptorily worded summons. Strolling down the hill from his command tent to the line of legionaries standing guard on the defensive line in the company of Julius, a century of armed and armoured legionaries and a pair of hooded prisoners, he found a dozen lance-armed cataphracts waiting impassively behind two lavishly armoured men on magnificently decorated horses.

'Good evening, Your Highnesses. Perhaps you'll join me? I find myself with a bit of a stiff neck after a day spent looking down at your failed efforts to knock me off my perch.'

He waited in silence while Narsai and Wolgash looked at each other and then dismounted at his suggestion, smiling slightly at Narsai's sour expression at having his attempted position of superiority dismissed.

'We demand that—'

'You demand, King Narsai? I wouldn't have thought you were in much of a position to be demanding anything. What is it that you'd like to *request* from me?'

Narsai took a deep breath before replying, clearly unused to having his pronouncements interrupted.

'Release our cousin, and then we can negotiate your departure from this place. I am willing to allow you—'

Scaurus raised a hand to stop him, shaking his head in genuine amusement.

'Let me guess. You're willing to allow my legion to march back to the west, just as long as I surrender my prisoners to you. Is that it, Your Highness?'

Narsai stood in silence, glowering at the Roman.

'I'll take your silence as an affirmation of my surmise, shall I? So, if I'm good enough to hand over the large number of prisoners I currently hold, you'll be magnanimous enough to let me scurry away back to Zeugma, will you?'

Wolgash opened his mouth to speak, but found himself silenced by Narsai's raised arm.

'Take the chance now, while you still have it, Roman. The alternative is—'

Scaurus shook his head emphatically.

'No. The alternative, Your Highness, is to sit here, eat some more of the excellent horseflesh you've been good enough to deliver to my doorstep, and wait to see which of us blinks first. And before you start issuing dire warnings as to what you're going to do to us all when we eventually surrender, let me point out one or two things to you.'

He waved a hand at the hillside, and the unbroken line of legionnaires resting in their places, ready to defend the position.

'Firstly, you will note that my legion is still effectively untouched. Your archers were unable to pierce our shields, your cataphracts did no more than ride to their bloody ruin against our defences, and your infantry . . . gods below man, what were you thinking? You had all the individual elements of victory, but you sent them at us one at a time, and squandered their collective power.'

He looked at the king for a moment with the disgust of a man trained from youth to spend his men's lives carefully.

'Your lack of caution has cost many men's lives today. And not just men . . .'

He looked along the legion's line in both directions, shaking his head in genuine regret at the slaughtered beasts that were still being butchered under the watchful eyes of the legion's archers.

'Ignoring whatever your motivation for sacrificing your foot soldiers might have been, I'd say you left a third of your strength in heavy cavalry up here, some of them literally skewered on the stakes that you can see are still ready to greet any further attempt to bludgeon your way through to us. Their deaths were hardly what I'd call noble either, their horses baulked by our defences, hemmed in by the riders behind them, then pulled from their saddles and bludgeoned to death by barbarians recruited in the far north. The remainder were taken down as they stumbled back down the hill, when they realised that they were beaten. It's a sad sight, a war horse dying with a spear shoved up its backside, but fitting, wouldn't you say, given the mess you've made of this battle?'

Narsai glared at him, and the legatus allowed the silence to play out for a moment before speaking again.

'So, you've been bested in battle. And your only consolation is that the moment we stir from this hill you'll have us at your mercy, on flat ground and open for the usual tactics that have served you so well, volley after volley of arrows until we're too weak to resist.'

He clicked his fingers, and a soldier carried forward a shield studded with the shafts of arrows.

'And so I thought this might interest you. Most of my men have cleaned up their shields, and the arrowheads will make a useful contribution to our stocks, but I kept this one as I found it, beside one of the few dozen men who were unlucky or stupid enough to get hit despite having such excellent protection.'

He peeled back the leather cover to reveal the layers of linen beneath.

'These materials make it almost impervious to arrows, unless they're loosed from so close a distance that your archers will find themselves with a face full of legion for their pains. And besides being arrow proof, my men have another defence available to them, kindly donated by yourselves.'

Two more men stepped forward with one of the Parthian captives between them, the armour stripped from his body and a roughly fashioned bag over his head. Scaurus nodded, and the centurion standing behind the prisoner pulled the bag away, leaving him blinking in the evening's sunlight. The black-clad monarch started at the sight of the young rider, his face swollen with the cruel bruising inflicted during his capture.

'This is your son, I believe?'

Narsai nodded, his jaw clenching.

'He'll be treated with all the respect due to a man of royal blood, you can be assured of that. But sadly, should you choose to attempt any attack upon our column, *when* we leave this rather dreary hillside to march on Nisibis, your son, and all our other prisoners, will be placed directly in the places where the arrows will fall the heaviest. I don't think you're going to want to order the deaths of that many members of your aristocracy, and even if you are, I'd imagine that the men waiting for news down there might be a little upset at the thought of their sons, brothers, fathers, and doubtless in some cases their lovers, standing unprotected under that storm of iron.'

He waved a dismissive hand.

'I suggest that you take a while to consider your options. And don't make the mistake of taking me for one of those people who won't follow up on his promises. One thing I am is a man of my word.'

The king of Adiabene stared hard at him for a moment.

'I will have the skin off you before you die, Roman. Slowly enough that you'll take days to die. That is my promise.'

Scaurus's only response was a shrug, but as the fuming king turned away, a hint of mischief touched his face.

'There is one more thing, Narsai. One question you *didn't* ask . . .'

He waited while the two kings turned back, hope in Wolgash's face, dark presentiment in Narsai's scowl.

'I can see you've already guessed what I'm going to tell you. It was the one thing you really wanted to know, wasn't it? After all Narsai, you suddenly find yourself in command of an army far greater than anything you could muster from your own insignificant kingdom. Doubtless you're already scheming to keep control of it, and perhaps even make yourself king of Media, eh? Of course, that won't be easy, not given that Media was a gift from the King of Kings to his son Osroes, but you can hardly turn away the chance to try for it, can you?'

He stared at Narsai for a moment with a calculating look.

'But here's the thing, Narsai. Osroes isn't dead. He's not even properly wounded. He was stunned on the battlefield by an enterprising young tribune of mine, and carried through our line into captivity without having the chance to resist, or to sell his life dearly and die like a king should under such desperate circumstances. And now he's my captive, entirely dependent on me for his life. So if the presence of your son isn't enough to inspire a little caution in you – and let's face it, there's a calculation there, isn't there? A son for a kingdom, perhaps?'

He smiled into Narsai's sudden outrage, patting the hilt of his sword.

'If you were truly furious with me, we'd have these out by now, wouldn't we? There's more calculation in you than meets the eye, I'd say. And remember this. If you attack us before we reach Nisibis, you'll be responsible of the death of the oldest of the King of Kings' sons by your own arrows. Do you think Osroes' father will take that well?'

He clicked his fingers to summon forward the other prisoner, reaching out to remove the man's hood to reveal Gurgen's impassive face.

'And so to make sure that the remaining members of your aristocracy down there get to make a considered decision, I'm returning this man to you, albeit temporarily. He's undertaken to accompany you back to your army, and to explain to his fellow nobles the condition of their king, and what will result from any further attempt to attack us. After which, as he has sworn to the Sun God, he will climb this hill in the morning and surrender himself to us once more.'

Narsai stared at his comrade for a moment, then turned away wordlessly, mounting his horse and pulling its head round to descend the hill, his escort falling in around him. Marcus and Gurgen exchanged glances, the Roman taking stock of the determined glint in the eyes that followed them down the slope.

'May your god watch over you. And if I were you, I'd stay away from that one.'

The prisoner nodded in silent reply, turning to follow his comrades down the golden slope.

'And what the fuck do you pair want?'

Otho's new chosen man hid a smirk behind his hand as the veteran centurion turned to the two soldiers waiting for him to notice them. Both men saluted with a briskness bordering on the punctilious, and the officer's eyes narrowed dangerously.

'Come on, spit it out!'

Sanga took a deep breath.

'Soldiers Sanga and Saratos, Centurion, sent by First Spear Dubnus—'

Otho snorted at the mention of the cohort's new senior centurion's name.

'What's young Dubnus sent me now, a pair of men to replace my casualties?'

Sanga ploughed on, still not meeting the big man's eye.

'Sent by First Spear Dubnus, Centurion, to act as replacements for your watch officer.'

The centurion raised an eyebrow bisected by a thick white scar, putting both hands on his hips as he looked the two soldiers up and down.

'Sent to me by Prince Dubnus, are you? Two men to replace one watch officer? Either you're both something special or so poor that he thinks it'll take two of you to do the job. Or are you special friends who can't be separated?'

A soldier tittered audibly behind him, and he turned to face his men with unexpected speed.

'I heard that, and I know who it was! If I hear it again you'll be out here for a short demonstration of keeping your mouth shut in the ranks.'

The century's men stared to their front with an apparent fixation on the horizon that spoke volumes for their belief that whatever Otho threatened was only ever a heartbeat from actually happening. He turned back to Sanga and Saratos with a questioning look.

'Well then, which is it? Are you future centurions or just the scrapings of another century's latrine sponges?'

Sanga spoke again, his face held in rigid lines despite an almost overwhelming urge to laugh at Otho's goading.

'Centurion sir! First Spear Dubnus and Two Kni . . . Tribune Corvus decided that we are two soldiers who are not entirely without merit, and has decided to assign us to your command in the hope that you'll beat some sense into us both! His exact words, sir!'

A slow, evil smile spread across the centurion's face.

'Did he now? He's a good judge of character, the prince. My character, that is, because beat some sense into the pair of you is exactly what I'll do, if either of you so much as farts in the wrong direction. Won't I?'

The question was directed at the newly promoted chosen man behind him, and the man's answer was both swift and crisp.

'Yes Centurion!'

Otho stepped forward, looking Saratos up and down.

'Nothing to say for yourself? Your mate here doing all the talking?'

The Dacian held his brace position, speaking at the empty air behind the officer's shoulder.

'I nothing to say, Centurion sir! When I something to say, I say it, Centurion sir!'

Otho nodded slowly.

'Good boy. You're the fighter who won the cohort boxing prize, aren't you, the Dacian animal?'

'Yes, Centurion!'

The grin returned.

'Well that *is* good news. I haven't had a decent sparring partner for so long I've almost forgotten how to hit a man.'

He swivelled and scanned the ranks of his century, but nobody was unwise enough to take the bait dangling before them. Slapping a big hand down on the Dacian's shoulder, he hooked a thumb behind him at the waiting ranks.

'Looks like I've got a new sparring partner. Welcome to

the Seventh Century! Your mate can stay too - for the time being.'

'None of you can meet my eye.'

Gurgen spat in the dust at his feet.

'And it's just as well that none of you has the balls to try.'

He looked around the fire where the surviving men of his house were gathered, shaking his head in disgust at them. Their joy at his survival had been fleeting, as his fury at being the only man to have stayed with his king had become apparent. Most of his knights were still armed and armoured for fear that the Romans would mount a night attack, their numbers grievously reduced by the battle's horrific outcome, but the bidaxs had more presence than any of them despite the fact that he was dressed in nothing more impressive than the padded jacket that he had worn beneath his armour before its confiscation.

'Your *king* fell. Your king's *bidaxs* dismounted to make a stand over his body. And you *women* rode for your lives! At least the peasants showed the Romans that they know how to fight and die.'

He lapsed into silence and stared into the flames.

'How many men fell in total?'

His master of horse answered, his voice gruff from the day's exertions.

'Three hundred and forty cataphracti, my Lord, and three times as many horse archers. The foot soldiers lost as many as both put together.'

Gurgen looked up at the stars and allowed a long breath to escape his lungs.

'One third of our knights? The holy fire must be flickering on the altars of Media tonight.'

He fell silent for a moment, then spoke again with a sudden note of curiosity.

'And do I need to ask which fool ordered the infantry to attack unsupported?'

'King Narsai, my Lord.'

Gurgen laughed hollowly.

'I should have known as much. The king's gundsalar would never have been that eager to see his men die for no good reason. Whereas Narsai . . .'

He left the thought unspoken, standing in brooding silence.

'Spread these words to the men of Media. The king lives, and it is our sworn duty to protect his life. These Romans will march east tomorrow, I am sure of this, and they will use him as a living shield, so tell our countrymen that the first of them to loose an arrow before Osroes is freed will pay for it with his life, with my knife to open his belly and my fist to rip his guts out through the bloody hole. And now you can get out of my sight.'

The noble's men left him staring at the fire, going out into the Median army in ones and twos to spread the word as he commanded, while Gurgen faced the flames in silence, brooding on his capture and humiliation long into the night.

'Really, Legatus? We just break camp and march out onto the plain? With that lot waiting for us? Do you think they'll be able to resist the opportunity to get revenge for what we've done to them today?'

Scaurus shrugged, sipping at his wine and looking back at his first spear with an understanding smile. The legatus had gathered his officers, as was now customary once darkness fell, and had led a discussion of the battle's conduct, pointing out where the Parthian leaders had made their biggest mistakes. In the course of the discussion more than one of the young officers had succumbed to sleep and the cups of wine that Scaurus had poured for them, but he simply shook his head when Julius mimed waking the closest of the sleepers.

'Let him sleep. This hill will be as quiet as a freshly dug grave tonight, with our men lying in their tents as still as corpses after the horrors of the day, and he'll need to be bright-eyed in the morning. What that boy needed most was a decent drink of unwatered wine to numb him enough to let him sleep. Let's leave the night's work to those of us who've been here enough times to cope with the shock, shall we? And while I know it seems unlikely that the Parthians will allow us to march, I'd bet that rascal Morban all the gold in my chest that they will. Pass me some more of that horse meat, will you Tribune?'

The flickering light of the fire around which the legion's officers had gathered coloured his face as he chewed a piece of cold meat, nodding with pleasure as he wiped his lips with the back of his hand.

'Splendid. How quickly we forget the simpler pleasures in life. With a cup of wine in my hand, my belly full of freshly slaughtered horse and a fire to warm my toes, it's almost enough to make me forget the fact that there are a rather large number of angry soldiers waiting for us just outside of bowshot. You *did* put out listening patrols, I presume?'

Julius snorted.

'I put out *fighting* patrols, Legatus, a selection of each cohort's nastiest soldiers. I also tasked Centurion Qadir to take a few of his best infiltrators forward to make sure that the Parthians aren't planning anything clever under the cover of dark. I've got no intention of being nailed to this fucking hillside by an arrow in my sleep.'

He took a sip of his own wine, winking at his superior with a hard smile.

'So, you were saying, Legatus?'

Scaurus grinned back at him, amused by the responses of those tribunes who were still awake to such familiarity.

'Don't look so troubled, gentlemen. The first spear and I have endured enough together that neither of us needs to stand on ceremony with the other. If any of you should rise to a position of responsibility for this many men, then trust me, you'll either be on very good terms with the man who does most of the hard work in leading the legion, or you'll regret it soon enough. And you could all do worse than cultivate an equally frank relationship with your own first spears. Which in your case, Vibius Varus, since Tribune Corvus has managed to get himself wounded, is a man almost as fierce as Julius here.'

He winked at Varus, who inclined his head in acceptance of the point.

'I'll be careful to treat First Spear Dubnus with the greatest of respect, Legatus.'

Julius snorted into his wine, and Scaurus raised an eyebrow at him in silent question.

'I was thinking, Legatus, that the task of keeping a close eye on Tribune Varus here ought to be meat and drink to *First Spear* Dubnus . . .'

He grinned again at the oddity of using the title to describe his former centurion.

'Given that all he's done for the last four years is pull another young maniac's balls out of the fire every time he tries to get himself killed. I think you'll fit in here just perfectly, Tribune.'

Gurgen climbed back up the slope soon after first light, stopping at the first challenge and allowing himself to be searched before he was led to the command tent. Scaurus greeted him with an easy smile.

'You came back then? Julius here was convinced you'd either think better of your oath or that you'd be face down with a knife in your back.'

The red-haired warrior turned a disparaging gaze on the senior centurion.

'He does not speak Greek?'

Scaurus shook his head.

'Then please be so good as to explain to him the importance of an oath to a man of honour.'

The legatus raised his eyebrows in amusement.

'He understands the concept only too well, but like most of my people, he struggles to connect it with barbarian peoples outside the empire's frontiers. You're much the same in that respect, I suspect. So tell me, what happened last night? How did your people take the news of Osroes' capture?'

The Parthian shrugged.

'Much as you would expect. Some argued that we should appoint a new king and declare Osroes lost, others that to abandon the King of Kings' son would be a disastrous mistake and bring even greater dishonour upon us all than already taints our worthless lives.'

'And?'

'And the army decided to honour the king. There will be no attack on your legion while you hold him. But what can you hope to achieve, Roman? You say you will march for Nisibis, but when you reach the city, what then? Narsai will lay siege to its walls, and you are a long way from your empire. Narsai is telling the tribes that your governor in Antioch will not raise a finger to assist you, corrupt and soft as he is, and that you are a single weakened legion, with no hope of reinforcement, marching into a sea of your enemies.'

He fell silent, and Scaurus shrugged with a smile.

'And he's right, of course. We'll march to Nisibis with your army trailing us all the way like a pack of hungry dogs, and when we arrive in the city we will doubtless present the man commanding the defence with a good-sized problem, being as we're carrying no more than two days' rations. But be assured, we will make that march.'

'Why?'

The legatus stared at his prisoner for a moment before speaking, finding the answer to the man's question in his eyes.

'You already know why. Because I'm a soldier in the service of my emperor. Because it's my duty. You would do exactly the same in my place.'

The Parthian nodded.

'I believe I would. Even if it meant my death, and those of the men serving me.'

The legion marched off the hill soon after, leaving nothing more than the stripped carcasses of several hundred dead horses for the flies, while the Parthian dead were laid out in tidy rows, their bodies wrapped tightly in their cloaks. The enemy's corpses had been carefully protected from the sorts of desecrations that were usual under such bitter circumstances. Each cohort formed up in their turn with swift precision and took their place in the line of march down the hill, the centurions pacing alongside them following the leading officer's example and striding out in front of their men as they led their centuries down the hill and through the Parthians in a deliberate show of bravado. Scaurus had attended Julius's centurions' meeting that morning, looking round at his officers with a grim smile.

'That army down there is too big to go round without making it look like an admission of weakness, so you're going to have to march straight through them. And I think we can be reasonably sure that they're not going to like it. I'm going to use the Tungrian cohorts as my advance guard, so they'll be—'

'Legatus?'

He'd turned to find that Cassius Ravilla had stepped forward, his punctilious salute at odds with the irritated expression on his face.

'Procurator?'

'My marines have marched with you, drilled with you, and fought with you, not that we saw much of the fighting yesterday at the far end of the line. To be frank with you, Legatus, we're getting a little tired of being regarded as just here to make the numbers up and be the butt of your men's ribaldry.'

'And you'd like to lead your cohort down into that angry mob as the vanguard? When any mistake might start another full-scale battle?'

Ravilla had nodded.

'My marines have discipline, Legatus, and they won't offer the Parthians a fight unless there's no alternative, but they also have more courage than you're giving them credit for. And I'll tell you what else they have . . .'

Scaurus had raised an eyebrow.

'They have Greek, Legatus. At least half my men have a decent command of the language, which isn't surprising given they've served all over the Middle Sea. If you send them down the hill first they'll be a lot more capable of communicating with those barbarians than your Tungrians.'

'And if the Parthians don't just move out of the way?'

Ravilla had turned his head to look at Julius with his lower jaw thrust out.

'My boys won't start any fights they don't have to, not with the situation already as tense as it is, but neither will they step back, First Spear, I can assure you of that. And neither will I.'

Legatus and first spear exchanged glances, and Julius shrugged.

'Why not? The procurator has a point about our lads not speaking the language. The only thing they'll be able to communicate will be with their swords and shields.'

Scaurus had nodded.

'Very well Procurator, get your men assembled and ready to march. You'll have to take them straight down the hill and through the enemy though, nice and slow but without any hesitation, and I'm sending the king's man Gurgen down there with you to reinforce the message. Gentlemen, I've warned Narsai that if his men so much as twitch in our direction then my officers are under orders to halt, turn to both sides and attack. In which case, the legion will launch a concerted attack from whatever position it has reached.'

He'd looked about him at the officers' serious faces.

'Officers of the Third Gallic, here is my direct order. An attack on any of us is an attack on all of us. Whilst I'll flog any man needlessly offering provocation to the Parthians, it's a case of one in, all in. Not that I expect Narsai to offer us any provocation . . .'

He'd grinned at them wolfishly.

'But if they do, I expect you all to get in amongst them like butchers on the day before Saturnalia!'

Each cohort was led by one of the tribunes, and alongside each of them walked a hooded prisoner with a soldier to guide his steps, and the rest of the man's tent party clustered around the pair, another dozen or so of the captive Parthian nobility distributed throughout the cohort's following centuries.

'Consider it a game of bluff.'

Scaurus had met with Narsai again that morning, the two men looking at each other with undisguised loathing across the line of dead horses.

'My legion is so long on the march that you might be tempted to engage my van, or my rearguard, with the expectation of destroying a cohort or two for no loss to yourself.'

He raised an eyebrow at the scowling king, his lips twitching as he fought the urge to grin at the man.

'After all, you do have some catching up to do.'

Narsai had glowered back at him in silence.

'And so, just to raise the stakes on such a gamble, each cohort will contain a number of prisoners, every man hooded and surrounded by a dozen soldiers. If your men attempt to recapture any of them, that man's throat will be cut. And an attack on any of my cohorts will result in all of the prisoners being executed in the same manner. That attack you're considering will kill the King of Kings' son, and start a pitched battle I just can't see you winning. Your men may be masters of fighting mobile battles across this empty desolation, but when it comes to bloodletting at close quarters, I think you've already learned your lesson. And now, if you'll excuse me . . .'

Marcus marched with the Tungrians, immediately behind the marines, the Britons indistinguishable from the legion's established cohorts now that their new equipment had been weathered from its initial gleaming newness. The cohort followed hard on the heels of the blue-tunicked troops, their eyes fixed to the man in front and giving no signs of recognition that there were thousands of sullen enemy warriors within a few paces on either side. Centurions and their watch officers walked ahead of and behind their centuries to avoid offering any unnecessary provocation to the Parthians, but where an enemy moved too close to the column, the soldiers whose path they blocked were as uncompromising as they had been instructed to be, using their shields or the heavy iron plates that curved over their shoulders to forcefully push back the attempted harassment. Beside the young tribune, on one of the legion's more docile mules, rode a no better than partially recovered Osroes, his words slurred by the concussion from which he was clearly still suffering.

'When can I remove this hood, Roman?'

Marcus looked up at him, meeting the man's eyes though the rough slits cut in the bag's rough fabric.

'I apologise for subjecting you to such ignominy, Your Highness, but the hood is essential, I'm afraid.'

'Ignominy is the least of my problems, Tribune. My head . . .'

Marcus nodded. Osroes' eyes had been screwed up against the early morning sun's rays while they waited to march, and his head was carried in a way that spoke of the pain that flooded him with the smallest of movements. The doctor had examined him carefully the previous evening before pronouncing his prognosis with a dour shake of his head.

'There's nothing much I can do without trepanning his skull, and I don't think he'd thank me for drilling a hole where one may not be necessary. It's a severe concussion at the least, and the flesh over his skull is so inflamed and swollen that I can't probe to see if the skull itself is cracked or not without draining the inflammation, an action against which Galen strictly advises in the seminal work on the subject. If it's just a concussion then he'll be unsteady on his feet for a few days, then it'll sort itself out. Keep an eye on him, and if he comes to then keep him on his back and well watered.'

He'd stood, moving on to the next man in the line of casualties with a grimace.

'Orderly! Pass me a bone saw please! That'll have to come off . . .'

Marcus looked up at the swaying figure beside him.

'Do you know where you are, King Osroes?'

The response was taut with exhaustion, but edged with an unmistakable anger.

'Of course I know where I am, Roman. I'm sitting on a mule with a bag on my head in the middle of my father's vassal kingdom of Adiabene, the day after I was stupid enough to let that halfwit

Narsai to push me into sending the best men in my army uphill at a prepared position, against an enemy with every trick in the history books to use against us.'

Osroes shook his head, visibly wincing at the pain induced by the movement.

'And so now here I am, reduced from riding the proudest war horse in all of Parthia to sitting astride a mule with a bag over my head.'

He paused for a moment before speaking again.

'Doubtless your legatus is now using the prospect of my death to keep Narsai at arm's length?'

'Yes.'

The king was silent for a moment before speaking again, his voice edged with bitterness.

'A smart move. He displays a high degree of cunning . . . for a Roman.'

He lapsed into silence, and Marcus stepped out of the column to look back down its length. Half of the legion was off the hill now, and the waggon train that formed its centre on the march was now rumbling past the watching enemy host. Supply carts loaded with the Scorpions and their bolts, transports bearing tents and cooking equipment and scores of waggons loaded with everything too heavy for the legionaries to carry, their passage raising clouds of dust that blew across the watching Parthians. In its wake came Felix's cavalry, and the young tribune smiled at the thought of the dark looks that would be directed at them by those men who had managed to escape the marauding Phrygians in the cataphracts' flight down the hill's merciless open slope. Behind the horsemen came the archers and slingers, followed by a rearguard of two more legion cohorts and the Second Tungrians, each one an imposing fighting unit in itself but taken together they were a fighting machine of incredible power and ferocity.

'Narsai can't allow you to reach Nisibis, you know.'

The Roman shrugged at his prisoner, his response phrased with the appropriate respect for Osroes' rank, but brutally frank nonetheless.

'He won't stop us, Your Highness. Not as long as we have you to deter another attack.'

Osroes snorted, his body jerking again at the sudden pain in his head.

'Then you'd better be sure to keep me safe, hadn't you? I doubt I'm much use to you dead.'

Narsai watched the Roman column marching down from its perch atop the hill with a mixture of frustration and calculation.

'No man is to provoke them, understood? Your king is at their mercy.'

Osroes' gundsalar inclined his head.

'Your command has been passed to the army, Your Highness, with a threat of a slow and painful death for the man who disobeys. But I must ask you . . .'

'How do I plan to free the king?'

The soldiers stared at him, and Narsai felt the weight of their expectations settle upon him like a cataphract's armour.

'In truth, gentlemen, I do not yet know. But . . .'

He waited ostentatiously for their muttering to die down, picking a piece of dried flesh from his mace.

'What I do know is that knowledge is power. So, Gundsalar, send out your scouts. I want to know everything that these Romans do as they march east. Any further trick that this legatus plays without our having predicted them will carry a bad portent for the man who had the chance to predict it.'

The general bowed in his saddle once more.

'Oh, and Gundsalar?'

'Your Highness?'

'There was a minor skirmish with the Roman cavalry yesterday, as I recall it?'

The older man nodded.

'Indeed, Your Highness.'

'Your scouts were overwhelmed, I believe, but they killed a number of the enemy?'

'We found thirteen dead Romans, Highness.'

'And the bodies?'

The Median general waved a dismissive hand.

'We left the barbarians to rot.'

Narsai raised a regal eyebrow at the man's apparent lack of foresight.

'Then I suggest you drive off the vultures and bring them to me. I have a use for them.'

The legion's column moved fast once the last cohorts had reached the road's smooth surface, trumpet calls for the double-pace march pealing out to pass Julius's orders to the most distant of centurions, and within a dozen heartbeats his men were moving at the fastest march pace short of a running gait.

Once the Tungrians were on the rough road and up to speed, Dubnus called for a song to take their minds off the coming exertions, and the marching soldiers roared out a ditty that had been several days in the composition:

'I'd rather have my balls cut off than sail the Middle Sea,
I'd rather go without my cock than sail the Middle Sea,
Sailors spend their lives on boats,
With nothing to fuck but goats
So I'm never going to sign up to sail the Middle Sea!'

Cassius Ravilla had dropped back to check on his rearmost men, and if his greeting to Dubnus as he waited for the Briton to reach him was acerbic, he was unable to keep some vestige of a smile off his face.

'I suppose this means that we're now sufficiently accepted to be openly abused?'

The procurator's brother officer grinned back at him.

'You haven't heard the rest of it yet.'

As if on cue, the Tungrians launched into the second verse:

'But I'd rather be a sailor than serve as a marine,
I'd rather pull a fucking oar than serve as a marine

They spend their lives on boats,
Pretending to be goats,
So I'm never going to sign up to serve as a marine!'

The Parthian host responded by moving out from the positions in which they had watched the Romans march off the hill, their loose formation pacing the legion to the north of the road's long ribbon.

'You really think they'll resist the temptation to attack?'

Varus had run up the column's length from his place at the head of the Seventh Cohort, grinning at the good-natured jibes that had followed him as he revelled in both his new-found fitness and the legion's sudden rediscovery of its pride. Marcus looked up at Osroes, lolling loosely on the mule's back and apparently asleep in the saddle, blessed with the innate skills of a man trained to ride from his earliest days.

'The king here thinks so, at least until we stop moving.'

'And you? What do you think, Tribulus Corvus?'

Marcus watched a fifty-man group of horse archers trotting back across the plain towards the enemy, one of several that had been dispatched from the Parthian army during the day to scout the ground before them.

'What do I think? I think that the man leading that host will be desperate to get to the king here, although whether he'll be hoping to rescue him or simply kill him . . .'

'Narsai won't care. All he needs is my body, living or dead. Once the tribes know I'm no longer a reason not to attack, he'll have you at his mercy. No amount of clever trickery will save you now that you've abandoned the security of that hill.'

Osroes had stirred, and was looking down at the two tribunes with a resigned expression.

'You think your own people will try to kill you?'

The king shook his head wearily at Varus.

'Not *my* people, Roman. Narsai's people. Explain it to him, if you will, Tribune Corvus?'

Marcus nodded.

'Parthia isn't one kingdom, there are at least a dozen kings who owe their allegiance to King Osroes' father, Arsaces, the King of Kings. Osroes is one of them, and King Narsai is another. Narsai rules Adiabene, a smaller and less important kingdom than Media, but were our guest the king to die in captivity, then Narsai will immediately have the right as the commander in the field to claim command of the Median army until another ruler can be appointed by Arsaces and his council. And if Narsai can present himself to the Great King as the man who defeated a Roman legion, and ejected Rome from a prize like Nisibis to boot, then his claim to that throne of Media would be hard for Arsaces to resist.'

'So if he manages to kill the king here . . .'

'He'll blame my death on Rome, and position himself as the saviour of Parthia.'

Both men looked up at Osroes.

'And if his killers come for you tonight?'

'Yes, Tribune Corvus?'

'Do you wish to live or die?'

The king shook his head tiredly, slumping back in the saddle.

'How should I know? The Sun God will decide . . .'

The legion covered thirty miles that day, the exhausted legionaries digging out a marching camp, eating their rations cold and then for the most part collapsing into sleep, unless they happened to have the misfortune to have drawn guard duty. A handful of centurions patrolled the camp's perimeter with unfailing vigilance, only too well aware that there were enough of the enemy to breach the camp's walls, given a determined assault and an unready defence. Julius had paraded the legion's centunions while their men were building the camp, expressing himself with a degree of robustness that had raised eyebrows among men who still harboured distant memories of a more relaxed way of life.

'I couldn't give a shit how degenerate a shower of arse-eating goat fuckers the enemy are, any man found asleep at his post will be beaten to death by his tent party in the morning, and any one of you that feels like making allowances can take his place. Understood?'

He'd looked across their ranks, his face hard with evident contempt for their collective abilities.

'Just so we understand each other, I'll be up and about during the night, and if I find any of your men with their eyes closed on guard then I'll be the one doing the beating to death. Think on that, and on who I might choose to pay the price for those few minutes of sleep.'

In consequence the duty centurions were harsh in their vigilance, taking their vine sticks to any man looking the slightest bit like sleeping, and when the sun rose it was the opinion of them all that while their new first spear might be a bastard, he certainly didn't spare himself, having been seen about the camp by several of his centurions during the night. The legion took a swift breakfast before forming up to resume its march at dawn, covering a good five miles before its Parthian escort managed to stir themselves and join the line of march, leaving the infantry to toil along to their rear.

'So, there was no sign of your assassins last night, Your Highness?'

Osroes was little improved on the previous day, and if anything, less animated than before, and waved Marcus's question away with a grimace.

'Too soon. They'll wait until you're exhausted before making their move.'

The Roman had smiled back at his prisoner wryly.

'They'd better not wait too long. There's a reason that Julius has us wearing out our hobnails this quickly.'

They marched all day with only brief stops for food and water, their rate of progress alternating between the burning pain of the double pace and the marginal respite of the standard marching speed, enough in itself to cover twenty miles in a day.

'Narsai will be getting twitchy, I expect. By the time we stop for the night we'll be a good twenty miles closer to Nisibis than he would have expected, and with only one more day's march ahead of us rather than the two he'd have been calculating. So if he's going to make an attempt to get to our prisoners, it has to be tonight. We'll double the guards, I think.'

The legion took Julius's decision with an uncharacteristic lack of complaint, and the first spear looked about him as the cohorts toiled to throw up the customary walls of the camp that would be their defence once night fell.

'Perhaps we've turned them into soldiers.'

'Or maybe they're just too weary to give voice to their complaints?'

Scaurus grinned at his subordinate's jaundiced expression.

'Yes, I know. Since when was a soldier ever too tired to complain? Perhaps they've realised that this is the last chance the Parthians will have to pull a victory out of this disaster. Tonight's the night Julius, there's no doubt about that.'

'You are certain of this?'

The old man spoke without taking his head from the dusty ground where he lay prostrate.

'Yes, Your Highness. I have ridden alongside the king since he was a young child. His seat on a horse is as evident to me as his hand on parchment would be to a scribe.'

Narsai nodded slowly, a grim smile of satisfaction settling on his face.

'And he was riding alongside the officer leading the first cohort?'

'Yes, Your Highness.'

The king turned to Osroes' gundsalar.

'Your scouts tracked each of their cohorts into the camp, and noted the place each one took inside its walls?'

The general inclined his head.

'They did so with precision and diligence, Highness. If my king remains with the cohort that led on the march today then he will be found somewhere here . . .'

He sketched a map in the dirt at their feet with the point of his dagger, quickly scratching in the roads that divided its rectangle into four smaller sections.

'Here. Where the roads meet in the camp's centre, that is where my king is held captive.'

Narsai stared down at the crude map for a moment.

'I will need the very best of your fighting men, Gundsalar. The bravest and the cleverest, men who can pass unnoticed in the shadows, but who will fight like uncaged beasts when the time comes for them to strike. I doubt we have a dozen men of this quality in our entire army, but we must assemble them quickly and make a bold strike into the heart of our enemy. This chance will not be offered to us again.'

The older man bowed deeply.

'As you command, Your Highness. I will bring the chosen men here.'

The king waited until he had vanished into the gloom before turning to his own general.

'Find Varaz and bring him here. Tell him that the moment of his glory is upon him.'

Narsai looked around the men who had been gathered from his army, taking the measure of them with a slow, calculating assessment in the light of the crackling fire. Each of them met his eyes with the appropriate deference, heads inclining in recognition of his exalted status, but the glint of their eyes and the set of their jaws betrayed supreme and untroubled confidence in their physical and martial prowess. Cataphracti nobility for the most part, they were big men with powerfully muscled frames, trained from childhood in the use of the lance, the sword and mace, on horseback and on foot, supremely conditioned to fight carrying the heaviest armour in the full heat of the day. His own champion stood among them dressed in the same unfamiliar garb they all wore, the neutral set of his body and the blank look on his carefully composed features masking the contempt that the king knew he was feeling for the men around him and for any man who lacked his unique and deadly approach to his craft. If the gathered soldiers were alike to swords and maces, weapons for hacking and bludgeoning at an enemy line, Varaz was an assassin's blade by comparison, forged with the intention of delivering a single unpredictable and lethal wound.

The man was untameable, giving his loyalty to none and his service to Narsai purely in return for gold, with an unveiled cynicism that would have long since earned him a swift death and an ignominious burial were it not for his unparalleled ability for swift and ruthless violence. He had bowed to his master on being brought before him, raising his dark eyes to stare unflinchingly at a man before whom he should in truth have been prostrating himself.

'So, King. Your chamberlain tells me that my moment in the sun has arrived.'

He looked up at the crescent moon, his mouth twisted in irony. 'And yet I see no sun. Only the moon, and a hunter's moon at that.'

Narsai had shaken his head in amusement.

'No man ever claimed to be your parent, Killer. No man knows where you were born, or how you came to be so skilled with blade and bone. You are nobody, as disposable as the water in which I shave, and yet you are the deadliest weapon at my disposal. You have served me well, and in return I have kept every promise I have made to you, have I not?'

The assassin inclined his head in acceptance of the point.

'And now, King, with an enemy army camped one day's march from a fortress so powerful that we may never break its walls, you call for me? What is it that you need that can be accomplished by a single man in the darkness? You wish the Roman general dead, perhaps?'

Narsai had smiled despite himself.

'No. He goes everywhere in the company of more hard-eyed men than even you could defeat in combat. I have a different challenge in mind for you. A kill worthy of both your skills and your dark heart. A kill that will ennoble your descendants . . .'

Varaz had raised an eyebrow.

'Ennoble?'

'You have a son, by the slave woman I gave you. He shows

promise with weapons for one so young, I hear. Would you like him to be raised as a royal prince?'

The other man stared back at him.

'You offer to take my son into your household?'

'Yes. I will swear the oath to the Sun God now, before my priest.'

His assassin's face creased into a hard smile.

'In which case it would be well if he were to commend my spirit to Ahura Mazda at the same time. For if you offer such a large inducement, I can safely assume that the price of delivering what you want of me will be that I have seen my last sunrise.'

Narsai had nodded, sharing a moment of understanding with his man.

'I think that assumption is realistic. In return for your death I offer you a life of privilege for your son, and his sons and grandsons. You will catapult your blood to the heights of nobility, and fulfil your destiny.'

'By killing King Osroes?'

Narsai had nodded tersely, aware that the man before him was quite capable of turning on him in an instant, even unarmed and in the presence of the royal bodyguard. The killer had looked at his booted feet for a moment before nodding his assent.

'It was never my expectation to end this life in my bed. Fetch your priest, King. Make your oath and have him shrive me.'

Narsai completed his assessment of the men standing before him, nodding his approval to the gundsalar.

'Time is short, so I will not waste it with unnecessary appeals to your virtue or duty. You all know why you have been gathered. You are the greatest warriors in our armies, the strongest, the bravest and the best of us, and your king has need of you. He is being held within the Roman camp, and while they have him we cannot mount an attack on them for fear of killing him. In the morning they will march again, and by nightfall the King of Kings' oldest son will be a prisoner within a fortress city so strong that he might never be freed. Tonight, my brothers, you must enter the camp of the Romans by stealth, find the king and bring him to safety.'

The most senior of them bowed before speaking, a black-bearded officer with a fresh cut down one cheek from the battle on the hill, the wound's edges roughly stitched together and black with dried blood.

'Your Highness, we may well find the king, but bringing him to safety may be impossible if the Romans detect us. What then?'

Narsai inclined his head in recognition of the question's ramifications.

'In the event that you find yourselves alone among the enemy, then you must follow the instructions of King Osroes himself, whatever they may be.'

The noble nodded.

'And if the king is not capable of making such a decision? His bidaxs Gurgen told us that he was suffering badly from the effects of a blow to the head.'

Narsai waited a moment, allowing the question's full implications to unfold in the minds of the men before him.

'In that case, you will have to make your own decision, for only you will be able to enact that choice.'

The noble held his eye for a moment, then nodded tersely.

'We will do what we must. Come, brothers.'

The king watched them walk away with a carefully composed face, his thoughts racing as he watched the assassin follow in their wake.

In the darkness between the two camps the infiltrators paused, waiting for their eyes to fully adapt to the darkness, checking by touch that each other's unfamiliar armour and equipment was as it should be. Then, following the big officer's lead, they moved slowly around the Roman camp until they were approaching it from the east, removing any risk of their being silhouetted against the glow of the fires burning in the Parthian encampment.

When they were no more than one hundred paces from the sentries guarding the camp's eastern gateway, the big man gestured for them to stop.

'Stay here.'

Narsai's killer shook his head, raising his hands to demonstrate the appropriate respect.

'Lord, you are a man of the greatest possible honour. This is a task that ought to be undertaken by a man who, through his long experience of the dirtier aspects of serving his king, has already sacrificed his honour. If you will allow me, I do have some small measure of expertise in such matters.'

The bearded noble nodded, quietly relieved to have the responsibility lifted from his shoulders.

'Go then. And do not fail.'

Varaz paced away into the night, smiling to himself in the darkness and permitting himself a whispered response once he was out of earshot.

'And in addition, Lord, where I am expert at moving quietly in the darkness, you blunder around like a blind bull. Now . . .'

He sank to the ground and watched the guards from no more than thirty paces, quietly calculating the best point at which to strike. The legionaries were most strongly concentrated around the gateway in the middle of the earth wall, keeping close to the fires that burned on either side, which would seriously reduce their ability to see into the darkness. A pair of men were positioned at each corner of the camp, their beats a good fifty paces from the nearest sentry and who, he noted, tended to spend more of their time getting as close to the fire as possible and as little as they could actually patrolling their section of the wall.

Retracing his steps, he found his fellow infiltrators waiting impatiently.

'I have scouted the best way into the enemy camp. Follow me.'

The noble tugged at his arm, whispering fiercely.

'Have you killed the guards?'

'No, Lord, not yet.'

'But—'

Biting down on his exasperation, he shook his head with an expression he hoped would not betray his frustration.

'Lord, from the very moment we make our first kill we will

have only a short time before their bodies are discovered. We must make that time as long as possible. Trust me in this.'

He turned and led them to the point from where he had watched previously.

'Stay silent and still.'

Pacing forward in the darkness, he waited until the guards to his left had turned and walked down their beat towards the fire, stepping quickly and lightly across the space separating him from the wall, easing noiselessly into its shadow and staring intently at the men standing at the camp's corner as he knelt to scoop up a handful of the dusty soil. When they showed no sign of reaction, he rose from the gloom and paced towards them with a measured, confident tread. He had no shield, but in every other respect he appeared authentic enough to stand up to a brief scrutiny in the darkness, his armour and helmet pulled from a dead Roman cavalryman retrieved from the open desert. Drawing his long knife, and reversing his grip on the hilt to put the blade in the shelter of his arm, he strode towards the guards, being careful not to speed up as he got closer.

The nearest of the two registered his presence in his peripheral vision at the very last moment, turning with a question as Varaz punched the knife through his throat and ran at the other man, hurling the handful of sandy dust at his target to buy a moment's confusion before the knife tore into his neck and severed both windpipe and vocal cords. The dying man gasped silently for air as he contorted into his death throes, then shuddered, and was gone. Dragging the corpses into the earth wall's cover, the assassin scowled as his comrades made their inevitably noisy appearance, feet scuffing in the dirt as they crouched low in poses.

'Over the wall!'

They obeyed his hissed instruction without question, their leader pausing for a moment to look at the bloodied killer.

'And you?'

Varaz looked at him with none of his previous deference, noting the hint of fear that had replaced the man's previous air of superiority.

'I'll stay here until you're well into the camp. As well for the Romans to see one their own when they walk back this way. When they turn back again I'll follow you in.'

The noble nodded, swallowing nervously without even realising it, and went over the wall in pursuit of his fellows. Varaz stared after him for a moment, calculating the odds that they would get close enough to the king to strike the fateful blow, then hefted a fallen shield and stood up, strolling out into the moonlight with a deliberate pace, quietly muttering to himself.

'Just another bored sentry.'

9

Exhausted, the legion's men had needed no encouragement to sleep on the hard ground in their blankets, rather than taking the time and effort required to erect the leather tents that could only encumber them in the event of an attack. Julius found himself accompanied by Varus as he walked the perimeter wall with a tent party of Tungrians, having disdained sleep once again in order to ensure that the legion was ready to defend itself against the attack he believed to be inevitable. The young patrician stopped, looking up and down the wall's length at the sentries patrolling their allotted sections of the defence, then turned to the senior centurion with as close to an apologetic expression as he was likely ever to get.

'I have to admit, First Spear, that I may have misjudged you. When the legatus first took command I was of the opinion that you were nothing better than a northern lunatic. When you had the entire legion sleep overnight without tents I called you a sadist, and then when you had the trumpets blown in the middle of the night I cursed you for a maniac . . .'

He paused, smiling wryly.

'I can only apologise. Clearly you had just such a situation as this in mind.'

Julius nodded at him, accepting the hard-earned respect with a straight face.

'It's not that hard, Tribune. Once you've seen a campaign or two, you find it natural to place yourself in the enemy's boots, so to speak, and ask yourself what he might do, if he's desperate enough. It's simple experience.'

The younger man took a moment to stretch his back before

resuming their walk towards the lone sentry standing at the point where the northern and eastern sides of the camp met.

'That may be true, but nonetheless, First Spear, you've become the heartbeat of the Third Gallic. If we survive this insane expedition on which the emperor has sent us, it will be entirely due to the legatus's cunning tactics and your iron control of the men that enables him to even consider them.'

He looked at Julius with unabashed admiration, something the first spear was ill-accustomed to receiving from the legion's senior officers.

'You won't have any problems from any of the young gentlemen either, not since that remarkable vic—'

Turning back to their path around the wall he stopped, frowning at something barely visible in the shadow of one of the camp's entrances.

'Is that a man lying down?'

Julius started and strode forward, putting a foot under the supine body and kicking the man onto his front. A dark, wet stain covered his neck and chest, and his weapons and helmet were missing. Another dead sentry was lying in the shadow of the earth wall, and, looking up, he realised that the lone figure they had seen patrolling the wall a moment before was nowhere to be seen. The first spear spun to face his superior, pulling the sword from his left hip.

'We're being fucked! Air your iron, Tribune, and stay close to me! *You!*'

He pointed to his trumpeter.

'Sound the stand to!'

The first notes of the summons to action broke the camp's silence with the power of a thunderclap, and before the first echoes had died away the legion was struggling to its collective feet, soldiers shrugging off their blankets and reflexively reaching for their weapons.

'Stand to! Prepare to defend the camp!'

The closest centurions heard Julius's bellowed command and repeated it in their own parade-ground roars, each successive cohort springing into action as the order rippled across the camp's expanse. Rushing forward to the walls, each century took its place in the wall of iron that was rapidly building behind the earth wall, soldiers swiftly arraying themselves into solid ranks despite the near darkness and settling into place as they had practised so many times before with a solid line of shields facing out into the darkness and another held overhead to protect against lofted arrows, their glinting swords held ready to fight. Julius looked about him, pride in the speed of his command's response tempered by a nagging sense that something was not as it should be.

'No arrows.'

Varus looked at him uncertainly.

'No arrows, First Spear? Isn't that a good thing?'

The Tungrian shook his head.

'No arrows, no attack.'

'And that's a *bad* thing?'

'They're not attacking. They managed to fool the sentries, which means they must have looked familiar, but having made their opening there's no follow-up.'

Understanding hit the two men simultaneously, and Varus gasped at the audacity of the Parthian plan.

'The prisoners!'

'Fuck the prisoners! They're after the king!'

The first spear spun, shouting an order at the closest centurion.

'You! With me, and bring your men!'

The infiltrators broke on the men guarding the prisoners in a wave of iron and muscle, their captured armour buying them precious time while the men who stood in their path wasted their chances to defend themselves, fooled by the sight of Romans running towards them. Drawing their swords at the last possible moment, the dozen-strong raiding party tore into the guards with the abandoned ferocity of men who knew that they were already dead. At the cost of four of their number, they left ten men dead and dying on the thin grass, hurdling the fallen with desperate haste.

'Intruders! Stand and fight!'

Marcus, standing by Osroes with an ear cocked for the sounds of battle from the camp's perimeter, started as he heard the screams and shouts of closer combat. Realising what was happening, he pulled the dagger from his belt and handed it to Gurgen, who stared back at him in amazement.

'Free your warriors.'

Marcus waved his good hand to indicate the men about them, then turned away, drawing the gladius from his left hip.

'And be ready to defend your king. This is a suicide mission, and it can only have one purpose.'

Stalking forward with the sword held low, he watched as the fast-moving attackers stormed into the tent party of legionaries who stood between them and their quarry. Alerted, and with their blades drawn and shields set, the Romans advanced to meet them in a solid line, but from the moment that the two forces clashed it was evident that the fight was one-sided. While the legionaries fought in the way they had been drilled for years, their attackers, each of them bigger and better trained than the soldiers, and with the joy of battle surging in their veins, gave battle with unmatchable speed and purpose. Hacking their way into the guards without regard for their own danger, they wrought swirling, lethal chaos, killing two of the defenders for each one of them that fell.

As the last few men under his command fought for their lives, their centurion took one of the enemy down with a perfect shield punch and brutal sword stroke, disembowelling the Parthian despite his borrowed plate armour, then died in his turn with a sword blade rammed through his neck. The last two men turned to run, falling to the attackers' swords as those of the raiding party still on their feet stormed through them, and came face-to-face with the gathered prisoners. Freed by Gurgen with swift strokes of the dagger Marcus had thrust upon him, they had been marshalled into a line that stood squarely in the path to the tent within which Osroes lay. Their leader limped forward, his sword arm red with the blood of the legionaries he had killed, his right leg a bloody ruin barely strong enough to keep him erect.

'The king! Where is the king?!'

The newly freed men looked at the noble in silence, only Gurgen having the authority to challenge him.

'Do you come to free him, or to kill him?'

Another man took a step forward, raising his gore-slathered blade.

'They'll kill him anyway, once they reach Nisibis! Stand aside!'

Gurgen shook his head, raising a hand.

'They've promised to free us all! The king needs—'

Osroes could be seen in the tent's doorway behind his protector, and the raiding party's leader looked down his sword at the red-headed warrior, his face white with blood loss and fury.

'I haven't sold my life this night to buy your lies, Gurgen! Get out of my path, the king must die!'

Gurgen pointed at the would-be assassins, bellowing an order at the freed prisoners.

'Defend the king!'

They stormed forward, the bravest of them dying on their amazed countrymen's swords before the remainder overwhelmed the infiltrators in a flurry of fists and boots. Marcus turned away, a flicker of motion at the edge of his vision the only warning he got before the last of them was upon him. The man must have lagged behind, waiting for the opportunity to strike in case the assassins lacked the nerve to carry through their grisly task. Raising his sword the Roman barely managed to parry the first blow, and was still turning back to face the threat when a swift fist to the face staggered him for an instant, long enough for the assailant to hook his ankle and send him sprawling and momentarily unfocused, laying him wide open to the death stroke.

He tensed, knowing that his stunned wits were no match for the man looming over him with a shining bar of razor-sharp metal in his hand, but the attacker was already past him with the sword raised, ready to kill and closing in on Osroes with clear intent. As the assassin ran the last few steps, drawing the blade back to strike, a legion-issue javelin hit him squarely between the shoulder blades, dropping him onto his knees with a foot of iron protruding from his chest.

Pulled backwards by the weight of the spear's wooden shaft

he struggled forward a step, inching closer to the king, and Marcus rolled to his feet, ignoring the pain in his wounded arm to put the spatha's blade at his throat. Shaking his head to regain his sense, he lifted the sword's point, forcing the dying man back from his intended victim.

'Give it up. You're a dead man, with nothing left but go to your grave with dignity.'

The assassin's head turned with painful slowness until he could see the Roman standing over him. Blood was running down the spear's shaft and pooling at the base.

'Should have . . . killed you.'

Marcus shook his head.

'I didn't throw the spear. He did.'

Gurgen stepped forward.

'No one kills my king, not while I have the breath to resist.'

He stared at the stricken killer.

'I know you. You're Narsai's man.'

The killer shrugged.

'Tell them . . . how close . . . I came . . .'

He snatched at Marcus's blade with quivering fingers, forcing it into his throat with a lunge that cut his palms to the bone and ripped through the veins in his neck. Bubbling an inaudible curse he sagged back onto the spear, ruined hands falling from the blade to hang on either side.

'That was a good throw.'

The bidaxs shrugged.

'I didn't see anyone else in a position to stop him. And there's your proof – Narsai wanted the king dead so that he could kill you all.'

'*Us* all.'

They turned to find Julius and Scaurus behind them, both men holding their swords ready to use, and the legatus strolled forward with a grimace at the assassin's corpse.

'We'll have the prisoners bound again shall we, First Spear? And I'd be altogether happier if that dagger you're holding was to find its way back into the tribune's sheath.'

Gurgen handed the weapon back to Marcus and held out his hands for the rope.

'Not you. Tribune Corvus here needs someone to help with the king, and you've certainly proven your dedication to the man. We march at dawn.'

The enemy horse archers were waiting when the legion broke camp in the morning, and Julius stared at them with a grim expression as his soldiers prepared for the day's march.

'So now we get to find out just how much power Narsai has over Osroes' nobles. If they're willing to sacrifice their king, they'll start loosing arrows at us the moment we're out of camp.'

Scaurus cocked an eyebrow at the king.

'What do you think, Your Highness? Do your nobles love you enough to resist Narsai's pressure?'

Osroes shook his head, still perpetually weary.

'Of course not. I've been their king for little more than two years, and the previous ruler was a much loved man. He may have died in his bed peacefully enough, but I suspect that his death was too well timed for some of them to accept as being without some other cause.'

'And everyone loves the idea of a conspiracy, especially where the possibility of what they fear holds some credibility.'

'Indeed. So in this case, Legatus, there are three factors in play.'

Scaurus frowned.

'Three? I can see the balance between their fear of what Narsai might do to them if they don't obey him and attack today, set against their fear of what your father might do to them if they do – what's the third factor in play?'

The king smiled tiredly.

'It isn't. Yet.'

Having tarried over his breakfast, calculating the likelihood of swaying the Median nobles to his side, Narsai rode through his army towards the Roman camp to be greeted by an unexpected sight when he reached the host's front ranks. His momentary look of bemusement darkened to one of anger as he realised who it was that the knot of armoured cavalry men were gathered around fifty paces from the army's ranks, a figure at once familiar by his rich blue tunic and proud stance.

'It's the king's bidaxs, Your Highness.'

Kicking his horse forward, the king cantered across the gap between his army and the small group of nobles, taking in at a glance which of the Median nobles had ridden forward to meet Osroes' man. A dozen or so faces turned to regard him as he approached, none of them kindly, several of them hostile. He noted the latter, half promising himself to have the more powerful of them meet with accidents before he remembered that his assassin had failed to return from the Roman camp.

'I warn you, my lords, you'd do as well not to listen to this man. His master has had his wits bludgeoned from his skull by the Romans, and this one wants nothing more than to pretend that the problem does not exist.'

Gurgen shook his head in disgust.

'I will repeat myself for those of you who may be hard of hearing, or who lack the old-fashioned virtue to arrive on the field of battle in a timely manner. Your king sends you his regards, and his regrets that he is unable to greet you in person. He wishes you to know that he is of sound mind, if still a little dazed from the way in which he was unhorsed in the battle during which he was taken. And he expressed his disappointment that you should have decided to seek his death, and sent the cream of our Median army into the Roman camp last night with orders to find and kill their own king.'

The reason for their hostility was at once apparent, and Narsai shook his head in a manner he hoped would emphatically give the lie to the bodyguard's words.

'I know of no such attempt on the king's life. If our warriors, being realists in all things, decided to take matters into their own hands, I can only applaud their determination to bring this enemy to—'

'They're all dead. They fought their way to the king's tent with the greatest of bravery and skill at arms, but in the end their sacrifice was without fruit. I speared the last of them myself, as he stood before my king with a drawn sword.'

Narsai swelled with genuine rage.

'You prevented your own people from removing a hostage from Roman hands!'

Gurgen shook his head, his lip curling.

'I killed an assassin who threatened the man to whom I have sworn lifelong loyalty, nothing more. And not all of the men who sought their king's life were pure in their intentions.'

He emptied the bag onto the rough grass, watching Narsai's face as the head of his killer rolled to a halt on the sandy ground, the dead man's eyes staring sightlessly up at him.

'You see this king's face when confronted with the head of his tame murderer, my lords? You see him recognise his man? A dozen of your finest fought their way to the king's side last night, determined to kill him only as a last resort, when they realised that they were surrounded. We restrained them with our empty hands, my lords, for love of our brothers and their ideal of their sacrifice, and several of my fellow captives paid for that fealty with their lives. But this man, this *scorpion*, lurked in the shadows behind them and sought to bring a dishonourable death to *your* king!'

Narsai snarled at him, turning his horse away.

'It was the only way I could see to prevent this legion from escaping our vengeance for the men we lost, back there on that bloody hillside! And I still see it as the only answer! If you fools lack the guts, then I will have to show you how it's done with my own archers!'

Gurgen smiled at his back, looking to the men gathered around him.

'A choice presents itself, my brothers.'

Scaurus watched the small group of nobles intently, waiting until Gurgen turned away and strode back towards the Roman camp, proudly heedless of the risk that he might find an arrow between his shoulder blades at any moment.

'So now we'll see how dearly the king's men value his life. And whether it's born of love of the man or fear of his father, whether that value can outweigh Narsai's need to see him dead.'

He turned to Julius with a nod.

'We'll march the legion now, if you will First Spear? Let's not give them any time to think it through.'

The First Cohort went out through the hastily demolished eastern gateway at the double march, the Romans clearly intending to make the most of the morning's cool, the soldiers' heads thrown back to suck in the air while their centurions barked commands and struck out with real venom at any man not displaying sufficient vigour.

'You've turned them into Tungrians, brother.'

Dubnus grinned at Julius as the Second Cohort lurched into motion, the air abruptly filled with the sound of Aramaic curses and imprecations that the Tungrians had quickly come to recognise.

'Listen to that! I swear I just heard that centurion call his front rankers a useless shower of cock suckers!'

Julius smiled quietly.

'They're not Tungrians. But they're something close enough that I'm starting to get quite fond of them, the dirty, idle bastards. And as for you, Your Highness, don't you have a cohort to be beasting?'

Dubnus turned away with a smug grin.

'No need. All my centurions know their duty well enough, as you'd expect given they're the best soldiers in their cohort. My lads will have had them lined up and ready to run before the rest of the legion had put their cocks away. It's discipline, that and the relief of not having to suffer under their former first spear . . .'

Julius waved him away, turning back to Scaurus to find the legatus still watching the legion's cohorts as they formed for the day's march.

'Today's the day, Julius. Today we'll discover if we're fated to die here, unlamented on a featureless plain, or survive to face death by starvation in Nisibis instead.'

The first spear raised an eyebrow.

'You don't believe that the city has food enough for us?'

'I might be wrong – but if they've been under siege for as long as I suspect, then they'll already be low on supplies before another five thousand mouths arrive.'

'But if we're marching into a death trap . . . ?'

'Not that we have much choice. But yes, if we're marching into a trap, then your next question is a valid enquiry. How do I plan to get us out again, given that if Narsai doesn't manage to turn the Medes loose on us, all he's going to do is ring the town with peasant soldiers and try to starve us out?'

Julius waited expectantly, and the legatus shook his head with a faint smile.

'The truth is, First Spear, that I really hadn't thought much beyond getting in there. That, I'm afraid, will be a matter for Our Lord Mithras to arrange.'

'There's still no sign of any pursuit!'

Felix looked back over his shoulder reflexively, finding the western horizon still free of any indication of pursuit. He grinned at Marcus, patting Hades' neck as the big stallion trotted effortlessly across the flat ground laid out before them, raising his voice to be heard over the thunder of his cohort's horses.

'With any luck the men watching Nisibis won't realise who we are until it's too late.'

Walking their horses across the plain until dawn's first light allowed them to mount, they had prevented their horses from alerting the enemy by the simple expedient of muffling their hoofs with rags and strapping on nosebags full of fodder while the beasts were walked out of the camp's southern side. Felix's cavalrymen had already covered two-thirds of the distance to their objective. Looking out to either side, Marcus saw only the empty plain running away in all directions as far as the eye could see.

'What do you think we'll find when we get to the city?'

Felix looked out over Hades' head to the east.

'I talked it through with the legatus. His expectation is that Osroes brought every horseman with him that he could, and most of his infantry too. There will probably only be two or three thousand of them, left behind to ensure that no supplies can reach the defenders.'

Marcus shook his head.

'That's still a lot of spears.'

'If they're levelled at us, then yes it is. *If* they're levelled at us . . .'

'They're just going to watch us?'

Julius looked to his left, at the mass of cavalry tracking the legion across the empty land towards Nisibis, the cohorts' every pace to the east reducing the amount of time available to Narsai if he sought to bring the marching soldiers to bay.

'It looks like it. Those that can keep up or who haven't already buggered off chasing our donkey wallopers.'

Dubnus coughed, pulled down his scarf and spat a mouthful of grit into the roadside dust, then replaced the flimsy protection and looked back down the legion's marching column. Far behind, almost lost in the dust that was being stirred up by the wind blowing across the plain, the Parthian infantry seemed to have given up attempting to maintain the pace that Scaurus was setting. To their left rode the cataphracts, their horses carefully positioned between the horse archers and the legion, their swords and maces on open display. Narsai had ridden ahead with his own men an hour earlier, hurrying away to the west in pursuit of the Phrygians with a thousand horse archers once it had become apparent that the Roman cavalry had ridden for the city under cover of the night.

'It's getting worse.'

Julius tightened his own scarf, shouting over the wind's keening, mournful note.

'The scout says it's not unusual to get dust storms at this time of year! I'm going to drop down the column and warn the officers to be ready for a surprise attack! We'd be on top of a blocking force before we knew they were there in this muck!'

The salar commanding the infantry that had been left to maintain the siege of Nisibis followed his deputy's pointing hand.

'Horsemen!'

A pair of riders were galloping towards them, the advance party of a much larger force whose strength was lost in the clouds of dust blowing across the plain that surrounded the city, their swords raised in salute as they reined in a dozen paces from the general.

'Peroz!'

The officers looked at each other.

'Victory!'

A soldier behind them had caught the riders' triumphant shouts and turned to his fellows, shouting the single word again loudly enough for hundreds of his fellows to hear, and with a roar the thousands of infantry men saluted the oncoming riders as their figures seemed to solidify out of the dust.

'What . . .'

The salar's deputy was quicker on the uptake than his commander, the first to realise that the cavalry trotting towards them were not what they seemed. As he turned to shout a warning, the advance riders peeled away to one side, and with a blare of horns the men behind them kicked their mounts into a canter, spreading out from their column of march into an arrowhead formation as they came across the open ground. The horn blew again, the horsemen pulling their bows from their gorytos cases and reaching for arrows.

'Spears! Present your spears!'

Turning to the men behind him, intent on gaining the safety of their ranks, the salar's stomach lurched as he found only terror in their eyes. Disordered and thrown off balance by the enemy's sudden appearance, their formation shivered, clearly on the verge of disaster.

'Present your—'

An arrow struck him squarely in the back, dropping him to his knees with the sudden agonising pain of its cold, iron intrusion. His deputy was already dead, sprawled across the ground with two arrows protruding from his armour, and dozens of the men in front of him were staggering with similar wounds. As he watched, a second volley of missiles whipped into his men, the regiment's ranks dissolving into chaos as yet more men fell under the deadly iron sleet.

'Hold . . . your . . .'

His voice reduced to no better than a whisper, the salar raised an imploring hand to the closest men, but their eyes were fixed on the oncoming enemy. With a sudden collective loss of will, the regiment broke, the ordered ranks reduced to a terrified mob in a single heartbeat as each man realised that those to either side were turning to flee. The noise of the Romans' oncoming horses was now loud enough to outweigh even the screams of his panicked soldiers, trampling their wounded comrades underfoot as they frantically sought an escape from the implacable enemy, and turning his head to look back, the salar realised numbly what it was that had inspired such terror. A line of horsemen was upon him, barely a dozen paces distant, each of them pushing his bow into the case on his right hip and drawing a long sword. But it wasn't the imminent onslaught that dismayed him, rather the fearsome aspect of their silvered cavalry helmets, rank upon rank of identical and cruelly emotionless metal faces offering their enemy no hint of fear or pity.

With another peal of the horn the riders came on with their swords raised, ready to kill those who failed to run or whose flight was too slow to evade their blades. The salar spread his arms, ready for the merciful blow that would end his agony and shame.

The last of the legion's cohorts marched into the fortress in good order, the massive wooden drawbridge that spanned the deep moat between inner and outer walls raising slowly to leave the city completely isolated from the Parthian forces now flooding onto the level ground surrounding Nisibis. The flat plain before the watching Romans was still scattered with the bloodied corpses of the spear men who had been routed and then slaughtered by Felix's cavalry as they fled, a trail of dead and dying men that ran away from the city to the north until it petered out in the foothills two miles distant. By the time Narsai had arrived with his own horsemen, the one-sided battle was already over, and the Phrygians were safely ensconced inside the massive walls encircling the fortress that had once been part of his kingdom.

'So, First Spear, what do you think?'

Julius looked out over the fortress, still struggling to come to terms with the scale of the city's defences.

'It's hard to take in, Prefect Petronius.'

'I understand only too well.'

The prefect commanding the city's garrison waved a hand at the scene laid out before them from their vantage point over the western gate.

'I was equally amazed the first time I laid eyes on it. A man gets used to the grandeur of the place after a time, but it really is quite surprising to find fortifications this strong out here in the middle of nowhere. I mean to say, there's nothing worth taking as far as the eye can see, and yet look at all this . . .'

Julius looked out across Nisibis, marvelling again at the tall brick walls that encompassed the city in two concentric rings, a deep dry moat having been dug between them.

'Not much use mining against these walls, I'd imagine.'

'No indeed! You might damage the outer wall, but to what end? The inner wall's at least as thick again, and both walls are buttressed, so mining would be more likely to make the outer wall slump, rather than collapsing it. And even if an attacker managed to take the outer wall, with the bridges over the moat destroyed it would be almost impossible to take the inner wall and force a way into the city, under constant attack and without any solid ground to work with.'

Petronius shook his head with a smile.

'I'd say the place is more or less impregnable, unless an attacker manages to starve the garrison out. I asked one of the elders why the place had been made so strong when there's nothing here worth having . . .'

He shook his head at the memory, and Scaurus tilted his head in question.

'The cheeky old bugger looked me up and down with a pitying expression, then folded his arms and gave me an ancient history lecture. He was a damned sight more interesting than my old tutor, I can assure you of that! Apparently, once we'd got past his repeated assertion that Rome was just another empire, and would one day surely fall, he pointed out to me that the city has been besieged at one time or another by all manner of people. Mesopotamians, Assyrians, Babylonians, Persians, Greeks, Parthians, and of course ourselves, all wanting the wealth to be had from possession of the only decent spring for a hundred miles. Everyone's had a go at the place at one time or another, and so, he told me with more than a hint of pride, they've got rather good at the whole fortification thing. And he has a point. After all, all we've ever done since the Parthians ceded the place to Avidius Cassius is keep the brickwork in good order, because the place was this strong when we took control of it.'

'Defences are all very well, but what about supplies?'

'If you're worried about feeding your men, First Spear, then put your mind at ease. Since the city sits right astride a major trade route, money isn't overly hard to come by and therefore neither are the staples of life. There's enough spare grain in the stores to feed your legion for a year, and those men out there will have vanished off to their homelands long before that. Besides, the first decent storm of next winter would clear them away even if they had the staying power to sit out there for the entire summer.'

He frowned.

'Exactly what it is that this Narsai hopes to achieve isn't clear to me, or for that matter why King Osroes thought it would be a good idea to sit watching a fortress that he's got no hope of breaking into. Surely they've both got better things to be doing than banging their heads against these walls?'

Scaurus shrugged.

'An interesting potted history, thank you Prefect Petronius. And I see your point as to the futility of whatever it is that the kings thought they might achieve by besieging the city, but to be frank I'm too relieved to have fought my way through to you to be giving much thought to what their aims might have been. My only concern now is to how we're going to get Osroes back to his father in Ctesiphon.'

Petronius raised an eyebrow.

'You're going to return the King of Kings' son to him, having taken him fairly in battle? What's the ransom?'

The legatus shook his head.

'The arrangement wasn't financial. I used him as a means of keeping Narsai from attacking us on the march, promising his nobles that I would return him to his father if he lived to see Nisibis. But the fact remains, getting him to Ctesiphon isn't going to be easy.'

The prefect raised an eyebrow.

'Your generosity amazes me, Legatus. After all, the payment that you could have demanded simply to let him walk from these gates would be enough to make you among the richest men in Rome.'

He pondered the thought for a moment.

'But never mind, we don't all want to be wealthy. And if all you need is a way out of the city that will set you on your way to the Parthian capital, I think I have something that might just work . . .'

'You're sure this is wise, Legatus? Sending a Roman officer to the Parthian capital might just be a very good way of getting him killed.'

Scaurus sat back in his chair, nodding in the face of his first spear's disapproval. Petronius had cheerfully vacated his office in the city's headquarters building in favour of the legatus, and from the windows on each side of the generously sized room it was possible to see the entire length of the fortress walls.

'I know, I'm asking a lot of him. If he manages to get Osroes away from here by means of this trick that Petronius has in mind, there will still be a long journey in front of them. And at the far end...'

'He'll be at the mercy of this King of Kings.'

Scaurus nodded again.

'Indeed. Although you shouldn't look at our enemy as simple barbarians. It's not as if they're Germans. The king claims direct descent from the men who ruled the first Persian empire, and the Parthian nobility have always prided themselves on being Greek in outlook. Since Tribune Corvus will also be an emissary of Rome, and as Parthia has no formal quarrel with the empire of which we are aware, bringing the Great King his wounded son by the most direct method can only count in his favour, so I'd be surprised if he were to be mistreated. He can take that monster Lugos with him, that will provide the Parthians with some entertainment, and perhaps Martos? The novelty of meeting a king from the far north will be something new, even for a man of Arsaces' age and experience.'

Julius bowed his head in acquiescence to his superior's command.

'I can see you're set on this, Legatus. I've got rounds to make, with your leave, sir?'

Scaurus leaned back in his chair.

'I'll consume a moment more of your time, if I may, First Spear?'

He waited until the older man had retaken his seat before speaking again.

'I know you don't want Tribune Corvus to carry out this task, and I understand why. You believe that his place is here with the legion, and that the risks he'll be taking are unnecessary. But you miss my point, partly because you're concerned for his safety and partly because you don't have my wider responsibilities. Your role is to provide this legion with leadership, to manage it in battle and to ensure as many of the enemy are killed for as few of our own as possible. It is a role you play as well as any man I've met, and better than most of them. I, however, am a legatus. That does not simply mean that I am a legion commander, but also, whether I hold the social rank or not, that I am effectively a senator of Rome. I have a duty to the empire that goes beyond simply leading her legionaries, but which also encompasses diplomacy. Diplomats prevent wars as often as soldiers win them, and it's clear to me that our one legion isn't going to snuff out the flame that Osroes and Narsai have lit here. One man with the right ear, however, might just manage it.'

He stood, walking to the office's window and looking out at the city.

'I have a greater need for the tribune's skills than yours, First Spear. You'd have him stand on those walls, looking out at Narsai's army and waiting for his arm to heal. I, on the other hand, need both his intelligence and the wit that his father made sure was developed by his education. Any other man I can send will simply be a soldier, whereas in Marcus Valerius Aquila I can present the Great King with as close to an old-fashioned Roman gentleman as the empire can manage here and now.'

He shook his head in amusement.

'In days gone by I would have elbowed him aside to have made such a journey. To meet the King of Kings? To set eyes on a man who rules a dozen kingdoms solely by force of personality and his ability to set one man against another, and thereby set them both to his will, a role so difficult that I doubt our own emperor would see out the week? Such a chance will never come again, be sure of that. The tribune's friends will be safe enough behind these walls, safe and bored beyond measure, whereas that young man will have the opportunity to visit a city that few Romans have seen in any other circumstance than from behind a sword.'

He stood, gesturing to the door and releasing the first spear to his duties.

'He'll thank me, when he returns.'

'This makes a pleasant change from the temperature up above, doesn't it? Standing guard duty down here is one of the most sought after places to be during the day, although I don't think the soldiers are quite so keen once the sun's below the horizon! How are you liking the tour, Centurion Avidus?'

Petronius's words echoed back from the bare stone walls, more tunnel than passage. The air was cool deep within the fortress walls, a draught at the party's backs making the flaming torches set in wall scones every twenty paces flutter and dance as they walked at a steady pace down into the fortress's lower depths behind the prefect, Gurgen and Martos taking one of Osroes' arms apiece to keep him steady on his feet. Avidus had tagged along with the party on hearing that they would be visiting the fortress's lower depths, and his reply to the prefect's question was wistful in tone.

'The men that built this place certainly knew what they were doing, Prefect. Although I can't say I've been surprised by anything just yet.'

Petronius laughed.

'Don't worry, I think you're going to find what I have to show you entertaining. One of my brighter officers discovered it a few weeks after we arrived for our tour of guard duty. He felt a slight breeze blowing through a gap in the bricks and had the wall pulled down to reveal this rather unprepossessing passageway, running straight down to . . .'

He chuckled.

'Well, you'll see soon enough.'

After another fifty paces he stopped in front of a thick black curtain.

'Safe to enter?'

The material was pulled back, and the prefect stepped forward into a gloomy near darkness, beckoning them forward with a ghostly pale hand.

'Step forward five paces, then stop and allow your eyes to adapt to the light.'

A rumbling laugh from behind Marcus spoke for all of them as Lugos shook his head, invisible in the darkness.

'What light?'

'Ah, wait a moment and you'll see. There are lamps in this place, just not very bright.'

Staring around himself in the gloom, Marcus realised that the prefect spoke accurately, for on either wall of whatever chamber it was that they had entered were tiny flickering sparks of light, their minuscule illumination barely enough to provide the meanest level of light to the open space, even once his eyes had become accustomed to the gloom. Julius was the first to realise what he meant.

'The floor. It's *moving.*'

Petronius laughed softly.

'It's moving, First Spear, but it's not floor.'

Scaurus bent carefully, touching a hand to the glinting surface.

'Water?'

'Water. It's the Mygdonius, what the locals call the Fruit River. A couple of hundred years ago some bright lad realised that the river ran so close to the city walls that they might as well do more than take water out of it. Look carefully and you'll see how I intend to get you all out of here.'

After a moment of staring into the gloom, Martos was the first to speak.

'Cocidius's hairy ball sack! It's a boat!'

'Indeed it is, Briton. You see well in the darkness for a man with only one eye.'

The vessel was painted black, its forty-foot length filling two thirds of the chamber's stone dock, a short mast lying flat against the planks that formed a series of rowing benches. Petronius waved a hand at it, his teeth a slash of white in the gloom as he grinned at them.

'This is the *Night Witch*, gentlemen. It is an invisible boat, or at least exceptionally difficult to spot on a night like this, as I can assure from my own experience while her crew were practising with her on the river at night. I've stood on the riverbank and not seen her pass within twenty paces, given the right conditions.'

With a flash of insight, Marcus understood the reason why they had been delayed in leaving the fortress for three days.

'The cloud . . .'

'Exactly. There is no moon, nor any starlight. On the river you will be a black hole, visible only to the keenest of eyes set to look for such a thing. And trust me, I doubt that there's going to be a single man looking at the river when you pass the enemy defences, given what I have planned. And now you all need to keep very quiet, we're about to open the river gate.'

He called out a soft command, and with a slow, low-pitched rumble, a section of wall began to slide across the chamber's face to reveal a gradually expanding rectangle of blackness. Avidus whistled softly, the professional envy evident in his voice.

'Building this must have been some undertaking. That piece of stone has to weigh tons . . .'

'It's a deception, Centurion. The door is no thicker than the deck of this boat, but it has been coated with thin stone tiles carefully crafted to resemble the walls to either side. When you consider that it can only be seen through the branches of the thorn bushes that surround the fortress, and that it is less than ten feet high, you'll understand why it's almost invisible from the river's other bank, and utterly undetectable from the distance at which our bolt throwers have kept the enemy lines.'

A dozen men in black tunics filed into the chamber through a low arched doorway and climbed carefully aboard the boat. At a signal from the prefect, a soldier handed each of the party a dark leather hide.

'As I said, you will be a dark hole in the river, but only if you take the right precautions. Once you are out of the fortress you must keep low in the boat, and keep those hides over you. One flash of pale skin will betray you to the watchers.'

Martos leaned forward, his disfigured face barely less than terrifying in the half-darkness.

'Watchers?'

Petronius shrugged.

'Of course. No besieging force is going to ignore the risk that the defenders might attempt to send a messenger out by means of the river, especially as this is the one time of the year that it's sufficiently full to be navigable. There will be men on either bank of the Mygdonius, set to watch for such an attempt, I'm sure of that. And if they spot you then your mission will be doomed, because even if you get past them, you will be hunted down by the enemy cavalry once the sun rises. The river takes many turns on its way south to the Euphrates and you will never outrun a swift horse even with the flow at your back.'

The Briton frowned.

'If I were set to watch a river in the darkness, my first thought would be to light a fire and illuminate the river. How can we pass unnoticed if the water is lit from either side?'

Petronius grinned back at him, quite unperturbed by the prince's scars.

'Ordinarily it would be impossible. But I think that they'll have more important matters on their minds than looking for boats when you pass.'

He nodded to the boat's master, a villainous-looking soldier with a face that rivalled Martos's for scars.

'On your way, Thracius, and remember to wait until the entertainment starts before attempting to pass the siege line.'

The party stepped down into the boat, the dozen-strong crew muttering curses when Lugos boarded, his every movement causing the boat to rock until he was seated, with the express order from the boat's commander not to move until they touched shore again. With their passengers aboard, the crew eased their vessel away from the stone quay, pushing gently with their oars to launch the boat slowly out into the short channel that connected the hidden chamber with the river.

'Lie down. And remain *silent*!'

Marcus obeyed the master's hissed command, flattening himself against the wooden planks as they slid into the shelter of the massed thorn bushes that covered the hidden waterway. Jerking as the first thorn stabbed at the skin of his leg, his muffled grunt of pain drew a glare and a fierce whisper from the closest of the crew, already sheltering from the bushes' fierce assault under his own hide.

'Use your leather!'

Diving under the heavy sheet of cow skin he felt the myriad

tugs at the thick hide's surface as the boat eased through the heart of the thorny camouflage, then there was a pirouette by the boat's bow as it emerged into the river's swift-flowing stream. Lifting the leather to peek out from beneath it, he found himself staring out across the plain to the east of the fortress, on the river's far side, at the distant light of picket fires that marked the Parthian line stretching around the fortress city.

Walking back up the tunnel with Julius and Avidus behind him, Scaurus asked the question he knew Petronius was eager to answer.

'So Prefect, just how are they going to get past the men Narsai's general will have set to watch the river?'

He could practically see the smug smile on the other man's face.

'It's a simple question of expectations, Legatus. One of the secrets of a successful siege defence, or so I've come to believe, is to persuade the enemy to trust their own expectations of any situation where doing so might give us an advantage. This is the moment when we show them that at least one of those expectations is *not* well founded.'

The boat was moving more swiftly now, drifting silently with the Mygdonius's flow as the waters that rose far to the north in the mountains rushed southward, their noisy burble disguising the occasional slap of water against the *Night Witch*'s side. The river curved briefly to the west, hugging the walls, then turned south again, and Marcus's view steadied as the boat master eased the boat through the bend without so much as a ripple to betray its presence before steering for the western bank. The vessel's bow kissed the rough earth for long enough that the crew were able to lean out and wield spikes, driving the iron deep into the soft earth where land and water met, then pulling on them to drag the craft into the shadow of the river's lip. Looking down the shimmering line of water to the south, Marcus realised with dismay that there were indeed watch fires burning to either side of the river, at the point where the Parthian siege lines ran down to the water.

'How are we going to get past those sentries?'

Thracius spat over the side, looking over the Roman's shoulder at the waiting sentries and considering the question before answering in a hoarse whisper.

'By means of a right nasty shock, Tribune.'

He looked back at the fortress with a grimace.

'When the prefect gives the order, there's going to be a few of them Parthian bastards wishing they'd not sat quite so close to the fire.'

The three senior officers emerged into the torch-lit street, Petronius leading them to a doorway that opened onto a spiral stair, climbing vigorously up towards the top of the city walls.

'Ever since your legion marched in here with that motley collection of soldiers at your heels, the Parthians have been busy digging siege trenches, and of course we've been equally busy trying to disrupt them.'

Emerging from the stairs onto the walls' broad fighting platform, he strolled across the flat stones to the nearest of the city's bolt throwers, larger versions of the legion's Scorpions, deadly engines of wood, metal and sinew. The weapon and its crew were lit from behind by a pair of torches whose flames guttered and spat in the gentle breeze.

'This beauty can hurl one of these . . .'

He took a bolt from the leader of the weapon's crew and handed it to Scaurus, an evil iron-tipped length of dense, hard wood with metal flights pinned to its tail to provide stability in the air.

'What's the slot for?'

Petronius glanced down at the bolt's metal nose, and the long rectangular hole that had been drilled through the iron spike. He took the missile back and passed it to the crew's leader, a keen-eyed chosen man.

'Demonstrate to the centurion how our night shooting works, would you?'

Deft fingers threaded a folded length of cloth through the slot, the material hanging out on either side.

'We soak the cloth into lamp oil, First Spear. Then we put a light to it, so that when we loose the bolt you can see it fly all the way to the target, which lets us adjust our aim just as long as we can see something to shoot at.'

The prefect patted the man on the shoulder.

'We'll get out of your way. Things are going to get busy very shortly.'

He led them away to stand by the parapet, looking out over the sea of camp fires that marked the Parthians army's closest approach to the fortress walls.

'You see gentlemen, we've been shooting the occasional bolt at them over the last few days, but the bastards have been delighted to see that we could only land the blasted things within twenty or thirty paces of their lines. Seems that some bright lad noted our initial shots and used them to set the siege line at a safe distance. We got lucky the other day and bounced a bolt off a piece of rock, and some poor unsuspecting soldier walking through their camp stopped it between his shoulders, but apart from that all we've done is waste good iron . . .'

He paused, grinning conspiratorially.

'That, and convinced them they're out of range of course. Which, as you might have guessed, isn't strictly true, not given that all those shots were taken with the springs only wound back to three-quarters of their full torsion. If, however, we wind them back until they're creaking . . .'

He turned to his first spear.

'I think it's time to provide our messengers with a little distraction. Shall we begin?'

The senior centurion saluted and turned away, raising his voice to a stentorian below.

'All bolt throwers – load!'

The crews leapt into action as the order was repeated by their officers in a chorus of equally loud roars, the command rippling round the city walls as each crew in turn leapt to their task, their swift and precise response to the order testimony to long hours of drill. Loaders laboured to wind back their weapons' thick strings with straining muscles while the crew commanders waited, cloth-tipped bolts in hand. Watching the nearest machine, Scaurus smiled quietly as the chosen man gingerly fitted the missile to the waiting machine's taut bowstring.

'Ready!'

A chorus of similar shouts rang out as the crews stepped away from their labour, each commander taking a burning taper and standing ready to light the waiting missile's incendiary cargo while the last fine adjustments were made to the weapon's point of aim.

'Shoot!'

The tapers dipped in unison to set light to the waiting bolts, and then, with a whip crack of unleashed power, the weapons spat their deadly missiles out over the space between city and besieging army, the bolts' flaming path describing a gentle arc down towards the unsuspecting Parthian siege line.

'Reload!'

The air above the waiting boat's crew was suddenly alive with screaming missiles, a dozen fiery streaks shrieking down into the Parthian lines to impact with audible thuds. Somewhere in the darkness a man was suddenly screaming, pausing only to draw breath before howling more helpless outrage at whatever it was that had happened to him. The sound stopped suddenly, silenced by a merciful sword stroke, Marcus surmised, and the sound of voices raised in fear and anger reached their ears.

After a short wait another volley of bolts whistled into the Parthian line, their aim adjusted to concentrate on the only available points of aim, given the lack of either moon or stars to illuminate the battlefield. More than one shot hit the target at which it had been aimed, sending showers of sparks and chunks of burning wood flying as the heavy bolts smashed into the enemy watch fires. Half a dozen missiles landed around the watch posts on either bank of the river, at least one finding a human target to judge by the wet, crackling sound of impact, and the chorus of imprecations and shouts from the hapless Parthians redoubled. A commanding voice was raised over the furore, bellowing a single repeated command. The boat master laughed, calling to his crew.

'Hah! He shouts to extinguish the fires! Cast off, but use your oars to back water and keep us from drifting. We must be ready, but the time is not yet.'

'See? That will teach these blasted easterners some manners!'

Another salvo of bolts arced out from the city's walls, slamming down into the Parthian lines in a random scattering of terror and death. Somewhere out in the darkness beyond the fires' light, a horse was screaming in its death throes, and Scaurus decided that it was the most horrendous noise he had heard in a military career that had contained more than its fair share of unpleasantness.

All along the siege line the enemy were struggling back from ground they had previously believed safe. Some of the enemy soldiers were running to kick sand onto the fires that were providing the Romans with such a convenient point of aim, others taking refuge from their deadly light by huddling in the darkness between the fire pits.

'Switch point of aim!'

Another volley of bolts was hurled from the city's walls, this time plunging down into the spaces between the fires where the press of men seeking the darkness's protective embrace would be at its thickest. A fresh chorus of screams and enraged bellows erupted as each of the heavy missiles killed and maimed with arbitrary brutality, redoubling the enemy soldiers' panic in the face of such impersonal and unpredictable murder. Petronius looked out over the Parthian line, more and more of the fires being extinguished as the besiegers hurled handfuls of sand to quench their flames.

'Two more bolts apiece and then I think we'll call it a night, shall we First Spear? I think we have the desired result.'

The watch fires overlooking the Mygdonius were suddenly dimmed, the ruddy pools of illumination they had cast over the waters masked by the dozens of men who had run at the command of their officers to snuff out the flames.

'Go!'

With the unhurried speed born of long practice, the crew flashed out their oars and bent their backs with a will, digging into the black water with swift, coordinated strokes that took the loitering boat from standstill to a swift marching pace in a dozen heartbeats. The master called out another command in the same harsh whisper.

'Ship oars!'

Ceasing their rowing and pulling in their wooden blades, the oarsmen slid under their hides as the *Night Witch* hissed through the water towards the river's gap in the Parthian line. With his night-adjusted vision, Marcus could see the scene on both banks with perfect clarity, dozens of Parthian soldiers still milling about around the glowing embers of the dying fires.

'They will still scc only thc fire. Cover yourself!'

The Roman slid under his own hide, leaving the narrowest of openings between deck and leather and watching with helpless fascination as the boat swept swiftly towards the point where their fates would be decided by the night-blinded eyes of the men gathered on either bank. A single Parthian was standing on the right bank and staring at the water, perhaps more aware than his comrades, perhaps simply fascinated by the Mygdonius's dark ribbon. With one last twitch of the rudder, the boat master eased her course towards the eastern bank, aware of the lone watcher, and then they were upon the point of maximum danger. To their left the Parthians were unheeding, still focused on completely extinguishing the fire's last glow, but on the right the soldier still seemed to be following their progress intently, as if, despite the fact that his eyes could not yet have fully adapted to the darkness, he suspected that there was something on the water that ought not to be present, a hint of foam at the vessel's bow, or the faintest gleam from her wet timbers.

Another volley of bolts whipped in, plunging down into the Parthian line with the remorseless terror of shots launched blindly into the dark, one last shake of the dice cup, chancing a few dozen wood and iron missiles against the possibility of killing a man on whom the battle for Nisibis might yet hinge. A soldier standing within a few paces of the watcher was caught squarely, his body burst by the horrific impact, blood and shattered bone spraying across the men around him. The soldier recoiled, his attention wrenched from the river before him by the stinging impacts of bone fragments, and, in the moment that it took for him to regain his equilibrium, the moment in which he might have realised what it was that he was looking at, was lost. As the boat slipped away into the night's deeper darkness, he shook his head and turned away, wiping the dead man's blood away from his neck and hair in obvious disgust.

'*Oars*.'

The crew rolled out from beneath their hides at the master's command, rolling up the thick skins and placing them at their feet as Thracius stared back at the fortress.

'Now we *run*.'

Petronius turned away from the wall, drawing a finger across his throat as a signal for his first spear, the officers watching in silence as the bolt thrower crews stood down and trooped away to their barracks with a general air of quiet satisfaction.

'Our men got away cleanly, from the look of it.'

Scaurus nodded.

'I think there would have been a good deal more excitement if they'd been detected. Well done, Prefect, that was a masterly piece of deception.'

He turned to the north, pointing at a spot low on the horizon where a flicker of light had caught his eye a moment before.

'That looks ominous though.'

The prefect followed his gaze, and as the two men watched, the lightning flickered again, so distant that the rumble that eventually followed it was almost imperceptible.

'Possibly. I'll issue an order for the night watch to wake me if it looks like coming this way.'

IO

Dawn found the *Night Witch* far down the river from Nisibis, the ship's speed the result of both the strong southward current and continuous rowing in which Martos and Lugos took their turn while the crewmen took food and water, and relieved themselves over the boat's side.

'It is fifty miles from the city to the Khabur river as the birds fly, but the Mygdonius takes many turns on the way, and so it is in truth double that distance. We have covered perhaps one half . . .'

Marcus looked down at the mast, still lying flat across the rowing benches.

'Why do you not use the sail?'

The master shrugged, putting the rudder over to guide his vessel around yet another bend.

'This river meanders like the path of a snake in the desert, Tribune. If I were to order the mast raised then much work would be required to continually trim and re-trim the sail. Rowing is easier. And besides, see how flat the land is to either side of the river as far as the eye can see? The sail will be visible for miles, and might betray our position to a horse patrol – and we have far to go before we can forget the danger of the Parthian cavalry. Although that worries me more . . .'

He pointed back to the north, and Marcus saw a distant mass of dark cloud on the horizon directly above the river's course, a bruise in the sky's otherwise clear blue vault.

'If that storm's coming south we could be in trouble. The Mygdonius floods quickly, when the water from the mountains is swollen by rain on the plain, and it could run so fast as to be impossible to navigate. We should all pray to our gods to send it away to rain on someone else and not us.'

Scaurus and Petronius struggled onto the windswept parapet at first light, both men huddled into hooded woollen infantry cloaks thick with the natural oils that made them the best protection against the rain that was lashing down on Nisibis. Down below, the river was already significantly higher than had been the case the previous evening, swollen by run-off from the mountains to the north. Petronius pointed at the closest of the city's roofs, water cascading from a drainpipe unable to cope with the flow of rainwater.

'Things are going to get interesting for the crew of the *Night Witch*, I'd imagine.'

After another hour or so of steady progress, one of the vessel's sharper-eyed crewmen called out, pointing to the northern horizon. Marcus saw what it was that had caught his attention, an almost invisible cloud of ochre dust, barely visible against the oncoming storm's dark grey wall as it swept down from the north in pursuit of the fleeing vessel.

'Riders. Only a few, but even one is sufficient to bring more of them.'

They watched grim-faced as the thin plume thrown up by their pursuers' horses grew steadily thicker, deviating to neither left nor right, and Thracius shook his head in disgust.

'As if that bloody storm wasn't enough. They're riding down the line of the river.'

He paused for a moment, rubbing his chin and staring back at the oncoming riders.

'Perhaps they've worked out that last night's attack was a deliberate distraction. Or perhaps it's just a patrol.'

'But if they see us?'

The master stared at the horsemen's dust for a moment before answering, and Marcus guessed that he was working out distances and travel speed.

'We're still hours from the joining of the two rivers, Tribune, and even then the Khabur winds just as bad as this. We need to buy ourselves more time, or they'll catch us before we make the turn. You, Tribune, will have to make sure the king's man doesn't try to escape, or to draw attention to us.'

While he issued a string of orders to the crew, then steered the boat into the shelter of the right bank where the river swung to the west, Marcus went forward to join the king, Lugos looming behind him.

'My apologies, Your Majesty, but I must restrain you both.'

Osroes nodded wearily, his eyes still dull and the set of his body listless.

'I was wondering why your captain has pulled into the bank. You have seen some sign of my people?'

'A patrol. Lugos?'

The big Briton stepped forward, Martos close by with a hand on the hilt of his sword, much to the amusement of Gurgen who held his hands out to be bound at the wrists.

'Whatever it is that makes you think I might resist this monster without so much as a toothpick, Prince Martos, you are much deluded.'

Martos waited for Marcus's translation, his face unchanging as he listened to the words.

'I sense danger in you, Parthian, and the last time I ignored that sense it cost me my wife and children.'

The noble shrugged, settling into the boat's curved side and closing his eyes.

'Wake me when you're ready to release me.'

Several of the crew had busied themselves anchoring the vessel to the bank's grass-covered earth, while others had brought forth several bows from a wooden box in the vessel's stern, each with a thick sheaf of arrows attached to the curved wooden staves, their strings kept safe from moisture in sealed waxed leather pouches. Stringing the bows and taking cover at the top of the bank, they peered over its lip across the flat ground beyond, and the plume of dust that was now close enough for the riders to be clearly visible.

'Four men.'

Thracius nodded at Marcus's count, waving his men down below the bank's lip and speaking loudly enough to be heard by everyone, his voice hard with command.

'They must *all* die here. If any of them escape to raise an alarm, then their mates will catch up with us within hours, most likely before we reach the Khabur. We'll only have one chance to finish them all without leaving any survivors, and that means waiting until they are close enough that we can't miss.'

Listening intently as the distant patter of hoofs on the hard baked earth gradually hardened to a drumbeat, the riders drawing steadily closer to their hiding place, the sailors waited with arrows nocked to their bowstrings, each of them looking to their leader for the command to attack. What it was that betrayed their presence was never clear to Marcus, perhaps a swift impatient glance over the bank's lip at the wrong time born of fear, or nerves, or perhaps one of the riders sighted the boat's black outline peeking from the bank's cover, but whatever it was that alerted the Parthian scouts, their reaction was instant. Shouting a warning that had his comrades reaching reflexively for arrows, their bows already strung and out of their bow cases, the closest of them hurled his spear at whatever it was that he had seen, the long iron blade catching one of the crewmen squarely in the throat as he rose to shoot an arrow at the scouts, sending him toppling back down the bank to fall backwards into the boat at Gurgen's feet with blood pouring from the deep wound.

The crew rose from their hiding places with brave determination and loosed their first arrows with more speed than accuracy, dropping one of the riders with the fletched end of a shaft protruding from his chest, and hitting two of the horses, but the Parthians' response was swift and deadly. Another of the crewmen jerked back with an arrow in his chest, as the scouts' return shots whipped into the ambush with the accuracy of men who had been using bows on horseback for most of their lives. Martos snatched the bow from his spasming fingers, nocking a shaft and rising from his place in defiance of the risk, sighting down the arrow for a moment before putting its wickedly barbed iron head squarely into the closest man's chest. The master loosed his second attempt with equal nerve, ignoring a shot that whistled past his ear and pinning a rider's thigh to his beast's flank with a deliberately aimed arrow. The last man fell with a pair of Roman arrows in his side, toppling out of the saddle to land on his head with a distinct snap of breaking bone.

The surviving scout turned his horse and spurred it away, ducking under the arrows that were sent wildly after him, both horse and rider badly wounded by the arrow protruding from his left thigh to judge from the beast's uneven gait and its rider's stiff, agonised posture. Martos loosed again, putting his last shot into the man's right shoulder and almost knocking him over the horse's neck, but by some miracle the Parthian stayed on his mount and rode on, too distant for any realistic attempt to bring him down. Marcus leapt to his feet, sprinting towards the spot where the only unwounded horse stood nudging its fallen rider with a gentle muzzle, uncomprehending of the fact that the man was already dead, his head canted at an unnatural angle. Snatching up the dead man's spear with his good left hand he stabbed it into the ground beside the horse, heaving himself into the saddle and then pulling the weapon's blade free of the earth in which it was buried, transferring it to hang from his right hand before wheeling the beast around with the reins gripped in the other, digging his heels into its flanks.

The wounded rider had a quarter-mile start, but his horse was clearly struggling with the effects of the arrow wound it had sustained in the short bloody fight, its pace slowing as the blood loss that painted its flank and its rider's leg dark red weakened its muscles. The Parthian looked back, and on seeing Marcus bearing down upon him raised his bow, blood-covered fingers groping for an arrow. Putting the shaft to the bow's string he drew it back as far as his weakened arm could manage, but the resulting shot was both weak and misdirected, the arrow striking the ground a dozen paces to the right of the oncoming Roman. He reached for another, but as he was struggling to nock the arrow, his hand shaking visibly with the shock of his wounds, Marcus dropped the reins and gripped the spear in his left hand, leaning in to stab the long blade into the hapless rider's chest, punching him out of his saddle to lie broken and bleeding in the plain's dust.

Reining the horse in and dismounting, he walked slowly back towards the fallen Parthian, looking down the spear's shaft at the dying man. The scout stared up at him uncomprehendingly, muttered something unintelligible and then spasmed, his body tensing for a moment before collapsing back onto the dry earth with a death rattle in his throat, the life leaving his eyes as the last breath sighed from his body.

The *Night Witch*'s crew were already hard at work digging a grave for their comrades when he reached the river, Thracius nodding his respect as the Roman pushed the bloodied spear's head into the ground, dropped the shield he had taken from the dead man beside it and dismounted. They dug in silence, Martos and Lugos taking spades from the first men to tire and working alongside the sailors to deepen the hole until the master judged it sufficient to protect their comrades from carrion animals.

'Get them in and fill it up. We'll say the words later, when we know we won't be joining them for a quick trip across the Styx.'

Marcus made his way down to the *Night Witch*, releasing Gurgen from his bonds and placing the shield beside the king, who had fallen into a deep sleep despite the hectic events taking place around him.

'This may prove useful for the king's protection.'

The noble looked dourly at the blood speckled across the Roman's tunic, then at the pool of blood left in the boat's curved bottom by the crew member who had fallen to the thrown spear.

'His blood, or another's?'

Marcus looked down at the stains.

'One of yours, a wounded scout. He probably wouldn't have lived long, there were two arrows in him.'

'A mercy killing then.'

The Roman looked up, but where he had expected to find a stare of irony, Gurgen's face was sympathetic.

'Perhaps. He was still trying to kill me, when I put him down.'

'No man can do any more to bring honour to his name. He would have been grateful for thc speed of your strike, at the end. As you may come to understand, when we reach Ctesiphon . . .'

Bodies buried, and with the dead Parthians and their horses left to lie where they had fallen, the vessel's crew reboarded and cast off, raising the sail at the master's command.

'They'll be too tired to row after that, and I reckon the river's running too fast for oars in any case. I'll let half of them get some sleep while the rest help me steer this bitch.'

Marcus watched while he skippered the boat through the seemingly unending succession of bends in the river. Those crew who hadn't rolled themselves into their hides and immediately fallen asleep worked constantly to adjust the sail's angle to the wind, while Thracius steered the vessel expertly around the river's meanderings. He looked round to find Marcus studying his expert use of the rudder to cut each bend in the river as closely as he dared, and pointed back at the storm-laden northern horizon.

'If you want to do something useful Tribune, you could keep an eye open back the way we came? I'd like some warning if we're going to be run down by several hundred of those bastards, because being taken alive by those animals isn't on my list of good ways to die. And wash that blood out of your tunic before it dries hard, you're supposed to be a Roman emissary but you look more like a river pirate.'

'A pirate? There are bandits on the river?'

The master laughed tersely.

'Why else do you think we carry weapons? You're not sailing the Middle Sea now, young sir, the river we're heading for carries enough wealth to make an unscrupulous crew who aren't afraid of the sight of blood rich very quickly indeed, if they don't pick the wrong ship to attack. And trust me, when you consider just how much fun it is to earn a living from fishing, it's no surprise that more than one village on the Euphrates harbours pirates.'

The *Night Witch* ran south before a freshening northerly wind, the oncoming storm's gusts bellying her sail, and after a while the master told his men to bring down the canvas and raise a smaller sheet in its place.

'The wind's getting too strong, the mast'll break if I leave that sail up! And the river's running so fast that all I really need is enough of a push to keep control of her heading!'

The shouted words were torn from his mouth by the wind's scream, barely audible to Marcus from less than a foot away, the two men watching the crew fight to pull the sail down without losing it.

'If it gets much worse we'll have to take shelter against the bank!'

A yell from behind made them both turn, to find a sailor pointing back up the river into the mass of darkness that dominated a third of the sky, his eyes fixed on the horizon. Against the brooding tower of iron-grey cloud, the smudge of ochre dust was almost invisible as it blew straight towards them, and Marcus shook his head as he realised that their pursuers were almost certainly riding into the gritty, choking fog churned up by their horse's hoofs. The master looked at the dust plume for a moment, then turned back to the river ahead of them, turning the rudder to accommodate yet another bend.

'That puts mooring up out of the question! There's another two or three miles to run before we reach the Khabur, so it's going to be a close thing whether they catch us before we make the turn, from the look of it! But if we do get there first, the river runs straight and true for a few miles, pretty much, a chance for us to lose them by running as fast as this bitch'll go when she doesn't have to make a turn every few dozen paces!'

Cupping his hands he bellowed an order at the struggling sailors.

'Leave that sail up! I want every last bit of speed out of the old cow!'

Listing violently under the wind's harsh treatment, with the crew taking turns to lean out over the hull's side to keep the

Night Witch from turning over, Thracius guided his vessel through the Mygdonius's remaining bends with cool-headed precision, never once looking back to check on their pursuers' progress, so intent was he on cutting each turn as finely as possible. After a few moments Marcus saw a second, smaller dust plume separate itself from the main body and begin to outpace the larger group. He shouted to the master, pointing back to the north.

'They've detached a party of outriders on the fastest horses! How much more of this river do we have to cover?'

The older man shrugged, putting the rudder over and aiming for the apex of the next bend.

'A mile or so? I've been concentrating on not sinking, not bend counting!'

The enemy advance party came on swiftly, thrashing their horses mercilessly as if they knew that they would lose the chance to stop the boat's escape if they didn't reach a shooting position before the *Night Witch* made her imminent turn south into the Khabur's course. Marcus momentarily considered getting Martos to string a bow and ready himself to shoot back at them, then realised that with the wind so strong in their faces the effort would be futile. The master shouted encouragement to his crew, pointing to a massive rock on the riverbank as he guided the vessel round the next bend so tightly that Marcus could have reached out and touched the enormous boulder.

'We're almost there! I recognise that rock! Just three more bends!'

The boat was heeled over in a turn to the west, and in the moment before the master snapped the rudder over to haul her around the river's bend to the east, Marcus stared over the vessel's right-hand side at the oncoming riders. The main body were too distant to be any threat, but the outriders were close enough that he could make out individual horsemen, spectral figures engulfed in the dust of their passage. Thracius flicked a swift glance over his shoulder.

'How close are they?'

'A mile or so!'

The older man's scowl of concentration hardened, his eyes locked on the next bend, and with nothing to contribute the Roman stared back over the stern, attempting to calculate the fast closing distance between the hunters and their intended prey.

'I'd be amused, if it weren't for the fact that I'll soon be dead if we don't outrun them!'

Martos had come to stand next to him, bracing himself against the boat's side as the master threw his rudder over and slewed the vessel into another hard turn.

'No means of shooting back at them! No way to protect ourselves against their arrows! We can only hope that the captain there has it right when he says we are almost at the next river.'

Cutting the bend's apex so close that Marcus could see the sand beneath them through the river's water, Thracius pointed forward, bellowing an order at his crew.

'Row! Row for your worthless lives!'

Marcus and Martos looked forward, realising with rising hope that the river before them ran straight for a quarter of a mile before seeming to meet a dead end, the junction with the Khabur. The crew threw themselves at their oars, pulling with all their might at the shafts in one last frantic effort, and the two friends turned back to stare at the oncoming riders, now less than half a mile distant. As they watched, the foremost rider loosed an arrow, the iron head a bright flash of polished metal against the looming storm's dark grey curtain.

'Is he mad?'

Martos's comment died in his throat as the shaft soared improbably high into the air, literally carried on the storm's arms, then tipped over at the apogee of its flight and flickered down towards them, vanishing into the water a hundred paces back in the vessel's wake. The two men looked at each other in dismay, Martos shaking his head. The entire group of horsemen loosed their arrows, which were lifted and strewn by the storm's fury to land in a wide scatter, none any closer to the *Night Witch* than fifty paces, but the next volley, sent skywards straight after the first, fell closer still. Flicking his gaze back to the junction with the Khabur, Marcus watched as Thracius eased his rudder over to the right, expertly leaning his vessel into a steadily tightening left turn designed to put them into the Khabur's wide main channel as swiftly as possible. He looked back with a grin, still unaware of the Parthian archers' threat.

'The Khabur's running fast! Once we're round this bend we'll be out of range so quickly that—'

A windblown scattering of arrows speared down across the *Night Witch*'s course, a pair of shafts seeming to spring out of the boat's deck less than a foot from one hapless rower, and while the master goggled at them, another arced down out of the black sky with the cruel accuracy of the random shot, stabbing deep into the space behind his collarbone with barely more than its fletching still exposed. With an upward roll of his eyes he sagged onto the rudder, forcing it hard over and sending the speeding boat curving round to the left, the taut sail's driving force throwing it bodily onto the mud beach where the two rivers joined. With a rasping grind of wood against gritty sand the boat ran hard aground, stuck fast in the deep mud where river and land met.

Shorn of their leader the crew dithered momentarily, long enough for another volley of arrows to fall in their random scatter across the beach. Most of them overshot the stranded vessel, but three struck the boat's wooden planks with dull thumps, further terrifying the sailors. Seeing the rising panic in their faces, and, as the first of them dropped their oars and stood with the clear intention of running for their lives, Martos jumped over the side onto the soft mud below, ploughing through the morass to firmer ground and then striding up the bank before turning to draw his sword, bellowing a warning down at them.

'Any man who tries to run, dies here!'

The crew turned to face Marcus, who had drawn the eagle-pommelled gladius and was looking down it at them with a furious scowl. He gestured to the stricken master, lolling against the rudder with the ashen face and quick, panting respiration of a man with little time left to live.

'Who's his deputy?'

The biggest of them raised a hesitant hand, flinching as another shower of arrows hissed down into the water off the boat's right-hand side.

'Get your men ready to row us off this sandbank, and get that sail down, it's holding us against the beach! Do it!'

Not giving the sailor time to question his orders, he turned to Lugos, who nodded his massive head and strode to the boat's bow, vaulting over the raised wooden prow and placing his massive hands on the wooden hull, straining his bulging muscles in an attempt to push the boat off the mud. Behind Marcus a deep commanding voice rose above the wind's bestial howl.

'He's not enough on his own!'

Marcus swung to face the Parthian captives, finding Gurgen on his feet and pointing at the recumbent Osroes.

'My only responsibility is to protect my king's life, and to stay here is to die here!'

The Parthian hurried up the ship's length and jumped over the side, ranging his strength alongside that of the massive Briton. Martos sheathed his sword and ran down the bank to join them, the three men heaving at the ship's hull with the corded muscles in their necks standing proud. A faint shiver ran through the boat's frame, and Marcus called out to them as he realised what had caused the slight movement.

'The river's rising fast! Keep pushing and she'll float off!'

Lifting the dying master away from the rudder, he laid the stricken sailor to one side, wincing as the pain of the movement contorted Thracius's face into a silent scream, then crouched into the stern's slight protection and looked across the river. The huge towering mass of dark cloud loomed almost vertically above them, flickers of lightning illuminating it from within and sending booming crashes of thunder across the empty landscape. Beneath it on the Mygdonius's far bank, the Parthian horsemen had dismounted, and were loosing arrows as fast as they were able, the shafts blown in every direction by the gusting wind. The *Night Witch* lurched again, lifted slightly by the river's inexorable rise, and the three big men at her bow threw their full strength against the deadweight of her massive timbers. Still the sandy mud's sucking grip held the vessel fast, and Marcus pointed his gladius at the crew with a barked command that had them moving before they had time to think.

'We need to lighten the boat! Over the side!'

Swarming over the *Night Witch*'s side, they slid into the water with terrified stares towards the bowmen on the far bank who were still shooting steadily at a target that was, were it not for the wind playing havoc with their archery, too large to miss.

'Heave!'

Lugos's voice rose over the wind's din, and the three men arrayed on the boat's left side strained their sinews again, Martos bellowing as his feet pumped in the mud that was denying them a clean purchase on the ground beneath them. The deck beneath Marcus's feet lurched as the *Night Witch* slid a foot down the beach, and all three of the big men threw themselves at the boat's side with roars and curses as her hull, lifted fractionally by the rising river, slid slowly back down the muddy slope. With a scrape of gravel that was more felt than heard, the boat eased her bulk gratefully down into the deeper water, drifting out into the fast-flowing water with a slow, uncontrolled pirouette that was turning her bow to point back up the river.

'Oars!'

The crew pulled themselves over the *Night Witch*'s side, one man jerking as he heaved himself out of the river, an arrow's long shaft protruding from his back. He stayed where he was for a moment, balanced between the effort that had lifted him out of the water and the iron's agonising intrusion deep into his body, then fell back into the racing water and was lost to view. The rest of the crew threw themselves at their oars, knowing what to do without having to be ordered, backing water on the right side while the opposite bank pulled mightily to swing the boat's prow back round to the south. Marcus sighted down the boat's length, waiting for the prow to clear the riverbank to the left before bellowing his next command, pointing with gladius down the vessel's length.

'Row!'

Another scattering of arrows fell like iron sleet as the crew strained their bodies at the oars, their bodies stretched back over the men behind them with each stroke in an explosive effort inspired by the prospect of escape from the murderous rain of arrows from the far bank. A man close enough for Marcus to reach out and touch screamed as an arrow pinned his foot to the deck, but kept rowing despite the sudden horrific pain of the shattered bones. Realising the danger to Osroes, Martos snatched up the Parthian shield that Marcus had taken from the initial skirmish, holding it over the unconscious king to protect him from the arrows' random paths.

With the river's spate at their back, the *Night Witch* gained speed quickly, spearing out into the racing current where the Mygdonius and the Khabur's courses met with her hull bucking against the chop, and Marcus threw the rudder over to his right to sling her into a sharp turn to the left, into the bigger river's stream. More arrows fell around them, but the shooting was growing wilder as the distance between bowmen and target lengthened, the gusting storm winds toying with the lofted arrows and dropping them across the Khabur's racing waters without regard to the archers' aim.

Marcus realised that while Martos had managed to climb aboard as the boat's stern had slid back into the river, Gurgen and Lugos were still clinging to the vessel's bow.

'Get them aboard!'

A pair of crewmen pulled their oars on board, rose and took a grip of Gurgen's arms, pulling him over the boat's side to flop exhausted on the deck in a pool of water from his soaked clothing, gasping for breath just from the effort of clinging onto the bow's timbers as the river had pulled at his body. As they were struggling to drag Lugos's massive weight on board, a final flight of arrows arched down out of the blackness that pressed down on the river from the north, one last volley loosed at a far greater distance than would have been possible without the wind behind the archers. One of the men hauling at Lugos's arms released his grip and scrabbled with both hands at the arrow buried in his back, dropping to his knees with his spine arched and his mouth open in a scream that was lost in the wind's howl. The big Briton pulled himself over the bow, his teeth gritted against the pain of his own wound, standing on the deck with blood running down his leg from the shaft protruding from the side of his thigh.

A bright flash of sheet lightning lit the bruised sky a sudden livid orange, the clap of thunder that followed an instant later seemingly loud enough to split the world in two, and with a hissing fury that tore the river's roiling surface into watery chaos, a sheet of rain ripped across the landscape, instantly reducing visibility to a hundred paces and putting paid to any further archery. The boat's exhausted crew slumped over their oars, the man closest to Marcus staring at his ruined foot in silent horror as the teeming rain washed away the blood that was still oozing around the arrow's shaft, his comrades' attention fixed on Thracius's corpse. The big man who had declared himself the master's second in command stood, walking down the boat's length and bending to speak into Marcus's ear.

'Best if I steer her now, sir. We need to moor up until this rain lets up, or we'll risk running into a rock and ripping her bottom out.'

The Roman stood, gesturing to the rudder.

'As you think best. I doubt the enemy will be doing anything more constructive under this deluge.'

'What the bloody hell do you think they're up to?'

Scaurus looked out over the city's northern wall, shading his eyes with a raised hand. The Parthian line that surrounded the fortress was unchanged, the soldiers busy at work deepening and extending the entrenchments that had been dug in a complete circle around the walls. A massive white tent had been erected across the Mygdonius's course just outside the range of Nisibis's bolt throwers, presumably to act as Narsai's headquarters and makeshift palace, a stream of officers coming and going while smoke from cooking fires hazed the air above it.

'King Narsai's not a man to forego his luxuries, is he? How many other men have a river running through their tent?'

The prefect pulled a face.

'If I could just get another fifty paces range out of the bolt throwers, I'd give that bastard the shock of his bloody life.'

Petronius had ordered his first spear to limit the bolt throwers to occasional harassing shots, not wanting to waste their stock of missiles, and so the enemy had dug more or less without interference while the prefect had laughed at their efforts.

'Completely without any military value, given they've no means of putting a hole in the walls. Whereas whatever it is that they're up to over there in the hills looks somewhat more interesting, don't you think?'

The legatus nodded slowly, staring out over the enemy lines to a spot a mile or more distant, where the walls of the river's valley ran down to merge with the plain, leaving the Mygdonius to run across the plain's open expanse. The repetitive sound of axes striking wood echoed distantly across the landscape, and as they watched, a tree on the river's banks toppled to the ground, the creaking roar of its fall reduced to a sigh by the distance.

'They want wood, and in some quantity given they've been cutting trees down all morning. If I didn't know better, I'd say they're building something . . . but what? As you say, siege engines might be their best bet, if they want to have any chance of putting a big enough hole in the city wall to attack through.'

'Indeed. Towers wouldn't be any use, because the moat's too wide for them to get close enough to the wall. And what else would they want all that wood for?'

Scaurus stared out at the mystery Parthian activity for a moment longer before replying.

'Damming the river?'

Petronius shook his head briskly.

'What would be the point? It's a well-known fact that the city has several fresh water springs within the walls, that's the reason why it was built here in the first place. They can piss in the river, float dead cows down it and yes, they could even dam it without my losing any sleep. No, it'll be something much more sinister than that, I'd imagine. I just wish I could work out what on earth they're intending do with all that wood.'

After an hour or so the rain abated from its constant roaring deluge to a relatively gentle downfall, and Marcus ordered the crew to stop bailing out the water that had been threatening to swamp the *Night Witch*. The sailors slumped exhaustedly onto their rowing benches, and the young tribune took a head count while they were temporarily still.

'Six men.'

He turned to find Gurgen behind him.

'And there were twelve of them when we left your fortress. Barely enough to handle the boat, I'd guess.'

Marcus shrugged.

'Barely enough will have to do. I'm not going to give up now, not having got this far.'

'And the horsemen pursuing us? What if they—'

'Cross the river while it's in flood? They won't dare that feat until the water's receded a good deal, and stopped flowing quite so fast. And their bowstrings will have been soaked in that downpour. No, we're safe from Narsai's men, for the time being. But we do need to put some distance between ourselves and the last place they saw us.'

He beckoned Thracius's deputy over.

'What's your name?'

'Tertius, Tribune.'

'Well then, Tertius, we need to move from here, or the Parthians may appear over that hill to finish the job.'

He pointed over the sailor's shoulder at the shallow rise in the ground that ran down to the Khabur's left bank.

'Not too far, just enough to convince them we're long gone, when they manage to cross the Mygdonius.'

'I don't know, Tribune.'

The bearded crewman shook his head with a look of exhaustion.

'The lads're pretty much all done . . .'

He waved a hand at the remaining crew members, half of whom were already asleep where they had slumped. Marcus stepped closer to him, lowering his voice.

'You have food and water?'

The sailor nodded.

'Not that anyone's going to want water, after that.'

'Wine?'

A knowing calculation crept over the other man's features.

'A little.'

'Then here it is. Get them awake, get them fed, and give me twenty miles, and then they can sleep for an hour or two. And you, Tertius, will be master of the *Night Witch*, if you think you can manage the added responsibility. Of course, you could just name Thracius's successor, if you're not sure you've got it in you?'

The crewman grinned at him, his fatigue forgotten.

'I'm your man, Tribune. Appoint me master and I'll have these lazy bastards on their feet and pushing us south before you've got time to work out my pay rate.'

Marcus nodded, holding out his hand for the *Night Witch*'s new master to clasp.

'Wake up, you rough-arsed refugees from a Syrian prick doctor's waiting room!'

The crew stirred, turning indignant faces to stare at their erstwhile comrade.

'Get your fucking feet on the deck, we've a sail to raise! You . . .'

He pointed at the youngest of them.

'You, open the food locker and make sure every man gets a double ration of bread, and a cup of wine as well! We need to get twenty miles between us and those dick-beating horse humpers before we can sleep, unless any of you helmet polishers wants to risk having your foot nailed to the deck like poor old Tarsus there!'

All eyes turned to the stricken sailor whose foot had been freed swiftly but brutally once the immediate danger was past. The new master, with a swift and decisive approach to the problem, had pulled a pair of pincers from the tool chest and taken a deceptively experimental grip of the arrow's iron head, as if sizing up the task at hand while the wounded sailor had moaned with pain at the arrowhead's slight movement. Raising his eyebrows at the men behind the sailor, he'd waited until they had taken a firm grip of their comrade's arms, wrapped a big hand around his ankles and, ignoring his mate's bulging eyes and babbled entreaties, clamped the pincers hard to the arrowhead and torn it free. The wounded man was now asleep on his bench, his foot wrapped in a bloody length of cloth, exhausted by the ordeal but still moaning with the pain.

After a moment of lethargic thought, the remaining crew members turned to their tasks like sleepwalkers, too tired to contest their new master's flatly stated orders.

'You chose well.'

Marcus shrugged tiredly at Gurgen's statement as the vessel cast off once more, slipping out into the middle of the Khabur's stream and heading south and east down the river's winding course.

'The man who taught me to fight was a retired gladiator. He showed me how to fight and kill an opponent with any weapon that comes to hand, but the most important thing I learned from him was always to watch the other man's eyes.'

'He was right. And in that man's eyes you saw . . . ?'

'The same flat-eyed lack of interest in anything other than getting the job done that I look for in my officers. The look of a man who wouldn't care what his friends thought of him if there was a promotion in it for him.'

The Parthian grinned.

'And what is it that you see in my eyes, Tribune?'

Marcus looked back at him levelly, but before he could answer a weak voice from behind them snatched the Parthian's attention from the conversation.

'Where are we?'

Osroes was awake, blinking painfully in the afternoon's dull iron light, and Gurgen hurried to him as the king's face creased in puzzlement at the hard wooden surface beneath him.

'On the river Khabur, my king, heading south to join the Euphrates. We managed to give our pursuers the slip.'

He helped the weakened king to sit up against *Night Witch*'s side, taking a water bottle from Marcus and lifting it to Osroes' lips. The bidaxs covered the king's legs with a thick cloak, the heavy wool still damp from the deluge, steam rising into the thick, humid air.

'We were blessed, it seems, and yet cursed at the same time. The gods sent a storm to cover our escape from your cousin Narsai's pursuit, but that same storm gave their arrows unnatural reach. Some men died.'

He waved a hand in dismissal of the fact, and Marcus's lips narrowed in anger.

'Forgive me, Your Highness. I have wounded to attend.'

He found Martos and the new master examining the wounded, the Briton's eyes alive with concern for his friend. He looked down at the unconscious sailor.

'This one will live to pull an oar, although whether he'll ever prance around the ship with the rest of these water rats is less sure. There's nothing we can do but let him sleep and see what state the wound's in tomorrow. Whereas this monster . . .'

He gestured to Lugos, who sat in silence contemplating the arrow shaft that protruded from his thigh with stoic disregard.

'This, I will admit, worries me. Their arrows are barbed, and this one is stuck deep in the meat of his thigh. I fear that its removal might well open a blood vessel and cause him to bleed to death.'

Marcus nodded thoughtfully.

'He needs a trained medic. How far are we from Dura?'

Tertius thought for a moment.

'At least one hundred miles, Tribune, perhaps another twenty or thirty besides.'

He shrugged.

'I was not responsible for navigation. With the river in spate we will cover perhaps ten miles in each hour, with the sail raised.'

'Gurgen?'

The Parthian stood, walking across the boat's deck to his side.

'Roman?'

'You said you have studied maps of your empire. Where are we? Is this still Adiabene?'

The noble shook his head.

'No. Where the Mygdonius and the Khabur meet is the point where Narsai's rule ends, and thereafter it is the King of Kings who is master. This, Roman, is Parthia.'

As the sun dipped to meet the horizon, Tertius shook his men awake from their two-hour sleep, ignoring their exhausted curses and groans and setting them to work to raise *Night Witch*'s black sail. The vessel was quickly moving as fast as a distance runner's best pace, the fresh northerly wind bellying her sail out. Marcus looked about him as the vessel ran out of the cover of the raised riverbanks, relieved to find the golden-hued landscape empty of the pursuing forces he had feared might be within sight.

'We may stick out like a bridegroom's prick now, Tribune, but give it an hour and we'll be nothing more than a black hole in the river.'

He nodded at Tertius's confident words, but the master beckoned him closer with a conspiratorial expression.

'But you should be aware that the crew ain't happy to be making this run in the darkness.'

'Why? Isn't this the entire reason that the boat's painted black?'

The soldier chuckled quietly.

'It ain't the darkness that scares them. It's the spirits.'

'Spirits?'

The sailor laughed again.

'Judge for yourself, Tribune. We'll be there soon enough.'

The boat ran south at a brisk clip, riding the Khabur's flow with the breeze filling her sail and, with little else to do, her crew watched with obvious concern as the sun sank slowly down onto the western horizon.

'There! Shadikanni!'

A sharp-eyed sailor pointed south, and Marcus followed his arm to find a barely discernible cluster of ruined buildings in the dusk's gloom. The man made a warding gesture with his index and ring fingers raised, his face pale in the gloom.

'We should not pass through Saddikanni after nightfall. It is a place of evil!'

Staring at the ruins, Marcus shook his head.

'Our wounded cannot afford to wait another day. If we wait for daylight before passing this place, we will then be forced to wait for nightfall before we try to sail through the Parthian settlements to the south. And besides . . .'

He looked to the west, where the sun was sinking beneath the horizon.

'It won't be dark for a while yet. If you want to be through the city before then I suggest you row.'

The man stared at him for a moment, then hurried to his bench and took up his oar, shouting imprecations at his comrades as he urged them to do the same. Propelled to the speed of a sprinting athlete by the oars' additional thrust, the *Night Witch* flew across the water, Tertius grinning at his mates' discomfiture as he steered her through the river's bends towards the ruined city.

'I know a little of the history of this place.'

Gurgen was at Marcus's shoulder, his face unreadable in the growing gloom.

'The name for it these days is Horaba, but when this was a great city of Assyria it was named Saddikanni. This place was built when your great city of Rome was no more than a collection of savages living in huts made of mud, and the empire of which this city was only a very small part endured for two thousand years, from the time when a weapon made of bronze was the deadliest thing a man could put in his hand. The men that built this city conquered Egypt, Babylon and Persia. They ruled the Phoenicians, the Syrians, the Jews and the Arabs. They defeated the Hittites, the Ethiopians, the Cimmerians and the Scythians. They rose to rule the world, Roman, in the same way that your empire aspires to control everything it touches, but it crumbled to dust, as all empires must when they no longer produce men with the strength and will to keep them vital. They became soft, and were overrun by the younger and more vital peoples around them, and now we do battle over the scraps of what was once the mightiest power in the world. Such is the way of all kingdoms, unless the strong act when they have the chance.'

He fell silent, and both men stood in silence as the boat rounded the last bend and slid into the ruined city's deep shadow. The wind gusted, rippling the *Night Witch*'s black sail, and while the crew stared at it aghast, their oars momentarily forgotten, the breeze suddenly fell away to no more than a zephyr, leaving the canvas dangling emptily. The ship's new master snarled an order at his men.

'Row! Row like fuck!'

Even the previously amused Tertius seemed to have taken his crew's nervousness to heart, bellowing at his men to put their backs into their rowing. On both sides of the river the wreckage of a once proud city rose above the river's banks, themselves lined in the remnants of what was once a stone dockside. On the eastern bank rose a single tall column, above which stood the silhouette of a winged bull, still visible as a black outline against the deep purple sky behind it, and the nearest sailor to Marcus quailed at the sight.

'It has no power! I am an acolyte of the light bearer, he who slew the bull and feasted in heaven above with the Sun God himself! The Lord Mithras will protect us from any evil that dwells here!'

The crew rowed even harder, caught between the ancient city's terror and the hard-voiced tribune's cast-iron certainty in his own god, but where several of them muttered their own prayers to Mithras, Gurgen simply shook his head and laughed aloud.

'*My* god is Ahura Mazda, which means "*the light of wisdom*" in your barbarous tongue. All other deities are subservient to his will, and the sun and moon dance to his command. And this?'

He waved a hand at the ruins passing on either side of the vessel. 'This is a warning, nothing more and nothing less. All empires come to dust in their time, when strong men are no longer to be found. Wake me when we reach anything of note.'

He sat alongside the once more recumbent Osroes, pulling the hood of his cloak down over his head and, it seemed, falling asleep almost immediately. With a final spurt from the oarsmen, the *Night Witch* left the last of the ruins behind her, columns and shattered walls almost invisible against the sky as dusk deepened into night, and Marcus stared back over the ship's stern with a thoughtful expression.

'You chose not to wake me, I see?'

Marcus shrugged at the big Parthian.

'You asked to be alerted if we passed anything of interest. Are you especially interested in fishing villages?'

Gurgen grinned at him.

'And it saved you having to bind me again.'

'Quite so. Although if you'd asked nicely I would happily have put you ashore to spend the rest of your days eating fish and making little warriors with the local women.'

The nobleman shook his head, raising a hand in mock terror.

'Spare me! A few days of untroubled wenching perhaps, but a lifetime?'

Marcus grinned back at him.

'Quite so.'

'So, master of my destiny, where are we now?'

The Roman stretched his weary body, pointing back up the river.

'Back there is Sirhi, the last Parthian outpost on the river before we re-enter imperial territory—'

'This is the Euphrates?'

The smile broadened a little.

'Yes. After our encounter with the spirits of long-dead Assyrians at dusk last night, the crew kept rowing for much longer than seemed likely. And the Khabur was running faster than any of them has ever seen before, doubtless something to do with the huge amount of rainwater that has fallen across the mountains to the north. So, whatever the reason, we passed through Sirhi before dawn, not that there was much to see, and we'll reach Dura soon enough.'

The desert fortress stood high on an escarpment above the river's western bank, and Gurgen stared up at its high walls with thinly disguised irritation.

'Everywhere on our empire's borders with Rome we are confronted by naked force. Do you wonder that men like Narsai dream of taking your boot off our throat?'

Marcus nodded equably enough.

'I understand. Just as I'm sure you know that this was a Parthian fortress, until the present King of Kings started the war that led to its capture.'

'And having taken it from us, you keep it for no better reason than its position astride a major trade route. Palmyra is a hundred miles that way . . .' He pointed to the west. 'Which means that your empire takes two bites at the caravans before their goods can enter Roman territory.'

'We probably also keep it because we're quite attached to Palmyra, I'd imagine, since the crossing here is equally as passable to your cataphracts as it is to baggage animals.'

The two men fell quiet as the *Night Witch* coasted up to the city's stone wharf, the exhausted sailors slumping at their benches as dock workers tied the boat to the quayside. An official came bustling along the wharf in high dudgeon, raising a hand to point at the disreputable-looking craft.

'You can't just turn up and moor up, you scruffy shower of—'

He took a step back as Marcus turned to face him, taking in the young Roman's bronze breastplate and deliberately aristocratic mien.

'Ah . . . my apologies . . . Tribune?'

Marcus nodded brusquely.

'Tribulus Corvus, Third Gallic.'

'The Third? You're a long way from home sir. I—'

'Quite. And you are?'

'A humble slave, Tribune, dockyard overseer. I report to—'

'Fetch him, please, whoever he is. I need this vessel resupplying with food and water, and I need a doctor immediately. There are wounded men aboard.'

Gurgen grinned at him as the slave turned tail and hurried away.

'You know how to treat your underlings, I see.'

The Roman pulled a face.

'It's not to my taste, I have to say, but there's no time to be lost. And no . . .'

He turned to face Tertius, who was hovering expectantly behind him.

'You cannot give the crew leave to go ashore, nor do you personally need to go up into the fortress for supplies or equipment of any nature. The local whores will doubtless manage well enough without your custom, and not only do your men need a few hours' sleep, but were we unwise enough to allow them off this vessel, I don't expect we'd see half of them again.'

When the doctor arrived he took one look at the sailor with the wrecked foot and ordered him to be carried away to the fortress's infirmary.

'I'll have a proper look at that horrible mess later, although there's probably not much I can do for him other than keep it clean and give it time to heal the best it can. Now, what have we here?'

He squatted down alongside the uncomplaining Lugos, pulling a thoughtful face as he unwrapped the bandage that Martos had put around his thigh the previous afternoon.

'You're a big bastard, aren't you? Thracian?'

'Briton.'

The deep rumbling reply caused him to raised his eyebrows again as he bent to sniff the wound.

'Smells sweet enough to me. Let's have that arrow out, shall we?'

He worked quickly, first pushing in the curved blades that would prevent the arrow's barbs from snagging the flesh inside the wound, then positioning a pair of hooked blades over them ready for the extraction.

'Ready, big man?'

'Ready.'

Marcus nodded his appreciation as the medic smoothly drew the arrowhead from his friend's thigh, the Briton's jaw clenching at the pain as the pocket in his flesh was forced wider to allow for its removal.

'It's usual to pack the wound with honey once the missile has been removed, but I have a preference for one small variation on that method.' He reached into his pack and drew out a small bottle. 'Vinegar. It'll hurt.' The Briton stared back at him impassively. 'But it seems to clean the wound out better than anything else. My father used it, and so do I, if you're willing?'

Lugos nodded, and the doctor clapped him on the shoulder, pulling a short length of wood from the bag and handing it to him.

'Good man. Here, bite on this and it'll be over before you know it.'

The Briton positioned the sawn-off piece of spear shaft between his teeth, biting down experimentally as the medic uncorked the bottle and positioned it over the wound.

'Ready?'

A nod was his only reply, and with a quick jerk of his wrist he doused the wound with the pungent brown fluid. Lugos's entire body convulsed with the sudden agony as the sour wine mercilessly stung his raw flesh, his biceps swelling like melons as he rode the pain, snarling as he bit down hard into the wooden shaft. As the pain lessened the Briton's eyes opened and he took the wood from his mouth, handing it to the doctor who stared at it in bemusement, his eyes widening at the deep gouges torn in the wood by his patient's massive jaw.

'I don't think that's going to be much use to anyone else . . .'

Tossing it over the side, he spooned honey into the wound, then wadded and bandaged the big man's thigh.

'I'll have some linen sent down. Make sure you change the dressing once a day until it's completely scabbed over, and the patient is to avoid physical exertion that might reopen the wound until the scab drops off.'

As he walked off the ship, a man in his late twenties wearing a bronze chest plate like Marcus's arrived on the quayside, deliberately waiting until the young tribune walked up the gangplank to greet him.

'Tribune Corvus?'

Marcus nodded, taking the offered hand.

'I'm Porcius, Legatus commanding the Sixth Ironclad.'

He acknowledged the younger man's crisp salute with a wave of his hand.

'Here with a five-cohort detachment of my men, which makes me responsible for the security of this outpost. This is a very sensitive and commercially important fortress, Tribune, which Governor Dexter believes merits the presence of a legion commander and half its strength to safeguard the trade route to Palmyra and ensure that the Parthians don't try to get clever with this particular frontier. And now here *you* are, with no warning, in a vessel painted black, which I'm told you've sailed here from Nisibis. When I found Nisibis on the map I was intrigued to discover that it's over two hundred miles from here, up a tributary of the Khabur river that isn't even marked as navigable. You've landed wounded, requested supplies and, I'm told, you intend to continue down river until you run into Parthian forces.'

He raised an eyebrow at Marcus.

'So, would you care to enlighten me as to why I shouldn't have you detained as a risk to peace and stability in the border area?'

Martos watched as the two men talked, smiling to himself as the detachment's commander followed Marcus's pointing hand and looked down at the sleeping figure of King Osroes with a startled expression.

'Gods below! That's the King of Media? The King of Kings' son?'

Porcius shook his head in wide-eyed amazement.

'And you've got him lying on the bare boards of a river barge? Surely . . .'

He fell silent as Marcus raised an apologetic hand.

'With all due respect, Legatus, this man has led a deliberate invasion of Osrhoene, and his ally, the king of Adiabene, has laid siege to Nisibis with the clear intention of expelling Rome from a possession ceded to the empire as the consequence of our beating them in a war for which we weren't responsible. My legatus has ordered me—'

'Your legatus? Which legion?'

'Legatus Scaurus, commander of the Third Gallic.'

'I thought my colleague, Magius Lateranus, commanded the Third. Scaurus . . . The name seems familiar, but that's not a family name I recognise as senatorial.'

Marcus nodded crisply.

'The legatus is a member of the equestrian order, sir.'

'An equestrian, commanding a legion? Whose fool idea was . . .'

He fell silent at the sight of the younger man's grim smile.

'The appointment was made by the emperor, Legatus. I believe it was suggested by the imperial chamberlain, as a reward for services rendered with regard to matters concerning the praetorian prefect and a charge of treason.'

Gauging that he'd said enough he stopped talking, watching as his words sank in.

'I see. And your orders are . . . ?'

'To take this man to Ctesiphon. Legatus Scaurus hopes that this intercession will provoke the King of Kings to call off the army laying siege to Nisibis, and restore peace to the Syrian frontier.'

Porcius shook his head.

'From the little I know about their imperial court politics, I'd say that's a slim hope. King Arsaces isn't really in control of the empire, it seems.' He shrugged. 'But, if you're acting under the command of a fellow legion commander, and a well-connected man to boot, it's not my place to put obstacles in your way. Your vessel will be resupplied shortly and I'll provide you with a safe conduct to show the centurion in command at the next fort down river.'

He raised an eyebrow at Marcus.

'Have a care though. He might not be quite as impressed by your legatus's connections as I am.'

'At least they've stopped felling trees.'

Scaurus nodded, staring out over the Parthian lines to the north. At the edge of visibility he could just make out a camp of tents clustered around the spot where the Mygdonius emerged from the foothills that fed it.

'It has to be a dam. Why else would they be felling trees there?'

Petronius shook his head in equal bemusement.

'Agreed. But why? I can only think that they don't know we've got enough spring capacity within the walls to provide more than enough fresh water for every man, woman and child in the city.'

'The only way we'll find out is to put a man in that camp. And that's . . .'

The prefect shook his head again grimly.

'Impossible. They may not be able to break down the walls, but we're not going anywhere until this siege is raised.'

Both men looked out at the force surrounding Nisibis, and the encircling trenches that had been dug just outside of bolt-thrower range. The river's path through the Parthian forces to the south had been barred with tree trunks set in the riverbank on either side of the route the *Night Witch* had used to make her escape. Petronius sighed and turned to look over the city behind them.

'No, either Narsai gets bored and rides away . . .'

Scaurus gestured to the scene on the plain before them.

'Which looks unlikely. I'd say he's settling in for a long siege.'

'Or someone else comes along and tells him to desist. I think we're going to be here for a while.'

Tertius looked out over the *Night Witch*'s bow with a grim expression, spitting into the water that was relentlessly driving the vessel ever deeper into Parthian territory. Another day's voyage had taken them past the last Roman fort on the Euphrates, and the master was clearly troubled at the impending moment of their surrender to the enemy.

'You're still sure you want to do this, Tribune?'

Marcus turned a wry smile on Tertius.

'Starting to wonder how the Parthians will treat you?'

The sailor nodded.

'The thought had crossed my mind. The crew's wondering more than a little bit too.'

Gurgen stood up from his place beside Osroes.

'I'd say you've little to lose, and much to gain.'

Both men turned to look at him, the sailor bowing his head slightly.

'How might that be, if I might ask?'

The Parthian grinned wolfishly.

'Have you ever bedded a Parthian woman?'

Tertius shook his head. 'Once had a couple of whores who said they were Parthian. Their pimp promised me the pleasures of the exotic east.'

'And?'

'One of them pulled me off while the other tickled my arse with a feather. I told him I didn't find it all that exotic, once I'd broken his nose and taken my money back.'

'Ah . . .'

The sailor stared at him for a moment.

'Ah?'

Gurgen smiled at him.

'I'm sorry. I was simply reflecting on the pleasures that lie just around that bend in the river.'

'Really?'

'Really. Far be it from a man of my status to discuss matters of the flesh with a barbarian such as yourself, but I can assure you that real Parthian women are very different from any experience you may have enjoyed before. And of course with you being . . . different . . . they'll be all over you from the moment you step ashore. Women, eh?'

Tertius thought for a moment.

'And they're not going to want to take us to this city of theirs then?'

Gurgen laughed.

'A handful of sailors? I'd have thought not. It will be the tribune here who has the opportunity to enjoy imperial hospitality, and possibly his escorts. The court does so enjoy being treated to the sight of men from far-off kingdoms. Especially men as . . . colourful . . . as these. You, I expect, will be required to wait for them to return, with nothing better to do than entertain a succession of curious females. I expect it will become boring eventually . . .'

'I think we can take that chance.'

Tertius turned to his crew.

'You heard the man. Get rowing!'

Marcus leaned closer to Gurgen.

'Really? It all sounded a little unlikely to me.'

The Parthian grinned back at him.

'Your crew needed motivation – I provided it. In truth, since the port of Idu is, I believe, the highest point on the river that is navigable to ships from the ocean to the south, it is already well populated by seafaring men from far more interesting places than Syria. I suspect your sailors will very quickly come to realise that when it comes to female company, they will be paying customers like every other man in the port. Let us hope they have heavy purses.'

If Marcus had expected any sort of reception, hostile or otherwise, he was swiftly disabused by the sight that greeted them as they rounded the river bend and came in sight of Idu.

The *Night Witch*'s crew stared open-mouthed at the port's

crowded wharves, both sides of the river solid with moored shipping from which bales, crates, bundles and casks were being loaded and unloaded by an army of toiling dock workers.

'This is the last port on the navigable stretch of the river. Some of these ships have sailed here from ports too distant to be recorded on any map you Romans will ever have cause to use, bringing goods for shipment on to your empire that will make the merchants involved, and many men besides, rich.'

Gurgen pointed to a stretch of dock where several smaller vessels were being unloaded.

'Put us in there.'

Tertius frowned.

'But there's no space.'

'Get me close enough, and there soon will be.'

Once *Night Witch* was within hailing distance, he shouted a peremptory order at the closest of the supervisors, pointing at the recumbent Osroes. The man on the dockside visibly blanched, turning tail and running for the office where the cargoes were tallied and taxes levied. He returned a moment later with an official who was clearly his superior, and whose evident belief in that superiority, already tottering, was punctured equally swiftly by whatever it was that the Parthian noble said to him. As the crew watched with increasing amusement, a man wearing a sword strode down the dock and pushed his way through the gathering crowd, waving away their protests and directing the half-dozen soldiers following him to push them back out of the way. Turning to the river he called out a challenge in slow and heavily accented Greek, clearly still of the belief that the whole thing was a simple misunderstanding between the dock officials and a hapless trader.

'State your business!'

Gurgen replied with equal pugnacity, his patience clearly at its end.

'The man lying here is King Osroes of Media, beloved son of the King of Kings, may Ahura Mazda bless him with continued good health. If you do not clear a stretch of dock to enable me to bring him ashore immediately, then your master will be given the choice as to whether it is your head or his that adorns the gates of this city, when I finally find someone to speak to who is not an idiot. Perhaps this will help you to decide . . .'

He fished Osroes' crown from the bag in which it had been carried from Nisibis, holding it aloft.

'This is the crown of Media! And that man is the son of your emperor!'

11

'Greetings. You are honoured guests of the King of Kings. I am Artapanes, and on the behalf of my chief priest Bagadates I am bidden to greet you to Ctesiphon, and to extend the hospitality of our city to you.'

The priest had appeared on the dockside moments after a century-sized unit of Parthian guardsmen, and after a brief and vigorous discussion had led Marcus and the two Britons away while the soldiers had lifted the semi-conscious Osroes from the *Night Witch* and closed ranks around the king. The friends were provided with transport, horses for Marcus and Martos and a cart for Lugos, then escorted from the port to the gates of the empire's capital, Ctesiphon, where they were met by a party of the priest's acolytes armed with staffs and knives. Leading the three men through the city, Artapanes delivered them to an unprepossessing building in the shadow of a magnificent walled fortress. Only in the apparent safety of what he had termed a guest house, was the priest willing to speak. Martos looked about him, taking in the opulent furnishings and wall hangings.

'Your city is vast, a place of wonders for a northerner such as myself. May I walk the streets and enjoy the sights that are to be found?'

The priest who had met the party at the dockside shook his head with a small smile.

'Regrettably not. My senior has ruled that your presence on the streets might present you with more risk than he deems acceptable to such important guests. Were anything to happen to you it is doubtful that Rome would consider the matter an accident. And as you know, our relationship with Rome is still more than a little . . . strained. The high priest has ruled that you are ambassadors of your respective nations.'

He looked up at Lugos, shaking his head.

'Wherever they might be.'

Marcus stepped forward.

'I am Marcus Tribulus Corvus, a representative of Rome, an ambassador if you prefer the term. I have come to Ctesiphon in order to return the King of Kings' son to him, and to ask the king—'

'In good time. That you are Roman is evident to all who see you, and your self-professed role is of no interest to the priesthood. And these two men?'

'I am Martos, King of the Votadini people in the Roman province of Britannia, far to the north of here. And this is Lugos of the Selgovae, my friend and travelling companion.'

The priest looked at Martos for a moment.

'King? Of how large a kingdom?'

The one-eyed Briton laughed.

'Small enough, compared to your King of Kings' empire. But enough to have given the Romans a bloody nose in battle, before my brother in arms here captured me.'

Artapanes shook his head again.

'A tale the King of Kings will wish to hear, I expect. You will meet him soon enough, and when that time comes I will instruct you as to your behaviour in his presence. For now, you are under strict instructions to stay within the confines of this building, for your own safety. Not all of my people will be as understanding as my master, and many still remember the atrocities inflicted on the city by your legions only twenty years ago. You will be fed and refreshed, and any other needs you have will be looked after by the staff assigned to watch over you. I must leave now, and take information to my senior priest.'

He left the room, and when Martos looked out of the door he found a pair of burly and implacable guards blocking any attempt to follow him.

'It looks as if we're here for a while. Perhaps you could use that Greek language of yours and get them to bring us some food?'

Marcus nodded.

'You realise we're effectively within the Parthian royal court now? If they've decided to have us quietly disappear then poison would be a good way to do so.'

The Briton shrugged.

'That may be true, but it's also indisputable that we can't go without sustenance. Get them to bring some wine as well. If we're going to die we might as well go to meet our ancestors with some style.'

'You called for me? I presume it's important, given the messenger gabbled out the request like a man with his arse on f—'

Still breathing hard from the exertions of climbing up to the northern wall's parapet, Scaurus followed his first spear's pointing arm.

'The enemy are breaking camp.'

The legatus took a long look across the expanse of plain before them. The Parthian infantry were parading in neat formations, while the camp slaves were rapidly striking their tents and packing them onto carts.

'So they are.'

Petronius grinned at him triumphantly.

'They've had enough! I knew they wouldn't be able to outlast us! More than one enemy has camped out there to no purpose, and this one's no different.'

His eyes narrowed at the expression on Scaurus's face as the legatus looked over the enemy army.

'Legatus?'

Scaurus looked down at the enemy army again, shaking his head as he realised what it was that was troubling him.

'They're not leaving. Look at them. Does that look like an army that's getting ready to slink away with its tail between its legs? Their flags are unfurled, the infantry are armed and ready to fight.'

'Why?'

Both men looked round at Julius, who was staring down at the enemy soldiers with a thoughtful expression.

'Why now? They've no more chance of getting over these walls now than they did yesterday, or last week. I'd presume they were just rehearsing for an attack, if they weren't striking their tents.'

Scaurus leaned over the parapet, looking around the wall's sweep to the west.

'But they're only striking their tents across a quarter-mile front on this side of the city.'

As he spoke, the huge command tent that had been the source of so much amusement collapsed as its central poles were removed, the movement catching Scaurus's eye as he turned and stared down at the Parthian army in puzzlement. The three men stood and watched as the structure's white canvas roof sank slowly to the ground, hundreds of slaves converging on the expanses of canvas and dragging it away from the river with no apparent concern for any damage they might do.

'And that doesn't make any sense either. Why treat such a valuable piece of equipment with so little care?'

As the previously concealed riverbed was gradually revealed, Scaurus suddenly made the connection that had been nagging at his subconscious since the river had ceased flowing days before, confirming his suspicion that the Parthians had dammed it in the mountains to the north.

'Gods below! Look at the riverbed!'

With the tent no longer obstructing their view, the reason for the construction of what they had taken for a palatial headquarters became suddenly, sickeningly clear. A ten-foot-deep trench the same width as the river's bed had been dug from the point where the Mygdonius swung to the east in its bend around the city, the excavation running arrow-straight from the dry watercourse towards the city walls for a hundred paces, the last quarter of its length gradually becoming shallower until the ramp this formed merged with the sandy soil. The soil from its excavation had been dumped into the empty river bed to form a fresh dam at the point where trench and watercourse met, its purpose immediately clear to Scaurus.

'They didn't build a dam in the hills to run us out of water, they were building a weapon!'

Petronius stared at him in consternation.

'They're going to break the dam?'

'Yes! And when they do, all the water they've got backed up in the hills is going to come down the river with more power than a hundred battering rams! That trench they've dug will point the flood straight at this section of the wall, and they've dammed the river to make sure the water has nowhere else to go. It will bring tonnes of soil and rock with it, which will shoot down that trench and hit this wall like a monstrous hammer.'

'But if that much water breaks through the walls . . .'

Scaurus nodded grimly.

'There'll be chaos in the city.'

Julius tilted his head.

'Listen!'

The distant sound of axes on wood turned Petronius's face white. Scaurus turned to Julius, pointing at the perfectly straight streets beneath them.

'If the water breaks this wall down it'll be channelled through the streets and do the same on the other side. Get the southern wall evacuated!'

The first spear saluted and ran, and the legatus turned to the prefect.

'I'll deal with the wall here, you get as many of the streets between here and the southern wall as you can evacuated to the east and west! *Go!*'

Petronius dithered for an instant, then turned and ran for the nearest tower.

'Centurion!'

The officer of the guard stepped forward and saluted smartly.

'Have this section of the wall cleared immediately. We take anything that we can carry and we leave everything that's too heavy to move. I want every man four towers away from this point and I want it doing *now*! *Move!*'

Clearly fighting the urge to question the command, the centurion turned away and started barking orders, sending men running to spread the order in both directions. Scaurus turned back to the scene below, nodding in reluctant admiration as the enemy troops on either side of the river started marching away.

'Perfect timing . . .'

In the hills behind the Parthians the sound of axes had died away, and an unnatural silence descended on the field as the enemy soldiers halted their march, leaving a quarter-mile gap in their line with the river at its heart.

'Legatus!'

Looking round, Scaurus realised that he was the subject of consternation from the men who had been cleared from the wall's platform a hundred paces to his right. The centurion who had called his name beckoned with frantic gestures, and he started walking slowly towards them, his attention riveted to the plain below. A sudden, tearing crack echoed across the plain, and for a moment the silence descended again. Then the roar of the released waters reached them, initially distant, then rapidly swelling as the Mygdonius's pent-up flow was unleashed down the valley, still invisible from the fortress's walls. As he watched in fascination, the torrent burst into view from the end of the river's gorge, a wall of furious white water speckled with tiny dots that the horrified legatus realised were boulders and uprooted trees, tossed effortlessly by the flood's elemental power.

'Legatus!'

With a start Scaurus realised that he was rooted where he stood, unable to move as the oncoming torrent ripped down the empty riverbed and tore through the trench that had been dug to direct its fury at the wall. As the seething flood reached the trench's end, the debris carried by its huge power was hurled into the air, flying boulders and tree trunks slamming into the brickwork, punching a dozen holes in the seemingly impenetrable outer wall in an instant, the impacts knocking Scaurus from his feet. The moat between the inner and outer walls was swiftly filling with debris from the destructive impacts and the missiles themselves, while the inner wall was already sagging in one place where a massive tree had punched through the outer rampart and struck its counterpart with stunning force. Grabbing the parapet he pulled himself up again, looking down at the unceasing, raging stream of dirty brown water as it slammed into the fortress's base.

'Legatus! Run!'

The stones beneath Scaurus's feet were shivering, a continual hail of debris spitting from the trench's end to strike the brickwork with hammer blows that either smashed cleanly through the outer wall or left great cracks in its surface. A dozen paces behind him a bolt thrower was torn from its mount by a flying rock, projectile and debris alike toppling a section of the inner wall onto the roofs below. Staggering as another heavy impact rocked the wall, he ran towards the beckoning soldiers, slowing his pace as the danger of being struck by a piece of debris lessened. Opening his mouth to shout his thanks to the centurion over the torrent's constant grinding roar, he saw the man's jaw drop at something happening behind him, and turned to see the entire one-hundred-pace section of the outer wall between two towers collapse into ruin. The raging waters, which had fatally undermined the structure, ripped through the gap, smashing into the similarly weakened inner wall and demolishing a section of equal length in a heartbeat, surging into the defenceless city streets with a crashing, grinding roar as the thousands of bricks from the collapsed defence were carried along in the foaming brown tide. The few people who stood helpless in its path, those who had been too slow or reluctant to evacuate their houses and shops, were washed away in an instant, lost in the muddy brown cataract that boiled through the city's heart. At the end of the long, straight street, funnelled by the buildings to either side, the torrent slammed into the inner wall on the city's southern side with the same awful power, crashing through both ramparts and raging out onto the plain beyond.

'Bastards . . .'

Scaurus turned at the centurions' whispered curse, looking out over the Parthian troops closest to the northern walls as they cheered the continuing jet of brown foaming water issuing from the river trench. Their raised spears and shields were the only sign of their rejoicing as their voices were lost in the unleashed waters' unceasing roar of power that sounded to him like the rage of a vengeful god.

'They're rejoicing in their victory over us. They think the city's wide open, and they marvel at the destruction that the water must be wreaking on us. They believe that when the waters have exhausted themselves they have only to march in through these shattered walls to have us at their mercy.'

Scaurus shook his head, looking back down into Nisibis's devastated streets.

'And they may well be right.'

Artapanes led the three men into a room thirty paces square, their entrance a man-sized door while a pair of iron reinforced doors wide and tall enough to admit a horse and rider were situated in the far wall. He had come to them an hour after dawn that morning, the fifth day after their arrival in the city, and had bidden them to dress in the garb in which they had travelled from Nisibis. Their garments had been cleaned and returned to them in the night; Marcus's bronze armour polished to a high shine, his boots similarly gleaming. The Roman's arm had been secured to his chest in a linen sling, the priest nodding his satisfaction at their appearance before beckoning the friends through their quarter's door. Following him through a series of dimly lit corridors, and at one point through a walkway so cool Marcus was sure it had to be a tunnel, they emerged into what the priest called the anteroom, blinking in the light of dozens of blazing torches.

'You are to meet with the King of Kings, as promised. The King of Kings wishes to express his thanks for your selfless act in returning his son to him, and may well compliment you on your sense of honour in sparing King Osroes' life. There are rules to be obeyed in the presence of the King of Kings, and any deviation from those rules will place you in grave danger from the men who serve him.'

Artapanes raised a finger.

'One. You will offer the King of Kings your abasement in proskynesis. Two. You will speak only when the King of Kings requests your voice to be heard. Three. You will under no circumstances contradict any statement made by the King of Kings or those members of his royal court who accompany him.'

He looked hard at Marcus, his kohl-accentuated eyes glittering brightly.

'This is not the meeting of a Roman ambassador with the King of Kings, it is a private audience to allow one man to offer his thanks to another for the safe return of his son. This is the only audience that you will have with the King of Kings, and when it has been concluded to our master's satisfaction, arrangements will be made for you to be returned to the place from which you sailed with King Osroes. You must translate these instructions to your comrades for they are as bound to this strict code as you yourself.'

Marcus nodded, masking his disappointment.

'And King Osroes? How is the king's health?'

The priest shrugged.

'I know little. The palace is a place of secrets, and the well-being of a royal prince is not a subject fit for the speculation of commoners such as myself. Since you clearly care as to the result of your journey to bring him here for treatment, however, I will tell you the little I have heard. And little of that is good. King Osroes remains unwell, and does not respond to the ministrations of the palace physicians, who have collectively decreed that only time and rest can aid his recovery. And with that question answered to the best of my abilities, I must tell my master that I have delivered you to this place, and that you are ready for your audience. Wait here.'

He left the anteroom, ordering his escort of guards to watch the three men while Marcus explained the rules of their forthcoming audience to his companions. Martos shrugged and sat down on the floor, grimacing up at Marcus.

'Hundreds of miles by boat being rained on, shot at and insulted by that Parthian animal Gurgen, and now we have to sit on our arses while that devious priest goes to do who knows what. I was hoping that this King of Kings would prove worthy of the effort it's taken getting to meet him, now I'd settle for not being executed for his amusement.'

Marcus smiled, but before he could respond, the commander of their escort prodded the Briton with the butt end of his spear, barking a command in Greek.

'Silence, barbarian! Your filthy language defiles this place!'

The Roman opened his hands and smiled broadly at the man.

'My friend merely wished to express his amazement at the majesty of this palace. I will communicate your wish for him not to speak Latin.'

His only reply was a cold stare, and, catching the Briton's eye, he shook his head.

'It seems that our escort do not regard the use of Latin as acceptable. It might be safest for us to remain silent.'

The priest returned, closing the anteroom door.

'It is as I told you. You are to be granted a brief audience with the King of Kings. This will be limited to the exchange of greetings and pleasantries. The King of Kings will express his pleasure at the safe return of his son, you will reply with whatever meaningless platitudes seem fit to you. You will *not* mention your battle with King Osroes, nor will you refer to the ongoing siege of Nisibis . . .'

Marcus raised an eyebrow at the priest, who was clearly better informed than he had previously indicated.

'And you will not in any way refer to your professed ambassadorial role. This will be a private audience between the King of Kings and three travellers who have been fortunate enough to find themselves in the happy position of being able to perform a service to his family, and for which he wishes to express his thanks. Do you understand?'

Marcus nodded.

'Perfectly well.'

'Very good. Explain it to your comrades.'

Lugos simply nodded, his face inscrutable, while Martos smiled wolfishly.

'I have done much the same in my time on the throne. A meeting of empty smiles, we used to call it.'

The priest gestured to his junior.

'Watch, and Ataradata will demonstrate how to show the appropriate respect to the King of Kings.'

The younger man sank to his knees, then lowered himself to the stone floor, prostrating himself full length before the priest.

'This is proskynesis. You will perform it as you see here when the King of Kings greets you, and he will then command you to rise. After this you may speak to him as to any other man, but with respect in every word. You will address him as "Majesty" whenever you speak to him, and—'

Marcus shook his head.

'As an ambassador of Rome, I cannot perform proskynesis. We reserve prostration for the gods. And my companion here is a king in his own right. Neither can he be expected to perform such an obeisance.'

The priest shook his head in disbelief.

'You must choose your own path, Roman. If you anger the men who advise the King of Kings it may prove to be a fatal error. What of the giant? He is included in this audience solely because of his entertainment value.'

Marcus turned to Lugos, explaining the act of prostration, and to his relief the big man simply nodded.

'He is king. I give respect.'

Artapanes nodded solemnly.

'Very well. At least one of you is likely to survive this audience. Come.'

He led them through the large door and into a vaulted chamber whose roof was supported by a forest of thick pillars, walking with a slow, stately pace towards the middle of the hall. Looking about him Marcus realised that the walls were decorated with weapons and armour whose design was instantly recognisable as Roman.

'Stop here.'

For a moment there was silence, and then a pair of doors in the far wall, their opening large enough to drive a cart through, swung wide. With a clash of metal on stone, a double line of guards marched briskly into the room, swiftly taking up positions on either side of the party. At a barked command they relaxed into parade rest positions, although Marcus noted that each man kept a hand on the hilt of his sword, ready to draw the blade in an instant if they perceived any threat to their king. A group of older men dressed in fine clothing and sporting the usual pointed beards followed them into the chamber, their attire denoting their place in the court's hierarchy. A soldier came first, his face scarred and his scale-armoured coat polished to a perfect shine, his gait at once pugnacious and martial. A herald called out his name and rank in Greek as he strode forward.

'Kophasates, chief gundsalar of the empire of Parthia! Commander of the King of King's imperial army and his lifelong companion in peace and war!'

A priest in flowing robes walked in the general's wake, his pace regal and stately, and with him came a hint of incense.

'Bagadates, most holy servant of Ahura Mazda, chief priest to the empire of Parthia and augur to his Majesty!'

Last came a tall, slim man in trousers and a tunic of red silk, a finely wrought gold crown on his head, his bearing and expression stating his unchallenged authority with no need for words.

'Vologases, first born son of the King of Kings! Commander of the King of Kings' immortals and most dedicated servant of his father!

Attendants swiftly set out chairs for them, and a larger and more ornate throne besides, but the three men remained standing. A magnificently armoured soldier marched through the doorway, raising a long cataphract lance to point at the vaulted ceiling as he strode past the seated courtiers, raising his voice to echo from the iron-clad walls.

'All hail Arsaces, the King of Kings! The Anointed King! The Just King! The Illustrious King! Friend of the Greeks!'

As the echoes died away, the sound of a horse's hoofs replaced them, a heavily armoured figure clad in silver and gold was riding slowly into the hall atop a war horse whose body was covered by armoured barding of equal grandeur that reached down to its knees. The beast's head was protected by scale armour studded with jewels and decorated with complex engraving, its eyes invisible behind delicately wrought gold wire discs. The king rode forward, past his unflinching courtiers, halting the magnificent horse a spear's length from the waiting comrades.

'Present your obeisance to the King of Kings!'

At the herald's command, Marcus and Martos bowed deeply, both placing a hand on the floor before them as Marcus had suggested to the Briton, and Lugos struggled to his knees, gritting his teeth at the pain from his wound, then eased his body down to lie full length on the stone floor. Silence reigned in the hall for a moment, before the seated general stormed to his feet, his voice an angry rasp.

'You dare to show the King of Kings such open disrespect!'

He put a hand to his sword, drawing it halfway from the scabbard, but froze as the king spoke, his voice hard and compelling.

'There will be no violence today, Kophasates!'

After a moment's silence, the horse emptied its bowels onto the stone floor, the warm, wet dung splattering as it hit the ground, its rich aroma filling the air. Arsaces laughed.

'Doubtless my augur will tell me that this was a poor omen, but I am a simple enough man to enjoy the absurdity of this moment! And hear me when I say this, my people, today there will be no violence offered to these men. Today I have put aside my hostility to Rome in order to greet the men who have spared my son's life and brought him back to me.'

He looked down at Marcus, still frozen in his bow.

'Rise, Roman. Rise friends of Rome. You . . .'

He pointed to one of the flanking guardsmen.

'Assist the giant in rising from his proskynesis, he is clearly disadvantaged by his wound.'

Two guards stepped forward, each taking one of Lugos's arms and straining to lift him from his prostration.

'So tell me, Roman, before we speak further of your valour and generosity, why you and this one-eyed barb—'.

Arsaces paused.

'This one-eyed . . . *man* . . . offer me no more than a bow?'

He pointed to Martos, and Marcus smiled.

'*King* Martos has come to understand the term "barbarian", Majesty, although he speaks little Greek. He also understands the reason for its use.'

'Does he speak Latin?'

'He does, Majesty. His father recognised that a knowledge of our tongue would help him in defending his kingdom.'

Arsaces chuckled.

'Although clearly it was insufficient to prevent him from becoming your slave?'

Marcus gestured to Martos, who stood impassively.

'King Martos is no slave, Majesty. His kingdom is allied with Rome, but not occupied by our army. He lost his eye fighting to free his people from the rule of a usurper who killed his wife and children, a battle that he won, with the aid of Rome.'

The king thought for a moment, then dismounted from the horse, handing his magnificent helmet to the herald.

'Then on this day of gratitude I shall break my vow, once and once only, and speak in a language you all understand.'

He switched seamlessly from Greek to Latin.

'And since I am greeting a king, I shall offer him the respect that his position demands. You may kiss me, King Martos.'

The Briton froze for a moment, but before the courtiers had chance to take umbrage, Marcus whispered a single word in Brythonic.

'Cheek.'

Nodding, Martos stepped forward, bowed deeply and then pressed his lips to Arsaces's cheek. The Parthian nodded, and, stepping away, Martos bowed deeply again before resuming his position beside Marcus.

'And you, Roman? Am I to receive no more recognition than a bow from you?'

Marcus raised his left hand in an apologetic gesture.

'Majesty, as a Roman ambassador I can offer you nothing more, for the Roman state cannot countenance any show of submission to a foreign kingdom, no matter how exalted. Nor do I have a gift to offer. Were I armed I would present you with my sword, handed down to me by my father and the possession of a long line of men dedicated to the service of our people, but since you already possess my sword, I have nothing to offer but my undying respect for your long and fruitful reign.'

The king swung to look at the general standing behind him.

'Such a weapon must surely be honoured. Bagadates, you have it safe?'

The chief priest inclined his head respectfully.

'I do, Majesty.'

Nodding satisfaction, Arsaces turned back to face Marcus.

'No gift is required, Roman. You spared my son's life in battle, and then you risked your life to bring him to me by the fastest possible route in order that he might be treated by my physicians. No man wishes to be so cursed as to bury his own son, even at my age. No gift could have been as precious to me.'

He bowed slightly to the Roman.

'And your companions. King Martos stood over my son in an arrow storm, I am told by his bidaxs Gurgen, and the giant was wounded ensuring his escape. You too both have my gratitude. And as tokens of my everlasting thanks for his return . . .'

He waved a hand at the herald, who stepped forward and presented him with a silk bag.

'Wear these gifts, my friends, and when you look at them be reminded that the King of Kings is for ever in your debt.'

He handed each of them a gold ring. Marcus looked at his, finding it decorated with the image of Arsaces's head in profile.

'No man in any kingdom I reign over will be able to deny that you have my favour, for the image on those rings is unmistakably mine. See the mark on my forehead?'

He pointed to his brow, showing them a skin lesion that had been covered by his grey hair.

'It is the mark of the men who ruled the first Persian empire, the proof that my dynasty can be traced back to Ataxerxes the Long Handed, ruler of an empire so great that it challenged the Greeks themselves.'

Marcus bowed again, and the king smiled.

'And so you will leave Ctesiphon with my gratitude, Roman. You will be escorted to your ship, and granted free passage back up the river to your own people.'

He paused, his face crinkling into a smile.

'And have a care, Marcus Tribulus Corvus, should you face my warriors in battle again. Many among my armies will mark you as a man whose death would make their name in an instant.'

He turned and walked from the hall, his courtiers turning to follow him. The last to do so was his son Vologases, whose stare lingered on Marcus for a long moment before he too swivelled on his heel and left the room. The priest Artapanes waited until the hall was empty once more, eyeing the pile of dung with disappointment.

'As well as could be expected, despite the poor omen and your insistence on refusing to follow the protocol I laid out for you. Come then, let us return to your place of safe keeping. Tomorrow you will return to your ship and leave the city, counting your blessings that you have survived your time in Ctesiphon and vowing never to return.'

'The walls are breached on both sides of the fortress. Our supplies have been depleted significantly by flood water, and while the mud is still being dug away from the grain stores it's estimated that we've lost over half of the food that was in storage. We have over five hundred dead, and bodies are still being recovered from the filth that chokes the streets and houses with every hour that passes.'

Scaurus paused, looking round at his officers.

'On the other hand, the fact that we had some brief warning of the flood gave us time to evacuate most of the off-duty soldiers who would probably have drowned. The legion is still effective, and so is Prefect Petronius's cohort. We can still hold out for two or three months with the grain we have left, most of the bolt throwers are still operative, and Centurion Avidus and his pioneers are supervising temporary defences. Does anyone want to add anything?'

Julius raised a hand.

'My biggest question is just how long it's going to take for the mud to dry?'

Scaurus acknowledged the question's pertinence with a nod.

'Good question. Centurion Avidus?'

The African raised his vine stick.

'For those of you who've been too busy digging out weapons and food, the river's back inside its banks now but it left a thick coating of mud behind as it washed away, so thick that when the Parthians tried to attack they weren't able to get anywhere close to the walls.'

Petronius's glum face brightened slightly. Predicting that the enemy would attempt to storm the breaches in the walls, he had ordered the bolt throwers to be hurriedly dismantled and rebuilt on either side of the gaps. When the Parthians had attacked, an hour after the waters had receded, their advance had first been slowed and then halted by the mud, horses and soldiers unable to move any faster than they could tear each foot from the clinging sludge. Faced with the onslaught from the Roman artillery, they had retreated back to their siege lines leaving several dozen men spreadeagled in the mud, their blood sprayed across the tan surface where each man had been targeted and brutally killed by the bolt-thrower crews.

'I walked around on the stuff for a while this afternoon, carefully, mind you. It's as deep as a man in some places, and I took my armour off first.'

'And?'

'It's hard to say, Legatus. There's a crust formed on the top, but if I trod down in the wrong place my foot went straight through. It's not going to get very much drier overnight, so I'd bet that crust won't be baked strong enough to hold a man's weight until midday tomorrow, when the sun's been on it for a few more hours.'

Scaurus looked at his men with a look of calculation.

'So, not much more than twelve hours from now we might find ourselves under massed infantry attack, because if Narsai can read the signs as clearly as we can, he'll dismount his entire force and send it in on foot. I'd put the spear men in first with the archers behind them, and then, once they have a foothold, the knights to punch a way into the city and open us for a full-scale assault. And if they get into the city then we'll struggle to stop them, because there are just too many ways for them to get around any defence we throw up. If we're going to hold Nisibis, gentlemen, then we have to stop the enemy before they get over what's left of the walls and into the city. Shall we go and take a look?'

On Avidus's advice he led them to the northern breach, where the walls had fallen inwards and presented the defenders with a hundred paces of brick-strewn ruin.

'They'll put their main attack in here, because once the mud out there is dry their advance to the defences will be nice and easy, unlike the other side where the walls collapsed outwards.'

The African waved a hand at the rubble-strewn street, illuminated by torches held up by citizens of the city who had volunteered to play a part in their own defence, working as fast as they could to tear up the rubble and carry it to the breach in the northern wall. Bricks from the walls' collapse were strewn five and six deep, mortared in place by the mud to form a vicious obstacle course where a man could advance only with the greatest of care.

'If you have the brick field on the other side of the southern breach sown with the caltrops we pulled out of the battlefield on the hillside, I can't see how they're going to get across it to attack us. Just try for yourself Legatus, and see how long it takes you to pick your way over this lot. One wrong move and you'll break your ankle, so take it easy sir. We're having to pull the bricks out with iron bars.'

He led them to the breach, and Scaurus stood and marvelled once more at the devastation visited upon the twin walls by the river's destructive power. Hundreds of legionaries were labouring at the point where the inner wall had stood, their arms and legs filthy with mud as they pulled bricks from the wreckage and passed them to the wall's foundation in human chains, one in every two being packed into a roughly constructed rampart while the other was hurled over the slowly growing wall into the muddy plain's slowly drying mire.

'We can't rebuild the wall the way it was, not without a lot of skilled labour and a month or two to spend on the job, but we can put together something to slow the bastards down. It's slow work though, and the men are exhausted after a couple of hours, so we're rotating the cohorts in two at a time.'

'How tall can you get that defence by dawn?'

Avidus looked at the roughly constructed rampart for a moment.

'No more than eight feet tall. I could go faster with some light, but if we use anything more than the moon's giving us then the enemy will realise what's going on and start sprinkling us with arrows, and that'll make us go a lot slower. It won't stop a determined attack, but it'll give them something to think about. And I've got one or two more tricks up my sleeve.'

'So have I. I think it's time you saw something I've been hoping not to have to use, Legatus.'

Slightly baffled, Scaurus left Julius to organise the preparation of the debris to the fortress's south for the sort of defence that Avidus felt would be sufficient, following Petronius back into the city. The prefect led him up a staircase to the top floor of an otherwise nondescript building, and Scaurus looked about him curiously in the light of the torch the prefect was carrying at each landing, noting to his bemusement that the rooms to either side were stacked with earthenware jars. On reaching the top floor, Petronius waved an arm at the hundreds of wicker cages stacked on all sides.

'We were fortunate that this little farm was built at the top of the building, to keep it as dry as possible, so the mud had no effect. As you can see.'

He handed Scaurus the torch with a broad grin.

'Take a look, Legatus, and tell me what you think.'

Late the same evening, as the three friends were readying themselves for sleep with the expectation of beginning their journey north the next day, Artapanes opened the door to their suite and beckoned Marcus to join him. Outside the door the same two guards were standing duty over the foreigners, but they ignored Marcus as he followed the cleric down the corridor that he knew from experience led into the palace.

'What—'

The priest raised a hand to silence him, and whispered a rebuke over his shoulder.

'Say nothing. I cannot answer your questions, for I do not know the answers. And, since I am already asleep in my bed as far as anyone other than those two guards is concerned, I was clearly never here.'

Bemused, the Roman followed him along the same route as before, but where they had previously forked left into the anteroom, the priest led him to the right, and up a corridor that climbed as it turned. Reaching a torch-lit landing, Marcus recognised the robed figure of the high priest, Bagadates. The senior cleric waved a hand to his subordinate, and Artapanes bowed, staying where he was as the older man led Marcus deeper into the palace, speaking quietly as he walked.

'You made a favourable impression on my master earlier. He has ordered me to effect a further meeting between you, a meeting that will never have taken place as far as the scribes and the bureaucrats are concerned. And which the generals must never even suspect. Here . . .'

He indicated a door.

'I will wait for you here. Enter.'

Marcus found himself in a room no larger than a good-sized office, a small fire burning in one corner. The walls were decorated with richly embroidered tapestries, the floor carpeted with ornately knotted rugs. A guardsman stood impassively by the door in the opposite wall, his unblinking gaze locked on the Roman. The door beside him opened and Arsaces entered the room, closing the door firmly behind him.

'Greetings once more, Marcus Valerius Aquila.'

Stunned, Marcus remembered to bow after a moment of indecision, and the king waited gravely until he was upright once more.

'You seem discomfited by our meeting, Roman. Or is it perhaps the fact that I have greeted you by your real name, rather than the alias under which you presented yourself, that troubles you?'

'I . . . *how*?'

Arsaces ignored the question, taking two cups from a table in the corner of the room.

'Rome sees me as a tired old man, does it not? Scarred by my defeat twenty years ago, haunted by the sacking of this very city, and kept on my throne mainly by the power struggle between my priests and generals. A weak ruler, I am tolerated by a dozen lesser monarchs who fear the civil war that would follow my death more than they dislike the current uneasy peace that I keep between them. Rome, Valerius Aquila, takes me for a man of straw.'

He poured two cups of wine, handing one to Marcus.

'Sit.'

The Roman obeyed his command, still clearly mystified by the king's knowledge of his true identity.

'At least you have the good grace not to hide your perplexity. I like honesty in a man . . .'

Arsaces took a sip of his wine.

'After all, I see so little of it.'

He sipped again, then put the cup aside.

'In truth, Rome's view of my abilities is not entirely unfair. I do pit my vassals against one another, reminding them that we face enough enemies to make my rule essential to wielding our collective strength against the threats to the integrity of our borders. To the north-east are a multitude of barbarian tribes, true barbarians, godless animals from the boundless grasslands who forever press up against the empire's northern kingdoms. They are horse archers without peer, taught from childhood to ride, and shoot, and kill, and their single intention is to steal, to burn and to rape at every opportunity. Against them we range our own horsemen, equally brutal, equally skilled, an imperial army larger than any force our individual kingdoms might put into the field. The day will come when these nomads swell to such numbers that they will burn a swathe of destruction across both my empire and yours, Roman, but not in my time!

'To the east is nothing but desert, through which the caravans from the distant silk lands struggle only because of the rich rewards to be had. No threat will come from there. To the south there is ocean, and peaceful trade with the dark-skinned men who sell us spices and the finest iron in the world. But to the west . . .'

He left the sentence unfinished, and Marcus realised he was expected to speak.

'Rome.'

'Indeed. Your empire, forever pushing at our western border. We have defeated you more than once, and brutally so back in the time of my ancestor, Orodes the Second. But each time we have beaten you, another general and another army have sought revenge for those defeats, and now your legions camp on our borders like hungry wolves, forever eyeing the next prize to be torn from my empire. You saw the fortress at Europos, or Dura, the Stronghold as you call it?'

'It guards the route to Palmyra.'

'It was Parthian, until Avidius Cassius took it from us, in the war with Rome that I was rash enough to start. Now it acts as yet another source of gold for your empire, taxes on the traders passing through it that should by rights flow into my imperial treasury, and fund my defence of the northern borders. And Nisibis, the city from which you sailed with my son, currently under siege by Narsai of Adiabene? Also once Parthian, again taken from us by Avidius Cassius. How I smiled when the news reached me that he had paid the ultimate price for attempting to wrest your empire from its rightful ruler. So now a puppet rules in Osrhoene, and your soldiers march freely through it and into Adiabene to garrison a city that was once the most glorious fortress in all the empire. And all the trade that passes through Nisibis funnels yet more gold to Rome.'

'But—'

The king waved a hand, silencing Marcus's interjection.

'But we started the war in which those fortresses were lost? Indeed I did. And I learned a valuable lesson from that defeat, Roman. I was minded to counterattack, as Avidius Cassius's army marched to sack my capital, but the priests would not allow it. The auguries were poor, and Mazda would be angry with my people were they to allow their king to die to no good end. Ctesiphon's destruction would be avenged, they told me, in good time. They were right, of course. Mazda sent a plague to punish your army, and the legions took the disease back to your empire when they retreated in disarray. I hear it has spread across your lands and killed a hundred times more than died in the city's sack, and I thank the god of fire for this fitting retribution. So, as the augurs predicted, all was as well as could be expected, given our defeat. By afflicting your legions with disease, Mazda showed his support for the empire, and for me as its King of Kings. The army, the priesthood and the vassal kings united in support of their ruler, and my empire recovered from the humiliation soon enough, as your empire suffered a just revenge in its turn. But as I rode away from this city with my Immortal Guard, turning tail rather than throwing the remnants of my army at your legions and dying gloriously, I knew the real reason for which I was forbidden to make that noble gesture, prevented from earning the glorious death that my younger self knew was required. There was no succession. No son of an age to take my throne. My death would have started the civil war we fear more than anything, weakening the empire and laying it open to invasion from the north. I accepted my humiliation. But I swore to avenge it, by one means or another.'

Marcus nodded.

'So you decided to wage war by other means?'

'The priests told me you were a quick one. Yes, by *any* other means. My spies watch your border provinces like hawks, and some of them rise in your service, working subtly to assist those among you who are either venal or stupid. The governor of Syria is an excellent case in point. I doubt he would have been quite as successful as he was at defrauding the state without a few well-placed ideas being dropped into his lap.'

'By a man who promptly disappeared when my legatus arrived on the scene?'

'Indeed. Legatus Scaurus had a prior reputation in the province, so the spy in question decided that he preferred the idea of a swift exit to that of crucifixion. Not, however, before he heard enough rumours about you to make for an interesting story on his return. Is it true that your father was murdered by the emperor's men, and yet you serve the same emperor?'

'I believe the exact phrase used was "confiscatory justice", Highness. The Praetorian prefect accused my father of plotting against the throne, had him murdered and then dismembered to deny him honourable burial. What was left of him was dumped into the main sewer and flushed into the river Tiber, I believe. My mother and sisters were presented as the centrepiece of a party for a group of perverts who count – or rather who *counted* – some of the richest and most eminent men in Rome among their number. They were raped and murdered, and their bodies were dumped outside the gates among the city's detritus. Only one of them was ever found, and her eyes had already been pecked out by the crows.'

Arsaces nodded, his gaze softening.

'So when you presented yourself as "Corvus" . . . It is the Latin for "crow", I believe?'

'It was a simple expedient at first, a means of changing my name to hide from my father's killers, but now I wear it as a badge of my hatred, and to remind me that my revenge is not yet complete. You decided not to die without purpose when Legatus Cassius turned his legions loose to sack your capital, Highness. I made much the same decision with regard to the emperor.'

The king smiled knowingly.

'Then bear my own example in mind. There is more than one way to have revenge upon an enemy.'

He raised his cup.

'To your eventual success. May you weaken my enemy in taking the revenge that you know must be yours.'

They drank.

'And now, to business. I didn't have you brought here simply to discuss our respective life experiences. I have a message for your legatus, a response to his attempts to make peace, and I wanted you to understand the context of that message as clearly as the words themselves.'

He fixed Marcus with a hard stare.

'My grip on this throne grows less certain with every year. On the face of it, of course, nothing is changed. The army and the priests bicker, always seeking an advantage, but neither will ever supplant the other. The army has the glory of defending the empire, and the honour which that brings. The priesthood has Ahura Mazda on their side, and the terror of his potential disfavour. They are like wrestlers locked in a perpetual struggle, neither capable of putting the other on his back. But the kings . . .'

He drank again.

'There are a dozen kings whose realms form the empire, and the position of King of Kings is wholly dependent on their willingness to be ruled. Which means that their fear of civil war must outweigh their dissatisfaction with their ruler. And kings, I can tell you, are never happy being ruled. I dream of such a luxury, having a man set above me on whom all problems can be blamed, fairly or not, but they only see how much better their own reign over the empire would be. And I have sons, men who look at me with impatience, given my age, and at each other with the calculating eyes of men who see only rivals. My second oldest son Arsakes rules Armenia. And Osroes, the youngest, I have given the kingdom of Media, for he is headstrong and needs to be kept busy. His march on Nisibis is a perfect illustration of that truth. If he recovers from his injury, he will make a formidable rival for his brothers. And the oldest, Vologases, is perhaps the most dangerous of them all, for which reason I keep him close. He is the oldest, the cleverest, and the man most likely to move against me. My gundsalar Kophasates watches his every move, and his command of my Immortals is in name only. I do not expect to die peacefully, but neither do I plan to make it easy for any of my sons to usurp my throne while I still live.'

Marcus shot a glance at the guard, but the king shook his head.

'He is deaf and dumb, profoundly so. He guards me when there is a need for discretion, giving me the absolute surety that my words will never be repeated. So, Marcus Valerius Aquila, my message to your legatus is this: you ask me to rein in Narsai, lift the siege of Nisibis and cease the harassment of legitimate Roman interests in Adiabene? I will not. I cannot. To do so would be to attract the ire of the kings I reign, while to condone Narsai's act of undeclared war is to provide them with evidence that my desire for revenge on Rome is undimmed by the years. Indeed, my son's defeat and capture, and his humiliating return to Ctesiphon, make it doubly important for Narsai to triumph. I will be compelled to providc assistance to his army, and to confirm his command of the army of Media while Osroes remains unfit to resume command. Nisibis will fall, eventually, when the grain stores are emptied. It may take a year. It will happen nonetheless. And I will accept the tributes that will be bestowed upon me, and smile as I ride my horse through the city's gates in triumph. And now that you understand my response, and the reasons I must make it, tell your legatus that if he chooses to march his men away I will see that their safety is assured.'

'If we will pass under a yoke, leave without our weapons and swear never to step on Parthian soil again?'

Arsaces smiled gently.

'Of course. And I imagine that the soil of Osrhoene would be included in that oath as well.'

Marcus nodded.

'I understand you, Majesty. When shall I leave?'

The king waved a dismissive hand.

'Soon. I have suggested to my son Vologases that he escort you back to Nisibis with a detachment of my Immortals. Not only will it be a good deal faster than working your way back up the river, but that way I can ensure that you are delivered to the gates of Nisibis unharmed, and that my message reaches your legatus without any interference from the more exuberant of my subjects. I shall make a formal farewell to you before you leave, and renew my gratitude to you and your companions. And return that sword you mentioned earlier today. After all, I am a man who honours his word.'

12

Scaurus closed the message tablet and handed it back to his clerk.

'The enemy are on the move, it seems. Which means, as we expected, that Narsai expects the mud to have dried sufficiently for his infantry to advance across it and take our makeshift wall. Our task is remarkably simple, but may prove to be the greatest challenge we've faced since we left Antioch. I expect every one of you to provide our men with an example of the virtue and discipline that built us an empire and have kept it intact, despite the best efforts of our enemies to take large parts of it away from us. We cannot afford to take a single step back, gentlemen, because if we do, then we'll be fighting in the streets of the city.'

He paused and looked round at them.

'And we all know how that will end up against superior numbers. Talk to your men, gentlemen, and tell them that they've broken these barbarians once and they can do it again. Tell them that they're the best soldiers in the world, and that these Persian animals will have to kill every last one of us before we'll surrender that reputation by leaving thousands of women and children at their mercy. Julius?'

The first spear stood and looked around him at the officers gathered around the table.

'We don't have long, so I'll keep this short. You're all the sons of men immeasurably richer than your soldiers can even imagine. For them, wealth means having enough silver in their purses to fill their bellies, drink themselves half stupid and stick their dicks up something warm and wet. Your men don't care about who the emperor is, or who gets seated where at dinner, they worry about the real problems in life. And right now they're stood waiting for an army of sun-worshipping heathens with twice their strength to come at them with fucking great long spears. What fighting skills can you gentlemen add to their strength?'

He paused, looking around him.

'Not much, if the truth's being told. You're all good men, but there's not one of you I'd call an old-fashioned hero, born to hold the blood-slicked hilt of a notched sword. But you can give them one precious gift, if you have it in you.'

The silence stretched out until it seemed certain that someone would ask the question.

'Equality. Today, just for a few hours, you have the opportunity to see the world from their point of view. You can fight alongside them, kill with them and risk dying with them. If they see you taking your part in the slaughter that's going to win or lose this battle for us, they'll fight with you and perhaps even fight *for* you, if you're really convincing.'

He shook his head.

'Enough. Just go out there and share the dangers that your men are going to be facing, and perhaps the men fighting with you will be moved to give that part of themselves they usually hold in reserve. For some of them that will include their lives, so don't insult them by asking them for anything you're not willing to give yourself.'

He paused and looked round the room again.

'Make the legatus proud, and you'll have done enough to earn my respect. Now, as to how this battle will be fought . . .'

With the briefing complete, the officers went back to their cohorts with serious expressions, while Scaurus, Julius and Petronius climbed the walls to stare out at the enemy formation marshalling to the city's north, just outside bolt-thrower range.

'It won't be long now.'

Scaurus nodded at his first spear's comment. The ditch in front of the Parthian siege lines had been filled with earth, and the flat ground behind it was packed with rank after rank of Median infantry who had been formed into a column fifty men wide and two hundred men deep, their spears and helmets winking in the sun. To either side looser formations of dismounted horse archers stood ready to advance, while at the infantry's rear a compact block of shining armoured figures stood perfectly immobile. A horn blew, and with commendable precision the spear men started their march towards the fortress's shattered walls, the archers walking easily alongside them with their bows strung and arrows nocked. Scaurus nodded at Petronius, who looked across the gap at his own senior centurion and pointed a finger at the enemy. The senior centurion's gruff voice grated out a command over the distant rumble of marching boots.

'Bolt throwers! Target, enemy infantry! *Shoot!*'

With a twanging thump the first bolts arced down into the leading Parthian ranks, punching one- and two-man gaps in the marching column. For every spear man killed by the missiles' eviscerating impacts, a dozen more were sprayed with the blood of a man who had been walking beside them a moment before, but for all the horror that was being visited upon them, the column's pace didn't falter.

'They've got discipline, I'll give them that.'

Scaurus nodded grimly.

'I can't argue with you on that, First Spear. Archers, Prefect?'

Petronius raised two fingers, and the response was instant.

'Archers! Target, enemy infantry! *Loose!*'

The legatus pursed his lips as the Hamians rose from the parapet's cover and launched their first volley, arrows whipping out from the walls and hanging in the air for a moment before plunging down into the advancing Parthian line, hundreds of shafts peppering the raised shields or flicking between them to kill and maim the unwary and unlucky. The officers had debated which would be the best target for their bows, but in the end a blunt statement from Julius had ended the discussion.

'It won't be archers who win this fight, it'll be infantrymen, and they have ten thousand to our five. Every Parthian spear man we kill with an arrow is one less man in the fight for that wall, and every man we wound is another obstacle in their way as they try to get bodies forward. Our archers have a parapet to hide behind, and the men on the wall have thick enough shields to keep the enemy arrows off. There'll only be one rule in this fight – if we kill enough of their infantry then we win the battle, and probably the entire campaign.'

The oncoming infantry's ranks were already looking ragged, with less than half the distance to the makeshift defence that plugged the walls' breach covered, but Julius stared dourly at the marching men.

'We're hurting them alright, but the rear ranks haven't even started moving yet.'

Scaurus looked down at the hastily constructed wall that filled the gap between the two ends of the inner wall, and the marine infantry waiting in its shelter, invisible to the enemy soldiers. Prefect Ravilla looked up at the same time and saluted, nodding in silent thanks for Scaurus's display of trust in putting his men into the front line.

The legatus gazed at the stolid marines' ranks, arrayed along the wall's fighting platform in the cover of the four feet of wall that was their main defence against the Parthians' spears. Avidus had been unable to do much more than throw up a rough stone rampart eight feet tall, backed by a twenty-pace long ramp that rose from street level to allow a cohort of legionaries easy access to the broad flat surface that the African's pioneers had constructed four feet up the wall's rear surface. At the ramp's end a fresh cohort was waiting for their turn in the line, successive units queued up along the length of the strip of pitted and lumpy ground that was what was left of the street into which the wall had toppled.

'I suggest we have the waiting cohorts prepare to come under attack from the enemy archers, First Spear?'

Julius nodded, and at the prearranged trumpet call, each of the units behind the wall moved quickly to erect unbroken walls of shields across their fronts. Another volley of artillery bolts snapped down into the advancing infantry, the leading units slowing their pace to redress their lines and allow men from the following ranks to fill the gaps, men dropping with each step forward as the Hamians poured arrows into them in a deadly rain of iron. The rattle of metal on stone and the whirr of flight feathers whipping past the wall's defenders announced the fact that the enemy archers had advanced sufficiently to loft arrows at the men lining the city's walls to either side of the breach. A Hamian to the officers' left turned with a shaft protruding from his throat before falling to the parapet, his body shaking violently as blood flowed out across the stone surface.

'Get him away from those pots!'

Another Syrian dragged his comrade clear of the earthenware containers that had been placed in the parapet's protection earlier that morning, making the warding gesture as he did so. Standing, he was struck by an arrow that pinned his hand to his thigh, tottered for a moment and then fell into the gap between the inner and outer walls with a shriek that was only silenced by his impact with the moat's mud and debris-filled surface.

The screams of the enemy wounded were now loud enough to break through the rhythmic footfall of thousands of boots, as the enemy infantry came on with the clear purpose of getting to grips with the men sheltering behind the city's last line of defence, taking advantage of the slackening in the Hamians' shooting as the archers took cover from the arrows being launched at them from below. As the greasy mud thickened underfoot, the spear men started to throw bundles of brushwood onto the soft, yielding crust that lay over the liquid layer beneath, repeating the action as more improvised fascines were passed forward to them by the men behind. Slowly, inexorably, the Parthian infantry crept closer to the wall, their pace increasing as they grew more confident with the firmer footing under their boots.

With twenty paces left to march, the enemy horns blew and the marching men lowered their long spears to point at the wall before them.

'Man the defences!'

The marines rose from cover, raising their shields and swinging their own long spears to point down at the oncoming enemy.

The Parthians were suddenly struggling, their pace slowing abruptly as they reached the ground where Avidus's men had laboured hardest over the previous evening, pouring buckets of water passed out to the walls by a human chain of the city's inhabitants to soften the dried mud, saturating it to the point where a booted foot could sink a foot deep without gaining any purchase. Reaching the space between the outer and inner walls, the gaps on either side between the two plugged with rubble to prevent any attempt to get between them, the footing got even worse for the attackers as they floundered into the deeper mud that filled the now invisible moat. The braver Hamians were leaning out over the walls, ignoring the Parthian archers' threat to pour arrows down into the struggling enemy infantry as they floundered forward, dropping more bundles of brushwood into the seemingly bottomless mire. As Scaurus watched aghast, an officer who had been urging his men forward paid the price for making himself too obvious a target and went down into the mud face first with a shaft sticking out of his back, blood staining the mud red as his men trampled him into the swampy ground, successive ranks stamping his struggling body deeper into the ooze until all that was visible were two hands, the fingers no longer clenched as he lost the fight for life.

With a clash of spearheads on shields, the Parthians staggered onto the Roman defences and the two armies collided at close quarters for the first time, the marines stabbing down into the mass of spear men, while the Parthians sought to fend off their iron blades, thrusting back up at the men on the wall above them. One of Ravilla's men fell back from the wall with his throat open, and his comrades pushed him clear for the bandage carriers, working their spears with renewed anger to reap the attackers whenever an opening allowed them to thrust in their long spear blades, but where an enemy soldier fell another swiftly stepped forward. Successive ranks of infantry crowded up behind the leading men, shields raised over their heads in an attempt to fend off the arrows raining down on them. A horn sounded behind the marines and they exchanged positions, the rear rank moving forward to take up the positions vacated by the men staggering back, already exhausted by the first moments of fighting.

'Look!'

Scaurus followed Julius's pointing finger, peering over the parapet at the dismounted cataphracts following close behind the rear rank of the infantry with swords already drawn. As he watched, a lone Parthian infantryman turned to run, clearly unmanned by the screams of the men dying under the city's walls, only to be cut down before he had taken the second step back.

'Gods below.'

The first spear nodded grimly.

'They're going to herd those poor bastards forward to be butchered, partly to exhaust us and partly to carpet the mud with enough dead bodies to give them firmer footing.'

'Can it work?'

Julius shook his head.

'I have no idea. But if they pile up enough corpses and get enough men over the wall to allow the rest of them time to get into the city, they'll hack us to pieces. Petronius, order your bolt throwers' captains to concentrate their efforts on the cataphracts!'

He leaned over the parapet.

'Rotate the cohorts!'

The horn sounded again, and the next cohort stamped forward up the debris ramp while the marines kept fighting, waiting until they were pulled away from the wall by their replacements, faces white with exhaustion, to take their place at the rear of the queue of cohorts that stretched deep into the city.

Tribune Varus saw Prefect Ravilla walking towards him, blood flecked across his face and chest, his eyes still wide from the combat he'd been pulled away from only a moment before.

'How was it, Prefect?'

The equestrian officer looked at him blank-faced, white with the shock of battle.

'Their column seems to stretch back to the horizon, Tribune. Every man we killed was replaced by another, and their wounded fall into the mud and are drowned if they don't die of their wounds. We were killing them, and killing them, and killing them . . . but there are *so* many of them.'

Varus let him pass, turning back to his own cohort with a thoughtful expression.

'What's going on, Tribune sir?'

Varus nodded at Sanga, smiling at the feathers poking upwards on either side of his helmet.

'Congratulations on your promotion, Watch Officer. As to what's happening, it's all very simple. The enemy are trying to overcome our defences by means of overwhelming numbers, and we're doing our very best to kill so many of them that they decide that the game's not worth playing.'

'An' who's winning, sir?'

Horns blew, and the cohort marched forward twenty paces. The tribune shrugged.

'Who's winning? It doesn't sound to me like anyone's winning.'

An hour later the enemy soldiers were no longer fighting against a four foot height disadvantage. As Ravilla had told Varus, any spear man unable to crawl away when the Romans' questing blades pierced his armour was simply trampled under the feet of the men behind to form the foundation of a ramp of human bodies, some dead, some still clinging to life and protesting feebly at the indignity of being so cruelly used by their fellows. Goaded on by the harsh commands of the cataphracts close on their heels, the Parthians were still flooding forwards, stabbing up at the Romans lined up on the makeshift wall before them.

'Petronius!'

Scaurus was having to shout to be heard now, the cacophony of agony from the battle below making it almost impossible to communicate in anything less than a parade-ground roar. The prefect turned to face him, then staggered and toppled over the rear of the wall's fighting platform with an arrow in his face.

'Shit! You!'

He reached out and took a Hamian centurion by the arm, shouting in the man's ear.

'Tell your men I want them to shoot at the enemy archers! Pass the word to your prefect!'

Julius strode down the wall, completely ignoring the arrows flying past him as the Parthian bowmen loosed arrows as fast as they could.

'Why have we stopped shooting at the infantry?'

Scaurus pulled him into the wall's cover.

'Because if they manage to put arrows into you and me then the odds are that this defence will fail! And because every man we kill down there is being used to improve their footing. Before long they'll be looking down at us from a ramp of their own dead! We need to try something else!'

He pointed at the earthenware jars.

'It's time for Petronius's nasty little surprise!'

Julius nodded, lifting one of the jars with both hands, apparently finding it surprisingly light. He raised the spherical object for the men around him to see, bellowing an order over the battlefield's cacophony.

'Pass the jars! And don't drop any of them!'

He pitched the pottery globe over the rampart, following its brief trajectory with a look of fascination as it arced down to land in the middle of a wave of fresh enemy infantry, the thin earthenware shattering as it hit the helmet of a hapless spear man. Out of the shards of creamy brown pottery came a fresh menace, utterly unexpected and clearly terrifying to the horrified Parthians. Unable to run in the thick mud, they floundered away from the jar's contents, seeking escape in any direction possible as the enraged creatures scuttled across the soft ground with their stingers raised, seeking a target for their ire. More pots sailed over the rampart as they were passed to the men closest to the enemy, each one splitting to reveal dozens of black-bodied scorpions whose venomous power was only too well known to the men onto whom they were being showered. As Scaurus watched in fascination, a Parthian who had taken the brunt of a falling pot jerked spasmodically as half a dozen of the deadly insects stung him. The men around him pressed backwards, climbing over each other to escape from the swarming scorpions, fresh chaos erupting everywhere that one of the jars landed.

'Throw them closer to the wall!'

More of the terrifying weapons arced down onto the spear men fighting for the makeshift barricade that blocked their path into the city, and the Parthians' concerted effort to drive the Romans from the wall disintegrated into farce as the infantrymen dropped their spears and frantically stamped at the deadly insects, drawing their knives to brush the scorpions from their shoulders and arms while the archers on the walls above them drew and shot again and again to force the enemy bowmen to look to their own protection.

'Rotate!'

The soldiers fighting at the wall looked over their shoulders as the Tungrians stamped hard-eyed up the ramp behind them, readying themselves to surrender their positions to the northerners while the attacking infantry were otherwise occupied.

Scaurus looked out over the parapet, realising immediately that something had changed in the battle's pattern.

'Look!'

Julius switched his attention from the handover taking place below them to the rear of the enemy formation. The dismounted enemy cavalrymen were pushing forward through the rear ranks of the spear men, bulling their way forward with their swords and maces drawn, their roars of command audible over the battle's constant din as they shouted orders for the infantry to move aside and let them pass.

'I've been waiting for this!'

He nodded at his legatus's shout.

'They're the only men on the field with any chance of surviving long enough to get over that wall, and if enough of them make it they'll hack our boys to mincemeat! But before that they have to—'

He jerked as if he'd been shot by one of the arrows, but when

Scaurus followed his gaze he too found himself horrified at the events that were unfolding before him.

The Tungrians gazed over the wall at the sea of dead and wounded Parthians with the dispassionate eyes of men who had fought on too many battlefields to be troubled by the sight of blood, Varus pushing his way through them to stare down at the enemy below. The spear men had lost all heart with the unexpected and shocking rain of venomous insects, and most of them were looking down at the corpse-strewn ground beneath their feet rather than the men lining the wall, stamping down at the insects scuttling about them without regard for the wounded men lying helpless under their feet. Something caught the tribune's eye beyond the men to their immediate front, the flash of a sword that rose and fell in the blink of an eye, and he stared out over the sea of heads to the cohort's front, unsure as to whether he had seen the momentary flash of polished iron. The Parthians before him were still backing slowly away, half crouched under the protection of their shields, but it seemed that they were meeting a gradually stiffer resistance, some force from their rear first arresting their gradual retreat and then actually reversing it, driving them reluctantly towards the wall.

Faced with the choice of being crushed into the makeshift defence or escaping, the spear men spilled out of their column to either side. Frowning in bemusement, Varus craned his neck to see what it could be that was causing such consternation among the soldiers. As the flood of men escaping to either side started to thin, his eyes narrowed as glimpses of what was happening behind them gave him cause to doubt his sanity.

Scaurus looked down at the oncoming cataphracts in disbelief, the threat posed by arrows flicking past the defenders' heads forgotten in the shock of what was happening at the rear of the Parthian column. Clearly realising that their attack was stalling before it had developed, the dismounted Parthian knights had taken action that rendered the two officers temporarily speechless. Fanning out to either side of the wavering column of spear men, they had drawn their swords, and were herding the infantry forward, summarily executing any man who tried to retreat. The legatus looked down at the scene playing out beneath them with an expression of horrified understanding.

'They're driving their men forward to be massacred. They know that every dead spear man makes it that much easier to get over the wall.'

Denied any means of retreat, the Parthian infantry had no choice but to advance across the acrid-smelling mire of blood, urine and faeces towards the makeshift wall, like cattle stampeding away from a hunting predator. All thoughts of retreat forgotten, as the crescent-shaped line of fully armoured men stalked forward and drove the infantry, now little better than a rabble, before them, the spear men washed back up against the defences, staggering almost apologetically back onto the defenders' implacable spears.

'Tribune?'

Varus shook his head, clearing the momentary spell of amazement, turning to find Dubnus at his shoulder. He nodded at the bearded centurion, drawing a deep breath.

'Front rank – spears!'

Three hundred long spears swung from their resting positions, pivoting to point down at the hapless infantry being pressed up against the wall, more than one clearly already considering scrambling over the rough stone rampart to escape the crush.

'Front rank – engage!'

Dubnus's voice bellowed out over the Parthians' terrified din, the unquestioned master of his craft calling his men to battle.

'Strike!'

The long iron spear heads lanced out as the Tungrians lunged their right arms forward, stabbing into unprotected necks and faces with a ferocity that was made all the more devastating by the lack of resistance being offered by the enemy soldiers.

'Back!'

Ripping their weapons free, the men around Varus leaned back, pulling their spear arms back behind their heads and waiting for the command, heads turning to the hard-faced first spear as he waited for the dead and dying enemy from their first strike to crumple, and for fresh targets to present themselves. Varus took a spear from a man in the second rank, swallowing his revulsion and swinging the weapon to point down at the milling infantry, drawing his arm back and waiting for the command the entire cohort knew was coming.

'Strike!'

Thrusting the long shaft forward, he watched as an empty-eyed enemy infantryman opened his arms wide to take the blow, the Parthian's body shivering as Varus's foot-long blade slid through the base of his throat and erupted from his back, both wounds spraying fine mists of blood past the blade's obstruction.

'Back!'

This isn't war, this is murder.

The thought struggled for escape through his mouth, the urge to murmur the heresy swelling to a need to scream it at the sky.

'Strike!'

Looking down the spear's blade he saw his next victim, a man who had been forced around in the panicking crush until his back was presented to the defenders, his helmet gone and the nape of his neck glistening with the sweat running from his scalp. The blade severed his spine as neatly as a priest's ceremonial axe taking a bull's life, dropping the stricken Parthian into the mud to increase the height of their ramp of bodies.

'Back!'

This isn't murder, this is slaughter.

'Strike!'

His spear head lanced forward with those of the men to either side, part of a finely drilled war machine trained until it had no equal in the bloody art of war, three hundred spears striking out in perfect unison to flense the enemy army of its strength. A small part of Varus's mind exulted in the joy of belonging, of brotherhood with the Tungrians' warrior tribe and killing along-side men who had terrified him only a fortnight before, but even as he embraced the sheer joy of their collective deadliness, he looked down the spear again, and saw a soldier clearly no more than a child looking back up at him, blood flowing from his mouth as the long iron blade took his young life.

The cataphracts were concentrating again, closing ranks from the long crescent they had used to terrify their infantry forward and into the defenders' spears, hammering their swords against their armoured shoulders in a rhythmic clash of iron that was slowly gathering pace as they stalked ahead. Spilling out to either side, the spear men scurried to clear a path for the oncoming knights as they headed towards the wall. Julius turned to his legatus with a grim expression, drawing his sword with an iron rasp.

'I'm no use up here! This is going to come down to a goat fuck, with us as the goat if we're not careful!'

He turned and was gone, running for the nearest tower with a snapped command to his trumpeter to follow him.

Realising the oncoming knights' intentions, Varus turned to Dubnus.

'They're going to try to break through!'

The Briton nodded, drawing breath to shout a warning to his men.

'Don't let them across the wall!'

With terrifying abruptness, it seemed, the armoured men were up close, striding through the scatter of arrows lancing down into them from atop the walls to either side. One of them staggered, a shaft protruding between two iron plates that had become separated rather than overlapping, and as he tottered, his eyes narrowed with agony, the man behind him stepped in and administered the mercy stroke, pushing his corpse forward to lie face down in the mud. More knights flooded forward carrying the fascines that had been dropped by their infantry, swiftly throwing them across the heaped bodies that were piled up against the Roman defences, clearly working to provide a firm path across which an armoured man could pass without the risk of losing his balance, then pulled back to the main body that had halted twenty paces from the wall.

'Oh no . . .'

The young tribune watched in horror as the cataphracts took the bows from across their shoulders, reaching back to quivers slung over their backs, and nocked arrows, drawing the strings until the flights touched their ears, forcing the power of their muscular frames into the weapons. The Tungrians needed no instruction, ducking behind their shields and into the wall's cover, shouting warnings at the ranks of men wanting their turn at the wall, but the marines behind them had no time to ready themselves. The Parthians loosed, their arrows whirring across the makeshift wall and wreaking havoc among the blue tunicked men, nocking fresh arrows and shooting again, and again, each volley aimed a little higher, to fall among the cohorts waiting further back.

'They're trying to isolate us!'

Peering carefully over the wall, Varus realised that the enemy had dropped their bows and were striding towards thc wall.

'Up! Here they come!'

Moving as quickly as they could across the treacherously uneven surface of bodies piled up before the wall, and slowed by the weight of their armour, the Parthians were advancing with swords and maces drawn. Before the Tungrians could align their spears, the fastest among them were at the wall, throwing themselves at the low parapet with savage battle cries. Varus realised their predicament an instant before Dubnus, and bellowed the order that he knew was needed if the line was to hold under such an onslaught.

'Rear rank! Swords!'

Leaping onto the wall's top, the first of the attackers was still for an instant, regaining his balance and looking down at the soldiers before him, only his eyes visible between his helmet and the chain-mail veil that covered his nose and jaw.

'Mazda!'

Striking down with the mace as he screamed the war cry, he smashed the closest soldier aside with brutal power, jumping down from the parapet and hacking about him with the sword in his other hand, seeking to drive the Tungrians away from the wall. The men in the rear rank came at him, three soldiers competing to be the one to claim his gold- and silver-chased armour, but the Parthian stepped into their attack with graceful purpose, allowing a stabbing sword to scrape along his armoured sword arm before backhanding the soldier away with his mace, a rising blow shattering his jaw with an audible crack. The other two men hesitated for an instant, and he was on them, stabbing his sword through the closer man's throat, ripping it out and swinging it wide to strike fast at the last man, hacking the long blade into the base of his neck. Dubnus stepped in close behind him as the Parthian delivered the decapitating blow, swinging his axe's pick blade into the square of the Parthian's back, punching through the armour and contorting his body with the sudden agony as the centurion kicked him off the iron spike. But the damage was done. Seeing their comrade's success in crossing the wall and engaging the defenders, a dozen more cataphracts had followed him up the grisly ramp and thrown themselves at the spot where he'd crossed the rampart. Hacking their way into the hedge of spears that sought to push them away, first one and then another of them succeeding in making it onto the wall's top and jumping into the fight.

As they laid into the Tungrian front rank, forcing the spear-wielding soldiers to retreat before their flashing swords, more of them followed, their strength growing as the defenders to either side were pushed back until there were more than a dozen of them facing off to the defending soldiers. The cohort's line was bowed around them, none of the men facing them eager to fight the armoured monsters who had hacked their way through their comrades, and with a sickening jolt of realisation, Varus saw that he was the only officer who could influence the rapidly worsening situation.

He looked around at the marines behind them, realising that Ravilla's men were in no condition to fight. Fully half the cohort was dead or wounded, the prefect lying on his back with a pair of arrows protruding from his body in front of their ruined line. The remaining troops were effectively leaderless, it seemed, many of their officers seemingly caught in the barrage of arrows that had torn the heart out of their cohort. Making an abrupt decision, the young tribune turned away from the fight, ignoring Dubnus's amazed stare.

Striding down the ramp he felt the eyes on him, knowing that Scaurus would be watching him from the wall above, and briefly wondered what the man would make of his apparent retreat from the fight that was developing at the makeshift wall. He stopped in front of the marines and raised his voice to a parade-ground bellow of the sort he'd heard the centurions using, but never expected to employ himself.

'Marines!'

A few eyes lifted from the dead and dying men around them.

'Marines!'

More men looked up at him, their faces hard with grief and anger.

'Your comrades lie around you, killed without warning! Your officers are dead, and you do not know what to do! Those Parthian animals have pulled your world apart! And mine, marines, and *mine!* I have sworn an oath of vengeance to Mithras, that I will take my revenge or die in the act, and now is the time I intend to deliver on that oath! Are you with me?'

They stared at him in bemusement for a moment.

'Are you with me? Will you stand here and cry over dead men or come with me and take bloody revenge on the bastards that killed them?'

A single marine stepped forward, drawing his sword and pulling the leather cord that held the cheek pieces of his helmet together to tighten their fit, ready to fight.

'I'm with you, Tribune! I'll have some of that . . .'

Another man joined him, and then, as if a collective decision had been made, with a low growl of anger that raised the hairs on the back of his neck, a flood of blue-tunicked soldiers stepped forward, until the only men not with him were either wounded or broken in spirit.

'Arm yourselves! Swords only, this is going to be a close-quarters fight! Those men are too well armoured to fight fairly, so we're going to kill them with weight of numbers! Get a man down, then find a gap in his armour and kill him, move on and do it again! My vow will be fulfilled when every one of those *fuckers* is either dead or on the other side of the wall! So if you're with me . . .'

Varus turned back to face the Parthians and ran towards the fight, his last command a hoarse scream of fury.

'Follow me!'

The gate opened, and Artapanes' guard shepherded the comrades through it into the biggest garden Marcus had ever seen. Walled on all four sides, the brickwork high enough to obstruct any view from the adjacent palace, it stretched away before them, groves of trees, beds of riotously coloured flowers and stone terraces artfully arranged to provide a vista that was at once restful and stunningly beautiful. The priest gestured to the path before them, stepping forward to lead the three men into the garden.

'This way.'

He led them into the garden's grandeur, along a footpath formed of different-coloured paving stones and into a copse of trees, emerging onto a smoothly clipped lawn of lush grass around which stood four heavily armed and armoured palace guards. Beyond the two closest sentries was the familiar figure of Arsaces, deep in conversation with a man Marcus assumed was responsible for the garden's maintenance, while a fifth guard waited close by with a short roll of golden cloth in his hands. Behind the king a pair of slaves were diligently working on a nearby flower bed, seeking out the first growths of weed and removing them with iron hand-trowels. Another stood close to the path, carefully raking away twigs and leaves that had fallen from the trees in the night, collecting them into neat piles before scooping up the debris with both hands and dropping it into a wooden barrow. Artapanes held up a hand.

'The barbarians will wait here. Roman, you will come with me.'

Martos shrugged and gestured to Lugos, leading him away to the nearby copse, both men settling comfortably in the shadow of a fully grown cedar. Marcus followed the priest forward, past the closest two guards who turned to watch the two men as they passed, their eyes watchful despite the cleric's trusted presence.

Prostrating himself, while Marcus bowed as deeply as he did at the first formal audience, Artapanes waited until the king turned from his conversation before speaking.

'Majesty, I have delivered the Roman as you ordered.'

Arsaces gestured for him to rise, smiling at Marcus.

'So, Marcus Tribulus Corvus, the time has come for you to leave us. As I promised, my oldest son Vologases will escort you to Nisibis in the company of a detachment of my Immortals. You are honoured. No Roman has ever ridden with them before, and I doubt the experience will be granted to any other. And here is your father's sword.'

He held a hand out to the guard, who went on one knee to offer him the cloth-wrapped object.

'I promised to return it to you. You would be wise not to draw it now, but I assure you that it is as it was when you surrendered it to my guards. Although I did suggest they sharpen it.'

Marcus reached out with his good arm and took the sword back, bowing again.

'I think you, King of Kings. It will never be said in my presence that you fail to keep your word.'

Arsaces inclined his head fractionally.

'And it will never be said in mine that all Romans lack *hunar*. I thank you once more for—'

Both men turned in surprise as the man who had handed the king Marcus's sword grunted in surprise, staggering away from them with an arrow's fletching sprouting from his chest. Spinning,

Marcus saw the two guards closest to the trees slump, their armour inadequate to protect them against the deadly pointed arrows at such close range, then flinched as another pair of missiles zipped past to either side, felling the two men behind the king. Stepping in front of Arsaces, he tensed his body as the pair of archers who had stepped from the trees nocked arrows to their bows and raised them, ready to shoot, but the bowmen simply drew their strings halfway, ready to loose. A stocky armoured figure emerged from the copse behind them, stalking forward with the bow-legged gait of a man born in the saddle, and a moment later a slimmer, taller figure emerged from the foliage behind him. The shorter of the two paced forward slowly with one hand on his sword's hilt, his words muffled by the silver chainmail across his mouth and nose.

'Well now, here's a scene I never thought to witness. The King of Kings hiding behind a Roman!'

Arsaces stepped forward.

'My guards will—'

'Your guards will do nothing at all other than take the blame for your death.'

The assassin stepped onto the grass, sliding the long sword from his scabbard. The polished steel sent reflections flickering across the trees behind him, and Marcus realised that the two Britons had sunk back into the cover of their branches.

'Even the most fanatical of your priests knows that once blood is spilled it cannot be put back into a lifeless corpse, especially when the army falls in line behind your killer. They will quickly decide to overlook the probability of your son's involvement in your murder, Majesty, and that of his brother, just as they will have no choice but to forget this!'

He struck with the speed and precision of a warrior trained from infancy, the sword stroke rising and falling in an instant. Artapanes staggered, cleaved from collarbone to navel, then collapsed backwards as the assassin twisted his blade and took a step backwards, ripping it from his body. He flicked the blade, sending a rain of blood droplets across Marcus and the king's clothing, then dropped back into the fighting stance with the sword held out to one side, ready to strike again.

'The priest's close relationship with Ahura Mazda seems to have availed him little. A new cleric will be appointed after your death, Majesty, a more malleable man, although not entirely trustworthy, as Artapanes would have done well to have realised. It was his junior cleric Atardates who informed us that his master and the chief priest had colluded to bring the Roman to you, Majesty, a meeting that can only be presumed was the first step in a further treaty with Rome. Who knows what else you might have ceded to them in your weakness? Clearly it was the duty of the nobility to prevent such an error of judgement, and to remove a man who has become so fallible from the throne. So now, my king, regretfully, your time has come. I will honour your long reign with a swift and merciful death.'

His gaze switched to Marcus.

'Whereas you, Roman, brought here by such divine providence . . .'

The eyes that were all either man could see of his face, narrowed with vicious amusement.

'Your death will be a little more . . .'

He searched for the right Greek word.

'. . . *protracted*.'

Tensing his body to attack, he faltered as a tumult broke out behind him, stepping back and sweeping the sword forward to deter any attack as he turned to see what was happening.

Martos had stormed out of the trees, launching himself headlong at the nearer of the two archers who still waited with arrows nocked to their bows. The Parthian loosed, but in his panic the arrow flew wide, and the Briton caught him in the mid-section, driving the breath from his body in an explosive exhalation. Rising onto his knees and knotting his fingers together, the Briton drew them back over his head, ready to club the reeling archer into insensibility, but the blow never fell. The second archer coolly raised his bow and put the waiting arrow into his chest, reaching into his quiver for a replacement as Martos tottered for a moment and then fell backwards. The fallen archer nodded his thanks to his comrade, getting slowly to his feet and reaching down to retrieve his bow.

With an ear-splitting bellow Lugos stepped out of the trees' concealment, taking the hapless man by the neck and pulling him upright, the archer's struggles helpless against his monstrous strength, then put a hand in the square of his back and threw him bodily at the second bowman just as he loosed. Struck hard by the flying body of his comrade, the archer staggered back, dazed by the crunching impact of their heads, but the arrow he had loosed flew straight, whipping across the short distance between bow and target to embed in the huge Briton's thick calf. Bellowing again, pain and rage combined as he took one pace forward on the wounded leg, then another, barely able to walk, Lugos staggered towards the felled bowmen, tottering with every step as his intended victims slowly struggled back to their feet. Fumbling for an arrow, the man who had wounded the Briton nocked it to his bow with shaking fingers, failing at the first attempt before feeling the bow's resistance as the missile's grooved tail found the string.

Raising the weapon he sighted down the arrow, drawing it back to his ear and raising the bow, ready to shoot at the oncoming Briton, then died as Lugos swung a heavy wooden barrow that he had grabbed by one handle, smashing the hapless archer's skull with a sweep of the improvised club. Fresh pain shot through Lugos's body as the other archer sank a dagger into his foot, and he lifted the barrow over his head with an incoherent scream of fury, sweeping it down onto his wide-eyed victim's face. Battered into the ground, the semi-conscious bowman raised an arm in supplication, staring up glassy-eyed as the giant looming over him lifted the barrow again, then died as the second blow smashed his windpipe flat and severed his spine. Staggering backwards, Lugos fell full length, unable to move for the pain in his leg and foot.

The stocky assassin turned back to Marcus with a chuckle. 'How conven—'

The Roman was armed, his own eagle-pommelled gladius in his left hand and a guardsman's longer sword in the right. The Parthian shrugged.

'As I was saying, how convenient. Your barbarians and my archers have neatly dealt with the problem of witnesses. I'll deal with your giant once this is done with.'

The second man walked slowly forward to join his co-conspirator, drawing his sword and ranging it alongside the shorter man's.

'And now there are two of us. Two of the best-trained warriors in the empire against a Roman aristocrat with only one arm. Give it up now, Roman, and go to meet your ancestors with dignity. I'll make it clean.'

Marcus crabbed forward, raising the swords with their points aligned.

'Who said I only had one arm? You're not the only man who knows the value of seeming to be somewhat less than he really is. Get behind me, Majesty.'

'Really? You think you can hold us off for long enough that help will come? Help isn't coming, Roman. By now my brother is already dead, and as far as the rest of the palace is concerned, the King of Kings is already in a place of safety. By the time the priests realise what's happening I'll have had long enough to gut you and watch you bleed to death, as you try to push your own intestines back into your gaping belly.'

Marcus danced forward, his blades flickering out to clash with the assassins' raised swords, forcing them to defend themselves as he stepped around to his left, threatening the taller of the two.

'You're the weak point, aren't you? This one will give me a proper fight, but you, Your Highness . . .'

He flashed the long sword out in a lightning-swift attack. The taller man stepped back, and his comrade stormed into the attack, charging forward with a shout and swinging his sword in short, chopping arcs that forced Marcus back half a dozen paces as he crabbed around to his right, retreating further from the king with every step. His assailant's eyes narrowed in fresh amusement as he readied himself to renew the onslaught.

'See? You can't back away for ever.'

Marcus grinned back at his attacker.

'I don't need to. Here will do nicely.'

He nodded, and with a jerk his assailant staggered forward, staring down numbly at the point of an armour-piercing arrow protruding from his chest. Dropping to his knees, the stricken man's sword fell from his numb fingers, and Marcus stepped forward to stare at him through the chain mail mask that disguised his identity.

'Go and meet your ancestors. Whether they'll consider death at the hands of a crippled barbarian worthy of that *hunar* you all make so much of will be between you and them.'

He swung the mortally wounded man around to show him the bow in Lugos's hands, another arrow nocked to the string and menacing the second assassin, then pushed him forward to fall face down on the immaculate turf. Stepping towards the taller man with a slow, catlike tread, the Roman raised his swords menacingly.

'That's enough, Lugos. The other one has to live, I'm afraid. See what you can do for Martos.'

The taller of the two would-be killers stepped back.

'No . . . I . . .'

'Thought it would be quick and easy? That it was for the betterment of the empire? Perhaps. And now you think you can talk your way out of this? Stand *still*!'

Quivering, the faceless would-be assassin froze where he stood, and Marcus stepped forward a slow, sliding pace.

'Like your father, I suspect, I find myself more disappointed than surprised by this turn of events. You sought to kill the king, and take the throne for yourself, confident that the army and priesthood would unite under your leadership. And what now, now that you've failed? Perhaps you think you can make it right by grovelling at your father's feet? Perhaps you can. Even if only because it's the pragmatic thing to do, to maintain a united facade for the world to see, you'll be expecting him to forgive you.'

He slid the other foot forward, his gaze intent on the other man's eyes.

'Yes, you know he'll punish you, but it'll be a gilded cage, won't it? You'll keep your rank, and he'll send you away from the court to lick your wounds, and remove your malevolent presence from his side. Where any other man would be roasted alive, your punishment will be to keep your crown.'

He took the final step, gently resting the point of the longer blade on his opponent's sword.

'But when you put an arrow in my friend, you made an enemy of me. And unlike the king, forgiveness isn't a word whose taste I find it easy to stomach when it comes to those who are close to me.'

The King of Kings started forward.

'Roman . . .'

Marcus struck, the long sword's thrust raising his opponent's blade in self-defence, the gladius snaking out for the other man's belly and drawing a frantic low parry while the spatha hacked down at his opponent's sword hand, severing the fingers wrapped around the jewelled hilt in a spray of blood.

'Arghhhh!!'

Shrieking, he raised the ruined hand, howling in pain and horror at the stumps of his fingers, severed at the lowest knuckle.

'My hand!'

Marcus stabbed the long sword down into the grass, allowing the gladius to fall point-down into the turf.

'And now, King of Kings, do as you wish with me.'

The king shook his head, taking the golden cloth in which the gladius had been wrapped and using it to bind his son's wounds. With a sudden crash the gate through which Marcus and the Britons had entered moments before crashed open, and a dozen guardsmen burst through the copse, their eyes widening at the bloody slaughter spread out before them. Their leader stalked through the trees behind them, sword drawn.

'Majesty! Mazda be praised, you live!'

He spotted Marcus standing to one side and his pace quickened, the sword's point rising.

'No!'

The officer faltered, finding himself faced by his king, then knelt on one knee.

'Majesty?'

'No man is to harm the Roman. He was not the assassin here, but my defender. This was the man who sought my death. My own son.'

He pulled away the wounded man's chain veil, and the guard commander recoiled, his reaction an astonished whisper.

'It cannot be . . .'

A man dressed in white silk splashed with dark red blood pushed through the guards, taking in the scene with a look that combined disappointment and resignation.

'You live, Father.'

He crossed to where Arsaces stood and kissed the king on the mouth, then went down on one knee. The king looked down at him, his expression unreadable.

'Yes, Vologases. As you see, I live. The assassin was this man.'

The prince looked into his brother's face without surprise.

'As ever, Osroes, everything you attempt eventually turns to ashes in your mouth, but this is your worst failure yet.'

He turned back to his father.

'He sent killers to murder me in my bath, but by chance I was awake early this morning. They broke into my bathing suite only to find it empty, and were overpowered before they could do any more than kill my attendants. You disappoint me, brother . . .'

He waved a hand at the scene, realising that Marcus was kneeling over Martos.

'The Briton?'

Lugos stared back at him, his leg covered in his own blood.

'He dead.'

Vologases walked slowly across to the spot where the dead Briton lay, placing a hand on Marcus's shoulder.

'We are dishonoured by this, Roman. For a guest to have been killed in the palace is unthinkable, but for that guest to have been a king . . .'

Marcus turned and looked up at him empty-eyed.

'Your dishonour means little to me.'

Vologases nodded levelly.

'And yet so much to me. And to my father. Your friend the king died in the defence of the most powerful man in the empire, which means that I will stop at nothing to wipe away that stain.'

He stood, turning to his father.

'This man died in your defence, Majesty.'

Arsaces nodded.

'He shall be buried as a captain of my household guard who has died in battle, in my own mausoleum. He shall sleep with the kings of Parthia.'

Marcus stood, inclining his head at the king.

'A great honour. His family will be proud to know he gave his life protecting one so powerful. I must nonetheless report back to Rome that a client king beloved of the emperor died saving the King of Kings' life, and without full retribution being exacted. That, combined with the siege of a legally ceded fortress town, and the destruction of an entire cohort of legionaries while going about their lawful business in a client kingdom, which had been invaded by King Osroes and his accomplices, Narsai of Adiabene and Wolgash of Hatra . . .'

He paused to allow the statement to sink in.

'We all know that wars have been fought over a good deal less. And Rome needs gold, King of Kings. Perhaps the man who stands behind the throne will decide to convince Commodus that your kingdom is ripe for another harvest, persuading the emperor to earn himself yet another triumph by unleashing his army. You know all too well that if Rome turns her fury east then no amount of astute intelligence work is likely to prevent half a dozen legions from repeating Avidius Cassius's march on this city. Of course, you could simply kill me too, if you think it will prevent the news of this infamy reaching Rome.

And if your pragmatism can overcome yet another stain on your honour . . .'

Vologases raised his hands.

'If I might add an insight to our discussion, before we talk of yet more bloodshed between our two mighty empires? It seems to me that whilst my brother here and his bidaxs Gurgen were the arrows pointed at my father's heart, another hand may have been on the bowstring?'

Osroes stared back at them defiantly, his eyes narrowed with the pain of his maimed hand.

'You think I'm not capable of making my own decisions?'

The prince shrugged.

'I know you best of all of us, little brother, and I think that while you're capable of attempting our father's murder, I'm far from certain that you would have done so without knowing you'd have the support of your fellow kings. Or at least those influential enough to ensure your coronation, were the king and I both to have succumbed to your plan.'

He reached out, taking a grip of the collar of his brother's armour.

'So here's what we'll do. Our father here is going to entrust the investigation of this attempt on the throne to me, both as his heir and a potential victim. He knows that I'll be unrelenting in my efforts, but he also knows that I understand the need to exercise the appropriate subtlety. The exercise of power is best achieved with the consent of the ruled. Isn't that right, Father?'

Arsaces nodded, a sad smile creeping onto his face, and his son continued with the same quiet fury in his voice.

'So here's what I intend. I will summon the twelve kings, in our father's name, and while we wait for them to assemble, you and I will spend some time together in the lower reaches of the palace. The old kings had a few cunning tricks when it came to finding out what they wanted to know, and I'm sure that you and I will soon enough come to a mutual understanding of what happened this morning, and what subtle discussions and alliances might lie behind it. When we assemble the kings there needs to be no further unpleasantness, simply a frank discussion with certain of them as to the thinness of the ice upon which they find themselves. Everyone will know their place in the world once more, and you, you may even still be able to walk among them with your head up. Or perhaps walking might prove a little too much – depending on how long it takes for you and I to reach that mutual understanding I was talking about.'

He paused, staring intently at his brother's face.

'Or would you like to spare us both all that unhappiness, and just tell me what I need to know now?'

'Reinforcements, do you think?'

The northern wall's duty centurion had summoned Scaurus and Julius shortly after midday on the fifth day after the final abortive Parthian attack, and the two men were looking out over the parapet, Julius using a hand to shade his eyes from the sun's powerful glare.

'Another thousand cavalry? They make an impressive sight, but it's not cavalry that Narsai needs. And besides . . .'

The men riding into the Parthian camp were clearly a military unit of some nature, each man uniformly equipped with spear, bow case and sword, and all of them wore helmets and had shields strapped to their backs, but there was one glaring absence from their war gear.

'What use would they be in battle without armour?'

First Spear and Legatus watched as the long column of white-tunicked riders trotted across the plain, each man mounted on a horse with the stature and power to carry a cataphract into battle. The legatus frowned as he stared out at them. The riders splashed through the Mygdonius at a fording point whose waters were already considerably lower than at their height a week before, an advance party of half a dozen men riding forward while the remainder dismounted and watered their horses. Pulling up in front of Narsai's headquarters, a cluster of tents close to the siege line with a direct view of the gaping hole in Nisibis's northern walls, their leader dismounted and strode forward with a pair of men on either side, while the sixth walked slowly towards the fortress, raising his hands to show that they were empty.

'I don't like the look of this.'

The newcomer was a distant but clearly visible figure, and as the Romans watched, the men guarding the tent threw themselves full length before him. A murmur of sound reached the walls, as the Parthian army woke up to the presence of the new arrival's apparently exalted status.

'Could that be . . . ?'

Scaurus shook his head doubtfully at his first spear.

'The King of Kings? I wouldn't have thought so. He's too old to be riding round his kingdom on a war horse, and I'd have thought that his arrival would have been announced with a good deal more fanfare. But I've an idea who it might be . . .'

The tunic-clad figure walked with deliberate care towards the improvised wall, now fifteen feet high, and stopped within shouting distance, his face partially hidden by the chain mail that hung from his helmet.

'His Majesty Prince Vologases of Parthia has ridden from the imperial city of Ctesiphon at the head of the King of Kings' Immortal Guard, at the direction of his father Arsaces, Forty-Fifth of his noble line, King of Kings, the Anointed, the Just, the Illustrious, Friend of the Greeks! His Majesty respectfully requests the presence of Legatus Gaius Rutilius Scaurus at a negotiation to determine the fate of the city of Nisibis! Further, His Majesty has bidden me tell you that time is pressing in this matter, and so further requests your attendance to be as prompt as can be managed given the obstacles to your leaving your fortress!'

Scaurus leaned out over the wall's rampart.

'I already have the fate of the city looked after quite nicely, thank you! And I decline the invitation to attend this *negotiation!* Rome still remembers the fate suffered by our general Marcus Licinius Crassus at Carrhae!'

The messenger looked up at him, putting both hands on his hips and allowing an impatient tone to creep into his voice.

'I suggest that just this once, Legatus, you ignore the lessons you've learned from the history books. Prince Vologases has assured me that he isn't going to be ordering any killing today.'

Scaurus started, and stared down at the man with wide-eyed amazement, while Julius shook his head and barked out a terse laugh, the sound drawing startled glances from soldiers who had grown used to his more usual saturnine view of their situation.

'You cheeky young bastard! Stay there!'

The legatus hurried down to the temporary rampart and gingerly lowered himself onto the desolate plain of sun-baked mud, picking a careful path over to the waiting Marcus, who saluted crisply and gestured to the Parthian lines, having removed his helmet.

'You're out of uniform, Tribune. What sort of effeminate fancy dress do you call that?'

His junior rubbed the material of his sleeve between finger and thumb.

'It's raw silk, Legatus, and worth about as much as my armour and weapons, in the right market in Rome. And it's the uniform worn by the King of Kings' Immortals, when they're not carrying enough iron to make a strong man's knees bend.'

He pointed to the Parthian siege lines again.

'If you'll accompany me, the explanations you're looking for are all over there.'

Following the younger man across the empty space between the fortress's walls and the enemy's waiting ranks, the legatus listened to a brief description of the journey down the Euphrates and the events that had unfolded in Ctesiphon, covering his eyes with one hand as Marcus recounted the death of their friend. Recovering control of his emotions after a moment, he shook his head apologetically.

'My apologies, Tribune. I distinctly recall telling Julius you'd thank me for sending you south, but if I could have predicted that as an outcome . . .'

'No . . .'

He looked up, to find Marcus staring back at him with emphasis.

'Martos died quickly, and he died doing what he did best. He could never have gone home to the Dinpaladyr again, he told me as much, and what life is it for a king to wander the earth yearning for the one thing he can never have, and mourning the wife and children who died as a consequence of his actions? He was buried in the King of Kings' own mausoleum dressed as a Captain of Arsaces' personal bodyguard, honoured with weapons and armour as fine as Osroes was wearing when we captured him, and with a war horse sacrificed to his spirit and entombed with him.'

The younger man shook his head at the memory.

'I'm not ashamed to tell you I shed tears over his corpse, and again at his interment, but all in all I'd say that if he'd known his fate in advance, he'd have been content. Now come and hear what Prince Vologases has to say on the matter. We may mourn it, but King Martos's death defending Vologases' father has put the King of Kings very much in our debt.'

The spear men manning the section of the siege line they had passed through snapped to attention as the Roman commander walked across one of the heavily guarded crossing points over the twenty-foot wide ditch, and the two men walked the short distance to Narsai's command tent. Dismounted Immortals were clearly in control of the situation, the king's own guard outnumbered three to one by white-tunicked men, every one of them a good six feet tall. Vologases turned from whatever he was discussing with the king and greeted Scaurus with a regal nod, smiling as the legatus bowed to a respectful angle.

'Legatus Scaurus, greetings.'

He waved Scaurus forward, dismissing his guards to stand out of earshot so that only he and Narsai faced the two Romans.

'Your tribune has told me much of your exploits while we've ridden here from Ctesiphon, and so I feel I already know you. Clearly you are an opponent of whom to be wary, an impression not dispelled by the news that my cousin King Narsai has shared with me. It seems you have handled his army roughly?'

The Roman returned the smile.

'Thank you, Majesty. King Narsai's men displayed all the bravery we expected of them, and the use of the river as a battering ram was inspired. We were fortunate to retain control of the fortress.'

Vologases shrugged.

'The affairs of state so often hinge on the smallest of things. However lucky you might consider yourselves, you are indisputably still in command of Nisibis, which is just as well, for if my cousin had managed to wrest it from you I would have been forced to demand in my father's name that he return it to Rome's control.'

Narsai was glowering at Vologases, and the prince continued with a grim smile.

'As I said, the smallest of things can sometimes be the fulcrum for great events. Your Tribune and his friends from the northern lands that are not to be named by the pious intervened in an attempt to kill my father, an attempt carried out by my brother Osroes and his bidaxs Gurgen. My brother feigned lost wits until he was returned to the palace, then used Gurgen to gather support among the army for an attempt to take power by the planned murders of both the King of Kings and myself, leaving him as the only man capable of ruling. I escaped death by good fortune, while my father was defended by his guests at the cost of the life of King Martos and the wounding of his bondsman.

'You have both the King of Kings' thanks and his abject apology that such violence should have been done to men who had been declared guests in the palace. His shame at this turn of events is only made deeper by the unavoidable fact that the very person who was the beneficiary of their bravery in journeying to Ctesiphon was then responsible for such infamy. He has directed me to pass on his most fulsome apology to you and to Rome, under whose protection these men were travelling. He hopes that it will not become the cause for a disturbance in the long peace since the end of the last war.'

Scaurus inclined his head in recognition of the apology.

'Your father's thanks are duly acknowledged and respected,

Prince Vologases. It dismays me to have lost such a friend, but for him to have perished in such a noble endeavour gives solace to my sorrow. As to Rome, however . . .'

Vologases raised a hand.

'Permit me, Legatus, but there is more I must make clear. My father was, as you can imagine, perturbed in the extreme to be so cruelly assaulted within his own palace and by his own son, with the apparent collusion of his most trusted gundsalar, Kophosates. Reprisals for this betrayal were swift and severe, a fact of which I can assure you, since I was the chosen instrument of my father's prosecution of the men involved. Five senior members of the court have been interrogated, admitted to their part in the plot and punished, four of them with a death whose grisly nature it would be unfair to burden you with. Suffice to say that an example has been made. The fifth was my brother, of course, who has been returned to Ecbatana, the capital of his kingdom, under close and attentive watch. During his questioning, conducted by myself, he swiftly confessed to having been only the spear tip of a cabal of several of the empire's kings, a group of dissenters which it seems has included my cousin Narsai.'

Scaurus looked at the king, whose eyes remained firmly fixed on his boots.

'You'll get no reaction there, Legatus. I've warned my cousin that the slightest reaction on his part, anything that might excite the ire of his guards, will result in their wholesale slaughter swiftly followed by his own public execution, here, in front of the very walls he sought to defeat and make his own. When we've completed our discussion, in which he will take no part other than to listen, I shall gather my father's Immortals and ride away, taking the king with me. His generals will disperse the army back to their various kingdoms, with express orders from the King of Kings to end these hostilities immediately, and to have marched away from here by this time tomorrow. They know better than to disobey such an order.'

He looked Scaurus up and down.

'And so, Legatus, you find yourself victorious. Were it not for my cousin and my brother's ill-judged intervention, my father would have found it difficult to overrule a king who sought to remove Roman boots from our soil. The siege would have continued, with whatever result. As it is, however, Narsai's imprudence has proved to be a sword with two edges. The other conspirators will be warned as to the potential consequences should they be so unwise as to transgress against my father's tolerance again, and provided with a practical example of the nature that his ire will take. An example provided by King Narsai.'

He turned to the downcast king, speaking swiftly in Pahlavi, spitting out the words with a vehemence that would have been simple contempt were it not for the edge of pure hatred. Narsai turned away without ever looking up, walking towards his private section of the tent. The prince watched him go with hooded eyes, his jaw set hard.

'He is to equip himself in his finest armour, array himself with weapons and mount the horse he rode into battle with you. I will greet him with solicitude and the respect due to a king, and invite him to accompany me to Ctesiphon for an audience with my father. We will ride out together, in the company of my father's Immortals, and I will escort him away to meet his destiny. He will treated with the honour and respect due to a man of his station, and will attend the gathering of my father's kings as a peer among his fellows. And then, at the right time, he will admit to his brother monarchs that he plotted to kill the King of Kings, but came to his senses in time to avert a tragedy that would have endangered them all. He will then retire to his capital Arbela, where he will rule in name only. I will find a suitably ruthless man to play the role of his bidaxs, and in reality that man will control his kingdom.'

'And you don't have any concern that the king, armed and armoured, might kill a dozen or more unarmoured men before he is taken down? Including yourself?'

'No, Legatus, in truth I do not. Narsai knows that if he were to attempt anything so foolish he would be overwhelmed by sheer weight of numbers, disarmed, and then forced to watch his family be despoiled and beheaded, one at a time. His fingers may twitch at the pommel of his mace, but he'll resist the temptation.'

Scaurus tilted his head again, his mouth twisted into a hard smile.

'A pragmatic solution, Your Highness. You will clearly make an excellent successor to your father.'

Vologases' laugh was tinged with a faint hint of derision.

'Forgive my disappointment at receiving praise from a Roman, Legatus, some habits die harder than others. I will indeed follow my father's path of keeping Rome at bay with soft words, and focus my efforts on the northern borders where the real threat lies, but in truth I fear your empire more than ever before. My father has presided over a period of gentle but inevitable decline, and the time may yet come when a new Roman emperor, a man stronger than the current fool, looks to the east and considers the wealth to be had by invading Parthia, stripping the western kingdoms of their wealth and enslaving the population. For all that I despise Narsai for his attempt on my father's life, a small part of me is shouting that he was right to confront Rome now, before it's too late.'

He shook his head.

'And you must forgive me my musing. I suggest you return to your fortress now, to spare Narsai the indignity of his departure from power being overseen by his enemy. And don't allow my bitterness to lessen the gratitude I feel to you, Marcus Valerius Aquila.'

He embraced Marcus, turned to Scaurus with a brisk nod, and then turned away.

'I will pray to Ahura Mazda for your safe delivery to those you love, and that your *hunar* will continue to burn with the same brilliance for the remainder of your days . . .'

Pausing, he turned back with a lopsided smile.

'Unless, of course, we meet on the field of battle. On that day, look to your blades, Aquila, as I will look to mine. And remember, I know what you are capable of, but you have yet to see my mettle.'

Scaurus watched him walk away, then turned to the tent's doorway.

'He's right. It would be unseemly to gloat over a man's fall from power.'

They walked from the tent into the sun's heat, a pair of Immortals to either side to safeguard their passage through the siege lines. Stopping to marvel anew at the destruction visited upon the fortress by the river's torrent, Marcus looked about him at a sea of dried mud in which the scattered detritus of a major battle had been baked.

'So Narsai used the Mygdonius to smash the wall, then sent his army to force their way into the city?'

Scaurus nodded, looking out across the scene of the battle from a new perspective.

'Yes. And we were lucky, Tribune, that your colleague Varus happened to be the man in command when their cataphracts managed to get a foothold on the wall that we'd thrown up across the breach. They looked unbreakable, all that armour making them almost impossible to kill, and when Varus ran from the wall I thought his nerve had failed him again.'

He shook his head ruefully.

'I misjudged the man. He rallied Ravilla's marines just when they were on the point of breaking, with the Procurator dying and half their men shot with arrows, and he took them into the Parthian knights like a pack of mad dogs. I watched the whole thing from the city wall, as the Parthians stood firm and killed three men for every loss they took, expecting the marines to break and run a dozen times over, if I'm honest. But there was something in Varus that wouldn't let them, some insanity that threw him at their line time and again, and in the end their sheer weight of numbers told. The cataphracts simply couldn't stand against their ferocity, not with men being pulled from their line and hacked to pieces before their eyes. In the end it was they who turned tail, fighting their way back over the wall in bloody desperation, but for a time it was too close to judge the likely winner. If it hadn't been for that young man and his burning urge for redemption . . .'

'Did he live?'

Scaurus chuckled.

'Live? He came through the madness without a scratch. You have a rival for the Tungrians' affections, Tribune, given it was they who were being battered away from the wall when he intervened. Even Dubnus seems to respect the man.'

He started walking towards the fortress, and Marcus followed him, looking about him at the battle's wreckage, weapons and discarded armour half sunk into the hardened mud.

'One thing does occur to me though.'

Scaurus looked at his junior as they recrossed the bridge into the empty ground between fortress and besiegers.

'What's that?'

Marcus looked at the walls of the city for a moment as they walked across the expanse of dried mud, waving a hand at the battered walls and the ground before them.

'I think Narsai was perilously close to getting it right. Indeed I think he only made one mistake.'

He turned to the legatus with an expression that made it clear he was deadly serious.

'He chose the wrong brother. I rode for five days with Vologases, and I can assure you that if we ever face that man across a battlefield, it won't be the easy ride Osroes gave us.'

Scaurus frowned.

'You think there'll be a war with Parthia? It sounded to me as if Arsaces was pretty much bent on avoiding such a thing. And Commodus's concerns only extend to the next place he's going to bury his manhood.'

The younger man shrugged, turning back to look at the Parthian lines.

'Nobody lives for ever, Legatus. Not kings, and most definitely not emperors, especially those with a gift for creating enemies. One way or another, everyone dies. One way, or another . . .'

Historical Note

There are several historical aspects of *Thunder of the Gods* that will bear some further and slightly more scholarly explanation than would be appropriate in a work of fiction.

To start with, Parthian history is a subject that the casual student of Rome may think they know well enough, but there's one big problem for the uninitiated – those who aren't studying Parthia with an ancient history degree in mind – the sheer lack of sources. Parthian historical tradition seems to have been oral for the most part (we seem to get most of our record of the Parthian kings from numismatics, the study of the empire's coinage), which means that the only place where we can find written evidence as to the empire's history is in the writings of those powers that opposed Parthian expansion – and most specifically Rome.

Parthia was indeed a great empire spanning the boundaries of ancient Persia, more or less, with a King of Kings in the Achaemenid tradition, and (at least initially) militarily the match of Rome due to a combination of highly mobile and deadly accurate horse archers and terrifying heavy cavalry, the cataphracti. In the standout battle of the two empires' early engagement, at Carrhae in 53 BC, Rome's heavy legionary infantry more than met their match, albeit on unfavourable ground and under questionable command. So began a period of apparent uneasy equality between the two empires that lasted until the fall of the Parthian Arsacid dynasty in the early third century and, for Rome, the horrifying events of the Sassanid dynasty's rather more effective response to Roman attempts at controlling Mesopotamia (for which read my colleague Harry Sidebottom's excellent *Warrior of Rome* series).

But this initial balance of power wasn't to last. The Parthians did indeed completely dominate Rome's might with a much smaller force at the battle of Carrhae, and then successfully defied Mark Antony's attempts to impose Roman hegemony over Mesopotamia in the thirties with considerable success. And for much of the first century AD an uneasy peace was the norm, with some Parthian success against Nero's armies in the sixties. But with the invasion ordered by the emperor Trajan in AD 115, to safeguard his recent occupation of Armenia, a pattern was established that would recur throughout the second century. Not only did Rome advance as far as the Arabian Gulf, sacking the Parthian capital Ctesiphon for the first time, but the scale of Parthia's defeat in the face of massed Roman legions was to be repeated twice more, with the capital falling once again in AD 165, to the Roman general Avidius Cassius, and for a third time to the emperor Septimius Severus in AD 197.

The Parthian empire had by the late second century gone from being a military superpower that had the measure of Rome's armies, to little more than a combination of convenient punchbag and piggy bank – indeed it is theorised that Severus's sacking and mass enslavement of Ctesiphon's population enabled him to prop up a tottering Roman empire whose crisis of the third century might otherwise well have come three or four decades earlier. And the reasons? Loss of absolute power over the empire's vassal kings? Internal divisions within the Arsacid dynasty? Incessant pressure from the steppe tribes to the empire's north and east? Whatever it was, the problem seems to have been one of Parthian weakness in the face of the same level of Roman threat that had been offered two hundred years previously by the republic rather than any increase in Roman military capability.

The reader who wishes to delve deeper is encouraged to read the following excellent works on the subject. Gareth Sampson's *Defeat of Rome in the East* tells the story of Carrhae, and attempts to do so in a manner that is fair to the Roman commander Crassus. Fergus Millar's *The Roman Near East* considers the period 31 BC–AD 337 as a whole, while Dr Kaveh Farrokh's

Shadows in the Desert provides a more Parthian perspective. And the usual excellent Osprey volume *Rome's Enemies 3: Parthians and Sassanid Persians* brings the Parthian army to life, and points out, as more than one well-informed student of Persia told me during my research (see the acknowledgements), that there was more to Parthia's military than archers and armoured cavalry.

A few other points of historical interest are worth offering to the casual historian without the time to delve deeply enough into the subject.

As described in the story, the Parthian kings did indeed make a point of emphasising their facial abnormalities on the empire's coinage, as a direct link to Ataxerxes I, who was known as 'Longhand', as his right hand was indeed a good deal longer than the left. While this might seem far-fetched, it seems that there may have been some basis for the claim. Modern scientists call the condition neurofibromatosis – a genetic problem that renders the victim prone to limb gigantism and wart-like tumours – and it seems from the numismatic record that it was suffered by both the Achaemenid and Parthian kings. Take a look at the coin representation of King Vologases IV (the birth name of Arsaces the Forty-Fifth, Arsaces being the dynastic name used by all of the Parthian kings) and you can see quite distinctly that there is the representation of a large wart-like growth on his head. I find it fascinating that a monarch would seek to emphasise a disfigurement in order to strengthen his claim to kinship with an ancient line of kings, but that seems likely to have been the case.

Speaking of Vologases IV, while I have exercised a degree of artistic interpretation of the state of Arsacid family politics in the late second century, we do know – from the numismatic record once again – that there was a King Osroes II of Media with a coin mint in his capital city of Ectebana in the late second century. It seems that many of the vassal kings were allowed to mint their own currency, an indicator of the way that imperial authority was quite significantly delegated by this point in the Parthian empire's trajectory to failure. Osroes II is believed to have revolted against the Parthian throne – and against his father – around the year AD 190, and to have been swiftly dealt with by his brother Vologases V shortly thereafter with his ascension to the throne. Vologases then ruled until the year AD 208, which means that he was on the throne in AD 197 when Severus invaded Parthia and sacked Ctesiphon for the third and final time.

And lastly, Nisibis. Whilst I was desperately keen to go and look at the historical site, cooler opinions prevailed (it being 2014 and modern-day Nusaybin being right on the Syrian border). In truth, it's clear that little of the ancient fortress has survived, which is a pity as it was clearly one of Mesopotamia's most impressive features. Changing hands several times over the course of the second and third centuries – including it being taken from Rome by its Jewish population during the little known but vicious Kitos War (a widespread Jewish revolt in North Africa, Egypt Cyprus and Mesopotamia) in the AD 140s, and then recaptured shortly thereafter – it was by the late third century back in Roman hands. Described as the 'bulwark of empire' by the fourth-century Roman historian Ammianus Marcellinus, the city was ceded back to the Persians in AD 363 as the result of the catastrophic defeat of the Emperor Julian, and indeed seems to have been surrendered for strategic reasons far more frequently than it was taken by force.

And that use of flood waters to breach the walls? Reader, I wish I could say it was my idea, but sadly I'd be lying if I made any such claim. The real genius involved was not King Narsai of Adiabene either – for all that he was a genuine contemporary vassal monarch – but some nameless engineer in the service of King Shapur II, who clearly took one look at the Fruit River and saw not a source of water but a battering ram. Just as I have portrayed in *Thunder of the Gods*, the city walls were felled by the flood water, but when Shapur's elephant cavalry followed up they became bogged down in the mud, and (ascribed by the Christian population of the city to a miraculous intervention but more likely as the result of good old-fashioned do or die), the walls were promptly restored to an effective height by the city's population.

And scorpion bombs . . . The first recorded use of highly irritated scorpions to put an attacking army off its stride was in AD 198, in defence of the ancient city of Mosul against a besieging Roman army. Although the concept might have been invented on some earlier occasion – and not necessarily by the Persians.

Senators and Knights – The Roman Ruling Class

The Roman empire of the late second century was composed of a population of about fifty million people whose fates were decided by an aristocracy numbering little more than five thousand men. Originally ruled by kings, Rome became a republic with the overthrow of Tarquinius Superbus (Tarquin the Proud) in 509 BC.

The establishment of the republic was not without irony. The previous king (Tarquinius's father-in-law Servius Tullius) had in the course of his beneficent forty-four-year reign done so much to promote the interests of the plebians that the aristocracy found themselves under pressure from the expanded franchise, and so used the excuse of his successor's tyranny to take control of the state. Controlling the assemblies through their disproportionate strength when it came to public decision-making (with more than fifty per cent of the voting centuriae), their firm grip on the city's political levers ensured that they would hold more or less absolute power over the republic for almost five hundred years.

Even after Rome had tottered through a century of civil wars that were made inevitable by the creation of a powerful standing army of legions that just begged to be wielded by men of wealth and ambition, and had been supplanted by the supreme rule of the emperor, the aristocracy remained not simply influential but essential to imperial power. Why? The answer lies in Rome's breakneck expansion from city state to a pan-European empire to rival that conquered by Hitler's armies two thousand years later. Despite his unequalled power, the emperor needed a host of bureaucrats and military men to safeguard Rome's frontiers and to control (and for that matter to tax) its vast population, a task beyond the control of even the most formidably intelligent of men. The first emperor, Augustus, recognised this absolute requirement for the aristocracy's continued role in public life, and was careful to keep the senate onside throughout his reign. Terming himself as 'princeps' – 'first citizen' – specifically to avoid a term like 'rex' – 'king' – that might reawaken the resentment that had proven so deadly to his maternal great-uncle Julius Caesar, he ruled with a deft (if somewhat firm) hand.

By the time period in which the *Empire* series is set, the late second century, the two major groups of men who composed Rome's aristocracy, the senatorial and equestrian classes, remained essential to the effective function of almost every part of the sprawling and increasingly threadbare imperial machine. Sometimes battered by the storms and vicissitudes of public life, often brutally exploited as a convenient source of funds by the throne, and with their positions at times the subject of gross venality in their distribution, they were nevertheless the lynchpin on which the imperial world was entirely dependent.

The six hundred senators, their positions dependent upon a property qualification of 250,000 denarii under Augustus (equivalent to about 70 kilos of gold), and needing the leading family member to have a seat in the senate to maintain their status, were Roman society's elite. Most of the really important positions in the empire's administration went to men from the senatorial class, including the role of governing the larger provinces (with the exception of Egypt which, as the critical source of grain, was the exclusive preserve of the emperor). Senators traditionally held the position of Prefect of the City of Rome, commanding the urban cohorts charged with keeping order in the capital, and as legionary legates controlled the empire's legions with the exception, once more, of the forces based in Egypt. With responsibility for most of Rome's highest ranked civil and military positions, it would at first glance appear that the senatorial class were effectively in control of enacting (and indeed influencing) the emperor's policies with regard to internal and foreign affairs, but this fails to take account of the pervasive influence of the more numerous equestrian class, the title meaning 'the Knights', in recognition of their original role as Rome's cavalry force.

While most of the positions open to knights were of a status lower than those reserved for senators, there were exceptions. The governor of Egypt was an equestrian, appointed by the emperor to keep that most vital of provinces well ordered, the position the pinnacle of such a man's potential achievement and without doubt only granted to those with the most distinguished careers in the public service. In the same way, other smaller provinces and sub-provinces were similarly available to knights at the emperor's behest.

Lower down the scale of public appointments, knights were *procuratores Augusti* (in charge of the province's finances), in the provinces controlled by the emperor and took many of the senior management roles that kept the empire's revenues flowing and its people fed in other procurator and prefect positions.

In the army, equestrians commanded the praetorian guard as Praetorian Prefects (usually two at a time to ensure their loyalty), the emperor's protectors and the chiefs of his military staff. Knights commanded the two main praetorian fleets at Misenum and Ravenna, and an equestrian commanded the *urban vigiles* – the City Watch – Rome's combination fire brigade and police force. Some equestrians followed a less conventional career path than the norm, such as those who specialised in law and became judges, and were given a dispensation from military service, but the knights were the backbone of the army's officer class. Many equestrians served well beyond the expected ten-year period that was initially spent achieving the *tres militae,* a three rank progression from command of an infantry cohort as a prefect, followed by a spell as a military tribune with a legion, with the command as a cavalry wing as the last and most prestigious office.

The increasing employment of equestrians by the emperors – perhaps as a counterweight to the senate – resulted in the development of a hierarchy within the class, probably as a means of preventing clashes over perceived superiority. There were three orders of prestige, the *Viri Egregii* (Select Men), *Viri Perfectissimi* (Best Men) and the *Viri Eminentissimi* (Most Eminent of Men). We don't know how these classes were organised or made distinct, but the assumption is that *Eminentissimi* was accorded only to the Praetorian Prefects (of which there were usually two at any one time), *Perfectissimi* to the major prefectures and offices of state, such as the governor of Egypt and the *Vigiles*, roles appointed by the emperor that effectively made these men his clients (in accordance with the long Roman tradition of patronage). The remainder of the equestrian class, it is assumed, were *Egregrii*.

Whatever the position, both senators and equestrians benefitted enormously from their service even before the obvious opportunities for corruption are taken into consideration. The prefect of an auxiliary cohort – the first step on the ladder of command – was paid 10,000 denarii, fifty times the basic pay accorded to his soldiers, and at the top end of the pay scale the governor of Egypt received 75,000 denarii a year. Even the lowest ranks of Rome's social elite lived in a manner to which most of the empire's population could barely have comprehended, never mind aspired.

The Roman Army in 182 AD

By the late second century, the point at which the *Empire* series begins, the Imperial Roman Army had long since evolved into a stable organisation with a stable *modus operandi*. Thirty or so **legions** (there's still some debate about the Ninth Legion's fate), each with an official strength of 5,500 legionaries, formed the army's 165,000-man heavy infantry backbone, while 360 or so **auxiliary cohorts** (each of them the equivalent of a 600-man infantry battalion) provided another 217,000 soldiers for the empire's defence.

Positioned mainly in the empire's border provinces, these forces performed two main tasks. Whilst ostensibly providing a strong means of defence against external attack, their role was just as much about maintaining Roman rule in the most challenging of the empire's subject territories. It was no coincidence that the troublesome provinces of Britain and Dacia were deemed to require 60 and 44 auxiliary cohorts respectively, almost a quarter of the total available. It should be noted, however, that whilst their overall strategic task was the same, the terms under which the two halves of the army served were quite different.

The legions, the primary Roman military unit for conducting warfare at the operational or theatre level, had been in existence since early in the republic, hundreds of years before. They were composed mainly of close-order heavy infantry, well-drilled and highly motivated, recruited on a professional basis and, critically to an understanding of their place in Roman society, manned by soldiers who were Roman citizens. The jobless poor were thus provided with a route to both citizenship and a valuable trade, since service with the legions was as much about construction

The Chain of Command
Legion

Legatus — Legion Cavalry (120 horsemen)

Broad Stripe Tribune — 5 'military' narrow stripe tribunes

Camp Prefect

Senior Centurion

10 Cohorts
(one of 5 centuries of 160 men each)
(nine of 6 centuries of 80 men each)

Centurion

Chosen Man

Watch Officer — Standard Bearer

10 tent parties of 8 men apiece

The Chain of Command
Auxiliary Infantry Cohort

Legatus

Prefect
(or a Tribune for a larger cohort such as the First Tungrian)

Senior Centurion

6-10 Centuries

Centurion

Chosen Man

Watch Officer   Standard Bearer

10 tent parties of
8 men apiece

– fortresses, roads and even major defensive works such as Hadrian's Wall – as destruction. Vitally for the maintenance of the empire's borders, this attractiveness of service made a large standing field army a possibility, and allowed for both the control and defence of the conquered territories.

By this point in Britannia's history three legions were positioned to control the restive peoples both beyond and behind the province's borders. These were the 2nd, based in South Wales, the 20th, watching North Wales, and the 6th, positioned to the east of the Pennine range and ready to respond to any trouble on the northern frontier. Each of these legions was commanded by a **legatus**, an experienced man of senatorial rank deemed worthy of the responsibility and appointed by the emperor. The command structure beneath the legatus was a delicate balance, combining the requirement for training and advancing Rome's young aristocrats for their future roles with the necessity for the legion to be led into battle by experienced and hardened officers.

Directly beneath the legatus were a half-dozen or so **military tribunes**, one of them a young man of the senatorial class called the **broad stripe tribune** after the broad senatorial stripe on his tunic. This relatively inexperienced man – it would have been his first official position – acted as the legion's second-in-command, despite being a relatively tender age when compared with the men around him. The remainder of the military tribunes were **narrow stripes**, men of the equestrian class who usually already had some command experience under their belts from leading an auxiliary cohort. Intriguingly, since the more experienced narrow-stripe tribunes effectively reported to the broad stripe, such a reversal of the usual military conventions around fitness for command must have made for some interesting man-management situations. The legion's third in command was the camp **prefect**, an older and more experienced soldier, usually a former centurion deemed worthy of one last role in the legion's service before retirement, usually for one year. He would by necessity have been a steady hand, operating as the voice of experience in advising the legion's senior officers as to the realities of warfare and the management of the legion's soldiers.

Reporting into this command structure were ten **cohorts** of soldiers, each one composed of a number of eighty-man **centuries**. Each century was a collection of ten **tent parties** – eight men who literally shared a tent when out in the field. Nine of the cohorts had six centuries, and an establishment strength of 480 men, whilst the prestigious **first cohort**, commanded by the legion's **senior centurion**, was composed of five double-strength centuries and therefore fielded 800 soldiers when fully manned. This organisation provided the legion with its cutting edge: 5,000 or so well-trained heavy infantrymen operating in regiment and company-sized units, and led by battle-hardened officers, the legion's centurions, men whose position was usually achieved by dint of their demonstrated leadership skills.

The rank of **centurion** was pretty much the peak of achievement for an ambitious soldier, commanding an eighty-man century and paid ten times as much as the men each officer commanded. Whilst the majority of centurions were promoted from the ranks, some were appointed from above as a result of patronage, or as a result of having completed their service in the **Praetorian Guard**, which had a shorter period of service than the legions. That these externally imposed centurions would have undergone their very own 'sink or swim' moment in dealing with their new colleagues is an unavoidable conclusion, for the role was one that by necessity led from the front, and as a result suffered disproportionate casualties. This makes it highly likely that any such appointee felt unlikely to make the grade in action would have received very short shrift from his brother officers.

A small but necessarily effective team reported to the centurion. The **optio**, literally 'best' or **chosen man**, was his second-in-command, and stood behind the century in action with a long brass-knobbed stick, literally pushing the soldiers into the fight should the need arise. This seems to have been a remarkably efficient way of managing a large body of men, given the centurion's place alongside rather than behind his soldiers, and the optio would have been a cool head, paid twice the usual soldier's wage and a candidate for promotion to centurion if he performed well.

The century's third-in-command was the **tesserarius** or **watch officer**, ostensibly charged with ensuring that sentries were posted and that everyone know the watch word for the day, but also likely to have been responsible for the profusion of tasks such as checking the soldiers' weapons and equipment, ensuring the maintenance of discipline and so on, that have occupied the lives of junior non-commissioned officers throughout history in delivering a combat-effective unit to their officer. The last member of the centurion's team was the century's **signifer**, the **standard bearer**, who both provided a rallying point for the soldiers and helped the centurion by transmitting marching orders to them through movements of his standard. Interestingly, he also functioned as the century's banker, dealing with the soldiers' financial affairs. While a soldier caught in the horror of battle might have thought twice about defending his unit's standard, he might well also have felt a stronger attachment to the man who managed his money for him!

At the shop-floor level were the eight soldiers of the tent party who shared a leather tent and messed together, their tent and cooking gear carried on a mule when the legion was on the march. Each tent party would inevitably have established its own pecking order based upon the time-honoured factors of strength, aggression, intelligence – and the rough humour required to survive in such a harsh world. The men that came to dominate their tent parties would have been the century's unofficial backbone, candidates for promotion to watch officer. They would also have been vital to their tent mates' cohesion under battlefield conditions, when the relatively thin leadership team could not always exert sufficient presence to inspire the individual soldier to stand and fight amid the horrific chaos of combat.

The other element of the legion was a small 120-man detachment of **cavalry**, used for scouting and the carrying of messages between units. The regular army depended on auxiliary **cavalry wings**, drawn from those parts of the empire where horsemanship was a way of life, for their mounted combat arm. Which leads us to consider the other side of the army's two-tier system.

The **auxiliary cohorts**, unlike the legions alongside which they fought, were not Roman citizens, although the completion of a twenty-five-year term of service did grant both the soldier and his children citizenship. The original auxiliary cohorts had often served in their homelands, as a means of controlling the threat of large numbers of freshly conquered barbarian warriors, but this changed after the events of the first century AD. The Batavian revolt in particular – when the 5,000-strong Batavian cohorts rebelled and destroyed two Roman legions after suffering intolerable provocation during a recruiting campaign gone wrong – was the spur for the Flavian policy for these cohorts to be posted away from their home provinces. The last thing any Roman general wanted was to find his legions facing an army equipped and trained to fight in the same way. This is why the reader will find the auxiliary cohorts described in the *Empire* series, true to the historical record, representing a variety of other parts of the empire, including Tungria, which is now part of modern-day Belgium.

Auxiliary infantry was equipped and organised in so close a manner to the legions that the casual observer would have been hard put to spot the differences. Often their armour would be mail, rather than plate, sometimes weapons would have minor differences, but in most respects an auxiliary cohort would be the same proposition to an enemy as a legion cohort. Indeed there are hints from history that the auxiliaries may have presented a greater challenge on the battlefield. At the battle of Mons Graupius in Scotland, Tacitus records that four cohorts of Batavians and two of Tungrians were sent in ahead of the legions and managed to defeat the enemy without requiring any significant assistance. Auxiliary cohorts were also often used on the flanks of the battle line, where reliable and well drilled troops are essential to handle attempts to outflank the army. And while the legions contained soldiers who were as much tradesmen as fighting men, the auxiliary cohorts were primarily focused on their fighting skills. By the end of the second century there were significantly more auxiliary troops serving the empire than were available from the legions, and it is clear that Hadrian's Wall would have been invalid as a concept without the mass of infantry and mixed infantry/cavalry cohorts that were stationed along its length.

As for horsemen, the importance of the empire's 75,000 or so **auxiliary cavalrymen**, capable of much faster deployment and manoeuvre than the infantry, and essential for successful scouting, fast communications and the denial of reconnaissance information to the enemy, cannot be overstated. Rome simply did not produce anything like the strength in mounted troops needed to avoid being at a serious disadvantage against those nations which by their nature were cavalry-rich. As a result, as each such nation was conquered their mounted forces were swiftly incorporated into the army until, by the early first century BC, the decision was made to disband what native Roman cavalry as there was altogether, in favour of the auxiliary cavalry wings.

Named for their usual place on the battlefield, on the flanks or 'wings' of the line of battle, the cavalry cohorts were commanded by men of the equestrian class with prior experience as legion military tribunes, and were organised around the basic 32-man **turma**, or squadron. Each squadron was commanded by a **decurion**, a position analogous with that of the infantry centurion. This officer was assisted by a pair of junior officers: the **duplicarius** or **double-pay**, equivalent to the role of optio, and the **sesquipilarius** or **pay-and-a-half**, equal in stature to the infantry watch officer. As befitted the cavalry's more important military role, each of these ranks was paid about 40 per cent more than the infantry equivalent.

Taken together, the legions and their auxiliary support presented a standing army of over 400,000 men by the time of the events described in the *Empire* series. Whilst this was sufficient to both hold down and defend the empire's 6.5 million square kilometres for a long period of history, the strains of defending a 5,000-kilometre-long frontier, beset on all sides by hostile tribes, were also beginning to manifest themselves. The prompt move to raise three new legions undertaken by the new emperor Septimius Severus in AD 197, in readiness for over a decade spent shoring up the empire's crumbling borders, provides clear evidence that there were never enough legions and cohorts for such a monumental task. This is the backdrop for the *Empire* series, which will run from AD 192 well into the early third century, following both the empire's and Marcus Valerius Aquila's travails throughout this fascinatingly brutal period of history.